Luther's An

Jay Margrave has been writing both fiction and non-fiction for many years but the author's recent fiction has concentrated on what could be described as mystoricals – novels that combine a love of history and literature to solve mysteries.

Also by Jay Margrave

The Gawain Quest

Luther's Ambassadors

Jay Margrave

GOLDENFORD

Goldenford Publishers Ltd
Guildford
www.goldenford.co.uk

First published in Great Britain in 2008 by
Goldenford Publishers Limited
The Old Post Office
130 Epsom Road Guildford
Surrey GU1 2PX
Tel: 01483 563307
Fax: 01483 829074
www.goldenford.co.uk

Cover design by Penelope Cline based on an original ceramic by Iris Davies

Printed and bound by CPI Antony Rowe, Eastbourne

ISBN-978-0-9559415-0-4

This is the second in the Priedeux Trilogy

Prologue

As the jigsaw pieces slowly came together, forming the famous picture, the men spoke to me, *tell our story* they said. You are the one we have waited for. Nearly five hundred years have passed, but now you are here.

Christmas is nothing without jigsaw puzzles and the 1000-piecer forming Holbein's Ambassadors was a gift eagerly opened and started.

Framework first; not easy with all that dark emerald curtain at the top. The floor was easier with geometric shapes, the patterning giving me clues. Except for that great diagonal slice of a twisted greyness cutting across the patterns. It was unidentifiable in this flat reproduction but I knew that, in the original, it would evolve into a skull if you stood in the right position; a reminder of mortality. The two men seemed not to notice, confident in their roles standing on either side of shelving, not treading on the symbol of death.

I continued with the pieces, some formed into such peculiar shapes that it was easy to place them; others were obvious because of the parts of the picture they represented; a piece of hand, an eye, a strange shape of finely grained wood, colours of bright fuchsia, ochre, and tassels of gold. Shapes and hues. It all added up to a rich, positive scene. After that, the bits of sextant, tilted globe, musical instruments with string-pinging broken - all easily recreated.

Then the two men's faces are fully formed. They both stare out at me. We know who we are, they are saying, two of the highest in the land of France, one of us in the Church, the other a diplomat. We are friends, we want the world to see us together. We are rich, and wish to show our positions in the world.

But I knew differently. This painting, so splendid, so large, was not displayed in its day; never mentioned in despatches. I knew Holbein's picture to be the strangest of his works; the largest, and dated 1533. It was lost to the world until found by a Victorian art historian in an obscure French chateau called Polisy. Even stranger is, if you look carefully at the globe lying askew on the bottom shelf, Polisy is shown as the centre of the world, at a time when Jerusalem was usually shown as such.

There are no records of the painting in Holbein's extensive notes of his work, as there are of others of his famous paintings, of how he came to record colours, lines, the profiles of his sitters. There are no preliminary sketches.

No-one knows why it ended up in Polisy, except that the place was one of the family chateaux belonging to Dinteville; the man who stands with the sword, with the richer clothes, the ambassador.

Even stranger is that at the time of the painting, there is great turmoil in England where it was executed; no-one should have leisure to sit for such a work. Henry VIII has broken from the Catholic Church and married Anne Boleyn in a secret ceremony. She is expecting her first child, an eagerly awaited son and heir to the throne. Everyone is gossiping, rumours fly.

Even across the Channel this is so. Francis 1, hemmed in between the two powerful leaders, the great Emperor Charles V and Henry VIII, is keeping his options open; should he follow Henry's lead and make himself head of the church in France as Henry has done in England, or should he condemn Henry? He sends spies, to watch at the Court of England but also to spy on each other. Dinteville can be trusted; or can he? So the Bishop of Lavour, one Georges de Selve, the other man in the painting, is also sent to watch. These two should not meet or be friends; they are supposed to be spying on each other. Dinteville writes to his brother in France, 'Tell no-one, but I met with our friend de Selve today.'

So a secret meeting is recorded. But would you then

commission a great painting, more than life size, from the up and coming Court painter, Holbein? All this I ponder as I work on my jigsaw; recognisable parts are in place now and I can appreciate the design, the colours, the narrative the painting is trying to reveal to me.

There is a nonsense here; and the two men know it. Look at the picture; they are surrounded by broken instruments, everyone a symbol, well-known to their Tudor contemporaries but only guessed at now, each item emerging as I fix more pieces; I have quickly compiled a great swatch of Dinteville's chest, with its gold chain, the Order of St Michael. Both men look relaxed, as if they are waiting for someone, as they lean nonchalantly against the shelving between them.

Like my jigsaw there are too many uneven pieces, too many dark areas, other aspects of their lives where the picture is confusing until all the parts are fitted together. I look at the completed puzzle; I need to investigate further. The feeling is compelling, they are imploring me to tell the truth, after so many years. Or am I imagining too much?

* * * * *

Trafalgar Square, The National Gallery.

I walk through the main entrance, up the stairs, turn left, push through heavy fire doors; through one gallery, then left again; and there it is – the actual painting in a gilt frame more than life-size, of two men, leaning lazily on the shelves between them. Holbein's Ambassadors. At this size the actual painting has so many facets it seems that, if it were cut into pieces, it would be impossible to put together again.

Now I can see it in their eyes, which glint as I move in front of the painting. Yes, they are talking to me, pleading with me. Despite being stowed away for so long, it is bright, the colours resplendent, much more so than my jigsaw puzzle. It stops gazers in their tracks; all admire it.

The gap between the two men is immense - as if there should be another person in the frame.

3

I stare at the picture, I am sitting now, really concentrating - de Selve looks at me with a diffident smile as if, if I wait long enough, he would explain - or confess, for he is used to so doing, being a Catholic Bishop. Dinteville may not tell though - he is more aristocratic, more reserved. He is trained in diplomatic ways; he is never going to tell such secrets. His feet are firmly planted in the mosaic that represents the world, or so it seems to me. The painting is not so much dominated but disfigured by the peculiar shaped skull slashed across the floor between the men's feet. It is a representation of death, and I wonder; is someone missing from this large painting? Having thought that, I become convinced. The more I stare, the more I believe it is uneven; there should be a third person in this design.

I am staring too much; the picture seems to judder, the men are smiling at me. They move, step over the magic skull before them and walk back into their childhoods where their story begins...

Chapter One

Blois, The Loire valley, 1514

'Let the blood of the lamb be spilt for the good of mankind,' Anne chanted as she cut into the tip of her forefinger. She watched as her blood bubbled for a second and then ran, catching on the extra crooked finger, and from there dripped on to the marble floor.

'And the Holy Catholic Church will be cleansed by our sacrifice,' she continued as she took the hand of one of her companions, Jean de Dinteville, and made a similar incision, mingling his released blood with hers.

They both turned to the third conspirator, who was a head shorter. He was hiding his hands in the dark velvet cloak he had deliberately donned for this occasion, looking already like the serious priest he was destined to become.

'Come, Georges, you agreed; it is even more fitting that you should join us, after what happened to you,' she cajoled but he kept his hands firmly hidden. He shook his head, whether by way of refusal or to shake away the memories.

'Georges, come we are doing this for you as well as for the world. We three will be ambassadors for reform, and you will be the bishop amongst us, so come…' Her voice was soft, persuading, and, after putting her arm around him, a soft caressing gesture, she gentled his right hand out of the folds of the cloak.

'Blood letting will release the pain, you know that, Georges, all the doctors tell us. It is as our good Lord showed us; He shed His blood for us, we will shed our blood now to show we are true in our aims. To show that we too sacrifice our lives for the reform of the church which has lost its way.'

She continued to talk, quietly, in a chanting hypnotic voice until

5

the boy relaxed and held out his finger. All the time, Dinteville stood by, watching, until the incision was made and Georges winced as the blood flowed. Anne held his hand to hers and joined Dinteville's hand, entwining their fingers together so that the gushing red mingled. She held their hands outstretched so that none of the blood touched their elegant robes.

This is the Genesis of my life, thought Anne Bullen.

She was quietly triumphant. She had engineered this ceremony. It was she who had persuaded those of higher rank to enter into her life's sworn aim of reforming the holy Roman Catholic Church.

'To us - and the cleansing of the Church,' she said aloud and the other two answered.

'And so we swear.'

'We will form a trinity like the French fleur-de-lys, entwined in our one aim as we go our separate fore-ordained ways.'

Being the youngest handmaiden to the French queen meant that Anne had had to learn quickly how to survive in the strange Court, and it had not taken her long to learn how to command these two boys, one of whom, Jean de Dinteville, was a head taller than her. They were at home at this Court where *she* was an English upstart. Despite that, they had agreed to mix their noble blood with hers.

Even young Georges, hesitant as he was at first, now spoke fervently. 'I swear that, when I serve in the Church, as I have been taught, I will do all in my power to change matters and scourge it of its corruptions.'

'Georges I thank you for your promise. I too promise to do what I can, as a woman.' Anne answered as large globules of blood fell onto the stone flooring. 'After all these years together, fighting our tutor, I know I can trust you both to carry out our mission.'

Jean said, 'Indeed, Anne, our four years together have welded us as one.'

He separated from them, wiping his finger on a handkerchief. This defused the charged atmosphere and he laughed. 'I remember when you first arrived, how quiet and unassuming you were. But then you told us of your time at the Court of Margaret of Austria, the daughter of the great emperor Maximilian, the regent of the Netherlands, and how young Charles was so pettish and childish, and that was it.' Anne smiled at his recitation, as if he was announcing her to the world. Jean continued, 'You had us in the palm of your hand from that moment. Your innate dignity always showed. We just cannot refuse you!'

Anne curtsied to the older boy. 'Thank you, Jean, you always were gallant and I shall always be your friend.'

Georges interrupted. His voice was not yet deep but it was firm.

'And as I am destined for the Church, I will work from the inside to reform it. None of the priests under my control will be...' His voice faltered.

Both she and Jean knew why the boy was so upset.

Anne guessed what he was thinking; he was transported back to only a fortnight ago; the beginning of fourteen days of life-changing events for all three of them.

'And, Anne, how will you deal with your part of our bargain?'

Jean was standing, legs astride, his left hand on the hilt of his dagger. Anne thought he had indeed developed the air of a dignified diplomat. He was dressed smartly in velvet, with an elegant belt and buckle, the belt holding the scabbard for the thin knife that had been used to make the cuts.

Anne did not answer immediately but lifted her head and looked towards the ceiling of the long gallery they had claimed as their secret place. She knew the answer now, as to why her father had sent her to the highest courts where he had been a visiting ambassador. He had told her she was to be trained in high-born manners.

I might be only a gentleman but you will be a great lady; you must learn the lessons of courtly ways and make valuable alliances. I married into the Norfolk family of England and now have great authority at the English court. You will perpetuate that. She had been only five when

7

he had drummed those words into her, just before she was shipped to the Continent, but she had always remembered them.

'Anne, Anne, answer us, stop daydreaming.'

'I will do what only a woman can do. I will marry a great man!' She caught sight of herself, her reflection distorted and dulled in the stained mirrors that awaited re-tinting in this disused place. Her new taffeta dress was clouded at the hem where she had forced a path through the thick white-grey dust on the floor. The robe had been prepared for the special banquet that night, and was shaped to her waist, the bodice just revealing her young, small breasts. She had put up her hair in a fashionable cap and held herself tall, imagining a train of courtiers behind her, some bowing low as she passed. There was a hush in the room, as the boys waited expectantly for her to go on.

'I will be a great queen!' she exclaimed.

Both boys stepped back.

'Anne! How dare you? That is treason.'

All three of them knew that to claim to be a king or queen, even in the future, might implicate you in a plot to murder the living monarch.

Jean, early trained in diplomacy, quickly recovered and smiled.

'Georges, look at her, how magnificent she is. She could well be a royal, and she is no doubt just daydreaming.'

He took her by the hand and led her down the long gallery, stepping over the debris of old statues and masonry. He played up to her.

'Indeed, my dear queen, and what will you have us do?'

Anne smiled back at him. 'Always be my friend – no matter what happens in the future.'

He nodded and Georges caught up with them. Jean turned to him, and saw he still looked worried. He let go of Anne and patted the boy's shoulder. 'Georges, we must obey her. Come; don't look so glum, no one knows we are here. It hasn't been used for ages, and there's no place for a person to hide and overhear. Let us complete our ritual.'

Once again they placed their fingers together, Georges hesitantly. Anne took his hand firmly and squeezed more blood from their fingers. It was difficult this time as it had started to congeal.

'Lord, help us in our venture.' It was young Georges, the future bishop who spoke, in the way he had been taught, chanting.

'Amen.'

Anne closed her eyes. Her only regret about today was that there was one person who was missing: their fellow pupil, Stefano, an Italian who had been sent to the court, like Anne, to learn its ways. If he had been here, she would have alluded to them as the four Apostles; going out into the world to preach new ways. But Stefano had disappeared, no-one knew where. She shook her head to get rid of his memory; nothing should spoil today. She was convinced that this moment would shape her life.

It wasn't just their ceremony, or the vision she'd had when she'd caught her reflection in the glass. It was something to do with the coming night's events. And being confident with these, her favourite companions. They had learnt together, their rhetoric, religion and their grammar. Soon all that would be finished and they would go their own ways in the world. The banquet was to be the event when Dinteville was to start his life at court formally; their school days together were over.

'How much blood flows from such little cuts,' she murmured.

'Hush, Anne, just pray for success in our venture.' Georges rebuked. Dinteville put the dagger he had used back into its scabbard, after wiping it with his bloodied handkerchief. He stood with hands clasped as if in prayer and the others followed his example. The girl looked up at him but his eyes were closed and his face was raised in a reverent ecstasy to the chandelier above them. Anne was too excited to close her eyes and took in the surroundings of the long gallery as if every part should be remembered. On many occasions they had sought refuge here, although for the first time she realised how gloomy and grey it was. She noted the dust-webs in the corner, the dirty glaze of the

9

windows which filtered the outside day into a dullness and the chandelier which she now realised was amber with the dirt of smoke from its candles.

Georges started chanting and she watched him, impressed by his gravity.

'Wherever we may be, wherever our paths may take us, here is our solemn oath written in our own mingled blood, to reform the church, to clean up the sewers of Rome, and stop the sodomy …' here his voice broke again, and he looked as if he would cry. Anne put her arm around his shoulder to comfort him. She knew what he was thinking.

Chapter two

She allowed herself to dwell on the awful events of the last two weeks. Two weeks! It seemed a lifetime ago. She and Jean had been so innocent then, when they had met in this very gallery, with no thought of the future except to get their dance steps absolutely right for the great banquet. Stefano had been with them that day, too. Anne recalled it was just as dusty and cold although the sun had shone, forming shafts of light that glimmered on the tarnished silver of the mirrors. They were practising their courtly walk, high stepping and formal.

'Jean, I am so glad that they see us as a dancing couple. Come show me those steps again. We must be perfect. And, Stefano, don't glower so much, you know you fall over your sword when you so much as take one step in the dance. It's just not for you, my dear.'

Anne loved dancing and the old king had asked for a team of youngsters to form a display after dinner. She liked to be observed even when practising, and was pleased that Stefano had agreed to accompany them, while Georges had been kept back by their tutor for being slow in his grammar.

She and Jean had been chosen to lead the dance. He took her hand and conducted her through the dust while their companion, a brooding expression on his face, looked on. Jean hummed the tune that the musicians had played at their practice earlier that morning.

The girl paraded up and down with her companion, her soft shoes hardly making a noise, the only sound being the crackle of her skirts. Her petticoats caught the dust and sent it swirling so that a thin cloud followed her, making grey shadows through the sun motes, as if she was accompanied by ghostly attendants.

'Well, Stefano, don't you think we make a fine pair?'

She addressed their watcher. He didn't answer. As they passed him, she saw Stefano turn round as if he would attend to his attire. He looked at himself in the mirror, adjusted his jacket, which was a little too short for him, and ran his hand through his thick dark hair, combing it into an even more unruly mess. She recognised that in reality he was watching their reflections, trying desperately not to show how jealous he was. She guessed he had strong feelings for her but would never say.

As they passed Stefano again, she laughed, a deep throated laugh which belied her youth, and looked over her shoulder and she and Stefano gazed at one another, while still concentrating on the stepping of the dance.

'Watch, Stefano, watch how we do the turn.'

He leant against the bowed glass, his arms crossed and smiled. He pushed one leg against the mirror as if to balance himself. Anne noticed the stance; it indicated nonchalance but she knew differently, knowing that although he had been sent to the French Court to train, his lot was to be a gentleman soldier, while Jean and Georges had pre-ordained positions at the Court, because of their families, and Anne would be married to a rich man: whether in France or England, none knew yet. She knew that Stefano was acutely aware that he was not a noble like Jean and Georges. He could not dress as well as them. His family were poor Italian noblemen, albeit with connections, from Sirmione, a spur of a town on the shores of Lake Garda, just north of the great Venetian state.

'Stefano, don't be jealous of the dance; you are learning your military craft well.'

He smiled at her, relaxing. She always had a way of bringing him out. 'You may be a bad student in the classroom but we will come and watch you when you next practise your fencing; you are brilliant at such sport.'

Stefano grinned and started to ape them along the line of the mirror, flattered now and not concerned that he might be making a fool of himself with his clumsy copy of their dance.

Anne caught sight of her reflection behind him, and then lost it as she came level with Stefano and blended into him for a second before finding herself again. She realised they were similarly dark, but her darkness was all in her eyes and hair, with the pale skin of the north, blue veins showing as delicate lines in the fall of her neck. Stefano had the dark skin of the south, as if he was glowing from too much sun. Because of that contrast between them, he always seemed to her exotic and exciting. Even though she was in Jean's arms, she wanted to touch Stefano, to feel the warmth of that amber skin. She found herself brushing the fabric of his quilted jacket as she passed him again but quickly danced on. Something in her knew she must desist from such longing.

She dropped her hand from Jean's arm and skipped back to the Italian. Dust rose as she reached him, clouding the air between them.

'Come, Stefano, you could dance if you wanted.'

He stopped moving, looking at Jean, who shrugged. Jean knew they could not deny Anne. Even so Stefano, against his better nature, refused to dance with her now she offered. He folded his arms in a defensive gesture, hiding his hands so she could not take them.

'No. I'll stick to soldierly pursuits.'

As he said it, he put his hand on the scabbard of his sword, trying to pull it out.

Anne stopped him 'No, don't show us, both Jean and I know how good you are.'

Jean picked up the hint. 'Stefano, in the field there is none better than you. We all have our own skills. Anne, for instance holds herself regally'

'But she isn't very good at her Latin.' Stefano's face broke into a grin which lightened his dark features and, as he did so, Anne looked away, embarrassed. His face had the beginnings of dark shadow to show that a future beard, when full grown, would be blue-black; his brows were thick, forming a line across the forehead. Even though his tunic was of cheap brown fustian and

13

the only elaborate item he had was his sword with a finely decorated gilt scabbard, Anne found him more attractive than Jean, for all his graceful ways on the dance floor and his refined French good looks. Her stomach felt strange when she gazed into Stefano's dark eyes, even when he was rude about her as now. How dare he mention the Latin? She knew she was lazy when it came to it, not for want of intelligence but because her deep seated feeling was that she – and others – should learn to read and speak their own tongue, and for that she had many a quarrel with their staid, preachy tutor.

'Latin! If I ever have my way, I shall make sure we all read the great book in my mother tongue – in English – and no one will gainsay me.'

Stefano moved towards her, bowed ceremoniously and took her hand. Kissed it and held his lips to it for a little too long, and said in his musical, Italian-tinted French, 'indeed, you are regal, Jean is right. A most beautiful lady.'

Jean clapped at this, but Anne glared at Stefano. He was not looking at her; he was grinning at Jean.

Anne was on the defensive now. Both Jean and Stefano knew how strong her feelings were towards reading the Bible. She had made it plain on many occasions that she would make up her own mind about what the Bible said, not trust the priests to tell her.

'Oh, my friends, never, never in Latin. All the world shall be able to read in their own language. So be it, I'll accept your French for now, but you'll see, if I become a great lady I will ensure that my vassals will be able to read the holy book in English. I will make sure of that.' She spoke firmly but then broke into a squeal of laughter, unlike the deep-throated laugh that she normally made. Jean and Stefano exchanged glances, and Jean started to speak. Anne, still fired up, did not give him a chance.

'I like speaking French as well as you, dear Jean, as it is what is spoken in this country. But I shall ensure my home country will not have to chant Latin. If I return home, that is.'

Her two friends recognised her tone; she was off again into her

14

familiar 'what she will do one day' and both Jean and Stefano listened, totally enraptured by her. As she proclaimed, she was still admiring her reflection. Stefano took up his old pose, arms crossed, hands hidden. Jean started to stride up and down.

'You will have to be very lucky to achieve that, Anne.'

'I will be so great that I will ensure you and all the world will speak English, how say you? All shall use my language, even for reading the great work, The Bible! No Latin for me.'

Stefano shrugged, a very continental gesture to show that he didn't care. Jean approached him and put his hand on one shoulder, still watching Anne.

'Very well, Anne, Stefano was wrong. What does it matter about Latin if all can read their own language?' Jean said to defuse the situation. Anne knew he always tried to curb her wild temper.

'Yes, Anne, Latin is not that important.' Stefano backed him.

They both knew that here, in their secret place, she would say anything, even dangerous things. Anne, quickly changing her mood again, accepted the conciliation and approached them, putting her hand on Stefano's arm.

'Stefano, you know your Latin, for it is so much like your musical language, but I'll not need it in my country, I swear.'

He shrugged again, unfolding his arms and opening his hands in a gesture of surrender. He did not move away from her but looked sideways at her hand on his arm and then at her, through dark long eyelashes, his eyes half closed.

'Dear Anne, let's change the subject. So long as I have enough knowledge to read what I need to read to find my way, I'll not care what language is spoken or written.'

Anne moved away from him, blushing.

'Come, Anne, 'tis only a game.' Stefano said, gently. 'But your dress ... I can see you are going to make a great Court lady,' he paused, knowing it sounded clumsy. 'One that might never acknowledge your old friends, what say you?'

Anne stopped her stylised walking and scampered back to the two young men who stood side by side. She put an arm around each of their shoulders even though Jean was the same height as her and Stefano a head taller, so she had to stretch up. As she did so, the loose folds of her dress caught on the ornament of the Italian's scabbard and, as she tried to pull away, the fabric tore.

'Oh, look, a triangle has come off. What am I to do? I shall have to get one of the Queen's seamstresses to mend this before the great day.'

She was not too dismayed, and pulled the piece of material away and put it hastily in a pocket. Her face was close to theirs and she looked from one to the other, softening.

'Oh, Jean, how could I ever forget you? And you, Stefano, even though you are rough and constantly tear my clothes. How can I forget those who befriended me when I was but a scared newcomer?' She paused and they all remembered the first day she had attended the class with the tutor. She was only nine and in a strange country, but still carried herself with dignity.

They were walking back and forth, their heads together, comfortable with their memories. They talked loudly believing they were safe in this long gallery, an unusual relaxation in the French Court with its formalities and protocol.

'How could I forget you – and Georges of course?' She said wistfully, suddenly nostalgic for all the training they had undergone together, wishing it could go on forever, knowing it was soon to end. It was something to do with the new dress she wore today, to practise the dance, and their strange talk. She was suddenly shy. There was an awkward pause between them. She broke away, and mercurially changed into the regal posturing again, stepping high and away from them.

Again, she stopped, and sighed, 'Ah, me, I am but only the Lady Anne Bullen and feel as if I am forgotten by my family.'

'Nay, Anne, how could you be forgotten when you are a lady-in-waiting to one of the greatest queens in Christendom, Queen Mary of France, sister of the king of England?' Jean listed all the titles in a ceremonious tone to emphasis her rank. 'Fear not, soon you will be married, and then you will forget your old friends.'

Anne impulsively kissed him on each cheek, in the French way, and took his face in her hands and answered solemnly, 'Nay, I'll never forget a true friend, such as you, dear Jean.' She then turned to Stefano and took his arm. 'And when we are great we shall shower each other with honours.'

Her ringing words were interrupted by a frantic tapping at the great doors of the gallery. They froze, tensed in their tracks at the noise.

'What ...?' whispered Anne. Stefano held up one hand, his other on his sword hilt, seemingly nonchalant but prepared like a good soldier for fight, and hurried to the door.

'Who is it?' He too spoke softly, through the great keyhole.

'Let me in!' The distressed cry distorted the voice, but they recognised who it was.

'Georges!' exclaimed Anne. 'Hurry; open it'. She nodded towards the door, and Jean, clumsy in his need for speed, turned the great key. As the door was released it burst open and a small figure fell into the room, twisted round and pushed the door shut quickly behind him. Jean, taking his cue from the newcomer, hurriedly turned the key again. Before them stood their younger friend, Georges de Selve, a childish version of the priest he was to become, dishevelled and sobbing, great gasps coming from his body.

He blurted out, 'I have been despoiled!'

Chapter Three

Anne immediately rushed to him and took him in her arms and he fell on her. They sank to the floor. The two older boys just stood there, helpless, as if taking part in a tableau. Anne gently tidied his doublet and buttoned him up, all the time whispering to him.

'Come, come, 'tis all well, we are your friends. All will be revenged ...' She looked over the head of the youngster at Jean and Stefano, who both looked away.

All three of them knew what Georges meant. In this Court everyone had to look to themselves and because they had been left by their parents to be trained in its ways, they had early formed their alliance, had learnt to stay close together protecting each other from those who would misuse them. As Anne stroked the sobbing boy, Jean moved, released from the numbing shock of the younger boy's revelation, and joined in, cuddling both Anne and Georges as if he would cloak them in forgetfulness. Still Stefano stood but when Anne looked up at him his hand remained on the scabbard of his sword and the knuckles were white. He made as if to leap to the door but Anne shook her head.

'Nay, Stefano, wait, let us hear young Georges' story, after he has cried himself out.' She smiled at the boy in her arms as she said it, wiping the dampness from his face with her fingers. Even so, she could not help thinking of her own position. What if the same had happened to her, parentless in this place of intrigue? She would have been shamed and her position at Court lost. Despite her bravado of a few moments before, she was well aware of her status. She was Lady Anne Bullen, a commoner's daughter but one who claimed to be a descendant of the English King Edward ll on her mother's side, and had travelled far for a fourteen-year-old. Soon the name would change to Anne Boleyn, to make it sound more French, more sophisticated.

The only sound was the sobs from Georges and the whispering of her taffeta dress. Anne had time to think as she soothed the boy and they all waited, not speaking. It was puzzling, this lust of men. She was on the threshold of womanhood and often she did not know whether to join these friends of hers or to sit sewing demurely with her older companions, the ladies in waiting, listening to their whispered confidences. All the other women who served Mary, the English queen of Louis X11, were calm and content to sew and gossip. Anne was not. She wanted to be moving, doing, reading. She loved this place, with its greyness and secret corners. She realised she enjoyed the stimulus of male company. But she had carefully avoided those men who seemed threatening with their hairy hands and rough, bearded faces, who, lately, had gazed at her hungrily. She could see from their eyes that she had something they wanted and was old enough to know what it was. To them she was a fresh innocent, and many tried to waylay her in shady corners. So far she had protected herself and intended to do so until marriage. Her lineage was such that she could make a good match to a nobleman if she were careful, but damaged goods would not catch such a prize. She felt safe with Georges, Stefano and Jean. They might tease each other but so far there had never been any hint between them of sex, except for her burgeoning feeling for Stefano. At every opportunity she would escape to these friends of hers. Now their closeness gave her strength but also a deep anger at what had happened to Georges. She repeated, 'I swear revenge on all of them.'

Eventually the sobbing subsided into hiccups and Anne pushed the boy a little away and looked into his damp, bloodshot eyes.

After a silence Anne, while still rhythmically stroking Georges' soft curls, said, 'Come, tell us, tell us what happened.'

There was a pause but, as if compelled by the girl's soft tones, Georges de Selve haltingly told. He did not look at any of those present, but stared into space:

'I was on my way here, for I knew you were all met and away

hiding. I had just left the garderobe, coming through that dark hall, when the Cardinal de Saumur stood in front of me. All I could see were his red robes and his flabby face leering over me. He charged me to go with him to his private quarters saying he wanted to hear my catechism. I said I had learnt it by heart, I would say it where I was, but he smiled, in that way he has, as if dribbling, and said he wanted to see it done in private.' Georges gulped, paused. Anne nodded, a stern look on her face which encouraged him more than a smile would have done.

The boy continued, 'When we reached it he gave me a rich honey drink that tasted sour underneath the sweet and I felt all comfortable and drowsy. As I knelt before him and recited, he started to stroke my head and neck. Then he took my head and put it between his robes and ... and ... I cannot go on.'

After a pause, he haltingly explained, 'He pulled me up onto his great lap and stroked my thigh and touched my privates.' The boy looked down, frantically wiped his hands together as if washing them. He was blushing, and Anne took his hands and held them still in hers.

'When he had played with me so I was excited, he was watching me, all glazed his eyes were and he opened his robes again and showed me his ... his ...'

There was a silence.

'Then he turned me over and I could do nothing.'

'How did you escape?'

'I was drowsy and I fell asleep. When I woke up he was watching me. Then he dismissed me. He said it was our little secret. I ran here using dark places and trust that none will ever know. I am so ashamed, so ashamed ... I am dirty.'

'Nay, nay, 'tis not you, 'tis him. A priest indeed. A cardinal who should be leading his flock. Oh, this world is wicked.'

Anne's face was shiny with spontaneous tears, and Jean was stony faced. Stefano had started to stalk up and down, his indoor shoes making a slapping sound. Jean and Anne looked at each other over the head of their younger friend, and in the exchange

20

was a resolve for the future which would never waver.

Anne was still holding the hands of Georges but now she stretched out and caught hold of Jean's hands and pulled them all together, so that they formed an unbroken group. Devastated, she made no attempt to hide the extra finger on her hand. She repeated like the credo, 'I swear revenge on all of them ...'

Stefano returned to them. 'I will kill him, kill him!'

But Anne answered, 'Nay that cannot be, he is too powerful.'

There was a silence in the room which Jean, always wanting action, broke by his questioning, 'Yes, revenge, but how, Anne, how? You say not to kill. We might poison him.'

Georges added tearfully, 'I would not want people to know. Please, let it be our secret.'

Anne nodded. 'Indeed, we will find a way.' She paused. 'And it will be our secret.'

She then gently disengaged herself and stood up, smoothing down the now ruffled dress. Her companions followed. She started to walk up and down, following the trails in the grey dust. She was oblivious to the tendrils of dirt which now clung to her petticoats. Her hand was at her chin. Their mirrored reflections were dulling now, in the late afternoon as the sun went down. For the moment she could think of no solution. They had to go soon or they would be missed and questions asked, and that was not what Georges wanted. Anne felt like a prophet leading her flock. Eventually she said, 'Come we must return to our duties. I will think of a way.'

Chapter Four

Anne was more perturbed than usual. Georges' experience had seriously upset her. She scurried through the galleries holding up the skirt of her dress to allow greater freedom of movement.

Georges' tale had left a horrid taste in her mouth and made her recall other unpleasantries, one of them being the way the king behaved. He would watch the dancers and entertainers, nodding indulgently but with a cold eye that made Anne shudder. He was old and ill and lay on a bower while the rest of the court, including his son-in-law Francis, desported themselves. Young as she was, Anne was aware of the undercurrents both political and sensual, as the old king declined into dotage. His daughter Claude was useless, not taking any notice of the debaucheries of her husband, Francis. Anne shuddered at the thought of them; Francis and Claude, the king and queen in waiting, not much older than her, with an air about them that made her doubly wary. It was whispered by the maidservants that Claude, disappointed in her father's choice of husband for her, had gone in on herself, with her own household, but she was friendly with the Queen, her stepmother, and Anne's mistress, for they were both in the same situation; great princesses being used by the men in their families for dynastic reasons.

Anne tried to avoid the older generation if she could, except for her companions, the Queen's handmaidens, even though she despised their demure ways. They treated her, the youngest of them, with some indulgence, covering for her when she disappeared as she had done this afternoon.

Anne felt sorry for her mistress, Queen Mary. She might be the sister of England's Henry Vlll, but she was virtually a prisoner and always watched mercilessly by her French relatives for signs of the quickening of her womb which would mean a possible male heir for Louis, however unlikely. That would put Claude and Francis in the shadows. It was the stuff of gossip amongst her maidenly companions.

That night, as she and Jean attended the evening banquet, she whispered to him, 'I have an idea how to comfort our young friend. We shall meet at the library, tomorrow.'

As Jean stepped away from her, he nodded imperceptibly. He heard her mutter, 'I'll have no more of these Popish ways, of the Roman wickedness.'

* * * * *

The next morning when she entered the library, Anne's demeanour had altered again as if with a change of clothes she would become the serious scholar. She wore a dark, discreet gown with a bodice that was laced tight and a collar that hid her long slender neck, more in keeping with a demure maid in the service of Queen Mary. The skirt was not full or long enough to touch the floor so her delicate ankles were exposed, giving her an air of virginal seriousness.

The boys were waiting for her, Jean running his finger along the shelves as if to test for dust, Georges sitting, with his head leaning on his folded arms, his eyes closed.

Anne smiled at them. By way of greeting, she said, 'Popish ways, boys; we must study them. Remember what Stefano says, we must learn our enemies' ways if we are to rout them. Let us compare the words of the Bible with what we know of our priests at court.' She reached for and opened a book.

All three of them had studied like this before, the scriptures and other works, and Anne started to leaf through the great volumes, chained to the walls, to find something to read. Jean also started searching. As she did so, she gently played with the curls on Georges' head, and he leant against her, for comfort. She smiled at Jean over his head. With these two, she was already adept at working out how to please men.

Anne left her book and moved to Jean to see what he was

23

reading, and leaned over his shoulder and read aloud, '*and the priests stood in the square and pontificated on adultery, condemning those who would sleep with all others but their wives, who had no loyalty to their marriage vows, who took whomsoever they should wish ... The same priests who were married to God; the same priests who had sworn loyalty to the Pope as Earth's representative of God, the very same stood in the square condemning adultery. And wherefore are they now, those same priests, after their sermons so just and so right? Do they now pray in their cell with their hair shirts beneath their robes? Do they but sleep a few hours and rise for their prayers in the night? Are they to be seen in their cloisters singing psalms?*'

She paused and turned the book over to see the leather bound cover, 'What are you reading?'

'I found it on the top shelf; it is a new treatise from the German states, I'm sure, but look, Anne, it is badly bound, the smell is of new leather.' He took the book from her and opened the book at its frontispiece, 'I've no idea how it got there.' Jean sounded apologetic but Georges interrupted, 'Have you heard about that Cardinal who was found defrocking his young priest, explaining that it was the way of the Court? And we all know what that means. He tried to tell the Priest he was privileged of God and this was another way to take the sacrament.'

Anne laughed, 'Indeed we have all heard of that. 'Tis old news.'

Georges opened his mouth and shut it again. Anne did not look at him. She sensed that he had only just heard of it, but then he had not been at the masque the night before. She also sensed his unease, it being too close to what had happened to him. She and Jean had caught the gossip as they had mingled amongst the courtiers. Anne took pity on him, and added, 'But it will surely be everywhere today, how the priest threw up his hands in mock horror and claimed he was not good enough to be so treated by his superior. He could not be worthy of such an honour.'

Her young friend just stared at her, but Anne continued, 'At least there were no stories of De Saumur's lust getting of bounds, no gossip about that. Georges, don't worry, your secret is safe; nobody mentioned you or de Saumur.'

Jean looked up at her, nodded slightly, and turned to look at Georges. Anne had moved round and was playing with his curls again.

'Little one, no-one else knows, only us – and we read today to hear God's words on such matters and then we will decide what to do, trust me?' Georges looked up at her, a sideways, upwards glance, and he smiled, relieved that he had the full story of the young priest but also comforted that his experiences were not Court gossip.

'Read on then ...' he prompted her

Anne was pleased. Her ploy had worked. By showing the lad how common such matters were among the courtiers, priests and other hangers-on at Court, she was sure he felt more comfortable about his own experience. Or so she hoped.

She took up the treatise again and explained, 'You do realise this has only just been translated from the Latin into French, so all the Court can read it? I wager it will be thrown at the Cardinal's face!' Then she repeated the last lines and carried on, '*Are they to be seen in their cloisters singing psalms? Holy people, my people, do not search for them in such austere places. For ye shall not find them so. Indeed no. Instead they are in the dens of iniquity. They lie in the bed of women forgetting those oaths of fealty to God and their Pope, their promises of chastity and marriage to the Church. Instead they are lusting and a-bedding with whomsoever they should wish. And the women flock to them for they think it good to lie with such as they, who are, for them, the representative of the good lord on earth*'.

Dinteville followed the words on the page with his index finger. Young Georges watched Anne as she read.

'Trust you to find that section!' Georges exclaimed when she paused for breath.

'And what do you mean by that?' she snapped back. He grinned and she mirrored his expression. The boys knew Anne was not fond of the priests who told her to be more demure, when they tried to quell her rebellious questioning.

Dinteville interrupted. 'And should we follow their example? Should we pray in one way and do another? No, we should look within our own souls as the Germans are saying. God gave us our reason and our hearts and we would look within our own hearts. We cannot follow such as they!' He chanted enthusiastically, as he had done on the many occasions they had discussed religion when their tutor was absent.

Anne though did not take up the challenge of Jean's questions. She picked up the book again and flicked through the pages, and read aloud from another passage, '*It is a basic belief of the good Christian that when he takes the sacrament he is eating of the body of Christ and drinking the blood of our Lord Jesus and as such he is part of the Holy Church and takes into himself*' - and herself, added Anne silently, but then carried on reading, '*... the holiness of the Lord and is absolved of sin and is cleansed. But what if that body corporate is rotten?*' She stopped reading and explained, 'That is called transubstantiation of the body of Christ' Then, without waiting for any comment from her companions, she carried on, '*What if the very priest who administers that sacrament as His Holiness the Pope's representative is not cleansed of his sins? What if the Pope himself, the earthly vessel of our Lord God Almighty with his many 'nieces' and 'nephews' has not been cleansed of his sins? The very sacrament itself must then be rotten, like a rotting body on the field of death, and those taking the sacrament from such as these must also be taking unto themselves the very rottenness and be tainted forever.*'

Anne looked up. 'By God this is true stuff, I say.' She looked at the two boys, her friends, and their faces were a-glow with the very strangeness and wickedness of reading such a tract that condemned the only church they knew.

'Go on, Nan, read on.'

Anne picked up the heavy tome and held it aloft, taking on the demeanour of their tutor, a serious man from Alsace, who taught them logic, '*And therefore I say unto you that when you take the sacrament it cannot be the very blood of Christ that you drink, it cannot be the body of Christ that ye eat. Indeed, no, it is the spirit of the Lord which descends from heaven, like the dove of the ascension, and blesses you with the spirit of our Lord and all those that purport to intercede; indeed, all those priests and bishops and archbishops and cardinals and, yea, even the Pope himself, are but weak vessels of humanity and thou shall not follow their ways ...'*

Anne stopped, threw the book aside. 'I cannot accept that. I like to see the Cardinals in their red robes and the large crosses carried before them on high days, and I like the music of mass and I like the services and I would not for the world want to follow my conscience in all things. How would we know what is holy if they were not there to tell us? Yes, we can read our Bible in French, but we need those to explain the contradictions.' She repeated, 'I like the music and the prayers of mass, they uplift my soul. And, after all, de Selve,' she faced Georges sternly, 'you are to be a priest and you would not be like that, would you?'

There was a silence in the room. Each of them was thinking of their futures, and all three knew they had predetermined paths to follow. Anne for marriage with a high born individual as yet unchosen; de Selve in the Church with a bishopric already reserved for him when he was old enough and Dinteville would follow his father as a courtier and ambassador.

De Selve stood up and walked to her, and held her two hands in his. 'We can reform our Church, we three. All we need to do is make our way in the world and then, from our positions of power, we can persuade the Pope to hold another Council like the Council of Basle, when he will issue bulls on how his priests should behave and I will persuade him to back up his instructions with the threat of excommunication. We can persuade our own bishops and cardinals to spread the word. I, in my priesthood; you through the influence of your great husband, whoever he might be, and Jean, here, as an ambassador.'

The girl returned his ardent gaze and knew that he burned with the same desire as her to change the world as only those on the threshold of life could burn. He had the added need for revenge

27

for being raped by a so-called man of God. As they stood there, Dinteville joined them, and put his arms round their shoulders, and said, 'Yes, all four of us may be parted but let us swear a solemn oath. With our blood. '

'But where is Stefano? Has anyone seen him since we last met in the gallery?' Anne interrupted. She always saw the three boys together, Jean, Georges and Stefano, and now, at a point where they were swearing fealty he was missing.

Georges let go her hands and his face creased in worry lines. Anne knew he was thinking the same as she was, 'No, I haven't seen him since ...'

'Nor I, he was not at sword practice this morning.' Jean also looked disturbed. It dawned on all three of them that Stefano had not been seen at breakfast, nor the mid day repast, nor at the morning mass that everyone attended.

'I did not like the way he reacted after your confession, Georges,' Anne whispered. 'He is impulsive. What if ...?'

Jean interrupted, 'We must search for him.'

They separated. They first went to the practice yard but the servants denied any sight of him that day. They searched all over the chateau, asked at the stables, in the kitchen, even took the liberty of asking the priests although Stefano was not known to visit them. He was nowhere to be found. When they visited their schoolroom, their tutor was angry.

'He will be in trouble, for he has missed today's lesson,' he explained.

After two days Anne was seriously worried, overlaid with a yearning to see him again. *If I see him, I will tell him how I feel*, she promised herself.

* * * * *

Then there was news, of a sort. The Bishop of Saumur had been found dead, blood-soaked and spitted through in a dark alley in the rough hovels that clung to the walls of Blois. All the gossip was centred on why he had been in such a place, and the charitable offered the suggestion that, like a good man of God, he had been ministering to the poor, while others scoffed and hinted at necromancy or even worse. It was not unknown for those at Court to seek out the poor for their own pleasures; even Anne knew that. The fact that he had been found not just stabbed but hacked by many violent blows seemed to be adding to the gossip. His body was brought back and he lay in state in the great chapel.

Anne. Jean and Georges followed in the train of their households into the funeral mass a few days later, an event which lasted all day and, when all was over, in the gloom of evening, they met in the long gallery.

'I spat at his body, and disguised it as a sneeze,' boasted young Georges, and Anne and Jean applauded him. Throughout the droning of the priests and the funerary ovations Anne had anxiously but discreetly looked amongst the host for the dark shiny curls of Stefano. He would have been there if he had been at court, she knew, as all the great dukes and their households were represented. Now she was seriously worried.

'And Stefano? Where is he?'

Jean shook his head. 'Indeed, it's very worrying about our young soldier friend. I think again of the way he held his sword that day. Nobody knows who killed the Bishop and his entourage are not saying, but nobody else was hurt, I hear, only the Bishop.'

'We must make enquiries, but discreetly, agreed?' The two boys nodded and they separated.

* * * * *

Stefano was never seen again. It was as if a door had been shut. Nobody mentioned him and when Anne asked tutors or swordsmen, courtiers or servants, she was met with an embarrassed silence. Eventually she realised she was being talked about and, mindful of her reputation, stopped making enquiries. Even Jean and Georges stopped talking about Stefano, not knowing how to deal with the loss.

'We must meet, us three, in the gallery.' Anne insisted.

Jean and Georges agreed, and when they met they swore their bloody oath which would shape their future together.

Chapter Five

Amboise 1516

It was a cold day. King Louis had died, his widow Queen Mary had returned to England but Anne was still at court. Queen Claude had insisted she stay and become part of her retinue and now she was rushing to collect a warmer cloak for the queen who froze on her daily outing. Anne had agreed to stay, hoping that if she stayed and Stefano *was* alive he would find her. She had grieved for her lost unrequited Italian lover for many months without mentioning him to anyone else. As the days, months and years passed he was built up in her mind as if he were Petrarch and Boccaccio in one. Although she was never to give any outward sign, she knew that her heart had iced up in some way by the thwarted feelings she had had for the lost boy. The only memory she had of him was a piece of torn taffeta, and the very sight of it made her smile. The service she gave to Queen Claude comforted her somewhat, as the young queen had begged her not to return to England.

'Please, dear Anne, your dancing is so exquisite you can take my place, for I cannot dance with this limp of mine, and I am happy to watch you. And your French is so good you could almost be a Frenchwoman! Perhaps some French noble will ask for you, and I promise you a dowry, as my lady-in-waiting.'

Her father had concurred. *Stay, you have the favour of the highest in the land, we are very proud of you*. The words in her father's letter echoed in her head as she raced back for her Queen's heavier cloak from her apartments. The queen insisted on her daily walk out in the formal grounds of the palace, feet crunching on the gravel path, the noise almost drowning out the conversations she had with one

30

of her maids. As Anne left, Claude was deep in conversation with Marguerite, her sister-in-law.

Anne was glad to tear away from the group. She was the only foreigner serving the new queen but she did not mind. She felt more French than English but sometimes it was good to be on her own.

She hoped she could stay in France, for she no longer remembered her English home and believed it to be cold and dark in the northern land. She also thought she would have more chance of carrying out her oath where she had the support of Jean and Georges, who were now involved in the politics of the French Court.

Despite the crisp air Anne was not cold, but she would always move fast and elegantly, enjoying the rustle of the rich cloth of her skirts, which fitted her now. The only disappointment was that, with the filling out of her figure, and added responsibilities, she found that it was not so easy to disappear and meet with her friends, Dinteville and de Selve. They were still at Court and she kept in touch with them when she could, exchanging pleasantries in the formal dances and conversing sedately with them in the clamour of the crowds. Sometimes they would arrange to meet secretly. Today, being sent on this errand meant she could find them and have a quick exchange of gossip.

As she scurried through the rich panelled corridors she was so intent on her plans that she did not notice King Francis's retinue approaching. King and queen kept separate households and only met for masques and banquets, and great state events. Anne did not mind this as she found the king and his lords threatening. She knew how to handle them on state occasions, where all she was required to do was to be seated demurely near her queen and dance occasionally when asked. Normally she would know the king was approaching by the rich smell of roses of attar that surrounded him, his vanity requiring his presence to be enhanced by such perfumes, and when she smelt this, she would slip into a side door. She found meeting with him embarrassing. He was always attentive to her to the point of it being remarked upon, and other courtiers would whisper, in loud stage voices, *'The English girl will be his next mistress, oui?'* and she did not know how to deal with it. She knew she would not want the dubious honour of being one of the King's many paramours. Today she was too late, for he was upon her.

'Qu'est ce qui? The little English maid. Bonjour, ma'amselle'.

He was so close she could almost feel the velvet of his formal coat, smell the garlic on his breath. He turned to his group. 'Look, how she blushes, 'tis an English trait that our French maids just cannot copy.'

The nobles laughed at his witticism.

Then he lifted up her chin with his long slender hand, and laughed into her eyes.

'We shall meet again, my little maid.'

She struggled free, curtsied and said in impeccable French, 'Excusez-moi, but I must fetch a cloak for my mistress who freezes, I cannot wait.' And she walked away quickly, head held high, down the corridor, trying to ignore the mocking laughter of the king and his retinue.

The encounter so troubled her that she forgot to try to find her friends and hastily found her queen's cloak instead and ran, using a back way to reach the garden again, eagerly joining the giggling girls surrounding her serious mistress.

* * * * *

She was woken by the rough hand of the matron who watched over their dormitory.

'Waken, maid, for you have been called and 'tis a great honour. You have been summoned by his majesty and must go to him.'

It was the lascivious smile that accompanied the words that frightened Anne, and she turned over, pulling the covers over her, and refused to rise. She knew what the summons meant and knew too that it would be the end of her dreams, for she was intent on no scandal attaching to her as it had to her sister Mary. She was determined to make a marriage as high as possible. Gossip from the English Court arrived by couriers and she had been teased by some of the King's cronies about her sister's antics with King Henry VIII of England. It had been expected that she too would grant such favours but she had coldly rebuffed the idea. Now the king had called for her she knew she would have to use all her guile to remain intact, as she fully intended. She was roughly hauled out of bed and the matron whispered, "Tis an honour, indeed. Now you must go.'

Anne did not think so but knew she would have to obey. She did not like the heavy-lipped king with his long nose and chin, and found the thought of him making love to her quite repulsive. She prayed that whoever her chosen husband would be would have some redeeming features but certainly King Francis did not have any as far as she was concerned.

Wrapping her velvet cloak over the cotton nightgown, she slipped her feet into soft indoor shoes. She made an attempt to hide her hair in a lace cap but, without the help of one of her companions who could braid it, the dark strands fell out so it stayed flowing around her shoulders. She tripped through the darkened corridors, lit at intervals by tallows, and all quiet now as most of the courtiers slept. *Help me Lord, bring your protector to me. She imagined a giant holding her safe, a warm and motherly smell emanating from the rough cloak as she tried to bury her face and forget what was happening. St Christopher, was that her patron saint? She hurried on, suddenly feeling confident. She would be safe.*

As she reached the royal apartments, she moved through room after connecting room but was suddenly stopped short by a muttering in a low-lit corner. She stopped and glided silently over to the shape. A dark-robed figure knelt at a prayer stool, muttering to himself. As she approached he looked up. His face was sharp in the dim light, with dark socketed eyes so there was no gleam from them. As she approached he moved so quickly that she jumped. Before she knew it, he was standing beside her, his breathing heavy on her bare shoulder. *St Christopher, help me now. My trial has begun.*

'The King's whore; surely a man of God should break you first.' He pawed her breast as he put his other hand over her mouth. She struggled, baring her teeth beneath the sweaty palm, pushed forward and bit whatever she could reach. He yelped.

'A man of God. You're the devil's priest. I'll remember you and yours,' she hissed as she slipped away and ran.

There were at least two more galleries to go, and now she was terribly afraid, and found she was trembling. 'Calm yourself, calm yourself, the king may be worse,' she muttered, surprised at how loud her voice sounded in the night-emptiness.

She reached the great golden doors of the king's boudoir, took a deep breath and knocked. It was chilly in the corridor and she shivered. The air in the enclosed space smelt foetid with the tallow from the flares. The door slid open noiselessly and, when she walked in, slammed shut behind her. Inside, there was the rich smell of perfumes strengthened by the warmth of the room, such a contrast to the chill and odour of the corridor. She could see no-one. The room was lit by soft candlelight. A fire roared in the fireplace, the light glinting on rich gold and jewelled furniture. A huge four-poster, draped with rich red hangings, soft cushions and sumptuous cloths, dominated the chamber. It seemed to be undulating in the flickering of the fire and the candles. Even the wooden uprights of the bed reflected the light, so well-polished were they. Instinctively she knew she was not alone, and turned round. There was the King, in a red velvet night robe, his white undershirt open at the neck. His face gleamed from the reflection of the many candles and the blazing fire, his large nose and eyes accentuated by the shadows. Anne's sight of the bed still echoed before her eyes as she faced her captor. He stood there, relaxed, smiling; his thick lips damp and half open.

She stood her ground. She knew that every step backwards was a step nearer to that sumptuous bed. She was only too aware of the gossip; that her sister was the mistress of the English king, and the way it was spoken about meant that Mary was debased, bad coin. Anne remembered she was an English lady and still a virgin. That was her passport to power: her only passport. As she thought of this her face set into a series of thin lines; thin lipped mouth, narrowed eyes, the nose pinched. Francis stopped his advance for a second.

'Mon Dieu, are you going to freeze me with that look, mon enfant?'

'I know not what you mean, my Lord, but I am cold and have been woken from a deep sleep. I would have my sleep so I can be jolly in the morn with my good queen.'

He nodded and surveyed her. She was gratified to see that her look had made him hesitate. Still he did not move but watched her, and she wondered what he saw. A young maid in the first stages of womanhood, ready to be broken into like a sweet orange, she guessed. She could see him slavering over the slight dip between her tiny breasts. She pulled back her hair and tried to hide it under the cap, knowing that it was probably darkly alluring and shiny in the candlelight. She stared back at him, feeling angry and cold. Francis shivered.

'You seem to have a halo around your head,' he whispered. Then he shook himself, and said with more assurance, 'No, it is a trick of the light.' He stepped nearer to her but, instead of taking her, walked round her, still looking at her. Anne stood still, waiting.

'Come; let me show you my collection of private paintings ...'

'Nay, I have heard of them and will have nothing to do with it.'

He turned to face her, puzzled now.

'Do you realise that if I take you as my mistress it will be a great privilege?'

'I think not so,' she answered pertly.

'And why not?' he demanded but she knew she had caught his attention. She had listened to him conversing with philosophers and artists at Court and had found it entertaining; Francis liked a good debate, and she resolved to keep him talking.

'I will save myself for my betrothed and no-one else. My sister is the mistress of King Henry and she is not happy. It seems to me

35

that such a duty does not lead to great things.'

'And you will do great things?' he asked ironically.

'I know I have a destiny,' she said, her head held high so that her long neck was accentuated.

'And what is that, young one?'

'I know not, but I am sure I will know when I am called.'

He laughed then and rubbed his hands together as if relishing a new experience. He was standing at the bed now, still facing her.

'Indeed, young Anne, you are attracting me to you as you speak. Come here.'

She stood a moment but his voice was stern and she obeyed. He moved back as she came to him, and stood leaning against the side of the bed, one hand on the bedpost. Even though she trembled inwardly, she would not show it and tried to concentrate on the patterns on the bedposts and the rich coverings. She realised the bed was raised on a daïs with gold-gilded carving on the posts. The ornate tapestry on the bed was blue embroidered with yellow fleur- de-lys: the King's colours. Now that she was so close she could see that on the curtains surrounding the bed there were gold stars. She glided towards the king and stood demurely before him, her hands held behind her back. She looked at him high up on the dais. He stepped down and took her in his arms and kissed her. His full lips pressed against hers, forcing them open and his tongue intruded into her mouth so that she felt faint. He smelt of sour wine and garlic, of sweat and stale clothes. His tongue pressed between her teeth and horrified her. She stiffened, her body not responding to his searching caresses and, positioning her teeth, she bit down hard on his thick lower lip, and at the same time started to pummel his chest. Suddenly he released her so that she fell to the floor.

She looked up at him aghast. He held his hand to his mouth and globules of red bubbled between the fingers. It reminded her of her holy vow with Georges and Jean.

'You'll not have me,' she hissed up at him, scrabbling away towards the door. She stopped as her back touched the wall.

Francis pulled out a lace kerchief and continued to dab at his bleeding lip.

Then he muttered, through his hand, 'Leave now, English lioness, I'll not play with a stiff doll. I like my women wilting and willing. Go on, go!'

She pulled herself up using the wall to assist, gathered her cloak around her and edged to the door. When she felt the handle, she turned it.

'I'm sorry ...' her breath came in short sharp gusts; she was trembling so, but still she tried to keep outwardly calm.

Francis glared at her and said thickly, 'I could have you assassinated for this, as we did your Italian after he murdered my friend the bishop.'

She fumbled with the door handle, which twisted awkwardly, her hands cold and almost useless but, with a surge of inner strength, she released the catch and was free. His words had made her even more determined to get out. Francis was still threatening her, his voice loud now. The last words she heard as she ran were, 'How dare you presume to be great from such a beginning ...?' She did not care what he shouted at her; she was in the cool of the empty corridor and now its very chill seemed welcoming.

As she ran through the corridors, his words about 'the Italian' stirred in her mind, and all she could see was Stefano, chopped down after he had taken his revenge. *She had to find Jean and Georges.* They had to know what had happened. She was hot now with horror at what she had learnt this night. No longer cold but burning with the terror of her escape. *Thank you my patron saint, for keeping me safe.* She was grateful that the matron was sitting in her chair, head lolled forward and snoring loudly. Creeping past her, she slid gratefully into bed but for the rest of the night stayed awake, fear and sadness mixing with a strange sense of triumph that she had not lost her virginity to the King.

Chapter Six

Was it coincidence that after this she was left to wilt at the French Court without hearing any news of a betrothal from her family? She was becoming impatient, knowing that she was fast growing past the usual marriageable age. But then a letter arrived: *'Be prepared to return to us in England.'*

Within a week her brother, whom she hardly knew, arrived to take her back to her birth-home. That was how she thought of it. An England she had not known for nearly ten years, to see a mother whom she hardly remembered and siblings she did not know at all, except by report. Yes, her father and her brother George had visited the French Court and she had met them so rarely she did not know how she felt towards them. Filial duty perhaps, a fondness for them as more than mere acquaintances. But she did not really *know them,* not like she knew Dinteville and de Selve. George though was the closest to her in age and he had been kind when they had met. She was curious and pleased he had been sent rather than a servant or, indeed, her father, who was so formal on the rare occasions she had seen him, almost as if he was embarrassed about her, but proud at the same time. She felt she could ask her brother what was afoot, but would never approach her father without great consideration.

For the moment though, her family situation concerned her less than the fact that she was to leave the French court. Why? True, she had disgraced herself by refusing the King, but she believed it had been so humiliating for him that he would not have revenged himself on her, for she guessed he would have had to reveal his failure in his seduction. Indeed, since that night, he had never even acknowledged her existence. There had been no repercussions and she hoped the whole situation had been forgotten, but she had kept in the background, surrounding herself with the Queen's other matrons of honour, when it was necessary for them to appear before the king. But had a letter been sent to England to her parents demanding her removal? It was not possible, she realised, not after all this time.

Her brother arrived in early spring, when the roads were only just opening up and the Channel would be choppy. He was obviously on a special trip to collect her for they did not stay long. Usually he would spend time with those he was familiar with at the Court, but that did not happen. Within a day the preparations had been made and now they were riding northwards.

Soon she was satisfied that her return home was pre-planned for George explained that he had left the English Court and his father some days before. She wanted to know about her family, and her future. George would, she thought, tell her what was amiss. They had been in the nursery together before going their separate ways of education. He had always been there, as long as she could remember but for the moment she could not even recall whether he was older or younger than her, she was so estranged from this English family of hers. He had started lessons before her so he must be older surely? As they travelled slowly north to the coast, Anne shivered, and remembered her times in the flat country of the Habsburg court and wondered if England would have that awful chill in winter. It had never been as cold in the French Court as in the quarters with the Archduchess, where winds blew straight from the north across the flat country. In France, as the weather chilled, the Court would travel further south, to the great chateaux on the Loire. Would England be horribly cold? She turned to her brother who rode with his face set firmly onward. Despite her stare he did not turn to face her so eventually she said, 'Why is Mary already at the English court? And so well established I hear. Surely I am the older?'

'She was in England. You have been in France,' he replied.

'But I am the older. Precedence has been breached.'

'What are you saying? Father would not do such a thing; he is too aware of his position. Surely he would not educate you in the way he has if you were the oldest and then forget to present you at the Court of our king before your younger sister?'

With that she realised she had puzzled him and she too was puzzled. She determined to ask her parents but now she would find out as much as she could to fit into her new life.

'Tell me about the English court. Is it as grand as the French?'

George paused, reining in his horse and staring ahead, as if he could compare the two places in the air before him. Eventually he answered, 'It's different. Where there is all white marble and golded-gilt in the French chateaux, there is red brick and wood panelling and floors at the English palaces, and there's a difference for a start, dear sister. In France, there are fortified places for living; in England there are castles made comfortable for occupation. He said nothing for a while and Anne, seeing he was thinking, left him to his silence. After a while, he looked at her and said, 'That's the difference; one is all lightness and movement, like you, Anne, and the other is dark and sombre, like our sister Mary who retires into matrimony, having done her duty by the king.'

They rode on, both of them contemplating what he had said. Then George added, 'The light is different, Anne, and I think the buildings reflect that. But our king is building some magnificent new buildings which I truly believe rival the French king's.'

The mention of the king made Anne think of her future. 'Am I to be presented at Court?'

Again her brother paused and spoke slowly. 'I know not but I think father has plans for you.'

'Yes, but what? What's to happen to me?'

George smiled then. 'You seem so impatient. I am sorry but you will have to wait until you have an interview with father. And, I warn you, he has great responsibilities at Court so don't expect him to be at Hever when we get there.'

'Hever? I am to go to Hever? But is that not in the country? I thought we would go straight to Court.'

They were on the merchant ship now, carrying them across the water. As they both watched the French coast receding, George answered, 'I believe it's only for a short time, until father …'

But Anne interrupted. 'Is it an old castle? A manor house? I do believe, George, that father did not own Hever when I left. I heard he had acquired it, from one of his visits. You know what he is like, always pleased when the king has bestowed more favours on him. All I remember is staying with mother's family in some grace and favour apartments and being looked down upon by our Norfolk cousins in the nursery.'

George was non-committal. 'Hever is a fortified mansion house, like several in the country. Father also has many good home farms and manors; there is plenty to eat from the same, but I am at Court most of the time. I do not involve myself in such mundane matters. Mary too is there, at Court, as you know, and father has great hopes of advancement.' His face lit up. 'She is a compliant good girl and her liaison with the king has given the family many favours. The king tires of her but he acts kindly towards his past mistresses and I believe it will turn out well. Now I must attend to the horses and you should go below, it is not seemly to be out in the sun in full view of the sailors.'

He turned from her and left her alone with thoughts that made her far from content. She did not go below but wandered to the bow of the ship and watched anxiously for the coast of England to appear, thinking deeply. Was she to moulder away in a 'fortified mansion house'? What was to happen to her ambitions and her dreams?

Chapter Seven

Hever Castle, Kent

'I must go out, even though it rains, I feel dull and cloistered here.'

Anne ran through the panelled corridors of what was now her home, feeling restricted and closed in after the sumptuousness of the grand palaces in France. Hever, she realised, was considered a large household by her neighbours but to her, used to thousands of people milling about, and the light of a more southern region, it seemed a poor place, dark and dingy. And more so on this wet spring morning, when the clouds were so low they hugged the distant rolling hills, blurring the landscape into nothingness.

It had been many years since she had seen the furnishings of home and everything had shrunk and become smaller to her young woman's eyes. The heavy oaken chests that had seemed huge and beautifully carved now seemed rural and rough, compared to the great gilded furniture in France. The brocade embroidered hangings, in deep reds and rusts, albeit keeping out the chill of the spring, seemed faded compared to her memory of the bright colours at King Francis' Court.

That morning she had jumped to the window only to find that the constant rain since she had arrived had not abated. She looked down at the moat, the water broken and serrated with huge rain drops, the colour of the mud the rain was stirring up.

Even though this part of the house was newly built, Anne felt it was old-fashioned. Her father, she knew, had ambitions and had kept the castle battlements to the west and the entrance still over the moat, to show he was the protector of the local populace, standing in on behalf of the king. Using new brick he had rapidly erected new apartments around the old courtyard and inside he had ordered it to be furnished well in the manner he had seen in Wolsey's palaces, so he had told her proudly on one of his visits, in the latest styles, of wood panelling, for warmth, and wooden floors for cleanliness. The work areas had stone floors to keep down the ever present dust, blood and debris raised by the preparation of food. Fine embroidered hangings hid the old stone walls. Despite these innovations, Anne thought it rural and almost obscene in its small size after what she had been used to. Even the smell of the place was cloying, with its herbal scents, after the rich roses of attar that had been newly introduced from the East in the royal Court of France.

She had been home for nearly a week and her father had not yet arrived from Court and summoned her and she still did not know why she had been ordered home. Her mother had welcomed her like the stranger she was, with dignity, assessment, and then approval at how she had grown and developed the hauteur of a Court lady, so she had been told by this mother of hers. Then Anne had been left to her own devices.

She had stepped gingerly down the narrow spiral stone of the staircase to reach the kitchen and burst into its warmth and humidity. In France she would never have dreamed of entering the working areas of palaces but here there was still a feeling of informality which in some ways she found the only refreshing thing about her situation.

'Muncy, where's Muncy?' she asked the cook who was plucking a swan, her red arms covered in the soft down as it escaped from the bag she was trying to stuff with the feathers.

'Madam, Muncy is retired, now all three of you are gone. There's no call for wet nurses or nannies in this house now. Your brother was weaned many years ago.'

'But where does she live? I have a mind to visit her.'

'On the estate – near the southern copse.' She breathed heavily as she tried to tame the feathers. 'Over the hill, and past the church. There's a small hamlet of cottages on the boundary. Her son is gamekeeper.'

'I'll go today. Now.'

The cook stopped her plucking and looked out of the window, high in the wall of the basement kitchen. Rain ran down the glass, not in trickles but as a steady flow. She looked back at her young mistress. Anne stood there, a grim smile on her thin lips.

'Yes, it rains, but I've a heavy cloak and if you can wrap the food in oiled cloth it will keep for Muncy. I will go now.'

'Food, madam? I am sure your old nurse has more than she needs.'

'Food. I want to take her something. She was good to me and, now I am home, I will check she has all she wants.'

Anne started to walk around the kitchen, collecting pies and dainties, bread and jellies. She placed them by the side of the near naked swan carcass and ordered, 'Pack these, and find some fruit as well. Are strawberries in season yet?'

'Strawberries, Madam? With this wet spring? You'll be lucky to have any at all, they're not usually ready until June.'

'So late here. In France the strawberries are ready in early May. Find something for her though, please.'

The cook grumbled but Anne turned to her and smiled, patting her shoulder in a conciliatory way and the cook melted. Anne knew she would have her way and left to clothe herself appropriately for the weather she was to face. She would wear wooden pattens to keep the rain from her feet and a long cloak of heavy hessian to protect her good dress.

She set off, across the moat and taking the long sloping hill easily, striding out, holding the hood close around her face, the basket of victuals hidden under the capacious outer robe. Because of the driving drizzle of rain, she kept her head down.

She only had to ask once in the tiny hamlet to be shown Muncy's home. It was set back, curtained by trees, as if the occupants wanted to disappear into the woods. When she reached the cottage, she knocked gently. There was no answer. She knocked again, hard and then walked in for there was only a latch to the door. Keys and locks were, she realised, for the rich.

44

Inside, the tiny windows, bare of glass, did not let in much light, especially on a grim day like today when the sky was armour-grey, even though the rough sack that stood for a curtainh was pulled back away from the window aperture. A draught from the door caught the embers of the fire which had died down and it sparked, one solitary flame rising. She called, 'Muncy, Muncy, are you there?'

The cottage had but one room with a large fireplace and spit, copying that in the manor house although the surround was of rough brick and not carved stone. As her eyes became accustomed to the gloom, Anne saw in one corner a rough bed. On it lay a bundle of misshapen bedding which, she realised, covered her old nurse. There was a smell of sour body, of illness. The person who had weaned her, who had cared for her, dressed her, cuddled her, until she left as a tiny child for her life's training. Anne almost recoiled from the smell of decay, but her concern for the person she remembered made her step forward.

She suddenly felt afraid. She kept her voice low as she spoke, 'Muncy. Why do you lie abed?'

'Who be that? Who be you?'

The voice was querulous and weak. Gone was the gentle firm voice of comfort the girl remembered. Her dread heightened, the dread of a young vital being for the strangeness of age.

She approached slowly, automatically placing the basket of viands on a table as she passed. She unconsciously held her dress high away from the musty straw which covered the earth floor. As she reached the pallet, she pulled back her hood, the collected rain water causing puddles on the floor which rapidly disappeared into the straw, raising a soft grassy smell.

'Muncy, 'tis I, Anne, your little Nan ...'

The bedding moved and a crabbed hand appeared and then the head, covered in a tight cotton bonnet. Grey wispy hairs, so unlike the abundant golden mop that Anne recalled, escaped on to the wrinkled forehead. The face was sunk into itself, the eyes deep, grey in a milky white surround of encroaching blindness. But there was still a dignity about the face that she remembered.

Anne took the hand and held it in her two. It was warm with a feverish dry warmth. She knelt so her face was on the same level as that of her old nurse's, to give the old lady a chance to see her.

There was a long pause. Then, 'My little Nan, 'tis truly you!'

She tried to raise herself on one elbow, but Anne stopped her. She moved to sit at the head of the rude bed, behind the nurse, and raised the shrunken body and placed her arms around her so that the old head was resting on her breast. Anne wanted to do it, so aware that it was a mirror image of the many times that she had been cradled from the world when she was an infant. But Muncy struggled, and cried out, as if in pain.

'No, girl, let me see you, I would but see you again before I die. You, such a bonny child, with those wicked dark eyes which flashed at me to get your own way.' She turned, and Anne eased her down on the pillow, and moved to stand before her. She undid the cloak so Muncy could see the fine raiment of dark satin beneath, the gold and pearl necklace fashioned in a capital 'B' at her throat, to show she was a Boleyn.

'Aye,' sighed the old nurse, 'truly when you were a babe I could see you would be a great one, like your father before you. It broke my heart to tell him so but I knew you had to be given the chances. You had to go away for your own good, to hide … .no, I will not say it. As you grew, you were not like that strumpet your sister, Mary, who only had brains in her legs enough to open them for the King, as I have heard! If you were not stretched you too would come to mischief with that sharp mind of yours. But it broke me, seeing you go. And then to nurse that pukeling of a brother of yours ... and the others who died ...'

'But Muncy, how do you live? Who cares for you?'

'Ah, my son, when he is at home. But he too has his duties. Do you not remember Tom?'

Anne tried to remember someone called Tom, but it all seemed dark.

'Aye, my little one, it was not the best of times for you. You

46

would be grieving, I'll be bound, for your home and your family. It would have been hard for you, that trip. Tom went with you in your retinue to the Court of the Hapsburg dowager. I charged him to hold you in the storm if there was one, and he did, he told me he did, and that you clung to him as if he was the very wet-nurse you had left behind.'

Her rheumy eyes were lit up now, and Anne realised she was talking about those she loved the most. Anne tried to recall the time. As she sat there, emotion swept over her. She had been very sea-sick, very ill, travelling across the Channel. So had the others of course, the other ladies who travelled with her, but they had been older, and had had servants of their own, being more established. Anne was so young that she had no-one to help and none had taken any notice of her as she whimpered in her own vomit, storm-tossed and lonely, but trying to keep her dignity as her father had ordered. The smell of Muncy, strange and old now, but still with that residue of herbs and milkiness, made her remember the feeling of being swept up, and pressing her face to the hard chest of a larger person where she had been comforted. Tom had lifted her in his arms and quietly crooned to her. His voice had been broken, not quite man, not quite woman, but the tune she recognised as a lullaby of Muncy's. She had hidden her face in his rough clothes and there she had smelt the milky residue of Muncy, and been comforted. *Her patron saint, her rescuer.* But when she had reached her destination she had been swept along by all the new sights and sounds and smells. New people came and caught her attention and the memory had faded. She had stopped thinking of what had happened to her saviour in the night. Now she realised she had always had a residue of the dream-like time and had always thought that person was her patron saint, an imaginary being of whom she had dreamed. Indeed, she realised that, in times of stress, that image had come to her as a comfort.

Now she could remember. So, that was Tom, Muncy's son. As she thought, Anne remembered what the cook had said. Muncy lived with her son, the gamekeeper. She moved back to the table and fished in the basket she had carried with her.

'I've brought you some sweetmeats. Pies, and game.' She pulled out a pie and proffered it to the old lady, who shook her head.

'Dear child, that is no good for me now. Sans teeth, I eat but gruel. I am not long for the world ...'

Anne dropped the pie on the table and ran to her side, 'Don't say that, dear nurse, I would have you nurse my sons!'

Muncy smiled and said breathlessly, 'Anne, my child, if there is but one more thing I would teach you, it is that death must come to us all, and I am prepared for it. The priest has been sent for but he does not come to the likes of me, except for gold, and we have none. So I must needs die and go to Purgatory until my soul is cleansed.' She took a deep breath as if to go on but Anne interrupted, 'Oh no, Muncy, you'll not go to Purgatory for you have been too good in your life! You must go straight to heaven!'

'Child, it is not for you to say so!'

'But I do say so, for I do not believe in Purgatory anyway!'

She started striding up and down the small room, knocking a stool over in her eagerness. 'No, Muncy, there is no such place. It is not described in the Bible, the good Lord's own words, and so it does not exist! It is just made up by the priests so they can be paid more for absolution.'

The old lady fell back on the rags which stood for pillows.

'Oh, mercy, mercy, the child speaks such wicked things. You sound like my son! What is the world coming to? I can but quit it soon!'

Anne stopped her pacing, sat at the end of the bed. 'Your son? Tom? What can a gamekeeper know of such things?'

'All he has been taught by the priests and more from his own questioning mind!' It was not the nurse that answered. Anne jumped from the bed and turned round. The deep voice had come from the door and at first she could see nothing, for the light behind just showed a tall broad-shouldered shadow. The shadow

48

moved and came in. From his left hand hung two hares held by the ears. Rain dripped from his battered hat, from his nose and bare chin, from his hands. As he came nearer, Anne could smell the sweat of a working man, could see the hard gnarled hands and the roughened face. But the voice, the voice had a timbre in it that hinted of something other than a working man.

'Tom? Are you Tom?'

He slapped the hares on the table and bowed. It was a mocking movement, and at once Anne felt anger at this inferior acting so disdainfully. She stepped back and looked at him haughtily:

'Do you know who I am?'

He pushed past her, just avoiding touching her in the small hut, and she could see, now that he was in the dull light from the window-aperture, that he had a sardonic smile on his face. He did not answer at once, but raked the fire to tinder up the flames and tested the pan for water.

'Mother, how are you? I'm sorry I've been out so long, you must be sore ready for your meal. But I can see you are being cared for by your visitor. Hey what do we have here?'

He had found the basket and was raking through. He took a bite out of one of the pies before Anne could stop him. She was almost tempted to gather all the viands together and leave at once, but did not do so for Muncy's sake.

She stood there and repeated, 'Do you know who I am?'

'Of course I do, young Anne! Don't stamp like that! I saw you being fed at Mother's breast as a baby. Aye, you've grown into a great lady, I'll give you that!' He was walking round her now, munching all the time. She flicked off a crumb from her shoulder, which he had spat out as he ate and spoke at the same time.

He continued, as she stood there trying to find fitting words to put this man down, 'More's the pity that you recognise me not! After acting as wet-nurse across the Ocean and nearly being killed on the way back!' He stopped in front of her then and bowed low, 'Master Tom at your service, Ma-am!'

'Tom Muncy, you deserve to be shot for your rudeness!'

'Priedeux, Ma-am, Priedeux is my true name, as I know full well from the locket and parchment around my neck.' As he spoke he touched something beneath his tunic.

'But if you are Muncy's son, why aren't you called 'Muncy?'

Muncy answered, her voice cracking, and they both swung round to her, 'Because he is not my blood child, but indeed he is my son, as I have truly raised him.'

Anne looked at him then and realised he bore no resemblance to her old nurse, Tom was fine featured beneath the damp grime, where mother Muncy had been round like a dumpling, with a snub nose and rosy cheeks; although she was now cracked and thin. He was dark where she had been Saxon fair.

Muncy had been watching them and when Anne stopped surveying the man and turned to her, she nodded, and sighed, 'Aye, Anne, another of my charges, but never reclaimed. A great lady brought him to me years ago and gave me gold to wet-nurse him. She knew I could be discreet. I was pleased.'

With this she held out her crabbed hand and Tom strode over and took it, held it against his chest and looked down at her with such a look of love that Anne forgave him his boorish ways. She was strongly loyal to those who helped her, like she would be to Jean and Georges, but if anyone should cross her, she would be strongly antagonistic. Now she added Tom Priedeux to those she would always trust and help, because of his absolute devotion to Muncy whom she always remembered with such gratitude and honour.

Her old nurse continued, 'All she said was that his name was Priedeux and I was to care for him as if he was my own son until he should be called away. To be honest, Anne, I was so pleased when the call for him never came. I prayed as he grew great in stature. I prayed that no-one would ever come. It was wicked of me, but as he grew so my love for him grew. I loved you all, my charges, and each time you were taken away my heart grieved. By the time he had been with me four summers I knew that if I could I would have lied my way to Hell to keep him. By the time a few more summers had passed she would not have been able to take him from me without tearing the heart from my breast. But I did right by him – I took him to the priests to educate him in the reading and the writing. She left money enough for that.'

'You can read and write?'

'Aye, Ma-am, I took to it right readily. Not to the monks you understand, I never liked their popish ways, but I took what they taught me right enough.'

'Why do you not like their ways?'

He looked at her then, a hard strange assessing look and then away at his adoptive mother. She understood. She moved nearer to Muncy. 'Dear, dear Muncy, I came because I believe I will not be staying at Hever long. But I will come and see you every day I am here, every day, I promise.'

She bent and kissed the dry wrinkled brow and the old hand reached up and stroked her black hair. After a few moments, Anne moved away, fastening her cloak.

Muncy cried out, 'Tom, walk with her back to the big house, and keep her safe!'

The young charges moved away together, but Tom stood back to allow Anne first exit, as if, she thought, he did really know rules of courtesy by birth. It was not an obsequious action, but respectful. She decided she liked him even more and was curious about him.

They walked along in silence for a while. It was Anne who spoke first.

'You don't like the priests! Tell me why.'

She looked up at him, the hood moving back from her face so that the large droplets from the trees in the avenue they walked along fell on her face.

He laughed, 'For one thing, they do not come to see mother, in her last hours, but that is but a small thing.' Then he added, 'To me, but not to her.' He paused, and continued in a low voice which Anne had to struggle to hear over the constant noise of the downpour and the dripping from the trees.

51

'They pretend to be holy and are blacker than the devil. They tell us to be pure but their actions are impure. They tell us we are sinful; they tell us to beware of the cardinal sins but then they are caught in the very acts themselves. They are cruel, unnatural men, priests and monks. Huh, forget them! I listened and watched and learnt. I learnt to keep quiet and keep my own judgement, to question in my own head, and assess what they told me and take to myself the truths I found whilst ignoring the falsehoods.'

Anne was impressed. As he spoke he looked ahead, not at her, and spoke as if in a daze. Surely, she thought, this invective was not just because he had been rapped over the knuckles as a child by the monks who taught him. There must be more to it then that. 'Shall I tell you of the French Court, and the priests who live there?'

He turned and looked at her then and nodded.

Anne started, 'There were stories of debaucheries and wickedness ... one which I shall tell you about and will truly shock. It is a truth that the French King, Kind Francis, has a gallery of pictures of nudity and ribald paintings ...'

'Did you ever see them?'

She shivered, the memory of that night returning. Spoke quickly, 'Nay, I was too well protected but nothing could stop the gossip reaching us. The king would take his mistresses to this gallery but the priests also would use it. One cardinal, dressed in the crimson robes of his office, so I have been told, took two boys to this gallery and showed them the Greek pictures of men together. He watched the boys' faces and one crimsoned the same as the cardinal's cloak, while the other merely looked puzzled, sad. The cardinal took the boy who blushed and placed his hands over his member and felt it was hard and played it until the boy fell on his knees with the exquisite pleasure of his first ... '

She watched Priedeux carefully. His face showed no reaction but the muscle in the arm she held seemed to tighten. He understood. She continued, 'The cardinal then took him to his room. That is the sort of story, which I verily believe to be true, that circulated the French Court!' Anne spat out the last words, to show Priedeux that she was disgusted.

'So, you can tell why I hate the priests,' he said slowly.

Anne had deliberately told the story, knowing that, as when she had comforted Georges all those months ago, sometimes one confession will give someone the freedom to confess themselves. Now she did not look at Tom but put her hand on the rough cloth of his sleeve, which was now damp, in sympathy and understanding. She knew no words could assuage the bitterness the man felt for how he had been treated as a boy. She also felt pleased that her guess had been right. Without him elaborating, she knew how Priedeux had been abused. She assumed that, like herself and her friends in France, he would never like priests and would always judge for himself. She was confident now that she could tell him about the new learning coming out of the German towns.

'You know, there is a great movement to reform the church?'

'Nay, I have no books or information except the gossip that comes from the house.'

'In France I read the Bible, in French and in English, and talked with many. There is a movement in the northern states, in the Hapsburg towns, that is trying to change the way we worship. They say we should listen to our own consciences and do what we will in the world, always thinking of the good of the world, and the Lord will forgive us. Confession and absolution from another human cannot save us, only the Lord himself.'

'Aye, Ma-am, that is what I have concluded.'

There was a silence between them as they negotiated a gap through a hedge to reach the land that sloped down to the home farm. She could see the glinting of the River Eden that skirted the buildings but not the moat which was hidden in a dip.

'Have you always been gamekeeper, here, on father's lands?'

'Nay, I ran away as I grew to manhood, angry at everything, even Muncy for I felt she kept me from my true state. I had dreams of being a great man. I wandered many a month and found London and found myself. Then I came back and your father was good enough to allow me to stay with Muncy and when the old gamekeeper died your father gave me the job. 'Twil do for now,' he said sadly.

Anne, young as she was, recognised thwarted ambition. A silence fell between them. They had reached the moat around the castle and would soon part. Suddenly Anne said, 'Priedeux, will you be my servant?'

'Tom, call me Tom. The name Priedeux is a private name.'

'Nay, I will call you Priedeux, if you become my servant.'

'Mistress Anne, I already serve you and your father. I am gamekeeper here and you will see me often bringing good meat to the house. That is my job,' he spoke bitterly, as if he would not be resigned to his lot.

'No, Priedeux. I mean, come with me to London, when I go to Court, as I mean to do, and hope that is what my father wishes. In my retinue. I shall have needs of a confidential messenger, someone I can trust to carry out my bidding. I think that one is you. I know it is you.'

Tom did not hesitate, 'Mistress Anne, I will serve you, if that is what you want, as I carried you in my arms when you were but a child and I not yet a man. There is nothing for me here but dull routine. If I can serve you in higher things then so I will.'

She stopped walking then and held out her hand in an unusual gesture of a handshake and he took it, in token of his loyalty. He almost bent one knee in reverence but she held the hand so he could not.

Then he qualified what he had just said, 'But not immediately, I must wait for the death of Mother Muncy. 'Twill not be long now. If only I could get a priest to her, she would die content.'

Then they continued to approach the moat. She was still curious about his ancestry.

'Do you remember nothing of your background, except the parchment?'

He shook his head. 'Only that you, your dark eyes, your

54

imperious but questioning ways … you seem to be part of my past, as if I have known you always, even before you were but the girl I remember.'   Now he was gazing ahead, as if he would see something other than the grey fields in the rain. 'As if you were in a book, or another time. Mere fancy, a dream of nothing.'

They had reached the formal gardens and he stopped.

'I'll come no further.'

'Thank you, Priedeux. I will speak with my father.'

'Thank *you*, Anne, for the kindness to mother.'

Chapter Eight

'If I am to go to Court, I'll need more than the one servant,' Anne said, turning to face her mother as the maid adjusted her under-bodice.

'Stand still and let the girl do her best,' her mother said. 'Your father comes down from London today to discuss your future.'

'But you must know, dear mother, why I have been recalled from France. Queen Claude would have provided a dowry for me, and I would not have minded marrying a Frenchman. Father must have great plans for me. You must be privy to them!'

The girl broke away from the servant who stood, forlorn, a torn ribbon from the garment in her hand. Anne put her arm round her mother's shoulders, an awkward gesture as she had to bend down to the older woman who was smaller than she was.

'Tell me, mother, please ...'

'Come this is not how a lady should behave,' her mother laughingly moved away. The girl certainly had charm, she thought. She knew what was planned, but it was not her business to tell Anne. Her husband was the head of the household and the father of the girl; he had made plans and it was for him to reveal them. She explained this to the girl who seemed so alien to her, with her mercurial temper; all quick enthusiasms one moment, sulking the next.

'Your father, as you know, is coming especially from London. He's a busy man at Court and you cannot expect him to come all this way to tell you something you already know. Great family matters need to be aired formally. Your father will tell you in good time.'

Lady Elizabeth turned and left the room, with a smile and a nod of approval to the young servant girl who was vainly trying to straighten Anne's bodice while Anne, in her impatience was stretching to clip the chain, with the large capital B, around her neck.

She would not be the one to tell Anne of the marriage plans; she was sure it would not be to the liking of this girl. Lady Elizabeth, albeit of noble blood herself, was a little afraid of Anne. She had a nobility about her, an hauteur that seemed beyond her years, coupled with a fiery temper as she had already witnessed. She suspected that the planned marriage to a minor Irish noble would not be to her liking. He might be a good match financially, but Lady Elizabeth could see trouble ahead. Anne, even in the short time she had been home, had proved headstrong. Not a good recipe in a girl forced into such a marriage for dynastic reasons. Lady Elizabeth was well aware, from her own circumstances, that a girl of high class could not choose her own husband and hoped that Anne had learned that lesson, although she feared she had not.

She had no qualms about such an arranged marriage in principle. After all, she thought, as she fingered the household keys hanging at her side, she had been 'sacrificed' when she married Sir Thomas Boleyn, but it had turned out well. Her father, the Duke of Norfolk, had seen in the young man many talents.

With her connections to the Norfolk faction at the new Court of Henry VIII and her husband's ability in languages, they had already risen in Court circles so that Sir Thomas Boleyn was one of the King's close band of advisers and a trusted ambassador. Elizabeth could hold high her head amongst her peers who might once have sneered at the match between her and a merchant's kin, despite her being of royal lineage. Indeed she could trace her blood to the great Edward II.

As she stood dreaming, there was a hubbub in the courtyard below and she saw her husband dismounting and the horse being led away. She looked down with a stir of pride in her spouse and thought him still a fine, upright man, his eyes with that clear look, and a tidy beard. She moved away from the casement and strode towards the stairs to meet him.

* * * * *

'Say, Liz, what think you of my daughter Anne? Has the expense been worth it?'

They were in his small study and Lady Elizabeth stood before him and assessed how she should say what she wanted to say. In the end she answered in a direct manner. 'Indeed, she has lived up to her great lineage.' After a pause, which was not lost on her husband, she added, 'And she follows in her father's footsteps when it comes to intelligence.'

Always acutely aware of her husband's low birth, she knew well to flatter him and knew he prided himself on his ability to learn new languages, and new ideas, quickly.

'And do you think the marriage with Ormond will be acceptable to her?'

The mother paused, countered his question with another.

'Do you think the marriage to Ormond would mean a successful outcome to your plea to the king for their lands?'

Her husband shook his head. 'I cannot tell, dear wife, but look what he did for our daughter Mary; married her well and settled lands and monies on her.'

'Aye, and Mary is content with that. I'm not sure that Anne ...'

'What are you saying, woman? Come, out with it, I can see you are trying to tell me something ...'

She hesitated to cross her husband directly. After a few minutes' thought, during which her husband looked at her sharply, she said slowly, 'There's no rush to engage her, surely?'

She detected a slight irritation in her husband's way of flicking his cloak away from him. He had rushed straight to his study without disrobing. She knew he had great responsibilities at Court and that his arrival was an especial dispensation. He had not seen his daughter for some months and that had been in the hubbub of the French Court.

'So. You have seen Anne. I do not know what she is like *now*. Tell me what you're thinking.'

58

'Perhaps give her more time …'

'It is true there are business matters to settle but I would start these as soon as possible if Anne is ready for marriage. She has proved expensive already.'

'Indeed my lord, the expense has been worth it, you will find her a true lady of the Court, her manners and deportment exquisite. I truly believe she can go far.'

There was a silence as her husband took in what she was saying, the words *of the Court* not lost on him. He had discarded the cloak carelessly over one of the heavy chairs and his wife absently moved and collected it, folding it deliberately over her arm, so she could put it away. He had looked up as she emphasised 'of the Court' but said nothing immediately, merely returning to the papers on his desk. He was handling them now, scanning each page quickly and then discarding it for the next, and appeared not to be paying attention, expecting his wife to continue but she said no more.

Eventually he spoke. 'As a lady of the Court? Dear wife, that is an expense that cannot be gone into. You know what is planned. What say you to the match? Would she do well as Lady Ormond?'

Lady Elizabeth paused, standing at the door as if to leave him, the cloak still over her arm. She knew the Ormond title was close to her husband's heart and he would pursue his claim to it in any way he thought fit, even marrying a daughter to one he despised. She could accept that. But even so, if Anne could do better?

'Indeed she is too good for a match with an impostor,' she exclaimed.

Her husband stood up quickly, walked around the desk and started striding up and down in front of her. After two or three turns, he approached her, his arms folded across his chest and barked, 'Indeed he is an impostor, claiming the title and lands when my back was turned. This is my last scheme. My arguments with the king personally and with Wolsey have failed. They refuse to countenance a return to our family, even though I am favoured by the king in other ways. Even though my cousin died without issue, the king does not see that we are the rightful heirs to those lands. This is the only way we can get them back into the family; Anne will marry that weakling and I will have control, as I should have, of valuable revenues from those lands.'

He built up into a crescendo of anger. 'If Anne marries that young upstart, then at least one of my family would benefit by the title and the rich income from the Irish and English estates. If it means sacrificing Anne to an Irish exile, then so be it.'

His wife draped the cloak over the arm of a chair and stood in front of him, so that he was forced to stop pacing, and laid her hand on his arm.

'Come, stop and think. Meet Anne and consider whether she would not be more trouble as a discontented spouse, even as far away as Ireland!'

Elizabeth would fight for this girl, she had decided. She had been lucky to be married off to an intelligent man, but had had to accept a lower status at first. Now Anne was to marry someone of lower status, and it was well known the Ormond brat was an idiot. Anne was worth more than that. Now Elizabeth had seen the girl again she knew that higher ambitions might be satisfied. The girl had developed into a young woman with a good complexion, clear of the pitted pox, albeit darker than was usually acceptable at the English Court. She had other attributes; that long neck, a good figure and, something that Lady Elizabeth could not put into words, but it was something special. Instead of a paltry semi-illiterate baron with lands over which a family quarrelled, why not a dukedom, why not a relative of the king himself? Why not, indeed, give Anne her chance at Court, where she would be feted?

'Trouble? Why think you she would be trouble? Whenever I saw her in France she was always quiet and discreet.'

Again she did not give her husband the answer she knew he wanted but answered the question with a question.

'How long would the negotiations take? I rather fear you must ensure a good marriage settlement and ensure all is written and agreed before we sacrifice the girl.'

Her husband turned and looked at her keenly. It was the word sacrifice that had caught his attention. They worked well together and she rarely argued with him. He respected her, not only for her antecedents but for wise and sensible counsel over the years, and consulted her on most business matters, which they discussed quietly and rationally. Now she had used an emotive term which he would not have expected from her. After all, girls had to be married off. She could see him thinking; yes, she could see he accepted that she had raised a valid point. He stopped pacing, sat at his desk, put down his papers, and placed his hands palm downwards on them, in an action his wife recognised. He was now going to mull over carefully what she said.

'Go on.'

'Think, my dear lord. We have but three children and we are well related on my side. Apart from what you have made for yourself and your position at Court, there are other family assets that could fall in. It may be that this Ormond match could work the other way and, if Anne should be fruitful, and others not so, her issue would stand to inherit much, from my family. She must be ensured of a good jointure for herself whilst limiting what that family would get if such should be the case. The marriage settlement must contain clauses that limit their entitlement to my family's wealth, after all.'

Lady Elizabeth stopped talking and waited for her words to sink in, her arms folded before her demurely. She stood quite still. She had said enough and now let her husband think. If she interrupted her husband's deliberations, he would become pettish and nothing would be achieved. He would take in what she said and consider carefully. They both knew that life was hazardous and although they had Mary, Anne and George, and they had all reached maturity, even now any one of them could be taken by sleeping sickness or plague, the girls in childbirth, or George murdered on one of the foreign expeditions he had started to undertake. Eventually her husband spoke.

'Aye, it could take months. And I agree with limiting their

claims on our estates, seeing as they have already stolen what is rightfully mine. So far we have not even exchanged initial valuations of the lands. I'll not be offering a dowry except the settlement of my claim. You are right; we need to ensure Anne and her children will be assured the title – and I would hope to have a reversion back to us if she should be widowed and left childless or die in childbirth. That could be a problem.'

He paused, stood up and turned to look out of the window at his lands. He was proud of the new mullioned windows, of the wood panelling and plaster that he had ordered but even more proud of the formal gardens which he could now see, with their promise of lustrous colourful growth in the coming summer. Anne was like one of his possessions and he needed to nurture her so she could reach her full potential, like his garden.

All the while, Lady Elizabeth waited. Suddenly he turned and faced her.

'What say you to her going to Court, and taking her chances? We carry out the negotiations in secret, but if in the meantime she uses her wiles ...'

Elizabeth smiled and approached her husband. She patted his arm and nodded. Success! Anne would have her opportunity. She was almost certain to use it wisely.

'Bring the child to me. I will see her now.'

As his wife left the room he muttered, 'I hope the promise she showed as a girl has borne fruit.'

The father's short audiences with his daughter when he had visited the French Court had not really given him a chance to know her well. More information had been gained from missives from those he had asked to care for her. There had been no adverse reports, but he wished now that he could have spent more time with her. He sighed. Everything was so rushed. He remembered now the heated negotiations he had had to carry out to make sure everyone was happy with the arrangements for the meeting later known as the Field of Cloth of Gold; the audiences he had had to have with the French King, with the numerous members of his Court who had all insisted on their correct place in order of precedence, and with the chamberlains who were dealing with the arrangements for provisions. He had almost lost his temper when he had been asked to agree the design for a giant brick-built oven to ensure adequate bread for the thousands who would be attending. In all of this, he had been reminded that his young daughter would like to see him. There had not been much time to attend to the girl, and he had relied on reports from first, Queen Mary, and then, after she had returned to England, the kindly Queen Claude, whom he had respected and trusted. Those reports had been full of praise.

He was particularly proud of the report from the Hapsburg Archduchess, who had thanked him, Thomas Boleyn, for sending such a charming and good girl to have in her retinue. And that was when Anne was but an infant.

There was a knock at the door. Now he would see if the girl had fulfilled that early promise and the faith he had in her.

Anne followed her mother into the room. She thought how alike they were except that her mother had thickened with childbearing and good living at Court, and Anne was proud to be called 'willowy'. She stood calmly before her father keeping her eyes down and waited as he appraised her. She held her hands before her as her mother did, mentally noting that her careful choice of clothes should impress him, having chosen a fashionable overdress in dark satin, with the Boleyn jewel at her neck. She had deliberately picked a demure lace head-dress, her hair tucked neatly away.

'Child, welcome back.' He approached her and lifted the pointed chin so he could see her face, her eyes. She returned his gaze as he held her there. Suddenly he took her in his arms. 'My own girl, welcome. Truly you have grown into a fine one.'

Then he stood back and she curtseyed and smiled at him, and turned to her mother who clapped slowly in reserved approval.

'Anne, your mother and I will tell you now what we plan for you.'

His daughter smiled and curtseyed again.

Now she would discover her future. She was sure she was destined for great things and knew that her father would be the one to start the journey.

'We are planning a marriage with Ormond, so that the dynastic lands can come back into their rightful family,' explained her father quite innocently, but stopped, surprised, when he saw his daughter's face harden.

'What's the matter, girl?'

'Ormond, father? Ormond? Surely I have not been groomed in the highest courts in the world to be hidden in the boggy no-man's-land of Ireland.'

'Anne, you will do what I have bidden.'

'But, father …'

Lady Elizabeth interrupted, 'Sir Thomas, I believe you were about to say …'

Her husband smiled at her and addressed his daughter, 'But the negotiations could take some time, so your mother and I will take you to be presented at Court.'

He did not need to say more: Anne understood. She smiled at her father and nodded, saying nothing. She could see he was well pleased with her.

'Thank you, I will not let you down.'

'Good, we understand each other. Be prepared to travel in a day.'

Anne hesitated, and then spoke, 'father there is one boon I would ask of you. No, two.'

He smiled. 'Only two? If this includes an account for clothes and jewellery then of course '

'Nay father, I'll not be so extravagant. What I ask is simple and can be carried out here at Hever. Father, I found mother Muncy ill, and near to death. She was despondent. If it is not too late, I would ask that our priest visit her and give her last unction.'

'Why, child, this is not a request you should be making. Has the priest been ignoring his parishioners again? Indeed, it will be done. But you said two boons ...?'

'Yes.' Anne spoke rapidly. 'I would take Mother Muncy's son Tom in my retinue, as my personal messenger.'

Her father looked puzzled. 'Tom? The gamekeeper? Why?'

'Father, he can read, he is intelligent. But he has no loyalties at Court for he has never been and I believe he would be true to me.'

'But, child, surely you can trust our house servants? I can allot some to you in keeping with your station. Indeed it is planned that your young cousin, Jane Seymour, would attend upon you in due course when she is older. Tom is rough, smelling of game and meal. He cannot be suitable. If you're to go to Court you'll take some of your young cousins as maids, and others of our household.'

'Father, interview him, see for yourself. He has a noble stature. Please'.

She looked at him, her dark eyes open wide, pleading. The mother watched and wondered and realised the girl could well become a persuading tease if she was not curbed. But in this request the mother could see no objection, so added her comment.

'The girl is right, she may have needs of a confidential servant who can run messages. Let us see this Tom and if Anne is correct that he is intelligent, then let him have livery, some house-training, and let Anne take him.'

The girl turned to her mother, 'Thank you, dear mother, you'll see I'm right!'

* * * * *

'Well, Tom, how do you feel about leaving the estate? You have heard what my daughter Anne proposes? What say you?'

Tom was wary.

"Tis the only home I am comfortable with, and I'll not leave until mother dies, albeit that will be soon.'

'But you left once before, Tom, and we thought you had gone for good.'

Tom smiled then, as if remembering a younger, more naïve version of himself.

'Aye, I needed to see the world to know my place in it, master!'

'And you came back here?'

'Indeed, to serve you and your family, sir, in whatever may be required. I think much of the Lady Anne, and would serve her as she wishes. But not until I do my duty by mother. I would have a priest for her, sir, if at all possible.'

'That has been taken care of, Tom; the priest has been ordered to visit her. And I will ensure prayers for her soul will be said every Sunday.'

Tom studied his master. The gamekeeper had had very little to do with Thomas Boleyn because he was so often away but now he stared at him carefully.

'Sir, I thank you for that great kindness.'

'Thank me not. 'Tis my girl Anne who asked it and I agree that no person, no matter how lowly, should be without the grace of religion. Now tell me, you can read?'

Tom nodded.

'Come here, and read from this.' Boleyn gave him a parchment and Tom read aloud.

'Now write the same words here ...'

Tom took the quill and held it hesitantly for he had not written much for many years. Slowly he copied the words in a neat but undeveloped hand. Boleyn took the parchment to the window and read it.

He returned to continue his assessment, and noted that the younger man stood there, his hands hanging helplessly by his side. His politeness and quiet waiting impressed Boleyn. He was used to assessing men, in his job for the King, and was valued for that judgement. And now, in this young man, he could see what Anne could see.

'So, do you wish to go?'

Tom Priedeux said nothing. Then he answered, 'Sir, there is nothing for me here, no sweetheart, no real home, no family once Mother Muncy dies, and I would go out into the world and seek my own way. So, if Lady Anne wishes me to serve her I can think of no other better way of living my life.'

'Good, we can spare a few days. Take the time; and we will wait on Mother Muncy reaching her natural end, however long that may be, and nurse her well. I will ensure help if you need it for her.' He circled Tom and added, 'In any event, you will need some training in the ways of household servants. Report to Lady Elizabeth and she will give you livery and show you how to conduct yourself as a man at court, even though you go as a servant. Can you ride a horse?'

Priedeux nodded, 'Yes, sir, I taught myself when a child.'

Boleyn smiled grimly. A boy of Tom's rank should never have been on a horse; that was for nobility or knights. At the same time, he knew there were many pranks which the estate children got up to, without the estate manager being aware of them. If it meant they learned skills that could be useful to him, then why not?

'Good, you will ride in Anne's retinue when we return to London.'

As Priedeux was leaving the chamber, Boleyn stopped him, 'One thing, Tom. You will discover that there are intrigues and gossips at Court and much silver passes hands from those who are great to those lesser mortals who, by the getting of that silver, are persuaded to tell tales of their masters or mistresses. If I hear you are accruing such silver, you will die in a brawl. Do you understand me?'

Priedeux nodded. He did not tell his old master that such a warning was unnecessary. He had already formed ties of loyalty and bondship to Anne that, as far as he was concerned, could never be broken. Not only was there the uncanny feeling he had that he had known her in a past life and, like all his station in life, he was susceptible to magic and superstition, but there was also his feeling of gratitude for what she had done for mother Muncy. He would never betray his lady.

67

Chapter Nine

'Mother, before I leave can I ask you something? Something that you may think sounds silly, I am sure.'

Anne had burst into her mother's private chamber and found the older woman sewing a shirt, with other linen by her side. Anne had not realised how involved Lady Elizabeth was in the day to day care of the household. In France the ladies would sew expensive tapestries or play with lace but not sew torn shirts or attach buttons. She was sitting at a window seat to take full advantage of the daylight and for once the sun was shining. Lady Elizabeth looked up at Anne and nodded, patting the seat beside her.

'Sit, Anne. Perhaps you can help. I have to get all these shirts ready for your father to take back to Court in a few days' time.' She handed her daughter a shirt and some lace and showed her where it should be stitched. Anne stared at the material and did not immediately start work. Eventually Lady Elizabeth broke the silence.

'What is it? You look worried. And you so poised and graceful from the French Court, and so excited and full of tales at dinner yesternight. I thought you would never stop talking ...'

Anne sat and placed her hands in her lap, not touching the sewing before her, the extra nail hidden by the other hand. The mother noted what she did, and patted those hands in an unspoken gesture of loving understanding.

'Well ...' Anne waited a while. For once she did not know how to begin. Then she sighed. Best to get it over with. 'When I was coming back, George said something which has puzzled me since ... I am afraid.'

'Afraid? What do you mean?' Lady Elizabeth spoke sharply.

'Mother, this seems silly, but I remember Mary and George in the nursery with me, and I swear they were younger. I know I was but a babe, but I am sure of it. So why was Mary presented at Court before me? It is against precedent! Father is trying to marry me off now when, if what I think is correct, I should have been married before Mary. Not only has she been at Court, she is now married and I have not even been presented. Am I the oldest or not?'

Her final question burst out, and her mother stood up and walked away as if she would move to a darker part of the chamber so as to avoid the light of understanding. Anne had not finished. She stood too and followed the older woman. 'And there was something Mother Muncy said the other day, although I am not sure whether she knew what she was saying in her illness. She said something about me being sent away "to hide" and then she stopped. She thought I hadn't noticed.'

Lady Elizabeth still said nothing. She turned to Anne but stood staring at her, a look of pity on her face. She paced back and forth for a while thinking of how dignified the girl had become, and realised she was very bright. She returned to the girl. She took her by the hand and led her to the window seat. They sat down.

'Anne, I am going to tell you something now which you must never acknowledge or breathe to a soul. You deserve to know.' She looked away and, as if she was talking to herself.

'It may protect you to know it, if there are any innuendos.' Then she looked Anne in the eye and continued, 'You come from a noble family and there are many who would see us fall, and such a tale as I tell you now would cause great joy to our enemies. Do you understand? You must swear to keep this secret; even if your husband himself tortures you.'

'I swear.'

The older woman nodded and stood up quickly, going to the door, opened it and looked out into the corridor. She shut it tightly, turning the handle in an exaggerated manner which showed she was deadly worried that anyone should hear her. She returned to her seat beside Anne and then began, in barely a whisper, 'It concerns your birth. We could not record it, your father and I for it must be surrounded in mystery. Yes, you are your father's first born brought to me after his sister died: do you understand? You were born a few months before we were married. Your father told me all, and I forgave him, for I was betrothed to him in a holy betrothal and it would have been shame to me to break it off, apart from the settlements and agreements that would have landed us in Chancery, with perhaps King Henry the VII at the head – he was a formidable lawyer who would have punished all who came before him! But I go off the point. Your father was repentant of what had happened in his youth, from lust and innocence with his sister. Only he and she knew, and mother Muncy. After we married, we first lived in Norfolk, in that remote Blickling Hall, and it was easy to hide the true facts. That is why he sent you away as a young girl and why we have been careful to confuse your age. You are, to the world, aged eighteen and that must be your official age if it is questioned. Do you understand me?'

Anne's mouth had dropped open and Lady Elizabeth did not expect an answer immediately. She was breathing heavily, after her long explanation. She waited, relying on the good training the girl had had, her intelligence, her poise, to be able to work out that the fact of her birth must never be revealed to anyone. She continued to hold the girl's hands between hers, mindful of that extra finger. They were cold with shock and the mother rubbed them gently.

'So I *am* older than Mary and George?'

Lady Elizabeth nodded.

'How old am I really then?'

Lady Elizabeth looked away and seemed to be calculating. 'You are nearing twenty-two. Not old, my child, but learned and wise, I would say.' She then put her arms around the stiff girl, and added, 'As far as I am concerned you are my first born, and my joy. For the sake of Thomas and his sister, whom I loved as well.'

70

But still Anne could say nothing. The mother continued gently, 'Now you know you can hold up your head, for you are a true Boleyn in more ways than one. You can do all you can at Court without trusting or having allegiance to my family, the Norfolks, if they thwart you at any time. I know my brother is jealous of my husband and that causes friction from time to time, so you must be true to yourself, only yourself, do you understand? He also suspects something but believes you were born of my loins before the betrothal was formalised into marriage. You must believe in yourself. And the Boleyn family name.'

Lady Elizabeth continued to whisper in her ear, about family and honour and keeping such a dreadful secret. Finally, the constant repetitions of the person that Anne had always thought of as her mother, penetrated. Anne slowly raised her head. There were tears in her eyes and her mother gathered her to her breast and let the girl weep. For a while they stayed like that but suddenly Anne sat up, wiped her eyes daintily and then looked at the woman who had generously taken her to her heart and nodded slowly, 'I understand, yes, I understand, and no-one will ever know this from my lips. I know you and father have kept the secret all these years to safeguard my future and I promise I will not let you down. I will make the best marriage I can at Court, I promise, and it will not be to the Irish idiot. I shall marry the best man at court, I promise, so help me God!'

* * * * *

Anne knelt at the altar of St Peter's church, on the cold brass of Margaret Cheyne. Her father's ancestors were buried here. She prayed.

'On whose soul may God have mercy. Amen.' Anne finished her prayer by reading the Latin inscription on the altar aloud. The small chapel was attached to her father's Hever estates and it was a comforting place, well known to her. She bent her head, her hands held together before her. The day had had too many shocks and she had come here to think. First the idea of the possible marriage to Ormond. She had but a short opportunity to thwart this and she

71

prayed now for guidance. She could not live in such a remote place as Ireland; how could she carry out her part of the bargain with Dinteville and de Selve in such a place?

But it was an even greater shock to find out the circumstances of her birth. She knelt and palmed her hands together at face height and gazed at the statue of the Virgin. As she stared, her fingers became distorted and changed into two people coupling: two people so alike that they could not be defined as separate. Legs and arms intertwined in the obscenity of incest. How could she face her father again knowing he would suffer in purgatory for such a sin? She dropped her arms to the altar rail so that the image of the Holy Mother was clear before her. Not only was she base-born but she was born of a cardinal sin – a coupling between brother and sister, condemned by God and the Bible. *And the sins of the fathers shall be visited on the children ... even to the seventh generation*. The words seemed to echo though she had not spoken aloud. She stared at the Madonna and child trying to find a way through to real prayer instead of the total horror she felt. Rationally she did not believe in purgatory; all the books she had read had explained that there was no basis for this in the scriptures, but here she was imagining her father in such a place and herself being tainted with his sin.

Being illegitimate was not so bad; others like her had been legitimised. It was the thought of her father with ...

'Holy Mother, Mary, help me. Help me see my way through this great trouble.' She prayed but only the cold of the church penetrated her soul and no answer came. All she could see was the plaster image. Surely this could not help her; she recalled the treatises she had read that condemned such statues as being worthless idols. Part of her believed them but now she was trying to obtain help from such an image. Deep down, she knew that no amount of prayer to such lifeless things could change what had happened, what she was. The mustiness of the church, from old incense and unwashed bodies, seemed to be a manifestation of the terrible horror of her situation. The enclosed silence was as death to her, despite the fact that she usually found the church a comforting place.

Lady Elizabeth, who was not her mother, had told her the facts and had just hugged and kissed her, a woman who had lived for years with the knowledge that her husband had betrayed her before their marriage in such a manner. She had forgiven and even accepted and nurtured the child, as Anne remembered from her early childhood. Anne thought on that and how she had been educated at the Court of the Hapsburgs, where a powerful Archduchess, Margaret, had praised her. How Henry's sister, Mary, had so recommended her to the new French queen that she had been left in France to be a lady-in-waiting when all the others had returned to England. None of these people, except her father's wife, knew the truth and why should they?

Now she knew why she had been sent away; her father could not bear to be reminded of his wickedness. Anne felt anger at this man who had so much power over her life. She knew he was ambitious; so was she, but for reform of the Church. She would have no chance to satisfy those ambitions except by marriage and such marriage would be controlled by this father who, if all the teachings of the Bible were to be accepted, had committed a cardinal sin. She muttered, as if in prayer, 'I swear that from now on I shall never obey my father unless it suits my wishes; he is not worth obeying!'

The oath comforted her and she returned to the memories of the women she had known.

'God's words condemn me, but living women have succoured me,' she said as if challenging the emptiness. The words had come involuntarily and she was grateful that she was alone. Her knees ached with the chill from the stone flags but, having reached this conclusion, she felt stronger. Rising stiffly she moved restlessly around the aisles, ignoring the writings on the wall of great texts from Jesus' words, until she faced westwards; there she saw the great fresco of St Christopher, a giant of a man holding on his shoulders the angelic child Jesus, haloed. This was the way, she now recalled with a flash, that Priedeux had strode up the gangplank of the ship with her on his shoulders, on that first journey from England. She had not remembered it until now, and it came to her like a palpable image. She recalled holding him around the neck, the chain and talisman he always wore chafing her soft hands. Priedeux, a man whom she already relied on totally, now she had met him again. He was her St Christopher. With his help, she could contact her old friends, de Selve and Dinteville. Priedeux would be her carrier of letters and messages. A small doubt came. Would her old friends want to stay friendly with such as her? She felt so sullied that others could tell, just by looking at her. She turned back towards the altar; even the plans she would make for her future were clouded by the truth of her birth. No, they would never find out for she would never say. She shuddered, imagining a time when she would meet them and they would see she was different. *But only if you let them see.* And she knew well how to hold herself, contain herself and not let others know what she truly felt. That was how she had succeeded at being a lady-in-waiting.

She turned back to the altar and knelt once again before the image of the Madonna. Now it seemed to be looking down on her compassionately.

What was the Bible after all? She had seen it in its original Greek and Hebrew, although she could not decipher the latter. She knew it was a work that could be interpreted in several ways. She herself had translated some from the Latin Vulgate into French and English. She knew how words could be twisted. The word Virgin, she knew, meant merely "maiden" in the original. So Mary was not necessarily a virgin who had received Jesus in her womb by divine command. Mary had conceived in a strange way, just like Anne's conception. So my mother was a maid who had received me by divine intervention, my father being that divine intervention, reasoned Anne.

As these thoughts emerged, further tears fell, and she looked up at the image before her, that of the Virgin Mary, Mother of God.

'So help me, Mary, help me to understand what has gone before. Help me to be strong for I am like you, a woman who is blameless.'

This time the image seemed to be slowly nodding as Anne's vision was warped by her tears. Then her head fell into her hands again and she despaired. What would the world think of such interpretations? Some might even consider her blasphemous to compare her situation with that of the Holy Mother of God. Anne did not care; she was now ready to say that she was right, she knew she was right; that she was who she was, and she knew, with a terrible certainty, that she had been made for a special destiny no matter her parentage.

'They shall see it my way; If only they would study their Bible, read for themselves, like I have done, to see that they have a little part of God in themselves, nay, that they are made in the image of God, that they are one with God, nay they are the God, that I am … that they have their own conscience and that morality stems from being honest with themselves and that coupling is a God-given privilege and that the progeny from such natural lust are blessed of God, like I am.'

She fell to the floor in prayer, frightened of her own revelations, the voicing of many matters that had only been half-formed. She lay prostrate while the shadows deepened in the corners. Slowly she became conscious of the stiffness of her immobile body, the tears which had coursed down her cheeks making them sore and red. 'I know my destiny, I know why I was born; I know why Stefano died, I know why Georges was defiled. I need to start the movement whereby humans can say to themselves: I take responsibility for myself, no longer listening to the Holy Father of Rome.'

Suddenly she stopped her ramblings. She was sure she had heard the soft clicking of a door latch. She thought she detected a slight draft and, yes, there was a presence behind her.

'My child, do you need help?'

The voice was reassuring, enquiring, with no sycophancy in it. She swivelled, looked up and saw a calm, long face, white robes at eye level as if an angel had come. She shook her head.

'But you are distressed. I can see that from the crying.'

She wiped her face with the cloth she held and was surprised to see it was her piece of the taffeta robe that had been torn on Stefano's sword. She shook her head again, not trusting to speak at first, hastily hiding the gaudy cloth.

'Nay, I pray to the Mother of Jesus, Holy Mary, for intercession for my soul, but I doubt she can help.'

'She can help those who would help themselves, my child. You have been wracked on the grill of doubt, but I see from your face that you have reached self-resolution, is that not so?'

Anne looked closer at the priest. His face was tranquil, plain but brimming with intelligence, haloed by straight cut hair. 'Your name, sir?'

'Thomas Cranmer, ma'am, at your service. A humble cleric. I am here to visit your rector John Shwayne, who is a friend of mine.'

He helped her to stand and they faced each other. They were of a height and she did not have to look up at him. She attempted a smile for the first time in what seemed months. He reminded her of Priedeux, and she liked what he had said which was in harmony with her beliefs. She guessed he could be useful to her in the future.

'Nay, not a humble cleric. A wise and astute man. You have read my soul aright. And I, Anne Boleyn, will help you, in your career, if I am able, as I must help myself.'

Chapter Ten

Hever was set in rolling Kent hills and the preparation for any journey was long and wearisome but when it was to Court even more preparations were need. Travelling would be slow. Pack animals were to be used to cart the finery needed for Anne.

'And you, young lady, will ride in a litter, covered so that the sun does not roast you,' her father ordered.

'But, I need the exercise, and I'll wear a veil.' She took her father's arm and led him to the nearest stable where a fine filly tossed its head. She stroked its mane and the horse nuzzled her shoulder.

'See, father, I can manage this.' She smiled up at him. 'You'll not want me to arrive at Court pale and stiff, surely?'

But her father would not budge.

'Nay, dear girl, I'll not have your first appearance at Court all bruised and injured. And if the sun comes out a veil will not be much good.' He turned aside to mutter to his wife, but Anne heard what he added, 'With that dark complexion of hers, we'll not want her becoming tanned like a peasant!'

Anne persisted. 'But, father, I *can* ride and to do so would make me fresh, fresh for my appearance at Court.'

Sir Thomas turned back to her impatiently. 'Show me.'

So she had ignominiously ridden around the home field on what she could only describe as the oldest, tamest nag in her father's stable. He had watched, stroking his thick beard, and then nodded. 'Very well, but you'll travel with the pack, and no cantering. George, I charge you with your sister's care.'

Anne could see her brother grinning, behind her father's back. She knew she could wheedle him to her wishes. She had seen him only rarely but when they had met she had been able to charm him. She knew that, once free of their father's watchful eye, she would be able to do what she wanted. But, as their father turned to him, he nodded in agreement.

They were to ride to Greenwich where they would join the Court. As they rode along, Priedeux was quiet, and the others respected his taciturnity knowing he was grieving for his mother who had died a few days before. Anne had attended the burial explaining to her father, 'I'll have no shirking by that lazy priest. She will have the full rites.'

Her father had agreed. 'Worry not, Nan, I'll shake up that old lazybones to his duty. I'll not have those at Court saying we could not afford to send our own to Heaven.'

As sister and brother rode alongside at a gentle pace at the forefront of the group, they said little. Apart from anything their voices would have been drowned by the rumble of the pack carts. The girl, almost new to her own country, looked around her. The day was overcast although it was not raining. She shivered for she was not used to this chill at the beginning of summer. The countryside seemed dull and the way her view was blocked by rolling hills irritated her. In France, as they travelled from chateau to chateau, there were wide flat lands where she could see for miles, only interspersed by the King's great forests and the glint from the winding River Loire. There the sky seemed forever a deep blue or sometimes interspersed by ever changing cloud formations which stretched across the wide sky. Here she felt closed in. She wanted to canter, to arrive quickly at her destiny. She spurred the horse a little faster, and her brother grinned and did likewise, until they were some way from the others. Anne turned and saw Priedeux disengage himself and canter too, as if he was of the same mind as she and her brother, feeling restricted by the slow journey in this hemmed-in land. Her reveries were broken by George as if he could read her thoughts, 'Well, sister, what think you of our dear country?'

'George, you were not much at the French Court?'

'Nay, not so much as you, I know the English Court more. Why ask you?'

'I can tell by the way you ask that you would want me to say I am much pleased at returning home, that it is all so green, so wonderful. But I cannot. Dearest George, forgive me, but it is so dull, dull, grey and gloomy, after France.'

'Aye, I agree it is dull at present, but wait until you see the splendours of Henry's Court. He is splendid too, standing way above others, noble and grand.'

'I have seen him from afar – at the Field of Cloth of Gold, when I was young. Do tell me, I so wish to love the English Court. Are the nobles learned? Do they debate on the new religious ideas? Luther's stand?'

As she asked she shifted in her saddle and half turned. Priedeux was a discreet distance away from them but she did not mind if he heard. She wanted George to know he could trust the man. She gestured to the servant and he caught up with them. George smiled but ignored him.

'On the ninety-five theses? You know about Luther, sweet sis?'

'But of course! You know de Selve and Dinteville, my great dear friends. Yes you do, George.' She chided him as a look of puzzlement came over his features. 'De Selve is a bishop and Dinteville you will remember is training with his father.'

She waited until George nodded. 'Of course, those youngsters who followed you everywhere!'

Anne smiled and explained, 'They have contacts and we acquired a lot of the new writings from the German cities. We even managed to procure copies of the prints titled 'Weibermacht' in their thick tongue.'

'And what does that mean?'

Anne laughed, '"The power of women." Women are not depicted well, I tell you. The prints all show what would happen if women did become dominant and they are not attractive pictures. But I find their honesty, like the honesty of their religion, appealing. And de Selve and Dinteville did too.' She lowered her voice conspiratorially, 'We would like to see reform of the Church.'

Her brother reined in his horse and took hold of Anne's reins to hold her back. He shook his head as if to clear it.

'Be careful how you debate such things at Court, dear Anne. The king wrote a pamphlet against Luther which was much liked by those in the Church, and he was then given a title by the Pope: 'Defender of the Faith'. So you can see the king and Queen Katherine profess to be violently against such division from Rome.'

'But the king writes such pamphlets? He is interested in the arguments?'

'Indeed he is, but also on many other subjects. He is great on the field when tourneying; he hunts and rides hard, exhausting many horses in a day, and he dances and sings, composing his own ditties. He is truly, Anne, a great man.'

'Aye, as I said, I saw him from afar at the Field of Cloth of Gold, for I attended in Queen Claude's retinue. But father would not introduce me, he said he was far too busy. He seemed a golden man to me then, with his hair flying.'

She spurred on her horse and George let her go, but called after her, 'He is also dangerous, Anne, for he has fits of great temper. And we courtiers jump out of his way when he raves. He can change like the wind!'

He spurred his horse to catch up with her and heard her laugh. As he caught up with her she said, 'But I believe all kings are like that. Francis was devious and Queen Claude had to devise many tricks to stop him deflowering – and worse – her whole retinue!'

'I have heard such tales. And you ...?'

She smiled and shrugged, to show George she was not offended at such a question.

'I was too young, and still learning. You remember; I was with Dinteville and de Selve under that horrid tutor.'

'Ah, yes, Dinteville, he is quite the ladies' man now. Are you sure you and he?'

He stopped as he remembered the servant. He turned round but Priedeux was staring away to the distance, as if he was not listening. Anne laughed again, that odd cynical laugh that George would get to know and find intriguing. Anne was sure that her brother would never have heard of her secret trysts and their blood ceremony.

'I? I, George, will take such secrets to my husband. No-one will hear of any such tales about me. What of Mary? How goes she?'

George laughed now.

'She has been well married by the king as reward for her services. Carew was given good recompense for taking her. She is still at Court and that is all she ever wanted. And our family have advanced because of it.'

Anne fell silent and they rode through a gully of white chalk which made his last words echo. As they came out, and the terrain became more populated, with the roofs of small villages in sight, Anne said in a faraway voice, 'I wonder if father thinks he can use me like that?'

'What do you mean?'

She looked at her brother. 'Father has told me of his plans for my marriage and I wonder why he sends me to Court and wastes his money on fine clothes and jewels. I know I need such to hold my own as maid to good Queen Katherine but if a husband has already been chosen, why let me go to Court now? You know father better than I, but I truly believe he does nothing without some ulterior plan. So I wonder if I am the stepping stone to even greater advancement?'

'Would you mind? Being a king's mistress brings many pleasures.'

They both laughed at that, but George went on, 'He is generous with gifts and jewels for his mistresses – and sons are precious to him; you'll find out about Bessie Blount's boy. He would acknowledge them.'

Sons, and power. Power to do good in the world. Anne held her counsel and after a while she changed the subject. 'D'you know Tom? He rides behind but I would have you be friends for I think I will need you both in my life.'

George nodded, and beckoned to Tom to join them, 'Indeed, I

learnt my first poaching exercise from Tom. So, you are elevated now into a personal servant, eh?'

The servant rode up, not at all bowed or subservient, but still he stayed to one side. He nodded. 'Aye, my lord, I would serve your sister, and carry her messages where she will.'

Anne noticed the reticence, the veneer of bowing to a superior and wondered if her chosen man would only ever be open with her.

'Tom has no love of priests either, George.'

Priedeux looked down, refusing to join the conversation. He did not use Anne's comment to elaborate. Yes, Anne was certain now, he would not have others know his personal thoughts. She continued, as if she was rebuking him, only a servant, 'But, Tom, heed well what my brother says; such thoughts must be kept amongst ourselves, for the king is still deluded by the Pope and his servants. Mayhap we will find a way to make him see the light.'

Her brother nodded and Tom was dismissed, but he continued to ride a short way behind them and neither Anne nor her brother ordered him away.

They were climbing now and the chalk downs had given way to heavy forests and verdant pastures. To one side she could see a huge river snaking. Anne asked where they were.

'Shooter's Hill, I verily believe. We cross a flat heathland and then ride down to Greenwich. The king hunts here, in these woods, and over that spur we can look down and will see the River Thames not far from Greenwich. Soon you will be presented at Court.' Then her brother turned to Priedeux, 'Tom, your first job – ride on ahead and you'll find a gatekeeper waiting at the palace. Tell him that the Boleyns, George and Lady Anne, arrive within the hour and would seek to present themselves as their father has instructed. Then ride back and tell us what we do.'

Tom touched the corner of his cap and spurred his horse past them and galloped over the hill and disappeared.

Anne took a deep breath. Soon, very soon, she would be in the midst of a new court, with all its excitements, intrigues and entertainments. And then she could carry out her promise to her French blood friends.

* * * * *

She curtsied low before him, hardly daring to look up. But she did so and he was looking down at her kindly, his little eyes wrinkled, so she could not see their colour. He was tall, his hair still had the golden hue she remembered, but it was thinning and he wore a velvet cap, feathered, to hide the thinness. He was bulky and impressive. He leant forward and raised her and she stood demurely before him, awaiting his pleasure. But there was nothing more in his gaze than passing interest, the courtesy of a King.

'So, you are Thomas Boleyn's younger daughter? Welcome to my Court and rest assured you will be protected here and treated well. You are to enter my dear Queen's retinue and we are pleased you have joined us. Mayhap some time you can regale us with tales of our brother Francis' Court and help us to make entertainments such as he has there. The masque master will be instructed to talk with you!'

Anne realised he was teasing her but also thought he was doing it to put her at her ease. He was treating her as if she was but a young child and perhaps to him that was what she was.

She bowed and stood to one side and knew she was soon forgotten as he turned to his ministers. A lady not known to Anne touched her on the elbow and gestured for her to follow. Anne turned away and obeyed, feeling a bitter disappointment, but could not tell why. What else had she expected from her introduction to Henry VIII?

* * * * *

Priedeux, left largely to his own devices, wandered through the myriad rooms, watching and listening. He was used to his own counsel, as gamekeeper, watching animals for hours to ensure he could catch them when the time came and he used the same techniques now to learn about this new terrain. He would explore a portion of the palace at a time, carefully working out his new

83

territory, knowing that he needed to be aware of ways and means of entry and exit. One day he stalked through a stone corridor, which, he guessed, was a connecting gallery between new, wood panelled apartments and the old stone castle that formed one wing of the palace. It was empty of the gabbling crowd and his steps echoed eerily. He pushed open a heavy oaken door at the end.

'Shut that door, shut it, oh, for God's sake how am I to create great pageants if I cannot have stillness?' The voice was shrill and womanly but came from a tall man so thin Priedeux wondered how he could sustain himself. He was richly adorned with embroidered jupon and hose which made his red-stockinged legs look even skinnier and he was jumping around and waving some light material. Priedeux was transfixed by the scene before him. There was a mock castle-entrance, with a moated gateway open, and tiny bow windows. The whole was painted grey and black, to represent giant granite stone-works, crenellated at the top. Ladies of the Court, some of whom he recognised, stood in false attitudes, with high pointed hats and silken shawls around them. They were positioned either at the windows or at the gateway. Their attire was exotic and old-fashioned, all being dressed in different colours, reds, greens, blues and yellows. The tall man was jumping around them, moving a hand higher, bending an arm at a greater angle, and muttering to himself, 'You are Constancy, always true, so it is even more important for you than for the others that you must not move.'

Priedeux had hastily moved inside and shut the door behind him but he stood now, quite still, in the way he had learnt as he watched the roe-deer at water so that the only thing that could disturb was the smell of him if the wind changed course.

He watched as the man continued to shape and direct his ladies. At one point he turned and nodded towards a dark corner and dance music began. The ladies moved as one, stepping sedately to the sound and the director of ceremonies tiptoed around them, nodding, smiling, or moving a lady's arm higher if he thought fit.

As the performers stepped from high platforms and gathered at the moated entrance, the structure behind them wobbled as if their weight at the front destabilised it. Priedeux did not think. He leapt with two great steps to the back and pulled with all his might at the rough wooden beams he found there. There was a concerted scream from the ladies as the mock-castle threatened to fall upon them, rocking violently before it stopped and stayed upright.

The master's screams were as high pitched as his performers.

'Oh, my God, my good God. Where are the scenes' men? What are they doing to me? The whole structure could have fallen on King Henry! Just as he was about to take his ladies. Where is that man who has saved us? Come here!'

Priedeux moved from behind the structure, holding it upright with one arm, as if he were Atlas holding up the world and gave an awkward bow, mockingly, at the older man.

'Priedeux at your service, sir.'

'I am Jonril, master of ceremonies,' he said as he came forward and put his skinny arms around Priedeux, as if he would bear-hug him. Priedeux struggled away, still trying to keep the structure upright, but the man held him tight.

'I can only heartily thank you, however you got here.' Suddenly he released Priedeux and stepped away from him. 'How did you get here? This is supposed to be a secret rehearsal for the King's banquet.'

'It would be well for you to think how this structure can be stabilised.' Priedeux stepped behind the mock castle with Jonril following him. He gestured to the rough wood, 'You need to ensure more weight behind if this is not to topple again. Look, let me show you.'

Priedeux moved further away from Jonril for he found it unpleasant for a man so feminine to touch him so closely. He pulled at the structure so that more of the rough supporting wood was leaning away from it, making the framework more triangular so it would bear the weight. The facade then leant backwards so he looked around and saw some large wooden trunks. He rolled these into place and then lifted the wooden struts until they were standing on these. Jonril scuttled around him, raising his skeletal hands and then dropping them in mock horror at the disruption to his set. His mouth opened and then shut as if it was a bellows.

Eventually Priedeux stood back and said, 'There, that should be much more stable. It does remind me of a rat-trap but 'twould work the other way too and be safe against all knocks now. See, this is the key.' He demonstrated again what he had done and Jonril clapped his bony hands together to make a dry slapping sound.

'Join me, become my scenery man, for these clods,' here he pointed to a group of rough-looking men who stood together, arms folded, 'these clods would have me beheaded with their lack of knowledge.'

'Nay, I am already bonded to my mistress, but I would help when I can for it fascinates me to see how things are done behind the scenes.'

'Come, drink with me, tell me of your history, Jonril owes you and I'll not forget that.'

After that, despite the disparity in ages and their characters, Jonril and Priedeux became friends. Priedeux was pleased to meet this new ally, already planning how it could serve Anne's purposes.

Chapter Eleven

'Boy!' It was a derisory call but Percy did not hesitate. He hurried to his master, and bowed as he dropped to one leg. It was one of the first things he had been taught when he joined this household.

'*You must learn humility before you can rule*' he'd been informed by his tutor on his first day in the household of Cardinal Wolsey and any protest was quailed by the way the tutor had raised the cane above Percy's head. Now, he did not move or show his dislike of the term 'boy', despite the fact that his voice was breaking and felt that he was no longer a *boy*. Cardinal Wolsey, after an impressive pause, continued, 'I want you to use your youth and so-called charm to find out about *that* girl.'

The Cardinal's chubby fingers were just about clasped over his rotund red-robed stomach, his feminine-looking lips hardly opening as his eyes, which seemed to be bulging from the folds of his rounded cheeks, pierced Percy. He was seated upright, his body wedged into the chair which barely held his bulk. The room was gloomy, lit by rush lights even though it was midmorning, and the face of the Cardinal was shaded and blotched in the gloom. Servants were hardly visible as they stood rigid, awaiting their master's orders. Percy was aware of the humiliation of being spoken to in front of these minions.

The youth said nothing. He was learning to listen, to respect his elders. He was totally bemused. To whom was his master referring? He waited, inclining his head slightly to show his master that he would do his bidding, as his father had warned him he must while he learned his way around Court.

'She's a wily one, and she has visitors. She seems to have much influence with our good Queen Katherine, even though she has been in her service but a few months. I like not the missives she receives from the French Court.' He did not look at the youth before him. It was as if the Cardinal, in his middle age, was becoming forgetful, mindless of those present. Percy had learned that that was the way he always spoke, thinking aloud, instead of talking to his minions directly.

Instead of noting those around him, Wolsey looked inward, thinking on the information he had gathered from those who prised open wax seals without the recipients of the letters knowing they had been intercepted. He knew the young daughter of Sir Thomas Boleyn received private letters from Dinteville, an up-and-coming young man at the French Court, and Wolsey wanted to know what they contained. That dratted servant Priedeux had always thwarted his efforts to intercept a letter. He'd watched the girl and saw the way she ingratiated herself into her Queen's favour. Wolsey had heard stories of her from his spies in France; and he wanted to know more. He carried on in his ruminative way, 'Not pretty, mind, not one to turn men's heads with beauty. But those sparkling eyes. I saw the way she eyed the King.'

The lad still did not know to whom he referred.

'My lord, I am sorry, but who is it that you speak of?'

Wolsey looked down at the youngster, still on one knee. He sighed. 'You may stand now, boy.' He paused, watching him as he awkwardly stood. Really, he thought, this lad of Northumberland's was not of the brightest. Then he spoke slowly, as if to an idiot.

'I refer to the Lady Anne Boleyn. She has been at Court some months now and all are talking of her, her coquettish ways, her skill at dancing, as if she were some great lady. Do not tell me you have not noticed her.'

Percy said nothing. Of course he knew now of whom his master spoke, but he had never been introduced and he was still learning Court ways. He would never dare try to speak with a lady of the Court. Now he was being asked to tell Wolsey about her.

'But how am I to find out about her, my lord? What do you

want me to do?'

Wolsey sighed again, 'You must talk to her, ask her about her life in France, what she wants out of life. You can converse, can't you, boy?'

Percy thought of his betrothal to Lady Mary Talbot daughter of the Earl of Shrewsbury, chosen by his father as was the way of the world, and he accepted what was decreed. It was easy that way. Now he was being asked to get to know another lady. Was this right? He remembered what his father had said: obey Wolsey in all he says; he is very powerful.

He could see Wolsey leaning forward, waiting for an answer.

'Yes, my Lord, I ... I can converse.'

'Well then, when we are next in the good Queen's chambers talk with her, ask her about herself. And report back to me.'

He bowed. He would try to talk to Lady Anne, but it would not be easy. Although he knew he should be learning to be relaxed in company at Court, he found it difficult and could not envisage talking freely with her. How did one start? And anyway, if he had to find out what she wanted out of life, surely this would compromise them? He considered protesting against his task. Surely his master knew of the proposed match, and would not thwart his patron, Percy's father. But Wolsey was still speaking, and Percy knew it was no use to remind him. Wolsey had plans, and nothing Percy would say now would deflect him; that much the young man had learnt in the service of the Cardinal.

'Percy, you are young, you must learn how to make those eyes shine on you and find out what she is like. I have heard she is intelligent and can speak many languages, like that clever father of hers. You must pretend to woo her and find out her innermost secrets, for there is something about her ...'

'But how can I approach her? She is in the Queen's household and I am in yours, my lord, and we seldom meet except on State occasions.'

'Aye, but soon I must see the queen about her pilgrimage to Walsingham; it will be a great religious affair and I would ensure

89

she has messages for my people there. You are distantly related to Anne and that will be enough to occasion an introduction and for you to talk with her. Be discreet, mind, if you can.'

The last was said with such disdain that Percy glanced up, showing for a second his annoyance at the way his lord treated him. Wolsey was not even looking at him, having reached out for his wine. Percy bowed again, and stood waiting further instructions.

Even though he guessed he was dismissed, he still stood there, unsure how to retreat from the room. Wolsey was not impressed with him, the boy knew, but he also realised, despite his lack of intellect, that as a lowborn Wolsey had to curry favour with the nobility of the land. Percy remembered how the Cardinal had preened himself when invited by the Earl of Northumberland to take Percy into his household. He thought with disdain of the Cardinal with his butcher's son's background. Even so, Wolsey was one of the most powerful in the land, answering to the Pope and the King, and a training in his household was not to be despised.

He thought sulkily of his position though and wanted to be gone. So far he had not been able to develop any of the wiliness a courtier was required to have, being too slow-tongued, at this Court of intrigues and back-biting. Before he had worked out an answer the conversation had moved on. He did not have the knowledge of worldly matters to take part in debate. Uninterested in such things, he was more at home on the moors of his northern home, hunting stag and wild boar. He found the Court dull and the work he had to do a bore. Now he was flattered to have been asked to keep an eye on Anne Boleyn; he was accomplished enough for that surely.

'You still there, boy? Go, surely you have lessons now?'

Percy hurried away, red in the face, not catching the eye of any of the others in the room.

* * * * *

'Your Majesty, have you made confession yet?'

The room was oppressive as usual with the crowds of women milling about, their dark weighty clothes swishing on the marbled floor which Katherine, a southerner, preferred. No herbal rushes here to soften a footfall. The air was heavy with the scent the women used to hide body odours, and the incense that Katherine used around her private altar. A large crucifix hung on one wall, and in a cornice the Madonna statue held pride of place before which a candle was burning. The hangings were rich damask, patterned with pomegranates, Katherine's symbol, and thickly hung, which added to the oppressiveness. Like a womb, thought Wolsey irreverently and then his lips twitched to think how inappropriate such a thought was with this woman who could only produce one sickly girl.

The queen stood regally and inclined her head in acknowledgement of his question.

It was their secret code to indicate that he needed to speak to her in private. Wolsey did not hear Queen Katherine's spiritual confession, for she kept to her own Spanish ways with the priests that had accompanied her from home when she had first arrived in England to marry Prince Arthur, but they liked each other and Wolsey was not averse at using the channels of diplomacy their friendship supplied to negotiate with the Spanish.

She fell back on her chair, richly carved as it was, raising a finger by way of order to serve wine. Wolsey thought she looked drawn and felt sorry for her. The last still-birth had drained her more than usual and now she wanted to make this pilgrimage to the holy place in Norfolk to pray that God would be kind to her and grant her the son both she and her king needed so much.

'Wolsey, ever kind for my soul. Come, we will talk in my private chambers.' She turned to her retinue of ladies, Anne amongst them, and said, 'Bring dainties and wine for Wolsey's train, and entertain them well until we are finished.'

As the Cardinal followed her, he looked towards the boy, who was standing quietly, his arms behind his back, his feet splayed out as if he needed to balance himself. Percy, feeling someone looking at him in that way that tame creatures know they are being studied, looked up and noticed Wolsey's glance. His master was eyeing a dark-haired slight girl who was sitting demurely in the window, apart from the other ladies in waiting. She was looking down, as if intent on her embroidery, so that Percy could not see her eyes. She was the only person in the room who seemed to be bathed in the soft morning light, and her needle, as it moved rapidly through the material she held so tautly, glinted and threw stabs of reflected brilliance onto her downcast cheeks. The boy understood what he must do and edged round until he stood in front of Anne.

He was sure that she sensed him standing there before her but she did not acknowledge him and he watched fascinated as she continued her rapid sewing.

For Anne, the presence of this young man was a surprise. Even with eyes down, she had noticed the slight gesture between the Cardinal and his page, and waited now. She did not know who stood before her but could tell by the cut of his hose and the soft leather shoes that he was nobility.

She kept her eyes down, calmly sewing. It would not do for her to start a conversation, but the time lapse was becoming embarrassing. She was ever attentive to protocol and knew that if they did not join others there would be gossip about them. She could see from the way he moved his feet that whoever stood before her was nervous, unsure how to start. This was unusual to her, used as she was to the quick repartee of a French Court and the ease of conversation between Katherine's maids. The English Court was more formal than the French but she was learning that, even here, easy conversation between men and women was expected. She began to feel sorry for the youth. She realised that, even though it would be wrong for her to talk first, she would be forced to do something to put him at his ease. She slowly looked up, smiled slightly and said quietly, 'Wouldst you eat with us, my Lord? Can I tempt you?'

Luckily the bustle and clatter of servants bringing in food

drowned her words to others. It was said so winningly that he smiled back, all shyness gone, and then realised he should introduce himself, 'I am Percy, the son of the Earl of Northumberland. I believe we are related through marriage, and I have been lax in not introducing myself before.'

He bowed and she stood and curtseyed, 'I forgive you, only because I believe you have not had an opportunity, is that not so?'

He warmed towards her. She was kind, soft and pliant and, when she stood up, she was nearly as tall as him. She held her arm in such a way that he knew he should proffer his, so that her small hand could rest on his forearm. He found it surprisingly easy to touch her, as if he had known her all his life and they moved across the room where the delicate foods, all sugar dainties and pasties, were being laid out. She helped him to choose, picking out the choicest and poured him some wine. Then she led him back to her seat at the window. She ignored the whisperings of her fellow maids.

Patting the cushioned seat beside her, she removed the embroidery she'd left there. It was his cue.

'Pray, let me see, what are you working on?'

'Oh, 'tis but a small thing. The story of Samson and Delilah – I am picking out Samson lying on Delilah's lap as she cuts off his hair.' She opened it and showed him and, as he looked closer, discarding the food behind him, he found his fingers brushing hers. She said, 'Would you be tempted by a woman, my lord? Would you lose your strength and secrets in such a way?'

Her voice was beguiling, the words carried to him as if they were but music in the air. Suddenly he felt strong and knew what he wanted in life, and it was not to do his father's bidding and marry Lady Mary Talbot.

* * * * *

'Where have you been?' She was striding the length of her chamber, her eyes deep orbs of anger but Priedeux stood watching, the curl of his mouth showing he was not moved or worried by her temper. Indeed, Anne could only describe his demeanour as sardonic. She became even more irate, particularly as she had been feeling triumphant and that triumph was dissipated by the lack of obedience in this, her favourite and most-needed minion.

'Come, come, Priedeux, you are my servant, not a man who can go here, there and everywhere at his own wish. I have need of you and when I summon you, you will come.'

Her voice grew louder, 'At once! It is not acceptable that you should go off for days on end.'

He still said nothing and she stopped her pacing. Standing before him, she raised her hand so that the index finger touched the dimple at her chin and rubbed it. She stared up at him. It was the man who looked away first, despite the fact she was half a head shorter than he was.

When she believed him cowed, she turned, immediately calmed, and said, 'Now to my business. Keep your secrets. No doubt you were at some whoring and I'll not need to know about that.'

As she spoke she turned to the table where lay pen and quill and parchment. Priedeux said nothing but watched as she picked up a document, sealed it with wax as it melted on the candle, and then handed it to him.

'I'll have you deliver that to my Lord Percy, in Wolsey's Household.' She added, 'And deliver it quietly, for 'tis confidential.' There was a tawny blush on her cheeks which made the servant look sharply at her.

'What, Northumberland's brat?' He was frowning.

Anne looked surprised, 'And what do you know of him?'

He paused before he spoke; she was staring at him and her look reminded him of her earlier wrath.

'Anne, I promised to serve you and I am doing so, for I see I am in the household of a great lady, and one who will be greater still. But beware, the game is hard, with many traps for the unwary, many wrong paths for those who are unwise. A paper can be used in evidence.'

Anne smiled, 'Indeed it can, oh wise one, but go on with your warning, I will hear it all.'

Her ironic tone was not lost on him but after another pause he continued, "Tis a dangerous game to try for a knight when the king is but behind ...'

She looked surprised. 'The King? Nay, Priedeux, you have ambitions for me far above dreaming. You guess my purpose. But not the reasoning. Come, let me explain.' She took his arm and led him to the window, away from the door and from any possibility of eavesdropping, although she was fairly sure she was safe in York Place, in her father's apartments. Then she said, looking not at Priedeux but out of the mullioned window at the walled courtyard beneath, 'The son will own half the northern lands when his father goes. It borders on that of Scotland and Scotland is ever an ally of France and France is where I have friends. 'Twould be easier for you to pass messages to those friends and back again through the Scottish coast than it is from here, even though we are nearer France as the crow flies. Northumberland controls a great tranche of this land of ours, is in the Privy Council and a close confidant of the King. The son does not have the character of the father. He is soft and would listen to a clever wife.'

She paused. 'And he has professed great love for me, even having poems written for me by Wyatt, and Wyatt writes willingly because he too ...'

'Aye, I have seen the love-sickness in his eyes when he watches you, but he is a poet and that can be forgiven. He is also a Kentish man and a good man. But Northumberland ...'

'What more could I achieve? With such a husband, I could reform half of England and hopefully influence the Privy Chamber to see how good those changes would be for the whole of the land.'

Even so, my Lady, I'll not take this note.' He was still holding it in one hand and pounded his other palm with it.

'Priedeux, I trust you, but ...' She had tears in her eyes, through total frustration. How else could she deliver the love note in secret, if it was not to be through the one she had chosen to be her messenger of secrets? 'Tell me why?'

'Because he is not good enough for you. You might as well accept your father's choice of the wild Irish Ormond.' Anne looked as if she was going to protest but Priedeux, confident in what he was saying, continued, 'Because all the Court knows he is betrothed to a lady who has a great dowry. Because, forgive me, Anne, for I have learnt much in these weeks at Court, you are much lower in station than he, and your father of a different faction than his father, and it would never be agreed. And you will then be disgraced.'

'But I will make it public; I will tell Percy that I will refuse to see him again unless he swears marriage. He is besotted by me, he will do as I bid.'

Priedeux grinned. He nodded at his mistress.

'That's as may be and, with such a missive, he may well feel compromised. We will try another way, but no letter, nothing in writing, my lady? Just in case.'

She looked at his hands, preparing to scrunch the parchment, waited a second, and nodded. Priedeux smiled and put the incriminating screwed-up ball into his waistband.

'I'll dispose of this later, my lady.' He turned as if to leave but she called him back.

'Now, where have you been?' It was a whisper but no less threatening for that. Her demeanour had changed again and now she was the demanding mistress. He smiled. Despite the cold whispering, he was never going to be afraid of her, for he remembered when she was but a mewling child in his arms.

'Serving my mistress in the best way I know.'

'Continue.'

'I have been scouring London for sources of interest.'

'Go on.'

'I have found a place. Off Cheapside, a small printer, outside St Paul's churchyard where most publishers are found. Sells tracts from abroad, in Latin and in English translations. I go there and they know not who I am as I am not known as a courtier or a servant and they tell me who is buying these tracts. You would be surprised.'

'Go on,' she said again, intrigued. Priedeux named Cranmer, among other young priests, and Oxford academics well known at Court. The girl raised her eyebrows in the gesture he had come to recognise, part excitement, part surprise.

'And you can buy some? Discreetly?'

He nodded, 'Of course.'

She put her hands to her face but quickly removed them as she realised Priedeux could see the extra digit. Her eyes were alight with excitement, her face all smiles. She seemed to have forgotten her wish to be betrothed to Percy in her intellectual excitement.

'Priedeux, you are more than I expected. Oh, well done, here is some silver, fetch as many new ones as they have. I am hungry for new ideas, for new theories, indeed I am.'

He bowed over the outstretched hand and took the silver. As he reached the door, Anne called after him, her face set to stern, 'Let me know when you will not be here to do my bidding; 'tis unseemly for a mistress to be beckoning a servant who does not come.'

He bowed, but she could tell it was a mocking movement. She let it go, turning so as to hide her smile.

* * * * *

It was true he had been searching London but not only on Lady Anne's business. He *had* found a bookseller and, after discussions with him, when the man had finally trusted him, Priedeux had discovered his under-the-counter wares.

But he had also been visiting bars and taverns. As he left the room, and found himself in a long gallery he reached for the pendant around his neck and stroked it. Not much to go on, but he would continue in the hope that one day he would discover his true ancestry. He had begun his search years ago and, unsuccessful, had returned home always with the thought that, later, when he had the chance, he would try again.

The first time he had reached London he was but a youth and had found it a bewildering, frightening place where the inhabitants spoke strangely and, it seemed to him then, with a rude, shortened twang that made him keep moving, unsure of his welcome anywhere in the tangle of streets. He'd found lodgings south of Tower Bridge, cheap, crowded and dirty, where he had a corner of a shared lice-ridden bed at night. During the days he'd wandered the streets just gawping, until some shopkeeper would yell, 'Gan with ya, gan, clear off, ya little thief. Can see it in yer eyes, so I can.' Priedeux would run and frequently find himself in strange quarters. Once he had been caught up in an apprentices' fight, along The Highway, running parallel with the river, but had managed to dodge down an alley smelling of fish and hid amongst the empty baskets while soldiers charged the two groups until they'd dispersed. Priedeux had carried on downhill to the river, his main point of reference in the whole confusing place, and dunked himself, fully clothed, to rid himself of the rancid fish odour. As he sat on the stony beach, watching the tide coming in, tears had mixed with the wetness, tears of loneliness and isolation. But he had not given up; he'd found a job as a pot-boy, then as a barman, living in, and spent what spare time he had searching the teeming alleys and courtyards of the great city of London, searching, always searching, for a clue to his parentage. The parchment, a tiny rolled up piece, merely had the word, 'Priedeux' and the locket which held it was of silver and shaped like a tiny tube with a levered lid on top. No pattern or mark on the silver.

The boy, like the man now, had no idea what to look for; all he knew was that he should continue to look. Over the months he had been in London with Anne he had devised a strategy and in his spare time he would wander into different parts of the great town. During his sojourns, he would find the inn that was at the centre of the local community. For he'd found that each part of this great place had its own speciality. Temple for the lawyers; the leatherworkers had their quarter eastwards, and, as he well knew, Billingsgate for the fishmongers. Each had its own drinking place, where the clerks and apprentices would gossip and vent their spleen against their elders.

On one such occasion he'd found himself in a long cellar of a drinking place near the Inns of Law. Priedeux took his stance at the bar, ordering the best ale in the place. He had a way of keeping still so that men did not notice him. Others would shove in and lean over his shoulder to pay their pence for their pint, some would push him a little further down the bar but he moved with a slight shrug which showed he wasn't going to fight back, and largely he was left alone.

'Quick man, give me a drink, for shoeing is thirsty work.' Priedeux looked up at the man who edged in beside him and was obviously impatient for his draught. He was muscular with solid arms and smelt of wood smoke and metal and sweat. His face, arms and chest were grimy with soot, and he wore only a sleeveless leather jerkin. Even in the gloom of this place, he was ruddy beneath the layer of grime. A blacksmith just come from his smithy. The barman slowly stopped his drying of a pewter mug, placed it on the counter before him in a deliberate movement and sauntered up to them. The man muttered, so only Priedeux could hear, 'That's right; rush, for we might all die of thirst.'

Priedeux's face creased into his sardonic smile and he nodded slowly over his ale. It was the cue the man was looking for. He addressed Priedeux, 'Best ale about here, slowest service. Perhaps that's how it gets to be brewed so well, waiting for it. Yes, Hal, a pint of the best – and what'll you have, stranger?'

Priedeux proffered his tankard and nodded for it to be filled again. When the transaction had been completed he agreed with his companion. 'Indeed, it is a good brew here. And I just passing through, I must be lucky to find it.'

'Aye, hidden as it is in this alley we usually get regulars, lazy bones that they are! I only come for to slake the thirst after the fire of my forge does burn my throat to a cinder. A warning, my friend, the brew here is good but it is mighty strong too.'

They leaned on the bar in identical positions and said nothing for a while. Priedeux was well content, recognising the signs for the beginnings of a short acquaintanceship where he might tax this man, to see if he knew the name 'Priedeux'.

'Not much call for great horses to be shod around here?' he ventured.

'Oh, I've seen them all: palfreys, packhorses and great war-horses. They pass up Cheapside, you see, bound for the City and out to country through Eastgate and back again with their loads – or they go south to the Tower and to the ports so I take all the passing trade. Or I catch those scurrying to the lawyers in the Inns.'

'Ah, so you have many a tale to tell.'

'Indeed, stranger, I could tell a saga, and sing it too, but for want of a cittern.' He paused and took a deep draught of ale, licked his lips, and took a deep breath.

'Once there was this old knight, a-boasting of his conquests in the time of old Henry, or even before that, in the Crusades, he said, while I shod an old nag that you or I wouldn't use for horsemeat, let alone fighting. The nag was a thin old beast and so was the owner but I let him rattle on and it was a good rattling on too for his voice was rasping like he had holes in his chest. I thought to myself, not long for this world, man and horse, so I shoed it thin, to last the time out, so I thought. Well, blow me, not six months later, comes this old knight a-roaring into my forge once more, a-complaining I'd done him wrong and sword out and at my throat, I had to shoe his nag on all four sides for free unless I wanted it cut. My throat, that is.'

'That's right; tell your best tale first, so there's nothing left.' That from the barman, who had stayed and was leaning on the bar, ignoring the other mugs still to be polished. The smith took no notice. He drew on another deep draught of his ale, as if the very thought of a slit throat made him thirsty. Priedeux said nothing, but mirrored the action. He'd found in his time that this encouraged the talking. He was right.

His companion took a deep breath, said, 'Aah,' in appreciation of the taste, and continued, 'And this time he spoke without rasping, as if he was bitter and it had all come to the surface, like: I

100

serve my king and my country and was turned aside by king and country when my usefulness was done, and now I am bereft except for my nag and you will not treat me like this. All I have left is to search for my kith and kin, I Sir Askham. He pronounced it Ask 'em. And I ride this country's breadth and height to find them, he said. And you, kind smith that you are, will do me no wrong, now, will you? You will remember Sir Askham and his relatives who are rich and powerful, when I find them. "Pray-do" that be the surname. And respect them and do not cheat them. Of course, after that, out of respect, you understand, I shod all four hooves with good shoes.'

Tom listened and nodded, it was a good tale. A tale told against the teller was always a good tale. And the 'pray-do' rang a bell which he would consider later, perhaps nothing to do with his search, so he tried to turn the theme, to his ends.

'Names, they are funny things. Have you ever heard tell of the name 'Priedeux?'

He waited, his tankard held half aloft.

His companion, in a similar motion, held his drink almost at the same height and put his head to one side. Thought a while and then slowly shook his head.

'Not as the name of a horse. Not as the name of a customer. Nay, I can't say that name has ever crossed the threshold of my forge's boundary.'

'Aah well, no matter. Let me buy you one, for telling me such a tale as that of the knight and his nag ...'

They had another drink but after that, Priedeux rose to his feet, 'I must away, good friend, maybe another time ...'

The smith nodded, ordered another, and turned his back on the departing stranger. Priedeux was disappointed. The story was a good one, and something in it made him think he might come back again but he would carry on searching.

* * * * *

It had been a damp and dark evening and now Priedeux was late. He would have to use the side gate to let himself into his sleeping quarters. He was a little drunk and depressed after another unsuccessful evening of sloping from one inn to another as he had not been summoned by his lady. He wondered what she had been doing. As on most occasions, his evening had been no more successful than any other.

He approached the high wall around York Place and walked alongside it. He knew well how to go in and out without being noticed. It did not matter if the side gate was locked; he knew how to open it, a skill learnt in youth. Even so, in the quiet of the night, his metallic fumblings with the gate seemed to echo in the dark void. When it eventually creaked open, he was sure he had aroused the whole household.

But in London night noises did not waken those sleeping. He had had to get used to the different sounds himself. Instead of the screaming of a vixen, the hooting of hunting owls and birdsong at dawn, there had been the raucous singing of revellers at all times of night, the tramp of night-watchmen, the creaking and rumblings of early morning wagons arriving from the country with fresh vegetables and squawking tied-up chickens. Instead of birdsong, there were the raucous cries of hawkers of warm milk, fresh bread and fish who called their wares as dawn broke, sounding at first to Priedeux like a devilish caterwauling until he had got used to them and had been able to decipher the words. Despite that, he thought, an unsleeping servant might detect a strange noise; there was a pattern to the city sounds, as there was in the country. As surely as he would recognise that the hoot of an owl as dawn broke was wrong, so a city dweller might know the squeak of a locked gate in the early hours was a warning. So he slid into the yard and pushed himself against the wall and waited. The only movement was the slow creaking of a leaning tree which bent gently in the soft night breeze. It was cloudy with no moon and Priedeux mentally thanked God for the skill he had acquired as a countryman, to be able to detect the shadows of night. He waited a while longer. No alert night-watchman, torch flaring, came from the house and after a while Priedeux started to walk across the yard, confident that he could reach his quarters without being discovered. His soft boots made no sound on the paviers.

But as he passed the stables, there was a rustling that had nothing to do with him. It was unlike the turning of a sleeping horse in straw. He did not stop but carried on, his eyes accustomed to the darkness, until he reached the stable door. Something inside was moving and Priedeux was sure it was not a horse. Surely he had heard human whispers mixed with the noise of rustling clothes?

He pushed open the door and entered. He was not afraid, just curious. Suddenly he could feel the sharp blade of a knife at his throat, a firm grip on his arms, a leg twined round his, in as good a locking vice as he knew. The body behind was slight and smaller than him. Even so, Priedeux went limp knowing that a false move would mean the knife would cut into his throat if he resisted.

'Keep quiet or you're dead!' the voice, even at a whisper, was cultured and Priedeux guessed a young man. He forced his body to become even limper so his adversary might relax. Then another, female voice uttered, 'It's Priedeux! Don't hurt him! He's a trusted servant.'

The knife was loosened. Anne! Holding a covered lamp which she now exposed so that Priedeux could see her. She was dishevelled, with straw hanging to the folds of her dress and in her hair.

Priedeux sighed, and not with relief. He turned to face the man who had now let him go. The boy, for that was how Priedeux saw him, stood alert, the knife still held aloft, almost crouching, ready to jump if he was attacked.

Anne and Percy! Had the girl compromised herself? Was this to be the end of her glittering career at Court? Were they both to return to Hever, she disgraced, and he to a life of a countryman? It was the last that made him despair and then think rapidly. The boy had relaxed at Anne's cry and Priedeux kicked the knife out of his hand, jumping away and at the same time unsheathing his dagger. In a second he too was crouched, ready for battle with his

103

attacker.

Suddenly Anne stood in front of him, a dark shadow against the dim light that came from the lantern she had placed on the floor.

'Put that down, Priedeux! Stop.' Then she turned and said, 'Henry, come! Stop it. We are in luck. Priedeux is the only one who can help us!'

Both men relaxed, and Percy picked up his knife where it had fallen, Priedeux watching him but when the lad placed his knife back into its sheath, Priedeux did likewise. His mistress continued, 'Priedeux, you must help us! Percy cannot get out. He hid today when Wolsey came to see the queen and we have spent precious time together. But now all is locked without and the walls have no holding places for a climber. You have come in, so must know the way out!'

Her companion interrupted, 'Anne, how much does this man know? Surely this was our secret!'

'My sweet love, Priedeux is my trusted messenger. He knows all.'

She trailed off as she saw her lover's face, which was one of disgusted surprise. Priedeux said nothing. Anne, shrugging, turned to Priedeux again. 'And I cannot get back to my chamber. I must be missed soon. Someone will wonder why I do not return from the privy after this length of time!'

Priedeux grinned, sure that his mistress could not see his features in the dark, although he could guess at the anguished look of hers. He could make out her lover now, foppishly dressed with much whitish lace gleaming in the dimness, outlining neck, hands and waist.

'Yes, you must help your mistress. Or we are all in trouble.'

Priedeux did not like the imperious way the boy had spoken, but then he was the son of a Duke, and likely to be a Duke himself and Priedeux assumed that was how great ones talked. He had not had much to do with other highborns at court, except by observation. Even so, he did not like being spoken to in such a manner so he ignored the youngster and turned to his mistress.

'Madam, if you are found in this compromising manner, all will be well with you, would it not? For you could truly be said to be affianced to this great man?'

She said nothing for a moment, but started to walk up and down, kicking the straw beneath her feet. Priedeux saw Percy back away slightly, as if he had been struck.

Percy muttered, stammering slightly, 'I know not how my father would take it. I would prefer to speak to him openly.'

Priedeux pursed his lips together. He guessed, despite what Anne had said, that her lover would keep his options open. Even if he thought he was in love with Anne, Priedeux judged Percy too weak to go against his family's wishes. The lace he sported showed he had expensive tastes, and if he were to marry Anne and his father disinherited him how would he afford such? All this sped through the servant's mind as the youngsters moved around him in a macabre step dance.

How had Anne and Percy organised this meeting? Maybe on the spur of the moment, without either of the youngsters thinking the matter through. Otherwise surely they would have wondered how Percy was to leave eventually. He would find out later. Now he had to address the task in hand, either to force the boy to propose and carry through that promise, or to ensure this meeting was kept secret. If he did not promise to marry Anne, she would be shamed if such a meeting as this was made public. At all costs, Anne should not be discovered like this. There would only be one conclusion drawn and, if the man denied her, then she would gain a reputation like her sister. After a pause he said, 'Come, I'll let you out the door, and My lady, wait here, I'll see you back to your chamber and think of something to explain your disappearance.'

He sidled out of the stable, not looking back, knowing the boy followed. He picked the lock again and creaked open the gate. Before it was a quarter open Percy had sidled through it. Priedeux whispered, 'Wait, I'll have words with you.'

Percy stopped, leaning against the outside wall. Priedeux, not

105

caring about the disparity in rank, grabbed the younger man's arm in a vice-like grip, so that his fingers sunk into the thick padded velvet of Percy's elegant clothing. He spoke through clenched teeth, his words menacing.

'My mistress will not be denied! If you tarnish her good name you'll answer to me and you'll not be able to say who killed you! Act honourably towards her, I say!'

The younger man said nothing but wrenched his arm away and disappeared without so much as a 'thank-you' for the help given him. Priedeux locked the gate again and returned to his mistress. She stood, just inside the stable, leaning against the wall, and he could tell she was drained.

'Come, I'll take you back and speak with one of your companions, say I found you half asleep. You have been very sick, understand?'

He saw her nodding. Her colour and look of exhaustion would add weight to that excuse, he thought, as he led her to the back door that servants used. He unlocked this and slid through. The servants' passage was unlit and, as far as he could tell, empty. He ushered her before him and they walked side by side until they reached the door which led to the main part of the palace. Priedeux slid through and checked all was clear. Here the corridor was wider and lit by dim flares which reflected in the oak panelling. The nobility are allowed to slope to their beds with light, he thought grimly. But it revealed more than just their passage to bed. As Anne followed him into the hall, he looked at her. There were still wisps of straw in her hair which he quickly removed. She pulled her bodice tight, lacing herself up again, smiling at him. It was not altogether an innocent smile but he smiled back, tolerant of her, knowing her to have failings, like all humans. He tweaked some stray straws out of the lace of her collar, then stood back and surveyed her. Nodded and moved on.

As they approached the double doors which led to the quarters of the ladies-in-waiting, Priedeux whispered, 'We must be brave for there's nothing for it. Come, lean on me and look ill.'

106

As he spoke they reached the doors and he rapped on them imperiously. The noise was so loud it made Anne jump and she thought it would waken even King Henry himself in his far-off royal quarters.

'Who's there? What do you want at this ungodly hour?' Various female voices twittered at once, and there was a rustling and mayhem within, but eventually the door was opened by a matron, her hair falling about her face, a cloak hurriedly wrapped around her shoulders.

'What do you want?' It was openly hostile.

'At last someone awakes. You should all be ashamed of yourselves, for here is Anne, one of your youngest companions, sick and none of you miss her! It is lucky for her that there is one good servant that keeps awake and alert. Here, take her.'

The door was opened and others flocked out, taking hold of Anne who hung limp and leaning heavily on them. Good, thought Priedeux, she makes a consummate actress.

'Well, tell us what happened, where was she?'

I found her outside the privy, half dead, having vomited her last dinner and all the food before it so it would seem. The vomiting has made her weak and she was but barely conscious. Care for her well.'

The matron, who had allowed others to take Anne, stared hard at the man and then said, 'Thank you, you are true! We will send for the doctor if she is not better in the morning.'

The door was shut on him and he stood there for a second before turning abruptly and moving slowly away. He had more work to do to protect his mistress.

Chapter Twelve

There was a bubbling and a-humming at Court and Priedeux soon found out the reason for it. When he had first arrived, he had not been able to discriminate between the normal chattering of idle courtiers and the twittering of those who would pass on tittle-tattle as if it were of political importance. One long summer and winter at Court had been enough for him to learn what the huddled crowds meant, with heads close together, an arm on a shoulder, the body leaning at an angle, eyes half-closed, so the ear could assimilate the whisper. Now he could even differentiate between the jangle of foreign accents, with their sibilating sounds, so different from the English hard talking. He could recognise the difference between the French courtiers or the Spanish ambassadors or one of the English factions. He could tell whether the gossip was of love-news, an exotic item concerning foreign courts or some horror of war. War was the worst; the way the men gloried in deaths and the destructions of towns and communities after it, leaving a wake of weeping women and unborn babes inside them.

Today he could see the Norfolk clan milling around and recognised their liveried servants being sent on errands. The gossip, he guessed, was scandalous, possibly of a love-intrigue at the English Court, but not serious. There was ribald laughter, ribs elbowed. If it had been war, the old men would be shaking their beards and looking dour and the young ones glorying. Priedeux had a sense of foreboding.

Bishops huddled together like overblown Lancaster roses, whispering.

A liveried boy hurried past with a salver and wine. He stopped the lad and said, 'What be the hurry? What's happening?'

The boy struggled free and reddened. 'I'll not tell ye, as you're Lady Anne's man, but it concerns her! You'll soon hear!'

And he scuttled off before Priedeux could catch him without making himself conspicuous. Even so, some heads turned and then looked away hurriedly, refusing to catch his eye. He decided to visit his mistress's chambers without being invited. He had a piece of news for her anyway and, even if he didn't have a reason for visiting her, he could excuse himself by showing he had a message. He sought in the folds of his clothes and found a paper he could use for the purpose. As he wove his way through the whisperings, he caught certain phrases:

'The young scamp!'

'She has charm but little dowry!'

'Way beneath him. Northumberland will never allow it.'

'The king must give his permission. Would he please Sir Thomas with his approval?'

'She dances well.'

'Dancing don't count when it comes to matches.'

'Surely he is betrothed elsewhere.'

Priedeux had heard enough. Had Percy declared himself?

He reached the door that had closed on him a few days before. He had not been summoned since then, and no news of his lady's wellbeing or otherwise had reached him. All had been as if a veil had been drawn over the whole night. That in itself was ominous, he thought. He rapped at the door.

It was opened a slit and a slim girl peered out.

'Is Lady Anne Boleyn there? How fares she? I am Priedeux, her messenger, come with news from home.'

The girl opened it wider and looked behind her.

'Let him in, Frances, let him in.'

He pushed open the door and strode in, as the girl stood to one side to allow him to enter the foetid air of an enclosed room with many women languishing in it. Queen Katherine was once more indisposed and her ladies-in-waiting had been incarcerated in her chambers for some days while they waited for her next move.

Anne was seated at the window, looking down at her unworked embroidery. Priedeux surveyed her. There was an air of quiet triumph about her. Her cheeks were glowing in a rare high colour. The matron, who Priedeux had handed her to previously, came up as if to chaperone her but she dismissed her with a hand signal. The woman huffed and slowly withdrew, with a frown. When she had moved sufficiently far away, Anne took Priedeux's arm and walked away from the group of ladies.

'Priedeux! You must send a message for me, soon,' she whispered. She then turned back to the matron. 'Ma-am, may I walk with my servant in the garden for a while? He would tell me news of home.'

The matron looked at Anne and at the man beside her. Priedeux stood still, his eyes lowered. She nodded and Anne led Priedeux out of the room into a side corridor. As soon as they were alone Anne whispered, 'Can you guess, Tom, what has happened?'

He paused for a moment and then nodded.

'Aye, from the prattling in all the halls of court. Your young lover has asked that he be betrothed to you! Is it not so?'

She nodded and walked away quickly, Priedeux striding beside her. When she reached the end of the corridor, she twirled once and exclaimed triumphantly, 'I am to be the Countess of Northumberland! Imagine! Lady of all the lands from the Scottish Borders to Lancaster with manors and privileges beyond compare. He is in line for the throne if Henry dies without an heir.' She paused, noting the look on his face, 'Yes, I know, there are others who would have to die as well, but life is short for many at the top. I will have power. A husband who will do all I ask for love of my sweet face! I shall educate *him* first, in the ways of the pure church, in the ways of following Christ's teaching, and then, together, we shall change the way the priests in our lands teach their people. You know what he said to me when I explained how I felt? *"Whatever you want, sweet Anne, whatever you want."'*

Priedeux tried to interrupt but she prattled on, 'We shall

110

educate the people so they, too, can read their Bibles in English and understand what our dear Lord taught and how they should lead their lives.'

She spoke rapidly, excitedly. She stopped walking and stood facing him. Priedeux stood watching her sadly. He knew that marriages were not made at the request of a lad hardly out of learning, who had been at Court but a few seasons.

He spoke slowly, 'I am but a servant, dear Anne, but listen to me. Marriages are the machinations of fathers and guardians to ensure the best match for their children. *You know that.* What makes this different?'

'Priedeux, you do not understand, he has *promised* ...'

Priedeux looked round to make sure no-one could hear him, as he continued, 'Anne; marriages are but alliances between equals. Alliances between kings, alliances between dukes, alliances between the lesser nobility, but rarely alliances between a duke's son and a girl from a family from such a lowly background, with only a 'Sir' in front of her father's name. Especially a girl who has a healthy grown-up brother who would take all the lands. Anne, you have no dowry, you are no match, even for a boy such as Percy.' Anne had stopped now and her triumphant expression sobered as Priedeux expressed his deep suspicions of her expectations. When he could see she was truly deflated, he changed the subject, and added cheerfully, 'Think of what I have said, but to cheer you I have some news for you, my lady, from your brother.'

She held her finger to her chin in the now familiar fashion and put her head to one side, waiting, showing no expression now except that of a dutiful person accepting news of family.

Priedeux explained, 'De Selve is in England, in the French train. They are come to avert the invasion of France that Wolsey threatens, to support the Emperor Charles.'

'De Selve, oh good de Selve, it will be wonderful to see him.'

Immediately she was cheered and, ignoring the rest of Priedeux's news, exclaimed, 'Oh, I can tell him of my betrothal,

111

how our plans for reform are finally coming to fruition.' Invasions were of no concern to Anne; all she cared for now was the returning feeling of triumph, Priedeux's warning forgotten, at her betrothal to the son of an Earl. To be able to share it with her childhood friend, whom she had not seen for some time, would be like adding pearls to a golden necklace.

'Where is he lodging? No matter, you can take a note to him, and he will come to me.'

She led him back into her quarters, ignored the waiting women and darted to a corner, took quill and parchment and proceeded to write, her tongue just obtruding as she concentrated. Then she straightened, 'Take this to him. I would hope to see him before tonight's entertainment and he can tell me all his news.' She paused, and smiled again, 'And I shall tell him mine!'

Priedeux bowed and left, heavy hearted. When he found himself alone he opened the parchment and read it. After reading it a second time, he tore the document into several pieces, and placed the bits in his pouch. Later he would burn it. *No paper, lady,* he thought, no record of who you know or your innermost secrets.

He knew where the Frenchmen were cloistered and had no difficulty in gaining an audience, using Lady Anne Boleyn's name. Soon he was in the presence of this friend of Anne's. Priedeux knew he was already a bishop but was surprised at how young he looked. *Another abuse of the church,* he thought, *too young to have the authority to officiate at services, surely.* He frowned at the absurdity, for he was well aware that, as a bishop, de Selve would be in receipt of the tithes and other payments from the Bishopric's properties in France without having to carry out parish duties.

The Frenchman greeted him politely but distantly. Priedeux mimicked his manner, repeating what his mistress had written in the missive in a dry and exact tone, except for the detail about a possible betrothal. De Selve listened to what Priedeux had to say and then left the messenger standing, while he played with a quill, stroking the feathers into a point, the action slow and deliberate. Priedeux had time to observe him and was surprised that Anne and he should be friends. Even though he was young, his face was closed, no emotion showing, his movements slow and studied, as if he was aware of his position. Priedeux guessed, from the way he slowly absorbed the message, that he was not an impulsive man. Indeed, to Priedeux, he seemed stolid and boring, completely the opposite of Anne's speed and intelligence, and he wondered why Anne had befriended him.

He did not wear the clothes of his office but a dark thick robe, fur-lined, and Priedeux realised he was used to warmer climes than the English summer.

Eventually he said, 'Tell your mistress I will meet her when and where she says, and, yes, tell her it will be a pleasure to make her acquaintance once again.'

Priedeux noticed that the accent was heavy and the words considered, as if carefully thought out beforehand. He nodded but as he bowed and made to turn to leave, de Selve raised a hand.

'Wait! I would ask you something.'

Priedeux turned, saying nothing, standing to attention.

'How long have you served the good Lady Anne?'

Priedeux answered quickly, 'As long as I have known her, my lord.' Then something in De Selve's face made him go on, 'I have been in her family's service since I was old enough to serve. She was but a babe when I first saw her and was ordered to assist when she travelled to Brabant. Since then, there has been a bond that will never be broken by me!'

Priedeux could not tell why he felt the need to explain so much but, as he spoke, he thought he detected a slight smile on the Frenchmen's lips, the neat beard seeming to twitch, but he could not be sure. Indeed, this foreigner was a deep one, and again Priedeux wondered how his mistress and de Selve ever became such loyal allies.

De Selve then said slowly, 'Be careful, for such loyalty may lead you into many strange adventures. The Lady Anne was always impulsive to the point of danger.' He paused. 'If you value *your* life, I would counsel you to value hers, and watch over her as you

113

would a young frightened doe who, when trapped, may do something that hurts only themselves.' He turned away from Priedeux and said, almost to himself, 'But she will learn and, when she does, her enthusiasm may turn to bitterness or cynicism. We shall see, shall we not, good man?'

Priedeux noted the reflective way that de Selve spoke, and realised that, despite his youth, the young bishop was disappointed in some way with his life. He stepped forward and took the man's proffered gloved hand and kissed the signet ring. Then he stood and faced his superior.

'Good sir, I have faith in my mistress and I will look out for her!'

De Selve nodded and waved a hand towards the door. Priedeux was dismissed.

* * * * *

'You stupid, stupid boy!' It was the way that Wolsey said the word *boy* that Percy knew he was in for a roasting.

'How can you engage yourself against your father's wishes, how can you disgrace me, in the eyes of your father, by trying to make such a foolish match?' Wolsey spoke to the air above Percy's head, his hands raised in exasperation, and then dropped to his knees.

'But you told me to...'

'...to find out about her. Not fall in love with her. Have you no control? What am I to do with you? *Fall in love* with her! That is a luxury reserved for merchantmen and dreamers, not for noblemen.'

'But 'tis because she is noble, a great lady. I am sure my father would agree.'

'A lady she may be. But not of the nobility, no title to bring with her. And no dowry, boy, no dowry. She has a brother and a sister, that sister with a child, who will take any inheritances. Anne will bring you nothing! Your father would never agree.'

'But if father should meet her, he would see that her character is such that she would prove a great helpmate to me.'

'Enough of this insolence. D'you wish me to summon your father to Court?'

'I shall tell my father the same thing. Anne is of the same noble birth as myself and I am nearly of age and have the right to choose for myself.'

Wolsey said nothing at this outburst. He just gestured to two of his burly retainers, who stood nearby and, without any further instructions they stepped forward and grabbed the astonished lad by his arms. He struggled but he was only slight, and they held him fast.

'Take Percy to his chamber and lock him up. I am sending for your father who must decide this issue!'

Chapter Thirteen

Dear de Selve,

Yes I am at Hever again and all seems lost as you have heard I am not now to marry Percy. A weakling he was, I know, but he would have served our purpose I am sure in that he would have done my bidding, and willingly, for love of me. No communication have I had from him. I blame him not. He never raised the question of marriage settlements, and he always said he preferred to marry a penniless lady such as myself whom he could nurture. La, la, let it be over! You have no doubt heard the news that his father disgraced himself by shouting and screaming at his son in front of Wolsey's servants and then packed my dear Henry up north where he has been forced to marry his father's – and Wolsey's – choice, Lady Mary Talbot, the daughter of the Earl of Shrewsbury.

It is Wolsey I must hold responsible for this cruel blight on my – our plans – but, trained as I am in patience and true resolve for the love of our church and its reforms in the ways we have so often discussed, I shall never give up. My hatred of Wolsey will spur me on.

I heard that the king had said, 'I shall not have that wench Anne marrying Percy' and 'twas told in such a way that he seemed to reserve me for himself. I was surprised but know of his lust with my sister so not shocked ... maybe this is another way? If only I could get back to Court. I'll write to Dinteville whom father knows well and ask him to petition father, for I am in disgrace and he'll not listen to me!

Please send me more tracts especially those from Germany. I hear all sorts of rumours from France, Italy and the German city states and that the Vatican is fearful at the revolt against its power. It pleases me to hear that some of our men of God can see the faults of the Popish ways and would cleanse the mother church.

How fares our dear friend Dinteville? I hear his language skills stand him in good stead and that he visits the English Court. My brother mentions him to me when he is at home but that is not much. Oh, I crave for men's society, for serious talk. My mother expects me to help in the management of our estate, to sew constantly so that my eyes feel sore with the staring. Oh, how different it is when one's eyes are skimming the pages of a book full of ideas and philosophy! I make good use of my time in organising the servants to hone my knowledge of man. I also read much so please send me more tracts. You can see how desperate I am when, as I re-read this, I realise that I repeat my request! Dear de Selve, God be with you.

P.S. the bearer of this missive is to be trusted, a true and intelligent messenger and more than a servant ... a friend, an ally – he delivered messages to you when I was at Court.

Priedeux smiled grimly to himself as he read this last sentence.

'Indeed, my mistress, more than you can be trusted, I'll say,' he muttered to himself. He was riding back to London, alone, and the old hack he had borrowed, so as to be incognito, was ambling along in the mid-morning mist as it rose from the marsh valley he was now travelling. There was no-one else journeying this way. He quickly tucked the first letter into his belt and extracted the next parchment from the leather pouch hanging by his side. He carefully slit the waxen seal of his mistress and unfolded the next paper.

My dear Dinteville,

I write to congratulate you on your success at the English Court, I hear all the young ladies-in-waiting admire your good looks and wit, and so they should! Yes, I am kept here at Hever in shame for my escapade with Percy but it was meant well, as you know.

Dear Jean, you know father; you have sat in with him on many talks between our beloved countries. Can you not suggest to him that I am wasted here in the country? I have faith in my future, in our plans but they will come to nothing unless I can do my bit, with only my womanly ways to catch a husband who will be of use to us to cleanse the mother

117

church. Can you not work on father ... I beg of you.

And, if you come across some interesting pamphlets, send them by my courier who bears this letter. Priedeux by name and ever faithful to me.

Priedeux sighed at the desperate note of the letter. He had been summoned to a pacing and excited girl who, as he entered, had still been sanding the papers she had been writing on to dry the ink. The letters were scrawled, the words joined up where she hadn't had time to lift the quill between them, with blotches where she had taken up too much ink. He opened the third letter.

My dear Queen Katherine,

I humbly petition thee as a true and faithful servant of your household that I have done no wrong and suffer greatly for my innocence in believing that I would be truly married before God and man to Percy. I know how honoured I was to be in your retinue and hope that I served you well as a lady-in-waiting but feel that my skill in so doing is being much wasted here at our country home, no matter how pleasant.

I humbly beg thy forgiveness in writing so pleadingly but if you can see your way to influencing your master and lord, Henry, to allow me to return to your side and the Court, ever faithful and true I will be.

Your loyal servant Anne Boleyn

Priedeux rode to London first and delivered this letter to the household of Queen Katherine, unknowing whether it reached her hands. Then he turned back eastwards, intending to take his mistress's messages to the two Frenchmen who had returned to their home country. As he rode along, he was conscious of the letters hidden in his pouch and it was not until he was on a lonely stretch of road that he opened it, took them out and carefully read them again. He muttered to himself, looking around him vacantly, repeating the lines.

The horse ambled on. When Priedeux reached a small copse he dismounted, collected dry scrub, twigs and then larger timber. Some of the wood was damp but he knew well how to find dry tinder from his gamekeeper days and he also sought out and found a cache of last year's leaves, still crisp and dry. Soon he had a small fire blazing and, when it was going well, he once again read his mistress's letters. Then he took one and tore it into tatters and fed it to the flames. He took up the other, read it again, muttered it to himself, and that too was consigned to the fire. He crouched around the warmth and watched as the paper turned into ashes, curling out of the shape of the original, then breaking into pieces, with those pieces rising on the thermals like drifting birds until they were lost. Even after some minutes there were still grey pieces remaining and swirling around in the warmed air. He waited a further while as the tinder burnt itself into ashes and, when there were only glowing embers, he trod out the glow and spread the still warm remains around with his foot, mixing it with the dried earth around it. He could feel the heat through the sole of his boot, and a slight burning odour reached him as his leather cindered with the heat. Eventually he stood and surveyed the scene.

Satisfied, he reached for his horse and mounted.

He muttered, 'No incriminating letters, lady, but I will ensure your messages reach their goal.'

He did not hurry but allowed his horse to amble along, in the gentle way it had, savouring its freedom. The sun had risen high now and the mist had cleared to a day of warm sunshine and no wind. Another reason for going slow was his reluctance to cross the seas again. His one and only time had been treacherous and only his care for the young girl who was his charge then and now had stopped him from giving into the foaming deep around him. He knew he had to go now he had burnt the letters because only he knew what the messages were, and who they were for, and if his mistress was to succeed in her mission, and Priedeux supported her fully in it, then he had to do all he could to get her back to Court. Besides, he had lost the will to live in the country and knew he might find out about his lost family if he were back in London.

He enquired of travel across the Channel and took passage on a merchant ship. The crossing was as on a calm pond and he leant over the prow, staring at the sun dappled flatness of water, surprised that a sea journey could be so pleasant.

* * * * *

Soon he was riding the flat lands of northern France headed for Polisy, the family seat of Dinteville, some miles southwest of Paris. He rode for some days, using his rusty Latin to communicate and was surprised at how large this country appeared. Eventually he arrived at the small village attached to the castle, the river snaking around it on a small hill, and crossed the two bridges which shortened the journey to the entrance. He was tired and bored at the constant need to concentrate on the strange twittering language around him in the marketplace and wished for good lodgings and some English conversation.

He was shown into the ambassador's presence almost immediately and wondered if he had been expected. Not by a letter, he was sure. Perhaps Dinteville had spies in the surrounding countryside who informed him of newcomers. Dinteville gazed at him for a long while until Priedeux lowered his eyes, and saw his hands were twitching as he held his cap in his hands. Why this one should make him nervous, Priedeux could not say. Unless it was the quiet way he sat, as if he were an animal staring at something that no-one else could see.

The room was spacious and airy and there were no shadows to mask the other man's face. Priedeux was impressed by the large marble fireplace, richly carved and decorated, even though in this place, at this clement time of year, no fire was needed. Rich wood panelling gave the room a warming atmosphere and large windows let in the southern light. The room contained heavily carved furniture, and Dinteville sat on a high back chair, richly cushioned with deep red velvet. He was full-lipped and hooded-eyed, autocratic. Priedeux could detect a faint smell of sweetness about the man and wondered if he perfumed himself.

'You have letters?'

When the question came, it had the sibilant sound of the French language. Priedeux thought of it as a secretive language, one where whispers were shelled into willing ears. Priedeux did not see the man's lips move, his thick beard hiding them. He suddenly felt afraid, as if this person was of a different world, totally unknown to Priedeux. The servant wondered if his mistress had the measure of this man. Was he really a true friend?

However, he trusted Anne's judgement and put his fears to one side. He had a mission to complete, so answered. 'I have no letters, sir, but I have a message from Lady Anne Boleyn, my mistress, which she has entrusted to me.' He hoped that Anne and Dinteville would never check on how their communications were transmitted.

'Oui, *continuez*.' Priedeux understood he should go on, so he took a deep breath and recited the letter he had memorised so well, word for word.

Dinteville leaned forward as Priedeux speeded up at the end.

'Repetez, s'il vous plaît'. Priedeux gathered he was being asked to repeat what he had just said, not only from the words but from the grand upsweep of the arm.

'And, if you come across some interesting pamphlets, send them by my courier who bears this letter. Priedeux by name and ever faithful to me.'

As he repeated the sentence Priedeux, who was usually too ruddy-cheeked to blush, could feel the blood thickening on his face, for this time he heard the word 'letter' in the phrase. Learnt parrot-fashion, he had not really taken in the meaning of Anne's message, except to realise that it might be used against her if it had been intercepted by a king's – or even a queen's – spies.

There was a silence. Priedeux waited. The silence seemed to go on for so long that he thought the man had gone to sleep. He was looking down; the only indication of alertness was his index finger tapping on the papers in front of him. Priedeux reminded himself that Anne trusted this man and, in order to break the silence, he decided to admit what he had done.

'Yes, sir, my lady did give me letters for you and de Selve, but I have learned that, at our English Court, you do not leave matters in black and white for strangers to read, so I burnt them before I left England. In case I was stopped, and they were found, you understand. I swear to you, on my lady's life, that I have repeated what I read word for word.'

Dinteville stood up then and came towards him, with a few quick steps. When he stood close enough to Priedeux so that Priedeux could see his eyes were deep brown, he raised his arms and Priedeux tensed himself for blows. Instead both arms were rested on his shoulders and the Frenchman proceeded to kiss him on both cheeks. Priedeux was so shocked he simply stood and took the gesture, totally unknown to him, although the Frenchmen at Court had, he now recalled, greeted each other in this manner.

Then Dinteville stood back and he was laughing.

'Sacré coeur! I always knew Anne could make many love her, but to have an intelligent manservant who not only loves her but protects her from herself! I congratulate you and praise you for such an action. Now, can you remember my French phrases to pass back to her? For you are wise and I will take Anne's words and trust you.

'And you go to de Selve now? You can carry a message to him in the same manner for he and I must not be known by others to be in contact. We three, Anne and de Selve and I, we will achieve our end with such as you to pass our thoughts and plans between us. And yes indeed I have pamphlets for Anne but if you carry them will they be safe?'

'Sir, I am but a small merchantman when I travel and there are few that can watch visitors to Hever and along that way, for the hills and forests round-abouts do protect it. If I am discovered I can merely say I am carrying them without knowing what they are.'

'Oui, you are right. Now, go to and we'll meet at dinner; you will sit at table with my household, as a merchantman you understand.'

Chapter Fourteen

Despite all the letters and the pleadings of her good friends, it took many months of machinations before Anne returned to the Court. It was Queen Katherine who eventually sent the letter of invitation, for she would only have six ladies-in-waiting close to her and it had been some time before there was a vacancy. Anne stubbornly refused to return to Court unless she had a position that she considered worthy.

When the summons came, it was an early May day and Anne was enjoying the soft spring rays of sun while she read beneath a tree. Her feet were damp with dew but she had never been able to bear to stay inside the dark close rooms of Hever. As soon as possible she had skipped out. She hadn't acknowledged the approach of Priedeux, although she well knew he towered over her now. Eventually she looked up and saw the messenger grinning.

'Your father has arrived and asked me to find you. Before you go to him prepare yourself. There is going to be a great meeting between the French and the English to discuss marriage between Princess Mary and the Dauphin. *Someone* in the French retinue of ambassadors mentioned one Anne Boleyn and that her knowledge of French would be much appreciated. The king knew the surname, so it is said, but not the girl. So he has prevailed upon his dear queen to grant you a place in her entourage.'

Priedeux had spoken in measured tones. He wanted Anne to be ready to greet the news from her father calmly.

Anne jumped up, dropping the missal she had been reading but quickly recovered it from the damp grass, wiping it on her petticoats, for it was leather-bound and precious.

'Priedeux! Thank God, I am called at last! Where is father? I have work to do.' She stood up and fitted her feet back into the pattens she had had the good sense to place over her delicate shoes.

'Wait, Madam, do not rush off. Listen to me.'

Anne turned to him impatiently, 'Priedeux, remember you are a servant. Do not order me!'

'Lady Anne, I may be a servant, but remember why you asked for me to serve you. I want to warn you. Do not seem too keen, in front of your father. Listen to him, for he could block this, if he wished it.'

'Surely not, surely not.'

She had started to walk back to the house and Priedeux could barely keep pace with her, for when Anne was fired with enthusiasm she was as nimble as a young deer.

'Madam, he is still pursuing the Ormond claim and may wish you to be charming to give effect to that.'

Anne stopped walking and turned to him, her face set.

'He may try to persuade me to agree to it, but inside here,' she touched her breast, 'in here, I will pursue my own ways. My father does not deserve to be obeyed.' She blushed then and changed the subject, worried she had said too much. 'You must go to Cranmer, the priest at Rochester, and tell him I am called. Tell him to prepare himself for I will find a way for him to be near me.'

Priedeux stopped walking beside her and she too stopped to turn round and face him, 'I know, a priest. Not like the others; he is a good man, I assure you. I have not been idle under the trees of Hever, sir, while you gad about with messages.' She was smiling and he was charmed by her energy, her ironic tone. 'I have been studying hard and making good allies, in the ways of my father. Cranmer, you know of, from your booksellers' visits, but now you will meet him. You will find he will be good for our cause.'

She continued striding to the house and the servant was forced to go with her. He was still not convinced.

'A priest, though! Is he really to be trusted to want to change the very thing that grants him authority over others?'

'Oh, Priedeux, he is not like that. For one, he agrees all should be able to read the gospels in their own language. He listens to my tales of Luther and wants pamphlets from Germany as much as I do.'

Anne had without ceremony walked through the home farm, which was the quickest way back to the main house. She was so excited she did not notice the cow pats she stepped into which, despite the high pattens, splashed the hem of her skirt and her stockings. They had reached the garden door to the house. Priedeux stopped and pointed at Anne's wet and besmirched shoes and hem.

'Madam, change before you go before your parents, for your mother is with him in his study. Pray tidy yourself, and show you are prepared to be a great Court lady!'

Anne turned and grinned at the man. She was not the sort to take orders from anyone but Priedeux said it so ironically, and had proved such a loyal retainer, that she accepted the advice. She patted her hair, encased in a country lace bonnet and nodded. As she entered the small outhouse, she removed the pattens and continued in her stockinged feet, which were not much drier.

'Indeed, I must impress father and if he approves, then I know the whole Court will admire me! Father is the hardest critic I can expect, God willing.'

She slipped into the main part of the house by the servants' entrance and it was some little time before she appeared before her parents. She didn't knock but burst in, as if she had just discovered she was wanted. She had removed the country bonnet and had wound her hair into a tightly coiled style. She wore a neat clean dress with white starched lace at collar and cuffs.

'Father, I have heard the news. Is it true? Am I to return to Court?'

Her father stood and gravely watched her. He put down the papers he had been holding and sat down, leaning back in his chair.

'Indeed, my child. Queen Katherine has need of another lady-in-waiting and rumour has it that your knowledge of French and your skill at dancing – so much admired when you were in the French Court – were discovered by judicious enquiries. It is hoped you will charm our guests.' He stopped and looked at her sternly, 'As I am sure you will. But not so as to make any more foolish liaisons. The Ormond marriage could yet be a possibility and I am petitioning for that so, in the meantime, besmirch not your name. Come, do a few steps for your old father and show me how you beguiled the French, for I must needs forget all that has gone before and look to the future.'

Anne grasped him by the hand, held it high and minced a few formal steps of a Court dance she had learned in France, shortly before she had come home. She was so entranced by the news that the memory of what her father had done was not uppermost in her mind right now. She hadn't seen him since being confined at Hever as his official duties had kept him travelling. This was almost their first family meeting and the anticipation of being at Court again was so great and her training in good manners so well learned that any repulsion at what he had done all those years ago was buried. Not only that but she was almost certain that her father had exercised his influence at Court and for that she must be grateful. Even so, she was sure that her friends, de Selve and Dinteville, and her brother George had spread the word about her. She finished the dance, curtsied and ran to where her brother's lute hung on the wall. She took it down carefully, settled the strings and then sang. Her voice was a sweet high soprano and each word of the French song she sang was as well enunciated as any French-born. She sang one verse only and then bowed and replaced the lute.

Her father acknowledged the performance with a nod of his head, 'Indeed, Anne, you need not try to impress me! Just be more prudent this time. I am convinced now that you are wasted on the Irish bastard, but I expect you to marry well, and this is the only opportunity you have.'

Anne said nothing; she had other ideas but realised this could be her last chance to follow her own plans. She ignored what he said about the Ormond match.

'Oh, father, someone must teach me the new dances at the court, or d'you think I can entrance them with a French round dance or even an Italian song – have they reached the English Court yet?'

'My child, I do not get involved with dancing. You'll have to find out from the ladies-in-waiting. But I do advise against being too forward; be subtle and careful.'

Anne decided to be practical. She approached her father and stroked the rich material of his sleeve, leaving her small hand resting there.

'Father, I must have new gowns, jewellery and a household if I am to do much good at Court.'

'Yes, she is right; we cannot have her lost this time, she is well past the marrying age.'

Anne turned to acknowledge Lady Elizabeth who had been sitting on a hard chair in a corner where Anne had not noticed her, even when she had been twirling in her dance, so preoccupied had she been with charming her father. Now she went to the woman whom she would always consider to be her mother and knelt down, placing her head in her lap, and hugged her. Anne knew she could always rely upon Lady Elizabeth for support.

'Thank you, mother, but 'tis not my fault and I will prove to all of you that it was right for me to wait! I'll not fail ye this time. But pearls, lace, velvet and damask I must have!'

She smiled as she said it and her mother stood up and patted her on the shoulder, helping her to stand.

Her father nodded, resigned, his hands held palm-upwards in a gesture of giving in to them. He moved to the fireplace and rang for a servant. Sir Thomas Boleyn was very proud of Anne but he would never have told her how much, for sometimes he trembled at her great confidence in herself. There was a recklessness that went with it that he thought might blind her to dangers. However he had seen her reading and studying and had been impressed with her resignation in her banishment. He had not been at Hever often enough to notice Priedeux's movements and had no idea she had been secretly communicating with her friends on the Continent. When the servant arrived he gave precise orders, in the presence of Anne, as to what was to be arranged for her. She was to return to Court with a large train of packhorses to carry what she would need to make an impression where all was rich jewels, rustling taffeta, ornate damask, and cloth of gold.

In the privacy of her own room, as she personally packed the tracts and books she had acquired from the Continent, she now excitedly discussed plans with Priedeux. He was to carry messages to Dinteville, for she had ideas.

'Priedeux, this time, I'll succeed, I know I will. With a little planning and organisation I will ensure success. I must devise a way to bring myself to the special notice of the King.'

'Madam, do you trust me?'

'With my life, Priedeux, you know I do.'

'Leave it to me, and wait. I have a friend at Court, a strange friend, but he will do as I bid, I am sure.'

Anne smiled and shrugged. Priedeux had proved his worth many times; many tracts and letters and trysts had he procured. She knew now the secret of 'nothing on paper' and would tell him her messages, and watch as his lips moved soundlessly in a mock copy of her words or of the words she had written. She knew he was memorising not only the content but any innuendo behind them, and she knew they were memorised correctly, even down to inflection and question marks. She knew from meetings with George that Priedeux never added anything or commented on what he relayed, except perhaps to add a description of how she was, whether ill or bursting with health. Now she would trust him to find a way for her to be brought to the attention of her King.

When they reached Greenwich where the Court awaited the French visitors, Priedeux disappeared. He hurried to the buildings where the work of the Court took place. Here there were stables and barns and sheds where the king and his Court would never be seen. He hurried from place to place until he found who he was looking for. Jonril, the Court masque master.

He followed the sound of hammers echoing against wood, of metal ringing out, of raucous shouting voices, of a strumming lute and a sonorous shawm. He soon detected Jonril's voice amongst the cacophony and headed for one of the sheds. As he entered, the thick smell of fish-glue and lead paint greeted him.

There Jonril was, jumping around as energetically as ever, his body seeming to twitch with the excitement of the work in hand. He was gesturing to a group of workmen, rough-dressed in buckskin, their arms bare, some holding saws, others hammers. One man had a row of nails in his mouth like ghastly black teeth that had been knocked out. Another burly workman, an air of authority about him, seemed to be arguing with Jonril, who was walking around a crude wooden contraption, gesticulating and pointing, his thin body jerking.

Priedeux watched his friend and smiled, for the masque master was so strange a companion for such as he. Suddenly, as Jonril circled around he caught sight of Priedeux and bounded towards him. Priedeux ducked to one side as Jonril opened his arms to give the unwanted bear hug and Jonril stopped short and shrugged and laughed.

'My great shy scenes man! You're back and it's a great joy to see you. We will drink ale tonight, but first I must nag and bully these men to finish this set.'

Priedeux nodded, 'I'll wait.'

He stood to one side and watched the carpenters and painters construct a wheeled contraption ready for the great pageant. It was on heavy rollers, little oiled-hinged doors in the front, high up and low, with small flights of steps hidden behind where the participants in the masque, both lords and ladies and musicians would be secreted. Away in a corner seamstresses worked to sew great drapes, decorated with flowers and tendrils of jewels and gold leaf. Jonril fussed round them, shouting and baying.

'Come, this must be finished before the banquet, what do you think you are doing? We are not building a flotilla here, just one barge but it must be finished soon.'

Priedeux grinned for he could see the contraption was nothing like a barge and knew Jonril spoke figuratively. Some of the men muttered about boats that would sink if they took his instructions. Jonril flashed responses back at them and so the work continued.

Eventually, with a flourish, Jonril finished badgering the men and returned to Priedeux, shrugging his shoulders in mock resignation. 'If only you would work with me! I'm sure we could construct great surprises for the king and his guests. Now, come and you can tell me what you have been doing in the country! Catching rats with clever contraptions? Eh?'

Priedeux laughed and shrugged. It would take him a whole evening and many tankards of ale to tell of his months of travel, if he were inclined to do so. He would not tell of those journeys on the Continent, though, for it might prejudice Anne's chances. He could not reveal his visits to Polisy, to Rome and to German city states to deliver messages to Dinteville and de Selve who now took his bishop's duties seriously, travelling to meetings with important delegates in the Pope's circle. On one trip he had to wait while de Selve attended upon the Pope at a hearing of heretics from the German states. De Selve had pleaded for unity, pleaded with the heretics not to break away from the True Church, explaining that only by keeping inside would reform take place. Priedeux had attended the meeting in the crowd and wondered about de Selve's stance, which seemed to be at odds with Anne's way of reforming the Church. He would not dwell on that now; he wanted to relax and catch up on the Court news and to sound out Jonril, to see if he would help with Priedeux's plans.

When they were settled in a quiet inn, their tankards full in front of them, he patted his friend on the arm and said, 'Jonril, I've come to call for that favour you owe me. I have heard there is to be a great masque in the presence of the French ambassadors?'

Jonril nodded and started to speak, 'A-ah, so secrets are out! It's based on a great story whereby the Greek goddesses of ...'

Priedeux interrupted, knowing he would ramble and try to tell

Priedeux the complete story of the masque, together with the details of how Jonril himself illustrated it, and the people who would take part, so he quickly continued, 'I want you to give my mistress, Anne Boleyn, a most important part. That of Patience ... here's how I want it to be.'

'But Priedeux, my friend, I already have my orders. A certain young lady called Mary who wants to catch the King's eye will have that part.'

'Mary will be indisposed and unable to take part in your forthcoming masque, I am sure.'

Priedeux's voice lowered as some men passed them and glanced at them. When they were alone again he continued by explaining precisely how he wanted Anne to appear. Jonril interrupted but the once. 'Can she dance? Can she act?'

'Judge for yourself! We have two days, do we not? Until the great banquet. Aye, I'll bring my mistress to you and you will see that not only is she a great lady, she can be a consummate actress when the need arises.' Priedeux laughed then. 'After all, my dear Jonril, what is this Court behaviour but so much play-acting and performance for the sake of diplomacy?'

Jonril nodded in acknowledgement of Priedeux's philosophy and agreed to meet Anne.

* * * * *

Priedeux briefed his mistress and she was quick to catch on. She scurried along the corridors following him until they came to where Jonril awaited. He said nothing as Anne curtseyed before him in an elaborate charade of presenting herself to a great man. He walked round her, his thin legs striding out, his elongated fingers stroking the bones of his face. That face was creased, the mouth drawn down, as if he was worried. Then Priedeux was surprised to see him stand still, his usual quick movements quelled. Suddenly he barked out,

'Dance, show me how you move.'

Anne said nothing. Instead she raised one arm, stepped one foot forward and started skipping a rill that she had learnt at the

131

French Court. As she danced she decided it was old-fashioned and added quick steps into the routine which made her feet peep out from the corners of her skirts as if they were independent of her body. The dance was energetic and involved her in whirls and curtseys to an imagined partner, dancing in a circle around the masque master who turned within that circle to keep his eyes on her, until he staggered with giddiness. Her arms moved sinuously, she pirouetted gracefully and landed gently without a sound, after a controlled leap. She hummed as she moved, a fast dance tune that she could keep in step with. Eventually she curtseyed low before Jonril, but in her eye there was a spark of anger at the need to show this man, a menial in her eyes, what she was capable of. At the same time she knew, if Priedeux said it was necessary, then she must do it to the best of her capability.

She waited. Looked at Priedeux questioningly but he did not meet her eye. Nothing was said for a while. Priedeux knew that Jonril was weighing up whether he could risk allowing this lady to take the place of the Mary for whom he had already been bribed for the part. The thin man had his head on one side and there was still a long pause. Then Jonril nodded and Priedeux was surprised at his controlled stillness. For once he did not speak. Then, ignoring the lady before him, he turned to her servant. 'Yes, she will do, I see what you mean. I will prepare her for the part. Come, lady, you have work to do, and be grateful that Jonril, the great masque master, teaches you.'

* * * * *

There were rumours at Court that the betrothal negotiations were not going too well.

'They have questioned Mary's right to sit on the throne of England!' whispered one.

'They ask about her small size.'

'The dauphin has asked for gold as well as her hand.'

Anne called for Priedeux, 'Tonight! He tells me it is to be tonight, before the Ambassadors of France! I'll not let you down.'

'You have heard that there is tension? Henry is said to be angry today for the French are as slippery as ...'

'As the Spanish ... and the Venetians and the Genoans. Oh, Priedeux, there is much going on at present, all states vying for power and the hand of those who would have it one day. But I agree with the French on this, that Mary is a sickly child who clings to her mother's skirts and her mother's piety. Too many pilgrimages has she been dragged to, and it has made her pasty. She is too devout without a spark of humour. If we tease her, she casts down her eyes and looks puzzled, and then turns to her mother. But enough! Tonight I must shine and perhaps, if all goes well, I'll be the jewel in the king's eye! Now go. I must prepare myself but when the signal comes you must lead me to Jonril so I can be set in the right place.' She called for her maid as he left.

* * * * *

The banquet started early and Anne Boleyn sat with the other ladies-in-waiting near the Queen, who was richly apparelled for this important state event. Anne thought she looked dull, despite the rich jewels. It was the rustling black broadcloth she favoured, even though she wore rich jewels which glinted in the lights of the great hall. The pearls against the matt cloth made her dull skin and eyes seem without spark. Anne also knew, from the gossip amongst the ladies-in-waiting, that the queen was disappointed that her daughter was not to marry her cousin, Charles the Emperor. Henry had not pursued the match despite his wife's pleadings. After a while, Katherine had not argued with her husband further. Anne thought cynically that Katherine could always act the loyal Queen, and outwardly accepted that her daughter could be queen of France one day. Anne though had seen her sulk and talk to her Spanish servants, and knew that messages were sent to the Holy Roman Emperor. Now she was being gracious to the French Ambassadors but Anne could see, from her vantage point at the corner of a long bench, that she was not being overly friendly. There was a frostiness in the way she offered the salt to her neighbour that belied any true amity.

Anne had persuaded the other maids to let her sit at the end of the long table so, when she slipped away, it would be unobtrusive. The purpose of the masques was to surprise and when Henry the king had taken part, no-one had known until he had led his fellow players into the hall. Anne was hoping to rely on that element of surprise but also knew that her queen did not really approve of the pageants and mumming and, while she did not discourage her retinue in the dancing, she had never instigated an exotic event. The only merriment the queen had organised, thought Anne derisively, was discreet accompanied singing at the end of a hunting day, praising the prowess of the hunters. Anne knew therefore that she was risking the disapproval of her mistress by taking part in the pageant, and there would be further disapproval when her role was seen.

She didn't care; she was reckless tonight with the excitement. She loved the French guests and enjoyed speaking French again; she knew her companions watched her in awe as she slipped easily into what they saw as 'French ways'.

She had enjoyed the rehearsals, too, and the studied attention and instruction from Jonril. She was in her element; she always revelled in learning new things, and she loved to show off her prowess in dancing and music. Anne was well aware that she was especially skilled in these, learning from masters at the French Court. Now she wanted centre stage to show all who mattered what she was capable of; especially King Henry.

For now, she picked at the food before her, the stuffed quails eggs and pies, and when her fellow lady-in-waiting whispered some gossip to her she hardly noticed. Her dark eyes flipped around the gathering, taking in the King, the Queen, the French ambassadors. She saw Dinteville amongst them and he caught her glance and acknowledged her and she nodded back. There would be time for private talk later, perhaps in the dancing. The ices were being served, the boys scurrying to reach the tables before the exotic concoctions, shaped like castles, should melt into water as if the castles had fallen into the moats around them. As one was placed before Anne she felt a tap on her shoulder.

'You should come now, madam,' whispered Priedeux and she nodded, handing the dessert back to the serving-boy but not before the chill of the food had made her hand cold and sent a shudder through her body. She slipped off the bench and followed Priedeux. They hurried to the back rooms where dressers waited with her costume. This was rich cloth of gold, with sewn on flowers in red and blue and green.

'Oh, there are you, ma'am, come hurry we only have a few minutes, but we know how to dress such as ye, don't we just, Flo?'

The other woman nodded and started to pull at the laces of Anne's gown while another unlaced the sleeve of the gown she would wear for the pageant.

The speaker was a red-faced buxom woman and Anne couldn't tell whether she was a rough countrywoman lost in town or a Londoner florid through drink, but she submitted to these two, as Jonril had ordered her. They were expert in unlacing and tying and soon she stood in the exotic costume. There was an elaborate gold head-dress and she was helped to fit this on before being led to the wheeled contraption where others taking part in the masque were being positioned. She was shown round the back where Jonril was jumping around pointing and muttering.

'At last, my star. My dear, you look magnificent. Now come, you stand in this arbour and when you hear the trumpets, release this little catch, as we have rehearsed and step out. Hold on to this hook as the pageant is wheeled into the hall, and now you're not afraid of blackness? You'll not faint from the tight quarters? You'll remember the words? The steps?'

Anne grinned at him. 'Jonril, keep calm; after you have rehearsed me, would I dare to let you down in such a way?'

'Priedeux was right – I was right to take this on. Good luck, my dear.' He moved so quickly she wondered if he had kissed her lightly on the cheek, before the door was slammed shut and darkness hid her sudden fear.

* * * * *

A slight shudder, as if the chill of the iced dessert she had handed back was still with her, made her lose her balance, and she held on to the hook that Jonril had pointed out as the lumbering set started to move. There was no going back now. At first there was an echoey silence but suddenly she could hear the laughter and bustle, albeit muted, that meant they had reached the banqueting hall. Indeed she heard the great doors being swung open and the varied smells of meat and other foods, which lingered in the air, reached her, filling the small space. Then all was still. She waited. There seemed to be a time of silence as if all had left and she was locked in this small space on her own. Before she had time to panic the clarion came. A burst of the metallic strong sound of many trumpets made her heart beat, and she imagined them being raised high, the banners flaring out beneath them to show the gold and red patterns that gave a clue to the theme of tonight's masque.

She waited but a second to unlock her door as her tune lilted towards her, then burst forth and caught her breath. She had been deposited immediately before the king and he was looking expectantly, excitedly, directly at her. She curtseyed and started the pageant by declaiming strongly, breathing from her diaphragm, as Jonril had taught her,

'I am but a meek maid, Patience is my name.
But it should always *be remembered that Patience wins the game.'*

She walked to one side and tapped on another still-closed door and out came another player, dressed as gorgeously as Anne who started to recite a similar verse about honesty always being true. But Anne was not listening. She returned to her position immediately opposite the king and, as she stood meekly by, she could see him appraising her as if he had seen her for the first time. Forget the times she had stood by the side of her queen and he had brushed past her. Forget the times when he had stroked her hair as if he would admire her but with that vacant polite smile. Forget the times when he had held her hand in a formal dance but moved on to the next dancer in the row without so much as a backward glance. All that was in the past when he only saw her as an addition to his wife's entourage at Court.

136

Now his face was all a-glow, and he did not turn to watch as each of the other 'virtues' came out of their hiding places. Instead his eyes remained on Anne, appraising her with a look that grew increasingly lascivious. Then the last of the maids said her piece and the whole hall erupted into applause. The king was still clapping as he came down from the royal daïs and took Anne's hand, gesturing to the musician's gallery to strike up a dance. He led her to the centre of the hall as the great lumbering set was wheeled away, and servants scurried to remove tables and benches. At first they danced a stately basse dance with their hands barely touching, and their bodies not touching at all. All the time, when they faced each other, he looked into her eyes and she returned the look.

Then he was laughing and shouting up to the musicians, 'An antimasque, a fast rill, anything that lets me remove my shoes and jump with this mistress!'

Then he caught hold of her at the waist and, as the music started again – a strong fast beat with the shawm and tabor and pipes competing – he threw her into the air, caught her by the waist as she fell and swirled her round until she was laughing hysterically at the success of her ruse.

At the end of this energetic dance he kissed her on the mouth, in front of the whole hall, and whispered, 'Lady Anne Boleyn, why have I not noticed you before?'

She laughed and replied quickly, 'Because you were not ready for me, my Lord!'

He looked surprised at this but the music was starting again and he took her hand for the next dance, another stately round dance where all joined in; this time they had to concentrate on the others in the circle. Anne realised that Sir Thomas Wyatt had taken her other hand. As they faced each other and walked round in a break in the circle he said through clenched mouth, 'I see I have lost you to a greater star!'

Chapter Fifteen

'Go, get me my doctor, for I will die. My Spanish doctor, mind, none of those English quacks. They poison me with liverwort or some such concoction.' The words were whispered through clenched lips, 'A priest, for the last unction.'

Anne hated days like this. The queen lay on her side, her body scrunched into a foetal position, her arms wrapped around her extended belly, her eyes screwed tight with tears forcing their way through the lids. She rolled and groaned. It meant that all her retinue had to stay inside despite the promise of a hazy summer day. Anne would have loved to have disappeared and taken a horse for a long ride, or walked briskly along the river. Instead, because the queen was ill, all the ladies-in-waiting were expected to wear dark clothes because bright colours offended her eye, wear soft shoes so there was no clacking to hurt her ears, and whisper to one another. Neither could they wear perfume because the smell piqued her nose and made it run. There was no playing of the lute or harp or even singing gently. Nothing appeased her pain. Another irritation was that the queen reverted to her native language, only talking to her favourites, and her voice sounded guttural and as deep as a man's.

Only her closest maid, Maria, who had been with her when she first came to England, could do anything with the queen and it was she who protested, 'Nay madam, no-one died of the regular bleeding, you'll not need a doctor or a priest. We'll staunch it and you'll bear with it, for there is nothing to be done for the pain.' Although she spoke in her own Spanish tongue, Anne was familiar enough with it now to pick up the gist although it was an effort. It was not unlike Stefano's Italian, except that where Stefano would say a soft 'i' these Spanish hardened it into an 'l' so that piano became plano.

Anne stood at the side of the bed, remote from the scene, watching with disgust. She could not understand this agony over what all women must go through once a month. If she thought she could escape without notice she would have done so, but she was sure that, if she moved from her post it would be noticed; it seemed that when the queen was indisposed she was super-sensitive to anything that broke protocol. As it was, Anne knew the queen had noticed her presence in the masque; how could she not? So far she had not made any comment. That in itself was ominous but Anne hoped the monthly pains would make her overlook the misdemeanour; she did not want to call attention to herself and upset matters any further.

The queen gripped the hand of her maid, as if she would hang on to it for any relief it would give her. 'Maria, you know this is not a monthly bleed. After four months I had hoped to tell my Lord the good news that I was carrying his son, this time, God willing, to full term, and now great globules of dead baby are forcing their way out of me.'

Maria, who was well trained in all aspects of birthing of both full term and premature births, protested, 'Madam, you exaggerate. 'Tis not fitting. There is no evidence of a dead baby!'

Katherine was not listening, 'Oh, sacred Mary, Holy Mother of Jesus, and all the saints that attend her, and my name-sake Saint Katherine, help me, help me through this.'

'Hush madam, hush, you will bear again.'

The woman on the bed thrashed suddenly, sending silken robes in a sudden ripple away from her body. The greying hair moved from side to side like tendrils of snakes writhing for a kill. There was an overlong gasp.

'No, time is closing around me, I know it.'

There was an imperious rap on the door as if the devil himself agreed with her, which made even Anne, usually so self-possessed, jump. Her mistress struggled on to one elbow.

'Tis the king! Nay, he shall not see me in this condition. Oh someone go, entertain him outside, tell him I am dressing and will be with him anon. No, not you, Anne.'

But Anne had moved with her usual graceful agility and was gone, without even bowing in the expected way to her mistress. She slid through the door before she had heard the end of the Queen's protests. As she pulled the door shut behind her, she found herself face to face with her king. She could smell the sourness of old wine on his breath. Even that was a relief from the claustrophobic sick bed scene within.

'My Lord, you catch us all of a tizz, for it is still dawn, is it not?'

Henry, a foot taller than her, looked down and she saw his eyes narrow with speculation. Then he smiled.

'Not quite dawn, my lady. Messengers from the Continent have arrived and business been conducted. I come with grave news for us all. The White Rose is dead. Killed at the Battle of Pavia!'

His face belied the grave news. He was smiling in a triumphant manner. Usually during the day he was morose and quiet, saving any jocularity for the evening's entertainments when he was well soused with wine. Some courtiers had begun to whisper that affairs of state, and by that they meant the succession problem, was taking its toll. Now he was truly elated. Anne pretended not to know why he was so pleased at the death of a relative, but crossed herself and muttered a prayer before asking, 'Not Richard de la Pole, your cousin, my Lord?'

'Anne, young Anne, he may have been my cousin but he was a thorn in my side, constantly inciting the French to raise arms against me, pretender to my throne that he was.'

Anne looked stern and he stopped in full flow, 'Why so hard? You were innocent gaiety itself last night!'

'Aah, I knew the young Pole at the French Court, my Lord. You remind me of him, for he was tall and fair, like you.'

Henry smiled down at her, and she could see that even a king could be flattered by such simple words. He nodded and continued, 'So, I must attend upon my queen and we must be seen to go to mass, to pray for the soul of my cousin. And hasten this union of our daughter with the dauphin, before the Emperor thwarts us with other plans.'

He turned from Anne and seemed to mutter to himself, 'I like it not, the way he has kept Francis in his train, a virtual prisoner.'

Anne, well versed in Europe's affairs, knew what he meant. The Holy Roman Emperor, Charles V, had captured his arch-enemy, Francis 1, and had invited him to 'stay' with Charles indefinitely. Until such matters as the marriage of their children could be arranged. Or some other treaty of peace between them could be concluded. In effect, holding the French king to ransom. Anne was quick to realise the implications. To Henry it could mean the failure of any marriage between the French dauphin and his daughter Mary. Even worse, if Francis united himself by marriage to the Holy Roman Emperor it would mean that all the great European powers would be aligned against him.

He turned to the closed doors of his wife's apartments again. He made to brush the girl aside, all the magic of the dance of the night before as nothing. 'My lady queen must write to her nephew and congratulate him and win him to our side now he has vanquished the French.'

But Anne stood her ground and bowed her head so he could not see her eyes. He noted the movement and put his hand under her chin, raising her face so she had to look at him.

'What's amiss, girl, that you refuse entry of a husband to his wife?'

Anne whispered, 'The queen is not well, my Lord, and will rest awhile. She will rise in due course. I have been asked to entertain you.'

'And pray, what is the matter with the queen this time?'

Impatience showed and Anne knew why. The queen was often ill and spent much time on pilgrimages away from Henry and even when she was at Court constantly prayed in seclusion. Henry himself attended masses twice a day but Katherine would often attend five or six times, as if she could not eat or sleep without

141

religious comfort surrounding each activity. At the slightest excuse she and her train would be off to some holy place to pray before relics while Henry stayed at Court. Anne had always enjoyed the travels to these remote shrines but not the journey's end of constant praying in cold remote churches, the chill of the stone floors making her knees ache. If the queen was not attending to such holy matters she would sink into a lethargy. Only great state occasions seemed to rouse her now. Anne knew that Henry tired of her ways, it was common Court knowledge. She could understand why he was exasperated but she was not afraid of him. She did not struggle against his imperious glare now. Instead, she looked straight at him, eyebrows raised, so he could see her glistening black eyes.

'My Lord, it is not for me to tell a man such things.'

He looked at her sharply, 'Not another lost child? Or just the monthly pains?'

She thought a moment before answering but he was sure to find out eventually and she could plead innocence or loyalty to her King, so said, 'A bleed after four months? My lord, you must guess for yourself.'

He turned away and looked out of the window. The birds had finished their early morning song and the yard below was well into its daily bustle, with women slopping out piss buckets, and men leading out horses to the trough for their morning draught of fresh water. Henry watched absently as the messenger who had arrived that morning inspected his horses' hooves. The shadows in the courtyard were long, with the sun not yet full in the sky. Anne stood quietly, her hands held before her, covertly watching him. He stared out into the growing brightness but his face was set, almost angry, his eyes lost in creases. She knew he was not watching the activity in the courtyard below but looking inwardly at his troubles.

'Aah, me, how can I rid me of this worry?' he muttered but Anne heard and moved to him and stood beside him.

'Come, my Lord, I have been asked to entertain you.'

He looked away from the window then and stared down at her hand, resting lightly on him. She knew it was dangerous to touch the king without his permission but something greater than herself was leading her on now. Perhaps it was the memory of the dance, and the conviction that she must light up those eyes again to have that special look in them for her and for her alone. She looked up at him, softly and gently. He leaned towards her but she whispered, 'Come, come with me.'

As she said it, she realised his face was too close, and she could feel a rising excitement at the knowledge that last night's attraction had returned to him and he was going to kiss her, but she would not allow this so she dodged under his arm, as it rested on the wall, moved to a side table where, in a trunk, were board games.

'Come, I, but a pawn, challenge my king to a game of chess!'

He was smiling now and watched as she set up the table, in the rays of light from the window, and laid out the pieces, his annoyance quickly dissipated in the anticipation of beating the girl at the game he knew so well.

'So you can play games as well as dance, my lady?'

He was standing behind her now and, as she set the pieces slowly, she knew he watched, mesmerised. Anne could feel his hot breath on her neck and she tingled. She moved to the other side of the games table and sat down. Gestured for him to sit opposite.

'Indeed, sir, and debate and speak French – if it so please you – and understand Spanish, Latin and the Bible.'

'And what will you give me when I win?'

Her eyebrows arched and she gave him such a sharp look that he almost recoiled.

'You, sir, will have to win first!'

The game began. Henry moved first.

'So you know your Bible?' he asked as he took one of her pawns.

She nodded but concentrated on her move. Time passed and she knew he watched her and deliberately kept looking down, knowing that her lashes shaded her eyes. By saying nothing, she created an aura of mystery as she surveyed the board before her. She had enjoyed their dancing, energetic and tactile as it had been, and hoped that Henry held a longing for her as if in a dream. She deliberately acted modestly but knew, from her experiences at the French Court, that men liked the odd quick riposte.

Anne also knew that for many months her king had felt jaded, tired of the routine of his days, and she now hoped to tease him into life.

'I wonder if it is the wondrous day of sunlight that makes my spirits soar, or is it that you please me much?' he asked as he watched her move a knight.

Still she kept her face downcast, as if the chessboard was all that would interest her, allowing a small smile to play around her mouth as she shrugged. She could tell that his excitement was tinged with annoyance. He was not used to being ignored, not used to a person concentrating so much on the game before them that they would not look his way. He moved his knee under the table until it touched her skirts but she continued to smile, reaching forward suddenly to pick up a piece, as her legs withdrew from him.

Anne continued smiling, knowing her prey was biting.

She moved her chess piece and said, ''Tis a shame your coz is dead, for you have few to choose as heirs now ... the young Mary, Fitzroy ...'

Henry's face darkened, 'And what would a girl like you know about such matters?'

She put up both hands in defence, but quickly dropped them when she realised her extra finger showed too much. She looked at him directly, 'Forgive a young maid her innocent enquiry, my Lord, but my father is well versed in such matters by you, is he not? I would help if I could.'

'And how could you, a mere maid, help me, the King?'

He said it as he impulsively moved a bishop.

'You need heirs. Strong boys. And your queen does not deliver such for you. Have you wondered why?'

Her courage in speaking thus had obviously shocked him. As she spoke, she realised he had left his queen exposed. Ruthless, she took the piece.

There was a silence as he placed his large hands on his solid knees and leaned forward to study the game. The sun was mid-day high now and the shadows of the pieces were short, the room bathed in light. Then he picked up a pawn and moved it rapidly. It made a resounding clop as he landed it near her bishop.

Then he said quietly, ''Tis true, I wonder if God is not punishing me for some wrong.'

She did not answer but looked up from her study of the game. She suddenly saw his eyes were wet and realised that he was crying. She began to feel sad for him, a big man, a man that ruled a great country, strong but weak for he could not get what he wanted. A man who commanded others to satisfy his desires. Commands which then inspired his envy of their skill in music, poetry, sciences – all the abstract talents that a man could wish for. All that he could not obtain was his own seed to quicken and grow. She sat back, ignoring the fact it was her turn. She whispered, 'My Lord, I can give you what you want, God willing!'

'How?'

'First you must read your Bible, and consider, and then confess.' She said it brightly, as if she were a tutor guiding a pupil.

Henry leapt up. The chessboard jumped in the air, the pieces falling higgledy-piggledy, pawns rolling into corners. Anne realised she had gone too far and fell back.

'How dare you! Me, a king and one trained for the Church before I became a king. How dare you presume?'

Anne looked up at him unflinching, through her dark brows: a coy look. She answered softly, 'Mayhap an innocent can see what those skilled in their craft cannot?'

As she spoke, she reached over to the huge Bible always kept in the antechamber of the religious Katherine. Anne sighed as she leafed through the thick pages. Katherine was religious but not good at theology; pious without knowing why; conscientious in her observance of ritual without understanding its meaning. The Book was in Latin and Anne skimmed the pages until she found what she wanted and then, slowly, translated, 'Here it is, "*And if a man shall take his brother's wife, it is an unclean thing; he hath uncovered his brother's nakedness, they shall die childless"*.'

She looked him straight in the eye and added forcefully, 'If you must use this to obtain a split with your queen, you can be rid of this sin. Then you can marry a fit and fertile woman.'

Anne knew she was taking risks but relied on the rumours flying around the Court. Henry was already doubtful, had already sent out questions to theologians. She had become a judge of men and knew that a doubtful person could be influenced by someone who expressed their thoughts in a positive manner. It was a risk, but she felt as if her time was running out. She remembered her birth date; she was lucky to look young but knew she was past the normal marrying age. Not only that but, with Queen Katherine as an example, she knew that child-conceiving and birth, always dangerous, became even more dangerous as a woman aged. She either captured Henry soon or settled for Ormond. She inwardly shuddered at the thought. She *had* to succeed at this game she was playing.

Henry was towering over her and she could feel his hot sour-wine breath on her cheek, smell the rancidness of his body, unwashed despite last night's exertions. Again she felt a tingling, as she had earlier, for the very power of the man. His whole bulk pressed against her as he read over her shoulder. Then he turned away, 'But I cannot suggest this; people know about my great knowledge of the Bible and will say I have tried to find something to suit myself. Indeed it would be wrong.'

Anne heard the slight whine in his voice, like a spoilt child. She knew he had to step carefully, and was looking for a way out. Could she provide it? She placed her hand on the rich cloth of his sleeve as she had done earlier, as if to pull him round to her, looked up at him in that way she had of raising her eyebrows and

146

widening her eyes. When she knew she had his attention, she looked down and whispered, 'But if you confess to the fear, and quote the scriptures mayhap your confessor will confirm it – mayhap he too will tell you that you should forsake this woman who has called herself your wife for so many years without male fruit from the tree. Mayhap he will suggest the way forward.' She continued to whisper such words until she felt her king move away. She stood where she was, facing away from him. After a while she turned round. He was standing, legs astride, one finger held against his chin, surveying her.

She smiled, 'My Lord, do this only if you think it is a wise thing that you would wish to do.'

Henry moved then, bending awkwardly on one knee, and started to pick up the pieces, a curiously penitent action from one so great. He set the board and she now watched mesmerised as he replaced the pieces in the positions where they had been. He sat down without saying anything and bent over their game, as if her words had not penetrated, as if there had been no conversation and all he had been doing was stretching his limbs before a difficult move. Anne too returned to her seat, sliding gracefully down opposite him.

After a pause she smiled, a thin-lipped smile, and moved a pawn, as if careless of the game. Then she chanted, in a priest-like tone, as if it was a magic charm, *'And if a man shall take his brother's wife, it is an unclean thing; he hath uncovered his brother's nakedness, they shall die childless.'*

His hand hovered over the board, indecisive as to what piece he would take. It stopped in mid air and she could not tell what piece he intended. He stared at her, his eyes screwed into a calculating look that made him look greedy.

Henry said nothing. He looked down at the board, and his hand started to move towards his bishop.

There was complete silence. Anne watched the sun glinting on the jewel at his neck. Henry deliberately picked up the bishop and placed it nearer to her pieces.

'Give me the chapter, the verse again!'

She answered, 'Leviticus 20:21!'

'Indeed, I had forgotten. It is an interesting thought.' He grinned. He leaned back ignoring the game. Anne studied the board. After a silence she called triumphantly, 'Check!'

Henry saw he had lost and held his hands up in surrender. He sighed and relaxed, saying as if to himself, 'I hear there are mutterings in the French Court as to the legitimacy of Princess Mary. They question her right to my throne. And now you quote the Great Work. As if all the world knows I have sinned.'

'Indeed no, my Lord, not all the world. This comes to me from the study I do, but dwell on it, and seek confession, for only priests can tell us the Lord's wishes. Surely your confessor will advise.'

'And then I would be free to marry again, as you say, a young lusty girl, who would provide me with the sons I need.' He was looking at her but all she said was, 'Like my sister ... it seems fecundity runs in our family.'

She spoke quietly, humbly, not looking at Henry. He reached out and raised her face to his. He kissed her, gently but possessively, as if she had given him new life. She felt the burning brush of his beard upon her cheek.

Then there was a thundering in her head. It was the door from the Queen's chamber, flung back so hard it banged against the panelled wall. It happened so quickly that the chess players had no time to adjust themselves before the queen and her retinue were upon them.

Queen Katherine attempted to walk in a dignified manner through the entrance supported on either side by two of her maids but, even with the double doors forced back by the need for three of them to come through together, there was not enough space, and there was a shuffling as the three vied for position. Anne suppressed a desire to laugh, as the queen and her assistants jostled and eventually seemed to fall into the room with one maid swinging sideways as if catapulted away. The Queen's face was puffy, her eyes red, and Anne thought she would burst out crying

148

at the indignity of it. It was obvious she could not stand on her own, despite a great effort. If any of her maids had let go, she would have fallen. Their entrance had been hampered by her stance, which was unnaturally erect. Her hair had been tightly coiffured, and hidden in a stiff bonnet, the severe style emphasising the tautness of her body. She had been dressed in dark clothes, which rustled now as they rubbed the taffeta skirts of the women who stood either side of her. It was the sound of dry autumn leaves falling, being trodden on and broken by thoughtless passers-by. There was a pause as they re-assembled themselves. They brought in a waft of the sour air from the chamber behind them. The trio moved slowly towards the chess table, the Queen's companions holding her by the elbows as if they were presenting her, and eventually she stood over them. Maids followed behind in stately procession. Anne realised some time must have passed while she and the king played, since it took many hours to dress the Queen, even when she was well. When she was suffering, her ladies had to cajole and persuade her to stand while they pulled on her petticoats. Each item of clothing had to be laced on carefully so as not to cause the queen more suffering. Her face now was impassive, but the colour had drained and all that was left was a dull grey, the reddened eyes screwed-up, pinpoints of darkness. Anne almost admired her stiff courage in rising from her pain-bed, but the feeling was soon lost when the queen spoke.

'You may play chess with my Lord, Lady Anne, but you will not win this game! Away with you!'

Anne stood up, curtseyed to her King, who said nothing, then curtseyed to Queen Katherine as she moved slowly backwards and out of the room, her eyes down, into the public chambers beyond. She pulled the doors shut behind her and paused, taking a deep breath. Then she turned and walked unhurriedly through the various courtiers and petitioners gathered outside, her head held high. If this was to be her last day at Court, she would not show that she was disgraced.

* * * * *

But she was not to be banished. Instead, after a few days of agonising wait, when she hid in her own chamber, she was summoned to Queen Katherine's presence in the same room as the chess game had taken place. There she found all the ladies-in-waiting gathered around their queen as if to protect her. Behind the Queen's high back chair, in shadow, was the King. The chess game had been stored away; the chairs re-arranged to create a temporary throne area for the Queen. Anne approached the tableau and curtsied deeply, keeping her eyes lowered. There was a pause until she stood upright again.

'I seem to have misunderstood what I saw, Lady Anne,' the queen chanted in a dull voice. Anne looked at her quickly and then at the King, who was smiling down at her. 'My Lord assures me you are pure. He has rebuked me for evil thoughts. My intention to send you home was unwarranted and cruel. My Lord wishes you to remain. I must accept that you will, so to speak, stand in my shoes, when it comes to dancing, for I know my bones are growing old and stiff now. If my Lord wishes to dance I cannot partner him.'

Anne curtseyed low again, catching no-one's glance for she was afraid they might see the triumphant gleam in her eye.

* * * * *

After that she found herself in a dangerous game where Henry would devise stratagems for being alone with her and she would try to ensure that such tête-à-têtes did not last too long.

One day, while hunting she had been told to pretend her horse was lame.

'Just as we reach the lee of the plain, where I can lead you to my lodge,' he'd whispered in her ear as they rode through the great oaks and beeches of Epping Forest. Not only had she pretended the horse was injured but also, in the excitement, she'd actually fallen off and Henry had lifted her in his arms speaking with authority to the surrounding courtiers, 'Go, I'll tend to the girl; she'll not ruin the hunting for the rest of you.' And he'd walked her to the lodge, carried her up the wide staircase and deposited her on a long settle which had been situated in the open viewing area upstairs. From here the hunt on the plain before them could be clearly seen. But Henry was not intending to watch the hunt. In the chamber a sumptuous feast had been laid and he brought to her a platter of dainties, 'Come, my poor injured girl, you must eat if you are to get well,' choosing a plum and dangling it above her mouth. As she tried to take a bite he withdrew it and kissed her instead.

His hands roved around her body stroking her. He unlaced her bodice and exposed her breasts and looked down on them with a look akin to hunger. Then he was licking her nipples as if they were steeped in some rich juices and she lay back enjoying the rising excitement within her. But, as he lifted her skirts, she pulled him to her and began to play with him, until he was satisfied, whispering all the time, 'Nay, my Lord, I cannot give myself to you while you are still married. I am pure, and will remain so.' But there was a smile on her face that encouraged him.

* * * * *

At the occasion of a great ball for ambassadors at Greenwich, Jonril as master of revels organised an outdoor party on Shooters Hill.

'You, my Lady Anne, will be Maid Marian to Henry's Robin Hood, and all the English are designed to be his merrie men,' she was told. Then the man laughed, 'Little do the foreign ambassadors know that, as the Sheriff of Nottingham's guests, they will be seen as the villains.'

The games culminated in jousts before the banqueting table set up at the top of the hill, with a view across the roof of the palace at Greenwich to the marsh-villages on the other side of the river. Anne noted that the trees had been cut back from the brow of the hill down towards the river to provide a grand driveway where the party would ride back to Greenwich palace at the end of the masque. Anne always enjoyed being at Greenwich, remembering her first attendance at Court had started here. It was also not so built up and smelly as London town. Apart from that the hill was covered in thick greenery, ideal for a Robin Hood party. It was the

151

journeying to the banqueting table that was the most fun. The men left first to hide in the woods. As Anne skipped up the hill with her attendant ladies, a group of masked men, all dressed in green, jumped from the shrubbery and each burly man carried off a lady.

The idea was to carry them to where the banquet was to be held. Anne was captured by the tallest, widest-shouldered marauder who could only be Henry. Instead of taking her to the rest of the party he carried her to an arbour deep in the woods which had been specially built. It was a tent-like affair, all of emerald silk. Inside, it was richly hung with tapestried wall hangings, and furnished with cushions and a luxurious mattress. There was a small side table upon which had been laid wine and goblets. Here Henry flung her on the mattress and hungrily attacked her clothing.

'Nay, nay, I'll not give in to a renegade,' she laughed, stroking his hair all the time and tugging at his beard. 'A man who commits a wrongdoing, a man who doesn't listen to his Bible.' As their lovemaking became more intimate, she climbed on top of him and rubbed her body against his, but never allowed him to penetrate her. She used her thighs, strong with horse-riding, to manipulate him until his pleasure was heightened into climax and then quickly removed herself and wiped his sperm from her underskirts.

'Truly you are a tigress and temptress,' he said to her. 'It is not seemly that you will not let me enter. I am your King, after all.' He reached over to the wine and poured them each a generous measure and handed it to her.

She sat up and looked at him, took a sip of the rich wine before answering him. 'If you insist on such rights, I will remove myself from the Court. You know how I feel. I love you righteously, according to God's law, and will not be defiled by an adulterous relationship.'

She stopped then and pulled his beard. Then she continued, 'You know what to do.'

'And you know I have approached the Pope. But while he has

Charles, Katherine's nephew, at the gates of Rome, he will never grant me the nullity I ask for. Please, Anne, love me as I wish you to.'

'I love you truly, as a virtuous woman should.'

With that Henry had to be content.

* * * * *

She decided to remove herself from the Court for a while after George teased her, 'So you follow in your sister's footsteps? Well done; you will reap a rich reward for our father. He will become a Duke soon!'

She laughed with him but protested that she was innocent of any wrongdoing and then she approached her brother and whispered in his ear, 'For I'll not end up an old has-been mistress, dear brother, not after all that I have planned. I shall be *queen!'*

It was then that she insisted on returning to Hever, using that year's plague epidemic as an excuse to quit the heat of London. She refused to return to Court despite the letters Henry sent her, increasingly passionate letters that proved to her that her ambition was not an idle one. Never one to let things lie she wrote letters of her own which Priedeux was commissioned to deliver, in his parrot fashion voice. Henry would listen, smiling, eyes closed, never noticing the voice-piece of his mistress, lost in the words she sent him. After he had given the message Priedeux would withdraw quietly so the king felt as if he was left with the ghost of his Anne, and carried on dreaming of her. Priedeux watched the king from afar as he remained with his eyes closed, and he realised that such dreams were heady stuff and led him on more than a compliant mistress would have done. Priedeux thought: *If he could not have Anne with the Pope's blessing, he would have her without, he was so besotted.*

Chapter Sixteen

Priedeux leaned on the ship's prow, staring out at the glitter-tipped breakers, the sea a-heaving, pewter-grey with greenish blue streaks where the sun broke through gusting white clouds. He knew they were near land for the gulls had started circling, looking like dropping scuds from the high cotton-wool clouds. The familiar white cliffs which Priedeux recognised as welcoming him home were not yet visible.

Anyone watching him would not guess that he was eager to be on land, an eagerness tinged with worry about what he would find when he reached England. He stood very still, staring into the distance, at a fixed point. In reality, he was exhausted and bored with journeying across Europe weighed down with gold for bribes and with secret messages. He had had his fill of exotic foods, turning the corner of a dusty street and smelling coriander and cumin in Greece and garlic and onions with casseroled meat in southern France. The raucous yells of bazaars in Spain, the sing-song of the Italians, and the guttural calls of hawkers in German city states had tattered his ears so that they rang permanently with memories.

Even worse than the sights and smells and sounds of far flung places were the meetings with academics and reformers and monkish men, who had all bent forward eagerly as he uttered his messages and, at the same time, paid them the gold he carried: bribes for the academic answer his mistress's master wanted. They would finger the coin diffidently and then enter into long debates, sometimes lasting hours. These men seemed to know nothing of time, with no idea of how to treat a guest. Priedeux had often been kept waiting, hungry and thirsty, while they deliberated about the English King's great problem, whether his marriage to Katherine of

Aragon, lasting over twenty years, was bigamous, unlawful according to the Bible. Priedeux was well aware these scholars played with him and the result depended upon whether the Holy Roman Emperor had won the last battle or whether the Pope was weak or strong.

When he had first set out he was pleased to have been chosen as one of the King's secret messengers and relished the freedom to carry out his mandate. He had been excited about the chance to see the cities of Europe, hoping that, perhaps, he would find mention of his own kin. Now he was sore with riding, his hands calloused with holding the reins, and his legs, he felt, were fixed into a permanent bow from being constantly in the saddle.

He watched the waves lapping the merchant ship that carried him home, hoping it was his final journey; the last assignment had been a marathon trip to Rome, Venice and even Constantinople, travelling via German city states where the convoluted guttural accents had defeated him. His Latin usually served, and he could in addition make himself understood in other languages which rooted from Latin. Once he had delivered his gold and obtained some decision from the academics, he had sought out taverns and tried to find out more about the name Priedeux. Disappointment always followed; he had been greeted with shaking heads.

The first few visits to the Bishop of Rochester, Thomas Cranmer, had been tame by comparison. These had become more frequent as Anne became better established at Court. Priedeux had been greeted with courtesy and respect, as if he was a man of substance, rather than a cipher of a would-be queen who might not easily succeed in her ambition. Now it was common knowledge that Anne was Henry's chosen next wife, if only the problem of Katherine could be solved. Even this Bishop who, Anne had assured him, supported her, prevaricated and hid behind theological argument.

The trouble was that everyone was scared to make a decision, even though coin-bribes were showered. They were afraid that if they agreed with Henry they would be excommunicated and dammed forever in hell or, with more earthly practicality, their town or city would be invaded by the Holy Roman Emperor, who supported the Pope. But if they sided with the Pope, especially if, like Cranmer, they were within the King's realm, they might lose their position as Wolsey had done.

Priedeux shifted slightly as he remembered his mistress's crow of delight as she heard that the Cardinal had been disgraced and had died. He knew his mistress had exacted the fine revenge of poisoning Henry's mind against his Chancellor for the way he had treated her and her first love.

He had objected. 'If you had married that upstart Percy, you would not be where you are now, my Lady,' he had gently reminded her, but she had seemed oblivious to such logic. That crow of delight had disturbed Priedeux and he thought about it now, as the lapping of the waves calmed him. As she had matured into her role as official mistress, sitting by Henry's side at state banquets, he saw her become more arrogant, losing the sympathetic charm that had first made him so loyal to her. Every time he returned from a mission abroad she seemed to be more ruthless. The reaction to Wolsey's downfall had been the first time he'd noticed that cold glint in her eye.

Then there had been the secret of how he had helped her to hide at Hever during the plague, and the carrying of letters between her and the King, who was persuaded that she had nearly died. Anxious love letters were sent. Only Priedeux was allowed in her chamber at that time; the other servants at Hever delighted that it was so, ever fearful that they would catch the plague. Only he knew it was a subterfuge by Anne to keep her lover panting, anxious and ever keen to see her again. She spent her time reading the tracts that Priedeux supplied.

Her brother-in-law, Carey, married to Anne's sister, had succumbed to that bout of plague and Mary was now a widow. Anne, fortified by the great love letters from her King-lover, had escaped. Recovered without a blemish. Some said it was witchcraft.

Anne had read the letters aloud to Priedeux, hidden away as she was, pretending sickness. *'My uneasy qualms regarding your health have much troubled and alarmed me,'* she read aloud from the paper he had delivered with a derisive bow. *'For when we were at Waltham, two ushers, two grooms of the chamber and your brother, the Master Treasurer, fell ill and are receiving every care have no fear nor be uneasy at our absence; for wherever I may be I am yours, although we must sometimes submit to fortune, for,'* and here Anne paused, looked at Priedeux, and hooted with laughter before she continued, *'who wishes to struggle against fortune is usually very often the farther from his desire.'* She was reading it aloud in the playful French that Henry had used, his 'love language' to her, and Priedeux understood all now, for his sojourns to Dinteville and the Bishop had educated him in that language.

Anne had been flattered by the letters and after reading them she had expressed triumphant hope, 'Soon I will be queen – *queen* – Priedeux, do you realise what that means? I can then influence him to reform the church. To clean it up, to ban indulgences, to have an English Bible in every church in England.' That had been eighteen months ago and still no progress had been made in the procedures for a Royal divorce. He wondered how he would find his mistress now.

He had heard how she strutted through the huge rooms at Hampton Palace, Wolsey's home, revelling in changing it, imposing her will on it, how Henry had acquiesced, following her like a tongue-lolling lapdog, hoping that, when they reached the royal bedroom, she would be his. It was rumoured that Anne still held out. She would have nothing less than the crown.

The whole business had made Priedeux totally cynical about God and man. He had long decided that each person interpreted God to suit himself and Priedeux now played but lip service to the church's dictates, enough not to be seen as a heretic by any controlling power. When in Venice he had worshipped at St Mark's and revelled in the new richness of gems, mosaics, exotic rugs and paintings that surrounded him. When in a German state he dressed soberly and worshipped in churches that were plain and where the sermons were long and heavily Biblical and in the native language. Priedeux had worked out what he thought God was, for he could not believe there was no God. He would observe the congregation at such services, and think that his God would probably damn most of them for vanity and self-serving. But he realised that he, too, was making the God he wanted.

He sighed, but his face remained impassive. He touched the pendant at his neck, as if that were the only tangible proof that he was a man with a God.

Many years he had been travelling and with no success in investigating his own affairs. Now he was going home once again, and he realised he was sick for the green fields and grey skies of Kent, even for the dirty narrow streets of London which had once seemed so alien. How would he find his mistress? He hoped he would not immediately be sent on another mission. He wanted to have some light-hearted evenings with his friend Jonril, who would put the whole world into perspective in his theatrical way.

Summer was a-coming and he was glad to be out on deck. It was musty below with the heat of many bodies, both animal and human, and he had never liked rats scuttling over him in the gloom. He felt they presaged death and destruction, plague and pestilence.

He enjoyed the solitude and the rich sea-salt smell, although the creaking of the masts were a constant background reminder of where he was. He was so used to these sea trips now that the noise hardly penetrated. This crossing was not a classic mill-pond smooth one, but was what he would describe as a gentle-rolling one, calming to the nerves, and he savoured it, remembering all the storm-tossed galleys he had been in, with praying passengers calling to God for their lives. He also enjoyed standing, and stretching his legs, after all the miles he travelled on horseback. The soft swaying of the ship was a comfort like the rocking of a cradle to a babe.

He thought he was alone but he suddenly became conscious of

being watched. Turning, he stared along the length of the prow. Some short distance away was another man, dressed in a fur-lined short cloak and a square hat that indicated he was a foreigner. He was alternately looking down and scribbling and then looking up, straight at Priedeux, with a keen-eyed stare as if he would penetrate his subject and see beneath the skin. As if he were recording the thoughts in my soul, thought Priedeux with some discomfort.

The man was not English, he was sure of it. Flemish perhaps? And what was he doing, with such writing materials?

The man realised he was being watched and stopped and nodded. 'Hail, fellow, I did not mean you to be disturbed by my activity.'

'What are you doing?'

'I catch your likeness, a portrait! In chalk, would'st see it?'

Intrigued, Priedeux nodded as the man approached with the rolling gait that landsmen adopt on board ship, and held out a paper which was pink-tinged. On it was a rough outline sketch and Priedeux recognised his own features, with the collar of his jacket petering out down the page. His personal pendant was a shaded oval darkness against his throat. How had this man seen such a small object from so far away? There was delicate shading around the nose and eyes, and Priedeux could see the man had captured even the tiny wrinkles that had developed as he squinted against the light. The tinge of the paper gave a skin-colour tint to the face. One part of the drawing was more polished than the other and it was obvious that there was further work to be done. The sun caught the blackness of the lines and they seemed to shimmer and move, as if the very picture were alive. He held the paper steady as the ship heaved, and then returned it, with eyebrows raised in question.

The man held out his now empty hand and said, 'Holbein, Hans Holbein, painter of Basel.'

Priedeux nodded, and shook hands. He had heard of the painter, who had portrayed Sir Thomas More. He knew that

Holbein had returned to Basel when no more commissions were given him.

'Why draw me?'

'That look of deep thought, a face lined with experience, but a discreet man, yes, discreet?'

Priedeux eyed his companion, but said nothing, as if to confirm the diagnosis of his character.

'Faces tell tales, they show the man beneath, that is why I like to capture features with ink, charcoal and paint.' He paused, and smiled, 'And I make a living from it!'

Holbein continued to smile and Priedeux smiled back. The man was right though, Priedeux had learned to keep secrets, but he would neither confirm nor deny it to this stranger.

He changed the subject, 'We will soon reach England, but I will stay still for you if you would wish to continue to draw me.'

Holbein thanked him. Priedeux took up his stance again staring out to sea and his memories.

Henry had shown his desperation in those letters. Anne had played well, alternating between coquettishness and virgin shyness. She allowed Henry to woo her to the point where he was so swollen with need for her that he was almost panting in public, and then she had withdrawn so that the man was left champing at the bit. Priedeux was amazed that a man, and a king at that, could allow himself to be drawn and teased so, but then he had to admit that he, Priedeux, had sworn loyalty to the woman because of her charm, her way of speaking with him on equal terms. He saw that she knew how to woo all who came within her sphere. He had been won over by her charisma so why should not Henry?

But he also knew that she had enemies at Court. He made use of Jonril to find out who and what they were plotting. Sometimes it was Norfolk's party, Anne's own uncle and cousin, who tried to prevent the girl's influence from growing, sometimes the foreign ambassadors, especially the Spanish, of course. Chapuys, the old Spanish diplomat, was a true friend of Queen Katherine and would say anything to blacken Anne's name. Anyone in the

Queen's retinue would swear that Anne was a witch and had cast spells on the King.

'There, 'tis done! Here, what is your name, sir?'

As he took the proffered likeness, Priedeux told the man his name and felt a strange stirring for, as he looked at his portrait, it seemed as if Holbein had captured his very soul; as if he could see all those secrets he had been thinking about etched into the lines of his face.

'Indeed, you are a great draftsman.'

He handed back the drawing but Holbein raised his hands, and pushed it at him.

'Nay, keep your secrets for yourself.'

Priedeux thanked him and Holbein leaned with him over the prow, after tucking his charcoal into the pouch at his waist. There was a companionable silence as they both looked at the Dover cliffs which had now come into sight. Priedeux could smell the warmth of the land before them now, a musty grass-like odour, and knew they would soon be landing. The sun was heading fast towards the west and he knew they would not be able to travel much once they landed.

'Where are you making for, great draftsman?' he asked of his companion.

'London. Where else?'

'You will not be able to reach London tonight, unless you travel in the dark. Pray stay with me at Hever. I am sure you will be welcome.'

'I thank you for that; to London I must go though, early on the morrow.'

'Why?'

'I go to seek my fortune at the Court once more. When Sir Thomas – Sir Thomas More – was at Court I had introduction. I know he is now disgraced. I have some letters with me, but I fear for the changes. I will play it carefully.'

'And from whence do you have letters? And for whom?'

Holbein hesitated. 'Why do you ask?'

Priedeux realised that all had to be careful now, if they were not to fall amongst enemies. Even a humble painter would fail if he chose the wrong faction. Priedeux was a good judge of character and quickly decided to reveal that he was at Court and for whom he worked.

'My mistress is the Lady Anne Boleyn. She could help you. She would listen to me. Could I show her this picture?'

Holbein stood upright and faced his companion, 'Truly God works in great ways! Indeed, sir, I would be delighted for you to effect such an introduction. Regard that as fee for the drawing.'

Priedeux bowed, 'And if you can ride a horse, we could reach Hever by dusk this very night and meet my Lady Anne after she sups. I believe she sojourns there at the moment.'

They shook hands and turned back once more to the sea-scene only to be confronted with the giant white cliffs of Dover like a great pure barrier before them, shutting out all the light of early evening. Even so, Priedeux's spirits soared – soon he would be home.

* * * * *

'May I introduce ...' Priedeux hesitated. He did not like the hard face of his Lady Anne: raised eyebrows, nostrils flared, tight straight lips. Usually she was gracious, with a face that belied her inward feelings. He was suddenly wary of her. How well *did* he know his mistress? The hard expression aged and uglied her. She imperceptibly moved her head as if in encouragement, the face softening. He went on, 'Hans Holbein, painter of Basel.'

Anne was sitting bolt upright on a high-backed carved chair richly cushioned in red damask, not unlike the French chair Priedeux had seen Dinteville sitting in at Polisy. So, Anne was introducing French ways to the English Court. The wide sleeves of her robe cascaded over the arms of the chair and hid her small deformed hand. Her body was erect and still and he thought for a moment that she would not acknowledge the visitor. Then she moved, stepped forward, the ugly mask totally dropped and she was radiantly smiling. Priedeux recognised the girl he had known, all charm again.

'Welcome, of course I have heard of you. I think you left our Court rather suddenly a few years ago.'

Priedeux recognised the slight inflection, and knew his mistress was not just making a statement. It was a question, and he knew she expected a detailed answer. Priedeux realised the charm hid a hardness that he had not seen before; where she had always been resolved to carry out her life's dream, it had been tinged with a generosity of spirit. She now came over to him as callous, the charm false.

She still waited for an answer, and the painter was obviously being careful how he responded. Priedeux said nothing. After all, he did not know how his mistress would like a stranger to arrive with him and he had risked his position by inviting Holbein, but the drawing he had made had convinced him the painter could be useful to his mistress, knowing that Henry loved new things. If Anne could introduce the painter to the king, as one of her protégées, surely it would advance her position even more.

Why should Anne like this man who had painted Sir Thomas More, the man who had done most to resist the King's wishes for a divorce? The portrait had been large, a cloying painting showing them seated altogether, a close-knit and loving family, so unlike Anne's who only stayed together for advancement, for ambition at the Court. Instead, More's family came over, in that painting, as loving, honest and uncaring for worldly ambition. The man had publicly opposed what Henry wanted to do with the Church, and had made his views abundantly clear. He blamed Anne Boleyn for the schism. Why should, then, Anne accept the painter of a family who were at odds with her own?

Priedeux stepped forward, taking out the drawing the man had made.

'Madam look at this, it is a consummate piece of work, done very quickly.'

Anne took it and held it to the light.

'Indeed, it is good – and I have seen others, but let the man

163

speak. Why have you left our home town of Basel, for no real reason?'

She dropped the drawing on the table as if to dismiss it for the time being.

Holbein spoke and Priedeux was relieved by his answer; the man obviously understood the situation. 'It may seem like that, my lady, but a painter must go where the work is. I know nothing of Court life, only that I paint people. And make my living by it.' Priedeux smiled to himself; it was a good answer. His new friend was more than capable of looking after himself. Priedeux moved to the window and looked out onto the bustle of the yard. Anne was obviously making preparations to return to Court.

As his hostess said nothing, the painter continued, 'My father earned his living by painting great altar scenes and I followed him, but with a slight difference. *My* patrons wanted to appear in the paintings they were paying for, so I portrayed them as visitors to the Nativity or part of the crowd at the foot of Calvary. They liked the scenes and, more importantly, the likenesses of themselves in them. It made them feel more holy to think they were taking part in the story of Christ.'

He paused and, seeing that she did not dismiss him, but was listening intently, carried on, 'Then, in the Swiss churches, it became not seemly to have bright colours and pictures. We must all read our Bible now and understand by reading. The pictures for those who cannot read have been removed. I have lost work, so I too must move on and find other subjects in other places. I know I can paint people's likenesses and so I seek commissions here, in England.'

Anne looked at him keenly, 'And what think you of the Bible-reading?'

'Madam, I would need more evidence before I can comment.' He said it humbly, head down, as if it was not of importance to him.

She nodded, seemingly satisfied. After a long pause while she stood, playing with the pearls that fell to her waist, she said,

'Welcome to my service, good Hans.' She clapped then as if an idea had been caught between her delicate be-ringed fingers, 'You will paint my king for me and perhaps me for him. Go now to hall and eat. Be prepared to travel with us tomorrow. No, Priedeux, you stay, for I will hear your tales now.'

She gestured to a waiting servant, in livery, who led Holbein away, but before the painter went out he looked back. Priedeux, watching him go, noticed the keen glance he gave to the Lady Anne and himself. Priedeux thought it was a painter's glance, observant and sharp.

'How dare you bring that sycophant into my presence?' she said grimly when they were alone. 'A popish man who would spy on me! And you, whom I thought I could trust, bring him to me like an asp in a basket!'

She was pacing up and down now, twisting her tiny hands together so he could hear the grating of the many rings she wore, at times twisting the pearls. Her rich damask clothes swished as she turned and the pearls rattled. As she passed him once, then twice, he caught the cloying smell of attar of roses, too rich a perfume for Priedeux's nose.

'I can trust no-one! Even my uncle Norfolk has come out openly against me, telling me I would lose my head for my ambition. Now you!'

The face was hard again. Priedeux stood in her path and stayed there even as she tried to push past him. He took the small hands which clenched around his, the nails digging into his wrists.

'Anne, my Lady Anne. Why do you think I have travelled the roads, sore-saddled and heavy with gold? Having no thought in my head but for you? Come, it is because you were my young charge, who ran to Mother Muncy with sore knees when you were but a child. The one who, when you were a woman, paid back the compliment and came to her and helped her through her last hours. Only I know what joy that gave to the only woman I ever loved, the only mother I knew. I have done your work because you were charming and caring and loving, so I accepted the ambition within you, because the ambition was in a good cause. How can you think now that I would betray you? Do you not know that Holbein has painted Erasmus? And he no longer paints exotic altarpieces but comes here to seek his fortune in a secular way.'

Priedeux went to the table and picked up his portrait and held it before her.

'Look at this; it is a consummate likeness is it not? You said yourself he can make great paintings of you and the King. If he is in your employ from the start, you will have great power showing the world that you and the King are one.'

She relaxed. Priedeux took his chance, knowing now he could say anything to her:

'What has happened to you to make you into this hag, who sees enemies behind every arras?'

Anne let her hands fall then, and her face slipped again into that of the young girl he remembered. She rested on him as if the anger, now gone, had sustained her, and now she needed support. He led her back to her chair and she fell into it. She gestured to another chair and he sat, but on the edge of the seat, angled towards her. She again toyed with the rope of pearls.

'Priedeux, I am growing tired of the fight. The years pass, and I long to be like other women, with many sons around me, as I have promised the king. But I *cannot, just cannot* hold on to him much longer. I believe he grows tired of me, as his legs grow tired, and he no longer dances with me. I know I can keep him with words but he is a lusty man and a desperate one. He needs a son and so do I, and there can be no son with the games we play.' Her voice was despairing. Then, mercurial as ever, she added brightly, 'I am glad you return, and I know I can trust you. Forget what I said. It is good to bare my soul to you, and confession is a good thing even if the Papists use it for spying.'

'And the result of the gold-spreading I have done? Did it have the desired effect?'

She laughed, an ironic sound, 'Of course some universities have played honourably and said Henry's cause is right and others have taken the gold and sided with the Pope.'

'Why doesn't Henry do what he has threatened, as I heard from the Bishop, and just split from the Church?'

Anne knew who he meant by 'the Bishop'. 'And how does de Selve react to that? I hear he is in Rome much now and has little time for his old friends.'

It was for Priedeux to stand now and start pacing. He had bad news for his mistress and there was no easy way of telling it.

'De Selve has spoken with me, my lady and I would repeat his words. You must let me finish first, before you speak. 'Tis said that in Greek times they would execute the bringer of bad news. I trust to your honest God that you would not do the same.'

Anne smiled at his words and nodded encouragement. He began, 'De Selve sends this message, and I repeat word for word, "*I cannot support you, my dear friend, if England splits from Rome, and at all costs you must prevent it. If we are to clean our Church and ensure reforms we must stay together, at all costs. Give up worldly ambitions.*"'

Anne half rose, the anger making her face hard again, but Priedeux lifted a finger and she slumped back. He had to give the message quickly now, '*Give up worldly ambitions for a crown and only work for reform, not for a total schism. Work for the reform we all agreed when we were but children.*" That are his exact words, I swear.'

He stopped. Anne said nothing, but he could see her face changing again. The cynical mask had returned. She struggled to maintain her calm exterior, but burst out angrily, 'How dare he? My childhood friend, whom I comforted when he had been ruined; we swore for reform and this is what we are striving for, and if it means I must be queen to do this, then I must be queen. What has *he* done, but toady to Italian bishops who know nothing about our northern lands? He would conciliate and if he does he will not achieve anything. Mayhap a Cardinal's red cap would please him more? Priedeux, I will find a way to make him stay with us, God willing, what say you?'

'Madam, I have repeated the message. I would not contradict

you and will do all you wish me to.'

'Good. I will think of a way – go now and eat. I am sorry to keep you so long. I will not have you travel much from me, as I need you to keep an eye on enemies at Court. We travel to London tomorrow, and you go with us.'

He bowed and left.

* * * * *

When he reached the hall, Holbein was still supping. Nobody else was there as it was past the normal time for eating, but the rank smell of food, left too long and cooling rapidly, a mixture of leeks and roasting meat, still hung in the air. The fires which had been used to cook the meats were dying down now and there were only dull lights from tallow candles. They were smoking and would soon peter out. Priedeux sat down opposite the painter and was served with a rich broth of meat and root vegetables, bread and ale. He set to and they said nothing for a while.

It was Holbein who, wiping his mouth with the linen napkin which Priedeux saw as a rich additional item in Anne's possessions, started talking.

'I see you are your mistress's confidant. Not so strange that it should be so with your name!'

Priedeux grimaced and said, 'Oh, that old chestnut! I know, Holbein, and am well sore with the jokes.'

Holbein, perhaps because he was a foreigner and took pleasure in his knowledge of languages, continued, 'A prie-deu is French-Latin for a confessional stool. Your mistress uses you as her confessional, does she not? Instead of a priest perhaps. How appropriate in this country where the king is attacking such things! Instead of a priest you confess to those you trust in your household. We all have the need to obtain absolution of some sort.' Holbein paused before adding, 'But perhaps you say pray-do in this country? For it is said on the continent, where I have travelled much, that the English do not speak the continental languages like others do, and make it sound much like your own strange language.'

168

Priedeux put his head to one side and thought about it. It wasn't the idea that he was Anne's 'confessor' but the way this man had said his name and the guttural Anglicised pronunciation that Holbein had just used. As a child, he had been teased by the monks who had said sarcastically, 'Well, Priedeux, you will learn to stay still and support those who need help.' But there was something else now, something about this other way of saying the name. Something dim in his memory. He had seen too many cities, too many countries, that all was muddled, and, in addition, he was tired. It would not come. Instead he thought he ought to deflect his companion from making more points about his relationship with Anne.

'I am only a loyal servant, having known her as a child. She is still young as you can see and sometimes needs guidance.'

Holbein nodded, and looked straight at Priedeux. 'I can see you are loyal. We will say no more. I must thank you for bringing me to her; she will make a good subject. She holds herself well, with dignity. I see now, a triangular portrait, showing that sharp pointed chin in contrast to a triangular design of dress.'

Priedeux continued eating, realising that the painter was in his own reverie, allowing Priedeux to go into his. It was something about his name, a prayer stool, and now the connection with 'pray-do'. He could not now recall where he had heard it, but he knew it would come back to him, and he knew how to recall it; by visiting those familiar places he had searched. As he thought, an inner excitement overwhelmed him.

He couldn't wait to return to London, to his old haunts.

* * * * *

But before he had a chance to investigate, knowing his duties had been completed, he was waylaid by his old friend, Jonril, who seemed keen to renew their acquaintance. It was the day after his arrival at Court, when he was checking his gear, polishing leather harness, that the familiar voice hailed him, 'Welcome, my good Priedeux, come, let us dine together. I know a quiet inn off Cheapside where privacy is guaranteed. I'll update you with what has been happening here and you can tell me of your travels.'

Priedeux did not immediately answer. After a pause, another shrug, Jonril added, 'Come, let me be your host for the evening, I can afford to pay for a quiet eating room with the gold from your mistress. She's generous to those she is grateful to and I owe you for the introduction to her.'

He agreed to go, even though such a visit to the poor part of London town that Jonril mentioned could be dangerous for such as he, with all the secrets he held. Priedeux was wise enough to know that those who carried secret messages for Kings could be seen as dangerous and therefore expendable. To protect himself, he knew he had to bring himself up to date with all the Court intrigues: which faction was popular and which being sidelined. He realised that Jonril, on the edges, so to speak, of Court life, would be more reliable than the gossip of courtiers or even servants who had their own axes to grind. As masque-maker Jonril could weave through the main action, listening and absorbing but taking no part in the formal life of the Court.

They made their way through dark streets, no lantern to guide them, with Jonril taking him by the arm when the corners were particularly gloomy. It was not that it was a dark night, being summer, but the overhang of the buildings in this commercial part of London where the merchants, hungry for commerce and greedy for space, built great bays and larger windows to display their wares, sent great shadows across the narrow walk-ways. Hanging from most upstairs beams were the signs of their trade. A silversmith's mark, a bale of cloth for the haberdashers, a great carcass for the butcher. At one point Jonril pulled Priedeux away from a great slime of rotting vegetables slopped into the middle of an alley and a rat jumped out and scuttled away. Jonril crossed himself, 'Rats I associate with illness, my friend. We should have bought nosegays against the smell.'

Priedeux agreed. 'Especially in ships, I have found; if they start to show themselves there is trouble aboard.'

As they crossed an intersection they were momentarily blinded by the rays of the setting sun reflected in a rich merchant's windows and thrown out in vibrant rainbow colours.

'Here we are,' Jonril pointed at a brightly lit premises, set obliquely in another tight alley, a discoloured sign showing a bloated wineskin swinging from the overhanging chambers above. Laughter and loud chatting came from a main large room. Jonril led him through this, wrinkling his nose at the smell of stale bodies and even staler ale, under supporting arches, through to the gloomy rear where there was a wooden staircase. As they approached, they were greeted by a great bloat of a man, wearing a grubby hessian-sack apron around his barrel body. He said nothing but nodded to Jonril in acknowledgement.

He led them upstairs and along a narrow corridor and into a back room where the noise suddenly hushed as the great panelled door was swung to by the departing host. There was a smell of rich wood-smoke and Priedeux knew they were at the back of the building, probably above the kitchens. The casement was ajar and he wandered to the opening and looked down to see an enclosed yard where barrels were piled high A lantern shone on a woman, heavily mantled, who was plucking a dead chicken, and a child lay asleep in a basket at her side. Stables edged the outer wall of the yard. The evening was growing cool now and he was grateful for the warmth emanating from the kitchens below. He realised he had been out of England too long and was not used to the chill of a northern summer evening. He turned to face his companion who was standing, arms akimbo, smiling. The chamber was not large, but had enough space for a table fit for six or eight men. Priedeux was surprised at the sumptuousness of the table-ware. It had been laid at one end on a rich eastern carpet which stood as tablecloth. Normally such an item would only be seen at Court or in nobles' houses and Priedeux speculated as to how it came to be in a rude inn. He also saw on the table a pewter candlestick holder, the candles glimmering as the breeze from the men's movements fanned the flames. Bread and some dried foods, including figs, apricots and salted fish, had been laid out. There were wooden platters at odds with the candlesticks, unlike the Court ware which would all be matching. Knives were placed to the side of them, oddly mismatched, although they were all silver, Priedeux guessed by the gleam of them. He realised they must be privileged guests if such precious cutlery was provided. One was elegantly carved like an Italian knife Priedeux had seen in that country, the other plain. There was also a flagon and tankards, finely made of polished wood. After a pause, Jonril ushered him to the table and, when they were settled, opposite each other, he poured out some of the liquid into the tankards. Priedeux sipped to find it was rich ruby port-wine. He was surprised, expecting rough ale or a badly made watered down wine.

'Not bad? I expect to surprise you entirely with good tales tonight.'

Jonril proffered some of the food: small herring, dried and salted. He cut the bread and Priedeux saw the coarse grains embedded in its centre and the dark crust. So, not like the fine white loaves of the Court. Priedeux bit into it tentatively but found it tasty, a type of barley bread with a hint of Mediterranean herbs which he recognised from his journeys.

'Yes,' nodded Jonril, 'this place was a great discovery. The landlord retired as a mercenary with an Italian wife who cooks great delicacies for those who stumble on it. I was told the secret by one of the Spanish ambassadors. I believe it is used to pass on information.' He said the last ironically, raising his eyebrows. Priedeux smiled, keeping his own counsel. So that explained the rich but odd collection of items. Booty collected by a mercenary including a clever foreign wife. Jonril cut off the herring's head, which he discarded into a bowl, left for that purpose, and ate the tender flesh of the fish.

Priedeux copied his host and waited for the salt-taste to dissipate before the remaining subtle taste penetrated. To his surprise the herring was not as salty as he thought it should be, and he held the remains high, in a gesture which indicated a question which would be put when he finished chewing, but Jonril beat him to it, 'Yes, I know! The best herring you have ever tasted?'

Priedeux grinned and nodded. He knew he was going to enjoy this evening and felt at home for the first time in many months.

The landlord entered, knocking discreetly, surprisingly quiet and agile for such a large man. He brought in two great platters of meats and sallats, soft greens half-cooked mixed with root vegetables, the plates resting in a row on his great arm. Despite his bulk, he gently laid the food between the two men, said nothing and left.

'A good discreet man and worth his weight in the silence he keeps,' joked Jonril.

'Indeed, I have suffered much from too talkative an innkeeper, when all I want to do is eat and find the bed,' laughed Priedeux. They took their knives then and approached the joint, Jonril nodding to allow Priedeux first go.

It was not until they were well into the meal, and all the fish had been consumed that Jonril leant forward conspiratorially, his elbows resting in the crumbs of bread, a lump of meat on the end of his knife.

'Your queen,' he said it ironically but even so Priedeux shushed him. The candles sputtered with the thrusting arm he used, but Jonril, whispering, continued, 'Your *queen* is in the ascendant. Matters have moved on apace. As you know, the Papal Court met in England and there were longwinded speeches and Queen Katherine refused to attend. Then she changed her mind and made a magnificent speech about her total loyalty to her master the King, which put everyone to shame.'

Jonril paused to wipe the crumbs from his sleeve.

'I believe the Pope's men knew not what to do. Here they were in a foreign land, with an angry king and they didn't know whether their necks would be wrung one night if they didn't bring in the verdict he wanted'.

He cut off another lump of meat, the juices from the centre of the joint now running reddish-pink. Priedeux watched him,

173

patient, knowing that Jonril would tell all in his own manner, 'Being Italian they wanted to return to their warm and cosy lodgings in Rome and knew, if they were to succeed, they could not grant the divorce for the displeasure of their Pope, who had the Emperor Charles at his back. It's lucky for Katherine that her nephew is the Great Emperor.'

Jonril chewed on a bone, took a breath and continued. 'So, the meeting has broken up in confusion for the lack of a strong man, without an end to it. The papal legates have gone back with no result, and we now await the Pope's decision from afar. All the great scholars and clerics of the world are arguing the question.'

Priedeux smiled. He said nothing about his mission to the universities of Europe.

Jonril went on, 'And Thomas Cranmer, Anne's man, has been appointed Archbishop of Canterbury.'

Priedeux was glad of the change in the conversation and answered eagerly, 'I have met Cranmer. A good Kentish man, like myself. He is a loyal friend of my mistress and favours the reforms that she wishes to make.'

Jonril nodded, paused and scraped a piece of meat from a back tooth with his little finger, took a draft of the wine and looked round. He went to the door, opened it quickly and shut it again before returning to his food. Priedeux waited. Jonril obviously had some secrets to tell. When he returned, he lifted his leg over the bench-chair, placed his elbows on the table, his chin in his hands. Only then did he lean forward and whisper, 'At the time, it is rumoured, when he and Anne were alone he had promised, *It would give me great pleasure to crown thee queen*. Anne had warned him to be quiet but had smiled.'

Priedeux interrupted, 'Oh, come, Jonril, you make up another masque. How could you know that? A rumour spread by my mistress's enemies.'

Jonril looked mock offended, 'Indeed not! It came on good authority from her maid Bridget, who is beginning to tire of Anne's pride and ambition.'

Bridget! Priedeux remembered her and believed her to be faithful to Anne although she was but a stolid housewife and would never be privy to Anne's ambitions for the church. Anne would only use her for dressing and domestic matters, Priedeux was sure. Perhaps she had heard something by mistake. It was easy for an imperious member of Court to forget that the person in the corner, perhaps mixing some paste for the hair, or testing the heat of a bath, had ears and a brain. Would Anne forget herself like that? Priedeux, remembering her high disdain when he had introduced Holbein to her, thought she might.

'Do you want to know more?' Jonril brought him out of his reverie. He nodded. The other man, now pleased with himself, said, 'Cranmer had then satisfied her more by suggesting that the country split from Rome, as it had been so long mooted, and, that Henry could claim to be head of a new church, just for England, and, when he was head of that English church, Cranmer would be the Church's Archbishop and he would have the holy authority to marry Anne to Henry. Anne apparently said that this was always her intention for it meant she would have greater power over her King.' Jonril stopped, as suddenly as he had started, breathing heavily.

Priedeux was stunned. How could Anne be so indiscreet? Was that really her intention? He had always known that she wanted to reform the Church, with a deep-felt wish that, Priedeux believed, was based on humanity and feelings towards the common man, such as he himself was. He remembered how kind she had been in her care for his mother. That was true charity and he believed that Anne possessed true Christian kindness. But he was beginning to doubt this belief now and wondered if it was all a subterfuge. Could she really be driven by mere hunger for power? And could the break from Rome be a reality? Even though Priedeux was not a Pope's man, and questioned the way religion was practised by the clergy, he still accepted that only the Pope, the rock, the descendant of St Peter, the favourite disciple of Christ, could be the head of a Church.

Jonril, taking a deep breath, went on, 'Katherine, the old Queen, still maintains she was a virgin when she married Henry and confronts him with it, to his anger. Henry has ordered her to a convent where Henry keeps a close eye on her so that her missives and pleadings to Rome are heavily censored. She is now powerless. She still refuses to agree to anything so the idea is to ignore her altogether. She no longer presides at Court.'

He stopped at last, his chest heaving with the rapid way he had relayed all the news, and broke off a piece of the remaining bread, offering some to Priedeux, who shook his head. Jonril wiped the platter of its rich juices from the meat and ate it quickly, lifting the bread in acknowledgement to Priedeux at the taste. Still Priedeux said nothing, and it appeared that Jonril took this as a sign that he could go on.

'We all knew Henry had seen Katherine once more over a year ago and had returned frustrated and angry and it had been a hard task for Anne to calm him. He stormed and raged, kicking the potboy and the dogs! It would be better for all of us if Katherine would agree to retire gracefully. After all, it's not unknown to have Royal divorces for the sake of expediency, is it?'

Priedeux agreed, thinking of Henry's own sister who had obtained a papal annulment some years before. But he wanted Jonril to go on so he gestured with his knife and asked, 'What of Anne? How did she take it? I would not want her to be undignified!'

Jonril nodded, chewing and swallowing, before he lifted his head again, 'Anne! She has a way with her. Honeyed words and a frolic, a game of bowls and a private dinner and he was in her thrall again, forgetting his anger with his almost ex-queen. It's as if Katherine does not exist, with Anne sitting at his right side at banquets and attending mass and Court occasions with Henry. She asked me to prepare a small entertainment for their private dinner and then leave when Henry started becoming amorous, which we did. She has great seductive ways with her.

'Even so, Henry is becoming more and more frustrated. If any suggestion is made to him that will lead to Anne's bed, I swear he will take it. And he is arrogant enough to think he could be head of a church. If that would give him what he wants – Anne as his consort in truth and the fruit from her belly.'

Jonril paused, and whispered, 'He is too concerned for the dynasty – he is desperate for sons. Anne promises him sons. That may be the way she bewitches him, I trow.'

Nothing was said for a while and they crunched the remains of the meal in a silent reverie, until the landlord appeared, firstly knocking and waiting until Jonril shouted, 'Come in, we have just about finished.'

Again they watched, in silence, as the great bear of a man removed platters and an empty wine flagon in one great movement, the flagon being hooked onto a plump finger. He looked at Jonril quesioningly, who nodded, 'Aye, bring in the sweetmeat now, I know it will be fit for a king.'

When they were left alone, Jonril explained, 'Wait for the biggest surprise of all. The man has a cousin who works in sugars, a confectionary woman, and it is possible to order specials, so I sent a runner this morning and ordered something for us – ah, he returns.'

The knock on the door this time was not discreet, but a loud rap and, when Jonril shouted 'Enter,' the door was swung open by some invisible hand, so they could see the dark silhouette of the innkeeper in the gloom of the corridor. He paused but a moment and then lumbered in with a piled concoction before him which caught even Priedeux, with his experience of worldly travels, by surprise. There before him was a tiny replica of the exotically decorated cart which had carried Anne into the king's presence on that historic banquet where she had first caught his eye, down to miniature doors which, when Anne had been hidden behind them, had opened to the trumpet fanfare. The colours were the same: bright leaf greens and yellows. As it was placed carefully on the table before them, Jonril leant forward and opened the decorated door before Priedeux. Inside was a female figure in a cloth of gold costume patterned with roses: a tiny Anne! Priedeux breathed in and nodded, 'Jonril, you are truly the great entertainer! And this is for us to eat?'

Jonril nodded, 'All made of sugar with an inner secret.'

He broke into the dainty with the large spoon that had been left and it collapsed onto the plate. He handed bits to Priedeux and they munched the crispy exterior, smiling at each other, but then Jonril began again, 'Now for the juiciest morsel of them all. The latest piece of news, which caps all else I have told you tonight. Henry is to meet Francis again in Calais and he hopes his French cousin will see the sense of supporting the divorce. This time the negotiations include the need for the King's consort, Lady Anne Boleyn, to be by his side and be accepted by the French Court. Francis wrote back and said he remembered Lady Anne well and would be pleased to dance with her again.'

Priedeux smiled, showing his pleasure at his mistress's elevation.

'This is all agreed and I understand Anne is jubilant. Admittedly the retiring French queen refused to meet with her which is not surprising seeing as she is niece to Queen Katherine. It's mighty strange that the French Kings' wives seem to die so conveniently – if Queen Claude was alive it would be best for our Lady Anne, so I hear, for she was mighty fond of the girl when she was her lady-in-waiting. But queens will die and their widowers remarry, and poor Francis had but little choice but to marry the sister of Charles seeing as he was hostage at the time. So the queen would refuse, would she not? However that problem has been overcome by leaving her at home!'

'What news. I am glad to be back but it looks as if my travels will soon start again.' Priedeux relaxed, savouring the food and the information. He laid his hand on his stomach, bloated with the rich fare, so surprising in this out of the way place. Now the room seemed too warm, claustrophobic, and he wanted away.   His palate was sticky and his teeth plaqued with the sugar, leaving an almost sour taste in the corners of his mouth.

'Come, Jonril, we have eaten and drunk enough, not only of our food. Mayhap you would walk with me a while?'

His companion nodded and they stood up, Jonril puttering out the stumps of the candles as they left the room. Priedeux waited downstairs, watching the drunken revellers in the main bars, as Jonril settled up with the innkeeper. As they moved away Priedeux realised he had not heard the man's voice at all and wondered if he could be dumb.

They headed west out of Cheapside, over the Fleet towards the King's palace at Westminster. It was summer dark now, and the river flowed glinting beneath them. Priedeux thought how the Fleet flowed to the Thames through the Inns of Court. The night was warm and he recalled an earlier evening when he had been wandering this way. That evening when he had heard the story of a knight searching for his family, like Priedeux searched for his. How he'd been told that the knight had said his family name was 'Pray-do'. *That was it! The connection with the word for a praying-stool, the way Holbein had said it..*

'Jonril, are you game for more drinking?'

His companion nodded. 'Indeed the night is young and soon to cool down. More drink would warm us.'

Priedeux took his arm and led the way down a side lane towards the Thames, and soon found the bar where the blacksmith had drunk himself into storytelling. How many years was it since he had last been here? Five? Seven? He could not now recall, the time had passed in a blur of intrigue and travelling, of conveying messages and collecting them. Would the servant still be polishing pewter tankards? The smith be recounting his tall tales?

They entered and he saw the long wooden serving-counter with dirt floor and silent customers in corners. Behind the bar were scurrying serving-men but at first Priedeux thought he knew none of them. Then, with a shock, he recognised the slow server of years ago. Now he had silver hair, and the large apron of an innkeeper, an air of authority. He was sitting on a giant barrel at the side of the bar, watching his men working, parchment before him, licking a stub of charcoal, his face a picture of concentration. Priedeux was sure the man would never remember him, for this place by its nature would take passing trade never to be seen again. Priedeux ordered ale and as he spoke the owner looked up, scanned the newcomers and continued to stare. As the brimming tankards were placed before him Priedeux turned to hand one to Jonril and caught the man's eye.

'I know you.' said the man slowly. 'I never forget a face. You've been here before but in the mists of my time, I'll swear.'

Priedeux smiled eagerly, delighted at the ease of it. He had forgotten Jonril now.

'Indeed, but many years ago. I seem to recall I was bored by some drunken blacksmith's tale!'

The innkeeper put down his paper and charcoal and slapped his knee and laughed, a deep-throated sound. 'In truth and with the only story he could tell well. He would wheedle a tankard of ale out of any stranger with that tale while all the regulars drifted into corners and yawned with boredom.'

'Does he still tell it?'

'Maybe so, but the devil himself wouldn't fall for it, would he? I trow he heard the story at his mother's knee and kept it going with his thirst, which finally drove him to hell!'

Dead then. 'So there was no knight, who came back? No Sir Askham?'

'Aye there might have been, I'll not deny it. There's many a stranger story which turns out true but I never saw such a knight.'

Priedeux drained the remains of his tankard and felt tired, light-headed. He turned to Jonril, who, unusually for him, was taking a slow way with his drink. He stayed by Priedeux's side but said nothing. Priedeux did not know what to say. He felt embarrassed that Jonril had been privy to a secret of Priedeux's. He knew that Jonril was astute enough to know that Priedeux did not talk about his background and would not want anyone at Court to know about it. Now, Priedeux appreciated that, for once, the masque-maker was not his talkative self. Priedeux slapped him on the back and said, 'Come away, a good evening comes to an end, as ever. Now you and I will return to our tasks and forget these childish things of strange tales and old knights.' Life is not a fairy tale, is it?'

Chapter Seventeen

'Jonril, you must arrange an entertainment, just for a chosen few.'

He bowed, waiting for her to continue.

'Only a few, madam?' She could see he was a little disappointed by the 'chosen few'. She knew he revelled in the flamboyance of large entertainments and loved to satisfy her frequent demands for such, and might feel insulted by her request.

'I know, here we are in the greatest palace of all, Westminster, with the greatest gathering of envoys at Court, where your imagination could soar and I am limiting you. But the devil is in the detail, dear Jonril, and this could prove to be the most difficult entertainment because it must be carried out in absolute secrecy, d'you understand?'

Anne was generous with gold to spend on costume and set and generous too with her praise with what Jonril produced, so she expected him to obey now.

'Madam, I serve you willingly. Tell me what you wish.'

'It is for my friends, Dinteville and De Selve; a discreet supper of old friends.'

She could see he was surprised, no doubt the connection had never been made between the three of them. Dinteville was a wily diplomat and de Selve a strait-laced churchman, so why should they be associated with Anne. She felt she should explain.

'I knew them at the French Court, dear Jonril, they are but childhood friends.'

He nodded, and repeated, more enthusiastically this time, 'Tell me what you wish me to do.'

She expanded. 'I want you to organise a little entertainment. This is how it should be ...' She bent her head near to his and spoke in a whisper.

Jonril edged towards her, placing his bony elbow on the arm of her chair. She didn't remark on the familiarity. It was as if the man was outside the general manners of the Court by virtue of his capacity to entertain. The King's jester, Will Somers, was the same. He could rib the King, hit him with his jester's stick, dance wildly around him, and the king chose not to notice the absurdity and rudeness.

He nodded as Anne itemised what she wanted in the revels. At one point he stepped back surprised, put his finger to his cheek to think about it and then nodded. He was sure her guests were not important enough to have an intimate dinner with someone who was considered virtually queen of England. The entertainment proposed was strange but not rowdy or exotic. For once Jonril could not understand the allegory behind it or the social standing for it. Despite that, he concurred and said at the end of Anne's discourse, 'I'll do what I can for you, of course, my lady.'

Satisfied she dismissed him. 'Go, I have an appointment with that dour painter Holbein.'

Indeed as she spoke there was a discreet knock at the door and Bridget entered. Anne stopped her before she could say anything. 'I know, Holbein is waiting. Jonril is leaving, so show him in.'

The men passed, nodding to one another. Anne gestured for Holbein to approach her but he stood in the middle of the room, considering her. She stared back slightly askance at this man she was not sure she trusted. He had a short curly beard on a round, genial face, small eyes that might be considered piggy, but even so they were keen, intelligent eyes. His hair too was curly and cut close to his head. The effect was of a dark painted frame to rounded features.

She spoke first, feeling strangely coerced. 'Welcome. I know you wish to paint me. How do you do it? What do I need to do?' She struck a pose, one hand hidden in the folds of the farthingale part of her skirt, the other held high, the fingers curled into a delicate 'come hither' gesture. Holbein ignored her. He turned and looked around the room. They were in a chamber which faced south and the late summer sun came filtering through the open casements to stripe the deep carpet of Persian pattern on the opposite wall. The polished floorboards gleamed and Anne could smell the beeswax scent the sun brought out from the wood. It was as if the man were surveying the room for its valuables, she thought, as she watched him take a circular turn, ending up facing her again. Perhaps that was how a painter assessed his subjects, as if they were jewels to be counted. By this time she had dropped the beckoning hand. He continued to stare at her. It was an acquisitive look, absorbing her into himself. Eventually he approached her and she noticed his guttural accent as he gestured, 'This will do; you can stand where you are, where none of the sun's rays fall,' he said, taking from out of his cloak a pad and charcoal. 'A sketch I make, of your features, quickly, like this.'

He demonstrated by making a few strokes on the page before him and holding it up. She saw he had captured her chin, the shape of eyes, a straight line for a nose, the forehead cut off with the triangular shape of her head-piece. She nodded, impressed.

'Then I shade it, to give me an idea of depth, make notes, of colours, textures, sizes, and it all takes but a few minutes of your ladyship's time. Then I go away and work in my rooms, quietly. I can show you a finished sketch if you wish.'

'Please.' He was in charge, with the authority of a talented craftsman who knows his worth. Anne accepted this, fascinated by his quick movements, the glances he made at her, devouring her, the hands moving again as if eye and hand were attached and one operated the other.

Within a few minutes, he was finished. He stopped and stared at what he had produced, looked at her again, slowly, considering, and then nodded. The room seemed to become so silent that she felt she was in a cell with this man, deep within the dungeons of the Tower where no-one would hear if she called out. While Anne stood still she was not idle. She continued planning the details of the dinner where she would confront de Selve. Another part of her was thinking further than that. Suppose even she could not persuade de Selve to continue their plans? What would happen then? Anne was skilled in the court ways of England, now, as well as being knowledgeable about European matters. She knew well enough that the game she was pushing Henry into, to become Supreme Head of the Church in England, could leave him vulnerable to attack from neighbours across the Channel. She believed the Pope had influence with other lords, city states though they may be, across the whole of Europe.

She, more than most women, knew the internecine connections between kings and doges, popes and emperors, princes and dukes. Anne's apprenticeship at the Brabant Court and then in France had not been wasted. She had developed first-hand knowledge of the web of European kingship, of relationships which were coveted and then denied, of marriages made of politics and of nullities following, sometimes because of lust and longings but usually for dynastic reasons. She and Henry were not the only ones who plotted together to maintain their love in the sanctity of holy matrimony. What about Henry's sister, Mary, who had eventually been pardoned for marrying Brandon? All knew that in Europe the Holy Roman Emperor ruled the territories from the flatlands of the Netherlands to the eastern outpost of Christianity and south as far as the Mediterranean coast of Spain, a power achieved by clever alliances. Anne knew well he had but a weak tenure on the German states, besotted as they had become with Protestantism. She also knew he was fanatical about maintaining the Catholic religion and constantly fought the rebels.

He and the French king were now bound together by marriage; consequently the Pope at present thought he could call on the Emperor for worldly support. In addition the small nation states of Italy – Venice, Florence and Milan – all vied with one another. Would all these factions group together against England if it truly broke from the one religion of all Europe? Some of the city states of Germany had professed to be independent and Charles, the Emperor, had invaded but had had to withdraw because of threats to other borders. Suppose the island nation of England incensed him so? It was even worse if Francis I joined him; Henry had discussed the situation with her.

'I'm worried about our French coz, for he blows towards the Emperor if it means he is safe. Ever since he married the Emperor's choice I fear he will invade if we go down this route.'

'Nonsense, my dear Harry; send missives to his Court, remember me to him and I too will write to friends I have there. A meeting with Francis where you can explain to *him* as another king that if you succeed, who's to say he wouldn't also succeed in his country by becoming supreme head of his church as well?'

Henry had sat back in his chair then as if hit. A moment later he'd taken Anne's tiny hand and kissed it fervently.

'Indeed, you have the brains of a man. Francis would like that, I believe. When I tell him of the means of extra revenue, of the tithes he could have instead of them disappearing into the coffers of the Pope's men, then he would follow for he has the same rich tastes as me and his coffers must always be hungry. To mimic me indeed.'

But then his face darkened. 'But it would be different for him; he does not have a channel of water between him and the Emperor, he would not ...'

'Come, if you promise him support. Two great kings, heads of their churches, such great power ... to persuade the people as well that the devil's man, the Emperor, would support the pope only because the pope has to condone his power.'

Henry had clasped his head in his hands and shook it. 'Anne, my dear Nan, you go round in circles, but I will see what can be done.'

So the negotiations had started and soon she would be in Calais, to meet with Francis again. She hoped he truly remembered her. The messages which Priedeux came back with claimed he did, but Anne knew of such diplomacies. She had been very young when at his Court. Would he remember that incident which even now made her blush with frightened shame, when she had bitten his tongue and escaped. She recalled the masques

186

where she and Dinteville had been partnered together, miniature imitation courtiers, and wondered. One part of her hated the French King, for what he and his Court had done to her friends when they were young. Anne did not forget how de Selve had been raped and her friend Stefano quietly disposed of, but she mostly blamed the priests for what had happened, not the French King.

She shook her head as if to ward off the horrible memories. She had almost forgotten the painter until he proffered the finished sketch. She shrugged and looked at the paper, admiring it. The very real representation of her was so good that it blotted out the old memories. Even so, she remembered well Francis' predilection for sexual excitement and had planned to send a highly confidential message by Priedeux to whet Francis' appetite before their meeting. She was recalled to the present. Holbein coughed, a deep guttural sound, still watching her. As she surveyed the drawing, another idea occurred to her concerning de Selve.

'My man Priedeux tells me you sketched him on the Channel crossing. Can you do such things in secret? If a man didn't know you were drawing him?'

Holbein considered a moment. Then said, 'To be secret I must not be seen. If I was given a good view of my subject, and could study the man a while. Indeed, it would be possible.'

'Good, you will be called when the time comes but you may have to miss your supper for it.' She laughed and dismissed him. As he left, she said to the servant, 'Send Priedeux to me.'

When her man arrived he found her pacing up and down, and he knew she was thinking rapidly. But this time it was not with red hot anger. He recognised the signs of cold determination and sighed. Did this mean he was to be sent on another mission overseas?

'Anne, at your service.'

She turned to face him, ignoring his familiarity. 'You've heard of the visit to Calais?'

He nodded.

'We are playing on dangerous ground and I want nothing to go wrong. I would have you go to Dinteville, and then to de Selve, who are both in England at present, and invite them to dinner with me, for old times' sake. In two days time, here at the palace, in my private apartments. De Selve must know it is not an invitation but a command. I leave it to you to make it clear. Have Dinteville arrive a half hour before de Selve for I would have quiet words with him first.'

Priedeux nodded and made to leave but she stopped him. 'One other commission you must undertake. I wish for new curtains to be erected in the dining hall: thick damask. You will arrange it so that there is a chair, a light and holes in the curtains through which eyes can peer. Then there must be light on the outer side of the curtain so that my guests do not know there is anyone watching. Can that be arranged, Priedeux?'

'Indeed yes, but it would help if you explained ...'

'A little scheme, a trick of mine. I would have Holbein paint pictures of my friends the Ambassadors. He must arrive before they are both present, I would have both of them in the picture.'

Priedeux raised his eyebrows.

'For a keepsake, you understand ...'

Priedeux smiled and bowed mockingly.

* * * * *

'What is Anne playing at, Priedeux? Doesn't she know I shouldn't be seen with de Selve? He is known as the Pope's man and that is how he succeeds. If it is known that we meet, especially with Anne, questions will be asked. I am Francis' emissary at the English Court; he for the Pope. We cannot be seen in England together.'

'I assure you of discretion. Anne has sworn to secrecy all those who will be present. The food is to come from her own kitchens and it will be served not by the usual servants.'

Dinteville surveyed the man before him. Over the years he had grown to trust him, not only for his remarkable memory for secret messages but also for the wisdom of the accompanying advice.

Dinteville had also grown to admire Anne's progress and knew it was by her own wiles that she could well marry the English King.

'Very well, I will attend, but will de Selve? You know he has already refused to help Anne further. And another point. We are known as arch-enemies and should never be seen together. That is the way it works. I have a reputation as a reformist. That is why Francis uses me to negotiate in England; de Selve is a supporter of the Church. He works secretly from within, making subtle changes to the doctrine. He needs not any scandal or attachment to me otherwise he cannot do his work and stay loyal to us.'

Priedeux explained, 'Anne has asked him out of friendship. My message to him is one of love and a need to catch up with old friends. She also promises an explanation of what she intends so as to put his mind at rest.'

'Priedeux, if you are to deliver that message you will have to use all your intelligence to get it through to him, for he is truly a Pope's man, as you already know from the messages he has sent through you.'

So, well armed with this information, Priedeux visited de Selve.

* * * * *

Two days later all was prepared. Anne directed her servants to dress her carefully, in a dark, discreet dress, which did not reach her ankles, so it made her look virginal. She remembered well how de Selve had admired her ankles, even as a pre-pubescent youth.

As her maidservant bent to pick up the perfume spray, she held up her hand, 'No, Bridget, not tonight, for I will have no feminine wiles with which they can accuse me of bewitching them. I am to meet old friends and we will talk of old times, of our studies together, of our interests in religion and philosophy.'

She had, however, insisted on hot water and had bathed carefully before dressing. Her hair she hid in a tight headdress, with tiny pearls edging it. The women were dismissed for although they knew old friends were visiting, they were not told who and, before the Frenchmen arrived, the only servants present were Jonril's band of scenes men.

Dinteville was shown in by one of these who, instead of stepping sideways to allow the guest to greet his hostess, turned a double somersault, bowed and skipped backwards out of the room.

Anne laughed. 'We are to be served by entertainers tonight but the main point is that they are totally discreet and loyal to me.'

Then she greeted him with the double-cheeked kiss of the continent and he returned it, enthusiastically. They had rarely met since their childhood times in France, but the closeness was still there, kindled by the exchange of news via Priedeux. They stood for a moment, arms held on arms and smiled at each other. No paperwork would survive to show these two knew each other or indeed plotted with de Selve, but they had achieved much. He stood back and surveyed her, 'You dress for de Selve,' he laughed.

She laughed with him, 'You are as clever as ever, dear Jean. Indeed, you are right. Tell me about him.'

'He has embraced his Church's teachings as a good bishop should, especially as he has the tithes from Lavaur – which, incidentally, he has never visited. Such income is enough to satisfy his craving for good food and company.'

He paused and watched Anne who was standing with her head on one side. 'Go on, dear Jean, even if it is unpalatable.'

'Well, my brother, the Bishop of Auxerre, who is, as you know, French Ambassador at the Papal court, saw how Georges behaved at the Diet of Speyer, when there was an attempt by the Pope to discuss matters with the German protestants. De Selve spoke directly to the renegades urging them to reconcile with the Pope. He does not, my lady, favour a split in any way. Indeed, he has even published the piece '*Remonstrances aux dicts Alemans*' where he makes it clear he believes the Pope is the only person who can rule the Church.'

'Indeed, Priedeux has relayed such information to me.'

Dinteville continued, 'In addition, he is a connoisseur of beautiful things. He has seen Venice, Florence and Rome and covets gorgeous jewels and icons and great paintings. All that he can obtain as a servant of Christ. I believe he has been corrupted and sees no future in our venture for reforming the Church, let alone breaking away from it. He would reform it if he saw a place for himself inside such an organisation but, as a good bishop, he sees that you are threatening his very livelihood.'

'You are sure of this? There is no possibility that he acts in such a manner to hide his true intent?'

'I see him at the French Court and my brother confirms it. But he is an honest man and would not, I believe, betray you or me, but he would go his own, holy, way.'

'Or unholy way, if what we hear of Rome is true!'

She stepped away from him, stood playing with the jet and pearl necklace holding a crucifix she had chosen for its very plainness. 'Surely he would help old friends, if he thought he could do so without being discovered? I have one thing I would wish him to do.'

Dinteville turned from her and ran his finger along the scrolled pattern of the fine Persian carpet that Anne had instructed be used to cover the table. Returning to her, he answered, 'It would be more that he would help if he thought his living was threatened, I believe. He is comfortable where he is and would not do anything positive to help unless he saw the danger of refraining.'

So, he felt safe on the continent, away from Anne's Court. Before she could say anything further, there was another knock and de Selve entered. He wore the sober clothes of his calling and his face too was sombre. Anne was surprised that his rounded boy's looks had matured into a sulky chubbiness that made him look self-satisfied.

He greeted Anne with a single kiss, a Judas kiss, she thought, before turning to his countryman.

'Jean, so good to see you.' He turned back to Anne, 'As your servant said, a reunion of childhood companions, an innocent dinner talking about old times.' His voice was tinged with sarcasm and enquiry.

Anne merely smiled and handed him a goblet of wine. He took

it but held it away from him as if to test the colour against the light, and did not take the usual polite sip. Jean saw this, took a sip of his own wine and nodded over the rim. Georges smiled and followed suit. Anne watched and, when this ceremony was over, she clapped her hands, the door was opened and food brought in by a bevy of young pages, all dressed in a livery which mimicked the French King's: blue with bright yellow fleur de lys. They held their trays high and music followed them. As they carefully placed the food on to the table, they all somersaulted backwards, bowed and withdrew, leaving three pages standing upright at the door. The three diners smiled at each other and Anne saw that her ruse had worked; it had put her guests at ease. The doors closed behind them and the music faded although it could still be heard.

When they saw the way the food had been laid out, the two Frenchmen exchanged glances but said nothing. The formal lay-out on the table emerged as the pattern of another fleur de lys. All the food was tinged with saffron yellow except the centre piece. This was a roast swan, its neck curled elegantly into its wing, re-feathered with its own white down.

'In honour of my French guests, all the food is taken from recipes my man obtained from the French cook at Henry's court. Please, sit.'

The table was laid so they were next to each other in a row. Anne sat in the middle with Dinteville on her right, de Selve on her left. The pages served them and then trooped out. All was silent until they had gone. Before them was the heavy damask curtain, a dark green, that Anne had ordered to be erected, with large sconces of candles before it. This ensured their table was well lit but behind the sconces all was shadow.

There was a silence before Anne leant forward to take a morsel. Before she bit into it, de Selve stayed her hand.

'Grace first, my lady.' She dropped the dainty and nodded, held her hands together and bowed her head and waited. De Selve muttered his Latin but Anne repeated when he had finished, 'We thank God for our daily bread, Amen'.

He looked at her sharply. She pointedly said, 'In English, Georges, so all understand.'

He said nothing but stretched towards the loaf of bread and broke off a piece, dipped it in his wine in the French manner and, delicately, so there was no spillage of the wine, placed it in his mouth.

Then the other two began. As Anne broke into the swan's meat aromatic juices ran, and it could be seen there was a cavity containing other, smaller birds. She gestured and Dinteville held out his plate to be handed a tiny quail. As they ate Anne said reflectively, 'The fleur de lys has a greater significance for us three. Do you remember, Georges, our discussion in the library?'

He looked away, and reached for another of the tiny birds inside the cavity but then turned to her, 'We swore to reform the Church, I remember that.'

Anne nodded slowly as she chewed. When she'd finished and had swallowed, she said, 'Aah, I thought my servant must have the message wrong when he told me you would no longer help, so I am pleased you came to my dinner tonight.'

De Selve stopped eating and put down the bone he was carefully stripping of its meat. He wiped each finger individually on the napkin, before he spoke. 'I am pleased to be invited to your ladyship's presence and our – err, correspondence – over the years has been stimulating. As you know I have been in Rome, Venice and in the German states. I have seen the Emperor Charles and was in the legation which negotiated the marriage between his daughter and Francis. I am a Frenchman, dear lady, and must abide by my king and country.'

Anne smiled then, respecting his honest answer. But in truth she was disappointed for she had hoped that all their training as children would have made him more of a diplomat.

'Indeed, I agree our kings and countries are of paramount importance to us, but we three also live by our consciences, do we not? Did we not discuss this many times in our youth? How it is with good works we set an example of our faith?'

He dipped more bread into the meat juices and chewed away, not answering.

Dinteville tapped Anne on the arm so she turned to him, 'It is very difficult for us, in our positions to demonstrate such beliefs, dear Anne. You must understand that our friend here has to be seen to be following his holy father.'

'Indeed, 'tis so,' interrupted Georges, who looked slyly at her, 'and, with my priestly training at Rome and Paris I have come to understand more of the true faith, Anne. I have said it before and will say it now, directly to you: I am concerned at how far you go.'

He paused. No-one said anything. The empty carcass of the swan fell in on itself. Both Anne and Jean had stopped eating.

'How far I go?' It was said in a quiet, deadly tone.

'Indeed. When we discussed these things in our youth we were concerned to reform the Church, do away with married priests, with drunken and debauched churchmen. To ensure the Church was cleansed. We never spoke about challenging the authority of the Pope, the Holy Father, or of breaking away. What has happened in the German states, in the Swiss cantons, is a sad thing, where the burghers take it upon themselves to say they are justified by faith. It is a scandal that they no longer listen to the edicts of the Pope. We must have one faith, guided by the rock of St Peter.'

He stopped. His face was red and his lips damp with spittle and fat juices and his eyes were watering at the corners.

'Oh, Georges, that *is* what we want. We would not want the whole of Christendom fighting, and that is something you can prevent. For I know my dear Henry does not wish for an out and out break. At least he would not want the whole of Christendom against him, that is for sure.'

'Why then does he persist in passing these statutes which prevent the priesthood from obeying the Pope? From seeking guidance?'

Anne sighed. She smiled at him. She knew Dinteville was breathing heavily beside her and she was not sure if it was because he was impatient with his countryman or whether he was waiting eagerly for her answer. She was playing a dangerous game – what she was about to say, if repeated to others, could well be interpreted as treason.

'The king knows his mind well. I temper this by advising caution. We are a nation surrounded by water and it makes my king feel safe and powerful. He is aware that France and the Emperor could work together and invade to stop him. So he must protect himself by ensuring there are no insurrections or trading with the enemy by those who might see him as wrong. He would make sure of this by asking for all, priests and others, to swear loyalty to him. That is all, dear Georges.'

She paused, took a dainty from the tray and bit into it, waiting for an answer but neither of her companions spoke. She went on, 'All he wants is boy-children, and a wife – me – to give them to him. It's not without precedent for a king to cast off a useless wife, so why is the Pope stopping it now? Answer me not. I know the reason, we all know the reason. Because the Pope is a lily-livered unprincipled wretch who sees his little Vatican threatened by the might of the Emperor!'

She relaxed back in her chair then so the Frenchmen faced each other. She looked from one to the other. Georges' face was flushed and impassive. Jean was still chewing, a small smile playing around his lips. After a moment she sat upright again and continued, 'Georges, you can help, help to prevent all-out bloodshed at least, if not total break from Rome.'

De Selve looked bleak and licked lips that were still greasy-wet with fat and spittle.

'How?'

'Persuade the Pope to grant the divorce.'

Nothing was said. She turned to Dinteville. 'Dinteville, you too can help.'

He raised an eyebrow in enquiry. He had been listening with interest to the arguments and admired Anne while sympathising with Georges de Selve.

'I would speak privately with King Francis. Can you arrange this? I know, it may be impossible, but I wish you to take a message from me. I would have you say that I would dance with him and, if he wishes it, he can show me his special paintings when we make a state visit to him. This I would do to help my king and my plans.'

'Is this wise? If Henry finds out … '

'He will not find out, will he? You will be your normal discreet self, yes? Priedeux assures me that you, Dinteville, are my man and I cannot see Francis telling Henry what has been offered to him. If Henry heard it he would believe it to be the ravings of a wily courtier. Of this I am sure.'

Dinteville thought about it and believed Anne to be right.

'I will see what I can do. But you, de Selve, you must promise to be discreet? Not mention this?'

The churchman nodded. 'I will try to talk to those in power at the Vatican but, dear Anne, I suspect you are right, in that the Pope, while having spiritual power, has very little earthly power against the might of Charles.'

Anne was partially satisfied but still felt that, while he would not report the evening's plans to anyone, he might not be as enthusiastic for his task in Rome.

As they continued eating, Anne recalled the presence behind the curtain and thought that, once de Selve saw the results of this evening's dinner, he would do what she had asked, for he would be too deeply incriminated to refuse.

Chapter Eighteen

Much later that night, when her guests had departed and Jonril's men had cleared away, she drew back the curtain. Holbein's head had fallen forward, the charcoal slipped on to his lap and his papers were just about to land on the floor. She gathered them to her, her gown touching his forehead as she moved. Startled, he awoke.

'Oh, my lady, I'm sorry.' His voice was more guttural than usual as if the enforced silence had dried his throat, or in his tiredness he sank back into his natural accent.

'Come, have some wine while I see what you have done.' She helped him up and took him to the table where there was still a full flagon. She continued to hold his papers. Flicking through them, she nodded approvingly. Holbein poured himself wine and inclined the pitcher to her but she shook her head and returned to his drawings. They were good. She marvelled at how he had captured the two men, looking straight at him, as if they knew he was hidden behind the drapes. There were several, some with scribbles on them of arrows and colours, descriptions of furs at collar and wrist.

'And you can change these scribbles into a painting, dear man?'

'As I have said before. You can be involved at each stage. I am at your service. Send your man Priedeux to me in a fortnight's time, when there will be something to see.'

He took his sketches from her, authoritatively, leaving Anne with her hands in the air. He left, bowing perfunctorily, stifling a yawn. She smiled to herself, realising that he had shown no respect for her at all nor had he asked her the reason for the work. She guessed that, as far as he was concerned, it was another commission. They had agreed a price, and he would deliver.

She admired his skill and likened it to her own; his skill was with pigments and pen and paper in creating an image; hers was with guile, intelligence and the use of her looks in creating a better world, God willing.

* * * * *

A few days' later she received a pricked-out plan, on good paper. Holbein explained to Priedeux, who relayed the information to her, 'This forms the cartoon which I will relay onto the material to be used. What do you want? Vellum? Wood? Any sort?'

'Priedeux, I know not what. Ask him what is the most durable, what will last, for I would have a painting more than life-size and on a good surface so that it would be indestructible. It should be easy to transport too, for if de Selve does not return to England, then Dinteville must deliver it to him and show him.'

A week after that, Holbein sent another message: what other items should be included in the picture? Anne shrugged and told Priedeux, 'The man was privy to our evening's conversation, tell him to choose.' She was confident that in his mastery the painter would deliver. Holbein enthusiastically produced even more than she had asked for. Priedeux relayed what he described at their next meeting, to Anne. *'A shelf of discord; one with symbols of the new religion. I can do this, to show they are implicated in it. Tools of time to warn that no man is immortal and that time is transient. I can obtain such instruments from a friend of mine, Nicolas Kratzer, to use as models.'*

She listened and nodded, not smiling but approving all he said. 'Priedeux, that is good, but return to him as I have more suggestions. I want representations of another in the picture, maybe a lute, a songbook. It will remind me of someone who should have stood beside both Dinteville and de Selve, but his life was cut short. I will always remember him even though he has been dead this long time since.'

Priedeux did not ask questions. He realised from the way that she spoke, with a catch in her voice, that she could not bring herself to name the person.

All Anne's feelings for Stefano welled up again. She knew Priedeux was standing watching her but she could not help dwelling on him. Stefano had been young and vibrant, unlike this king of hers, who could be fierily angry or morose and businesslike. Stefano had been slim with the vibrancy of youth; Henry was large and running to fat, with ulcers developing on his legs. Despite that, Anne had grown fond of him; fond of him as a person would love a loyal dog that could be used to hunt down prey or be stroked in a comforting way. Those feelings were totally different to the way she thought of Stefano. She remembered Stefano as being generous to his friends. Indeed he had given his life in rash revenge for what had happened to de Selve. Anne could never imagine Henry doing that. Henry could be generous to those he loved, sometimes to excess, as she well knew from the jewels and titles he had lavished on her and her family. She knew her feeling for Stefano had been a young immature attraction, made more poignant by never being consummated or even developed into innocent love; what she felt for the king was loyalty for someone who was useful to her, someone she could manipulate for her own ends.

'Go, and make sure Henry does not find out I have commissioned this painting. He might rebuke me for my extravagance and question why I want a grand picture of Frenchmen! I confess he has been generous paying off my gambling debts but may not be as generous in giving me funds to pay for the painting. Besides, it is not part of my scheming with *him.*'

As Priedeux was about to leave, she called him back. 'One last thing. Tell Holbein he must make the painting so that it is clear it is set on a particular day, Easter Friday 1533. There is a good reason for this. Make sure he understands that.'

Priedeux did not mind being the go between and would relay Anne's instructions to the letter, as he normally did, not asking the reason. He enjoyed his visits to the studios, being intrigued by the process. It took some months before the painting was ready to be taken down from the easel and mounted. Priedeux visited Holbein's workshop many times to see how the work developed and marvelled at how the likenesses of the two men had grown, from just the original pencilled sketch to flesh and blood colours. Holbein had used the damask green of the curtain he had hidden behind as a backdrop and Priedeux smiled at this.

He had taken the rich brown of de Selve's cloak and had copied the medallion of the Order of St Michael on Dinteville's chest, which Holbein had seen at a later Court event. Anne approved when Priedeux told her. 'It will give weight to Dinteville, and de Selve will realise we are important people not to be crossed.'

On one of his last visits, Holbein was copying a detailed small drawing, crosshatched with squares, onto to the lowest part of the picture, 'What're you doing?' Priedeux asked.

Holbein looked up, brush poised. 'The most difficult part, not to be interrupted. It is to give effect to the wishes of your mistress. She has asked me to create an oblique skull, representation of death, of one who should be in the centre of the picture.'

Priedeux nodded, intrigued. He had never heard about this aspect of Anne's life before he had received those last instructions from her and marvelled at her ability to continually surprise. *That was how she keeps Henry he thought.*

This was one of the last times he visited. Priedeux was always taken aback at the number of people at the workshop, for Holbein had apprentices and assistants who helped with the mixing and preparation of paints and canvases, the making of wooden frames and other materials. As the master worked, Priedeux wandered around the studio while Holbein continued to paint, mixing his palette with the powders he used to make the paints, the room heavy with the odour of linseed oil and the glue used to fix the frames. Around the walls were other half-finished paintings and on a large table were piles of sketches. Priedeux rifled through these as the painter worked.

'Who are all these people?' he asked, holding up a particularly clear picture of an older greybeard, his head held in his hands, his eyes sad and watery.

'Commissions, more work,' answered Holbein without looking up. There was a silence as Priedeux continued to study the old man's likeness. Eventually Holbein put down his palette, stretched himself and came to Priedeux, looking over his shoulder.

'Ask not about that one. He commissioned me to paint a reflective self portrait, but after that sketch I never found him again. Lodging here, in London, he was, up Eastcheap. Explained that growing old – which was obvious – he would not be able to search much longer so wanted such a painting for posterity. In case, he said, and never finished his sentence. Sometimes when I spoke with him I thought perhaps his mind was wandering. Priedeux, I put it down to old age and thought that as my work progressed so would his tale. I took the initial sketch, and we agreed a price, colours, materials. But I never saw him again. His landlady said he had left her without paying his dues.'

'Did you ever know his name?'

'Ja, but I suspect it might be false now. Sir Askham... she said he was always asking questions, and showing a neck amulet.' The painter paused and his glance swept towards Priedeux's neck. 'Not unlike your amulet which you try to hide. But if someone does not pay ... pah.'

As he spoke, he returned to his work. He made a vicious swipe with his brush at the canvas in front of him but wiped the resulting streak away quickly. Taking a deep breath, he picked up his tankard, took a swig and started again. His method of painting was deliberate, using small brushes, and he usually worked precisely, each brushstroke a careful mark, leaving clean lines and defined areas of light and shade. Priedeux realised that, even when he painted black it had different colours in it to recreate the texture of the cloth it was depicting, which made it come alive as embroidered damask or thick fur. That was why people admired his work and wanted his portraits, for he could demonstrate their very wealth in their clothes, their pewter, their pets or room hangings.

Priedeux was still holding the sketch. The portrait of the old man intrigued him. *Sir Askham! That name again.* The face was so tired, even though he looked straight at the viewer, as if he would ask another question. Then Priedeux looked deeper at the folds of the cloth around the wrinkled neck of the old man. In amongst the generous lace collar there was a hint of something. Priedeux tingled with excitement. It was as if there were echoes of an object or revelation he could not quite see. It was the same feeling he had had when he was out with Jonril, that night of the grand dinner celebrating his return.

What excited him so much was the vague outline of the pendant. He fingered the old silver case at his own neck beneath his clothes. Holbein stopped painting, placing his brushes carefully into the cleaning fluid, and turned to his guest. They had become trusted friends now.

'Aye, like the one around your own neck, as I said; almost the same. I could paint it larger if you wanted me to, so you could see the detail, for I forget very little once I have drawn it. No doubt they are common trinkets in this country.'

'I know not, for I have never seen another like mine.' Priedeux paused. He had learned not to discuss his private life with courtiers, and although Holbein was not such he was a confidant of many at court. Holbein simply nodded and moved to the corner where there was a pitcher of ale and some bread.

'Come, eat with me, for I am hungry after all this concentration on these two Frenchmen.' Priedeux approached him and took the piece of bread his companion broke off. They chewed in silence as Priedeux moved back to the picture of 'Sir Askham'.

'You've no idea where he came from? Did his landlady know?'

'Ja, of course I asked for I would want the shillings he had promised me!' Holbein tempered the answer with a smile, and took the drawing from his guest and held it to the light, assessing it, like a builder would stand back from the house he had just completed, proud as well as judgemental. 'She said some place on the marshes following the Lea, on one side of the king's forest near

Epping but there was no way I would travel to such foreign parts.'

Priedeux looked over at his friend to see if he was joking, but he seemed to be quite serious. Priedeux grinned. Here was a man who travelled halfway across Europe but would not travel a short distance into the country of his adopted place of work.

Priedeux knew of Epping Forest for had not Henry and Anne hunted there on Chingford Plain, eluding their entourage, to emerge laughing and embarrassed from some copse hours later? While Priedeux was never of the royal hunting party, he had heard of such goings on and had been in the entourage awaiting his mistress' command. He badly wanted to go there *now*; all his instincts told him that a man who had a pendant the same as his *must* be related. How long would it take him to get to the place? Could he ask Anne to allow him the time to go? He knew the meeting between Francis and Henry was imminent and he might be involved. Surely he could ask for permission to leave his post for a while?

He had to find out about this old man; his whole body tingled with anticipation and hope. For the last few months he had felt as if he was becoming ever closer to solving the mystery of his birth. He'd never had time to dwell on his own life before but he suddenly realised he had no family, no ties to anyone except his lady. What would happen to him once she was queen? Would she still have need of him? Would that be the time he could do his own hunting on the plains? He did not want to wait, for he had no idea how long all his mistress's plans would take.

Holbein was moving away back to the work in hand.

'I will have something to show your mistress soon. You can see 'tis nearly complete.'

Priedeux returned to stare at the painting his mistress had commissioned, tucking the picture of the old man in his breast, absentmindedly. Holbein saw the movement but said nothing and guided his friend to the frame which held the painting of Dinteville and de Selve. Priedeux looked at it again. It was good, very good. He would tell Anne she must see it soon.

But when he reported back to his mistress she was none too interested for another event had overtaken her busy life.

He found her in the gardens around the King's tennis courts in the new buildings at Hampton. The courts themselves were indoors but there were large open hatches where the players could be watched. He knew she liked these buildings not just because they smelt of fresh paint and wood but because they had no memories of the old queen; there were none of the pomegranate wood-carvings, Queen Katherine's emblem, engraved on the ceilings. It was a thorn in Anne's side that the pomegranate patterning remained in some of the rooms, too difficult to eradicate.

Anne walked in the knot garden with her father, their arms entwined, her head bent towards his shoulder. The garden had been newly created under her orders, from a complicated plan acquired from French friends, comprising a pattern of entwined knots. A convoluted arrangement not unlike the ways of the Court, thought Priedeux. It was a cool August day, the sun slanting from the horizon to signal the waning of the year. Seeing the father and daughter together, a rare event now, Priedeux thought of Hever where there would be the smell of new cut corn and laughter to be heard across the fields as the labourers completed the harvest home. He remembered the smell of the first apples that Mam Muncy had stored away carefully. Despite the wide walks between the plants here and the rich smells of flowers he felt claustrophobic in this walled garden. The path was of shale and the clipped box surrounding each bed accentuated the feeling of formality and keeping-in. As he approached father and daughter they stopped and turned to see who was coming. Their discreet conversation tailed away.

They stood, watching him walk purposefully towards them and waited until he was almost upon them. Priedeux thought that the father looked more bowed down now he had been given the greater title of Lord Rochford by the King, a reward for some secret diplomacy that he had carried out. Or, Priedeux thought cynically, a reward for producing a daughter such as Anne. He had been given lands and manors so that he was richer than the Duke of Northumberland, meaning he could now hold his head high with his wife's relatives, the Norfolks. He was certainly dressed in a rich robe, edged with deep fur, the material sheeny in the slanting sun-rays.

Lord Rochford was the first to speak. 'Well, dear girl, here comes that elusive servant of yours. Priedeux, I haven't seen you for many moons, do you drift in and out by side gates? How goes it with you?'

'Well, my lord, I would want to stay a-while but the Lady Anne sends me on many errands.'

'Aye, but she assures me you have proved your worth and her trust in you. In faith, I see you blend well into the court. I'll not ask what she does with you, so long as she treats you well. So be it, I truly begin to think that Lady Anne has the better of me in some things these days. Hey ho, I must be on my way.' He turned to his daughter and kissed her on the cheek, she proffering it with dignity. 'Remember what I told you; high office means a higher fall. Beware of the Norfolk faction.'

Anne nodded to him, fully understanding, and watched her father stride away. She had never let him know she knew the secret of her birth. As she had climbed higher in the king's affections so her father had confided in her more. He was a valuable ally in her game at Court and her personal emotions regarding him could be well hidden. As he closed the gate in the wall which led to the stables, she gave that triumphant twirl which Priedeux recognised but now thought affected and annoying. 'I am to be made a marquess – note, a marquess, not a marchioness – and my lord proves his love with many lands and manors. Oh Priedeux, surely my day will come soon.'

He said nothing but fingered the talisman at his throat. He was still thinking of 'Sir Askham' and small glimmerings of wishfulness for the network of family were making him inattentive. Seeing his mistress with her father had made him remember the only mother he knew and the possibilities of his new-found information. He had evidence that his father could be a knight, a gentleman, and he was not low-born, if only he could have time to find out.

Anne, sharp as ever, noted his lack of comment or criticism.

'Come, Priedeux, you are usually quick to warn me not to be so forward, what is wrong?'

She stared at him, her finger to her chin, and went on, trying to gain his approval, 'Does it not excite you? Your mistress raised to one of the highest in the land? D'you not want to know why?'

The man shook himself like a damp dog and smiled at her.

'I apologise. I was still a-wandering in that painter's workshop and full of admiration for his skills. Very well, tell me.'

She took his arm, as she had done on that first walk back from Nan Muncy's cottage, a confidential gesture, and walked him to the edge of the garden, through another gate. Now they were on the banks of the Thames where building works were being carried out to create a new landing stage. They heard the muted sound of banging as the carpenters went about their labours. On the horizon could be seen the spires of Westminster cathedral built some hundreds of years ago but still showing cleanly white against the sky.

'I have just come from my dear Harry who kisses me and tells me why.' She stepped back and waited. Priedeux said nothing, so she continued, speaking quickly and fiercely, 'He negotiates to meet with Francis. My idea, of course. Now that they have signed a treaty of support, they would meet to discuss ways and means. We will persuade that king of his powers and he will join us, I'm sure. Harry wants me by his side, more than a consort: his helpmate and equal in status, and this cannot be so unless I am his lawfully married spouse. If not that, then as the highest in the land. So I am created a marquess; higher than dukes and lords. I must be more than his sister who is but the wife of a duke, or the Duchess of Norfolk, more than all else.'

Priedeux stepped back and bowed low. 'Soon you'll want none

of your humble servants from wild Kent. You'll need grand ladies of the bedchamber and stewards who will mind the books for you. Shall I be sent a-packing?' He said it mockingly but Anne assessed him and suddenly she saw him in a different light. She led him back to the arbour and, taking his arm, made him sit beside her. The air was rich with the perfume of the tired late summer flowers of musk rose which surrounded the seat.

'Priedeux, my dear Priedeux,' she leant forward and took both his hands in hers so he had to face her. 'You have travelled far and long for me and you are tired. I see that. You have developed grey hairs in my service, wrinkles around the eyes, and your cheeks are becoming sunken.' She said it ironically but Priedeux, for the first time, realised that he indeed felt old. He felt as if his life had slipped away. Oh, yes, he had had women, both here and abroad, but there was no lady awaiting his return, no son to pass on his strange name, no sister to lament his passing.

Perhaps Anne was a witch, and could see into men's hearts, as she surprised Priedeux by almost repeating what he thought, 'Aye and nothing to show for it, no wife, no child. That comes with wealth, I assure you. Let me promise you, ye shall have at least three manors to mind, with the rents that are due to you for looking after my interests. I have neglected you, have I not? But you are valued, you must know that for all the times you took my messages and brought mine to me. Now shall come your reward and you can live in the country, a fitting respite for one who has travelled so far and so well.'

The man lowered his eyes for her dark brown orbs were earnest, wide and he could not meet her gaze. Once again, he could see why men did her bidding, for when she spoke like this she was all fire and passion and he felt now that he was the most important person in her entourage. He felt he could ask her now for the time he needed.

Their tête-à-tête was rudely interrupted by loud shouting.

'Nan, Nan my dear bubs, where are you?' Henry could be heard scrunching closer, his step so heavy that the shale was raised in small clouds of dust, but he continued to shout, 'I have had a great idea. I will ask that old witch Katherine for her jewels. Your long beautiful neck will be adorned with the royal pearls for your inauguration. Where are you?'

'Harry. My Lord, how comes he here?' she looked at Priedeux but before he had a chance to disappear their king was upon them. The servant jumped up but not before the king saw Anne's hands upon his arm. King Henry stopped and stood, his face changing from one of eagerness to tight-eyed anger.

'What dost here? Not another lover under my very nose.'

But behind him scurried a maid in waiting, 'Lady Anne, I am sorry, he would push past me in his eagerness.'

Lady Anne stood upright then and her dark eyes turned on the great man before her and the trembling maid.

'Susannah, go back to your porch. I quite understand that a king cannot be refused. Now my Lord, come. How can you expect me to be making love to a dull servant from the country? And how come you do not recognise the loyal servant who travelled to all the colleges of the world for you?'

Priedeux hung his head, for he could sense those sharp small eyes of Henry looking him up and down and felt he should not meet his gaze. Priedeux's clothes were dull apart from some pale yellow rose petals which had fallen onto them, disturbed when they had jumped up, and were now resting on his shoulders. He knew the clothes would show he was of lower rank than a gentleman, but not quite a lowly servant. He did not move, not sure whether to bow or not. He decided not; the lack of courtly manners would make him seem even more of a bumpkin. But he was adept at judging men and seeing them without looking directly. Although he had taken messages for Henry, he knew the man did not always see well with his middle-aged eyes that had been exhausted by reading so many Court papers. The king used underlings and did not always remember them.

'I do not recall having seen this man in your household before.' Henry said it defensively but still held the pose, as if he would pull a sword any moment if he carried one.

'Of course you do.' Anne said angrily. 'He is my man who took the gold to the universities for us. He is come from Hever and carries messages between me and my family. Come, my Lord, how could you forget such a thing. My father has shortly left and also gave Tom messages for home.'

Priedeux was embarrassed. How could Anne talk to the king in such a manner? Surely such a great man would not put up with that. He had never seen them together in an intimate way, usually being the harbinger of verbal messages between them.

Henry opened his mouth to speak but Anne held up her hand, one finger pointing at him. 'You would never gain a great lady if you think ill of her like that.' She sounded as if she was ranting now, 'I'll go to a convent before such accusations are made and you are lucky it is just my plain servants who heard you say such a thing. How dare you!' She drifted towards her lover and pinched the flesh on the back of his hand, 'And now, dear Henry, would you wait a while, in the chamber, until I have finished with old Tom here and sent him on his way?' She pecked the King's cheek, and spoke so softly that Priedeux was not sure he heard the next words aright, 'And I will find a way of punishing you for thinking I have any other lover but your dear self.'

Henry softened as she touched him and visibly wilted, his wide shoulders seeming to sag a little as she moved away with him. Priedeux almost expected the king to turn back to him with a sheepish grin on his face, but he did not, so engrossed was he with his mistress. The whispering between them continued and Priedeux at last moved, brushing off the damp petals impatiently. Then Henry parted from Anne, and made his way up the path again, almost trotting, to her apartments. The servant realised that Henry was no longer young and was stiffening with old age and worry. Anne turned back to him.

She smiled. 'My dear Priedeux, forgive me. A country bumpkin you are not. I know, it is surprising how the king is so soft for me, and me only. That is why I go on with this.' She tossed her head and then became businesslike. 'Now, what were we talking about? I fear I have overlooked you and insulted you all in one day.'

She led him back to the bench and they sat down again, Priedeux still feeling uncomfortable. He would go on with it, though, for he feared now for his future. Henry's stare had been uncomfortably observant and hostile and he doubted whether he would get his manors. He started, 'Anne, there is something I must do for myself but I am loath to leave your service without your permission.'

She said nothing but her straight eyebrows were raised in question. He knew she would think it was a woman.

'I need to be released for a week or two. For a private matter. Ask not.'

She nodded. 'But of course, I'll not need you for this grand ceremony, which I am sure I will find tedious but needs must be got through to be a marquess. All I'll need are my loyal maids who will dress me with pearls and raiments so that all the world will know I am the most important woman in the land. To think, Tom, the queen's pearls.' Her mood changed again. 'I do not like the King's idea, no matter how much I would love to feel those cold seeds around my throat. I fear the people will not like it, the way they gossip. That old queen has bought their love with alms, and prayers.' Then she sparkled again, 'Hey ho, let them grumble. I shall be queen and the mother of a great king. That I'm sure of, if God be with me.'

Again her mood changed, back to businesslike efficiency. 'The ceremony is to be on September 1st and if you would return by the autumn then you can go. For then you will need to take messages to my friends at the French Court.'

He stood up, carefully, for the damp had penetrated the thin cloth of his hose. He nodded, 'I'll be back by then, I promise.'

She took his hands in hers and pressed them in affirmation of her bond with him but he turned rapidly and scrunched down the path, not looking back. Already his mind was on the way he would travel out of London town.

* * * * *

For some reason he dressed carefully for his journey, taking clean hose and jerkin. Even so it did not taken him long to prepare himself; he was not a vain man. As he travelled along Cheapside he took off his cap and ruffled his hair and then scratched his chin. He realised he was unkempt and in bad need of a haircut, but why he should think of such a thing now, he could not say. He dismounted before a barber's sign and entered. Inside he saw there was a queue and he was about to leave when he heard the strumming tones of a cittern being played. He leaned against the door post and listened as the player sang in a soft, but insidious tone.

'Let your lady lay
Where she do choose
For her we shall play
Like a cittern. fast and loose.'

The men waiting laughed as the singer took breath and then continued along the same bawdy lines. Priedeux understood the innuendo for he knew well that a cittern was known as the lady of the barbers, being strummed by all who would.

'Wherever she does lay
Whatever state she play
Whether with king or Frenchie
We'll strum her on the benchie ...'

Priedeux frowned, not at the common words, but because he knew who they referred to. He felt like protesting but said nothing. Soon the singer was called to the chair and Priedeux took his place, though not taking the instrument.

'Ye'll not play then?' asked the next man in the queue.

'No, I'm not a strummer. The penny whistle is more in my line, for I'm a travelling man. Even that I gave up when my horse pricked up its ears and threatened to bolt with the horror of the sound I made.'

The others grinned at Priedeux's joke and another took up the

211

cittern and began to strum and hum, but sang no words. The air was heavy with the implications of the previous singer's doggerel. Soon one of the barbers, perhaps embarrassed by the unusual silence in his shop, asked of no-one in particular, 'Have you heard the latest of the palace?'

'No, but do tell,' answered the man who sat next to Priedeux. Priedeux tried to back away from him but there was no space.

'The king is now known as Nan's monkey, for he dances to all the tunes she plays.'

Priedeux said nothing, pretending to listen to the humming, trying to make out the tune. One of the men under the razor said, his mouth tight-lipped for fear of being cut, 'And 'tis said she casts spells on him, for why else would he stay with her? It is said she doesn't open her legs for him, not until she be queen.'

'Let her be queen then, for what does it matter? None of it will change my lot for I'll still be sitting in my tally house listening to the moans of people who pay their taxes.'

'And more taxes to be collected once she be queen and starts to produce the sons our king wants; have you thought of that?'

'No. I've heard that the King's mistress knows a thing or two about raising money. Already she suggests fining the priests if they collect indulgences.' Priedeux spoke, for he could not help but support his mistress, although he knew it was dangerous.

'And how do you know, stranger?'

Priedeux shrugged. 'It's all the talk of the alehouses around Westminster where I travelled through earlier today. But, as you say, I am but a stranger, on my way to manors in Essex to find out what merchandise they may need, so I'll say no more.'

He grinned and the others smiled back. Then he was called and he sat patiently as he was trimmed and shaved. The others continued talking and he listened, glad that he had an excuse not to join in the conversation.

'I still say the old queen was good and dignified. She gave alms to Spital Priory where my girl was cared for after her brain became addled and the gold paid for good food. What has this Kentish upstart, not even a lady, done for us?'

'You're right, Ned, the monks and nuns do good as well as bad. Just think though, if we don't have to pay tithes to the church, we'll be that much better off.'

'Aye, but then they'll want us to pay more taxes.'

The customers continued to mutter and argue. Soon Priedeux was done and he left. As he mounted his horse he felt pleased to be on his way and his spirits lifted. It was suddenly a welcome thought that he did not have to watch over Anne for a few weeks. He had seen how she could manipulate the king and, surely, once she was a marquess she would be secure in her position. He knew she did not worry about public opinion. She had been so long living at courts around Europe that Anne had no concept of the ordinary people. He admitted she could handle men on a personal level but as a crowd ... that was different. Even on the day when she and the king had been spat at returning from hunting and jeered by an angry mob, she had been more furious than scared. He would see to his own affairs for once and leave Anne to hers.

He rode eastwards leaving the City by the Postern gate close by the Tower, passing that grim place of imprisonment on his right and shivering a little at its dark hovering presence. The low autumn sun sent a long shadow of turrets around him and he fancied he saw clouds gathering behind it.

Once out of the noisy City it was like another world. Here there were small homesteads with fields full of sheep and cows, strutting chickens and geese. By the side of each was a pigpen where the hogs were almost fatted ready for killing and preserving for the winter months. The food for the great crowded populace was stored or grown in these places. It was a low-lying country and he could still smell the smoke and fumes from the leatherworkers and smiths on this edge of the city. It would be some time before he left the lingering miasma behind and could enjoy the scents of the country. Some children ran along by the side of his horse and tried to grab the reins asking for small coins. One pretty miss offered him some eggs, 'Fresh sir, honest sir, give us a groat, sir.' He

213

grinned at her cheekiness, for four pence was far too much, but he dropped a coin in her hand for the trying of it. He'd done the same years ago when he was a child, to passers-by on the main road near Hever, when he could skip off from the monks. He'd reasoned then that travellers were always foreigners and wouldn't know the value of English coin. Sometimes he'd been right and he'd glowed as he'd handed the coin to mother Muncy.

He continued to travel east until he came to a small hamlet and was told it was Bromley-by-Bow. It huddled around a stream, which Priedeux guessed, meandered its way to the Thames. Here he asked directions to Epping of a youth who sat on a low bridge over the water, which trickled its way over marshes, with rivulets, which split and joined again.

The boy looked up from his whittling and pointed, 'Follow the river upstream for it'll take you away from the Thames. But there b'aint nothing there 'cept marshes. There be a manor and fields far over and then you'll come to the forest.'

Priedeux thanked him and turned upstream. The boy was right. As he followed the stream, the path became increasingly muddy underfoot with mounds of reeds to catch his horse's hooves. It didn't help that the clouds he'd seen over the Tower had travelled fast, following him eastwards and now a thin drizzle started, causing a mist that reduced visibility to a few yards. The river was not so much a flowing torrent as a trickle of many little streams, moving around islands of reeds and rich water-grass. At some points Priedeux could not tell whether they stepped on damp earth, which gave with their combined weight, or whether they travelled in the water itself. He reined in the horse and dismounted and decided to lead it. His feet squelched underfoot and as he walked marsh birds and ducks rose in the air with great croaking noises of annoyance at his disturbance, then disappeared like wraiths in the mizzle. Soon some of these birds would be travelling away for the winter.

With his unerring country sense he continued until he came to another bridge, which he decided to cross. He knew the Epping

Forest was on the Essex side of this marsh. Here it was still flat and misty and he had no idea how long he travelled but soon the mist turned to greyness and he knew night was coming. He would have to find an inn soon or sleep out, which he did not relish in this inhospitable place. He imagined cut-throats and murderers gliding in the marshy mist, just waiting for such as he. He had not brought much coin with him, but some poor beggar would think it a fortune. As he made his way along, the land slowly became firm again and he knew he was going uphill. The drizzle continued. Suddenly his cloak was caught, as if grabbed, and he instinctively reached out, pricking his hand on a bramble. If he was not careful he would end his days torn to shreds by the simple blackberry. He slowed even more, cursing the weather. Now he was leaving the marshes and reaching firm land, perhaps the rough area around a small hamlet where the forest would creep back if the serfs didn't regularly cut back and tidy. Then he caught the dark shadows of trees. Perhaps this was the start of the great forest of Epping. The tree-shadows stood out more because of a glow of light at some distance. At the same time, he smelt the welcome odour of baking bread mixed with that of cooking rabbit. A hamlet was ahead, he was sure, and he guessed it was probably a small place where all the inhabitants cooked their food at the great baker's oven. The evening's baking was well on its way, he thought.

As he approached, he halloed, 'Hey, is there anyone there?'

Out of the mist came a youngster who trotted beside him. 'Hail, stranger, who be you?'

'A traveller, looking for food and shelter for the night. Where am I?'

'You be at the baker's who has great power around here. He'll give you shelter for the night but he'll charge as well. Would you like me to lead you there?'

Priedeux hesitated. He could be led to bandits who would slit his throat and no more would be heard of him. A trickle of rain dropped off the hood of his cloak onto his nose and then into the slit of his shirt, and down the front of his chest. He shivered as the

215

wet spread down. That decided him. He had travelled over the known world and been safe. Why should it be different in his home country? Besides, he did not want to spend the night on this damp marsh.

He concurred, 'Aye, take me there.'

The lad jogged in front of him and soon they had reached the light. Priedeux was surprised to see it was a substantial complex of at least four ovens, forming one side of a square. All of them were blazing, tended by men who were either stoking the fires or using big flat trays to slide in batches of dough, eight to a tray. There was a great mist of hot steam around each oven where the mizzle fought with the heat. On another side, at right angles and some way from the ovens, was a substantial brick and timber frame house and Priedeux wondered if he was at a manor house of some local knight. His guess was discounted when, at the door, he saw outlined by the good light of tapers and candles a rotund man, bald-headed, whose large frame was covered by a huge white apron.

'Hey, Will, what have you bought me here?'

Priedeux heard the lad mutter something about a stranger, found and lost, before there was a great guffaw from the man, 'Will, you should take more care. You could be leading a great army of bandits to us to murder us all in our beds. Go, lad, to the kitchen and have some ale. Oh, and leave the rabbits outside.'

The man moved out of the light and came towards Priedeux, 'Come, sir, and welcome. We don't get many strangers this way so it will make a change. I can leave the men to work.' As Priedeux dismounted and looked about him, the man said proudly, 'Aye, it's a goodly sight, is it not? I bake bread for the City and my men leave before dawn to ply their wares in the streets so I must be baking in my great ovens all evening. Come in out of this dampness.'

He turned lightly on his toes, a surprising movement for one so rotund and reminding Priedeux of Jonril's innkeeper, and called, 'Madge, Madge, come and see. We have a guest for the evening.'

A woman appeared, wiping her hands on her apron. As her husband was fat so she was thin, so thin that the apron strings were twisted twice round the body and tied at the front and her nose and chin was sharp. She smiled and Priedeux recognised a kind-hearted soul, with no guile in her, 'Welcome, stranger. Simon, you are cruel, bring the man inside. Help him off with that cloak and stoke the fire. I'll fetch some ale, and bake a good pie with those rabbits that Will has brought.'

She nodded and disappeared as quickly as she had appeared at the door. Her husband turned back to Priedeux and helped him off with the cloak. Gesturing to a chair near the fire, he pulled a fireguard near and used this to drape the cloak over it facing the blaze. His wife came shortly after with a tray with tankards and stoneware jug. She put this down on a side table and turned to her husband again and laughed. 'Simon you are stupid. Don't leave that cloak there to dampen my best room. Look, even now the windows steam up. Take it to the kitchens and hang it over the fire in there.' Her husband for all his bulk jumped and did her bidding and while he was gone, his wife poured a tankard of ale from the jug she had brought in, handing it to Priedeux. When the baker returned he was not given a drink, but instead his wife good-naturedly said, 'And then set up the trestle in here, for we'll eat in this parlour rather than take our guest into the kitchen to eat with the men.' She took a deep breath, and her husband said quickly as if to stop his wife's prattle, 'We are Simon and Madge Cranders, master bakers.'

Priedeux nodded and answered, 'Tom.' They shook hands and he continued, 'I am a stranger and traveller in these parts, ma'am, and am most grateful for your hospitality.'

She brushed his words aside, with a gesture like she was waving away a fly. 'Nay indeed, 'tis our pleasure. Although we have all these men a-working for us, this is a remote place and there are not many passers-by, so you can earn your night's hospitality by telling us of other places. Not about the City though, or about the king and his queen and the arguments. We

217

know all this. Our men find out more by selling bread in the streets than the town crier.' She busied herself as she talked, finding a fine cloth in a trunk and shaking it open to lay it on the trestle table which her husband was still setting up, pushing large wooden pegs in holes to steady the legs.

Eventually her husband stood and stretched, surveying their work. Madge bustled out of the room, but soon returned with food. As the warm aroma of game pie reached Priedeux, he realised he was very hungry. As they ate Simon asked, in a guileless tone, 'And, Priedeux, what brings you to these parts? You say you come from Kent but your accent is mighty strange.'

'I have travelled many miles as a merchant, or a carrier. I know not my family, and must make my living as I can. Thankfully I am blest with intelligence and can read and write, so I take commissions, taking messages for those who cannot or will not read, and carry them out.'

His host nodded, said nothing, and Priedeux realised he was waiting to know what such a man was doing travelling in the Lea valley marshes.

'I am on a private mission now,' he said no more and there was a silence in the room, which became almost palpable. Somehow, maybe it was the kindness of these people, their simple trust in him, or something about Madge that reminded him of Nan Muncy. It may have been the locally brewed ale, or the game pie. Maybe it was because they were strangers, and had nothing to do with his life at Court, or as Anne Boleyn's servant. Whatever it was, he felt as if he could trust these kind folk, and tell them what he was searching for. He stopped eating and looked up at them. He began, 'It is time I found out about my family and certain clues have led me to these parts. I look for someone called Sir Askham.'

The baker nodded, as if his comment was the most natural statement in the world. 'And you believe he lives hereabouts? What makes you think that?' He leaned forward as if he would grab at Priedeux's answer.

'Certain clues.' Priedeux hesitated, but thought *a groat has been*

218

spent; might as well spend the whole purse and untied his collar to reveal the pendant. 'This … I have been told that another travels with something similar and that he lives hereabouts.'

Simon and his wife glanced at each other and Priedeux could have sworn Madge gave an imperceptible nod to her husband. He said slowly, 'A man of that name lives but a mile or so into the forest. At a place called Wilcomstou. A small hamlet sustained by hogs. But many come and claim … no matter, only you have shown the pendant.

'It's nothing much, except for an old manor owned by Sir Thomas Ascham, for we spell the name in the old way, near there. He is old now, and they say dying.'

He had pronounced it with a soft sound of 'sh' in the middle, as if he would whisper it, but Priedeux could not believe the coincidence.

'But I thought it was *Sir Thomas Askham*? As if he were asking questions?'

The master baker laughed. 'Like you do now! Nay, we soften the middle of the word about here but you may say it so. I have little to do with him for he too was a travelling man, and came to these parts without any history, claiming to be a relative and next of kin of the old Ascham who had owned the manor since Doomsday. A soldier he was, you could tell that, turning up with an old nag. He says he searched for his family, like you say, and is always ranting and raving about trying to find them. Sometimes he goes off and sometimes he comes back. We are tolerant and know that old age addles a man's brain. And if 'tis true that he has lost a family then it is a terrible thing.' Simon sighed, looking at his wife as if for support for what he was saying. She said nothing but patted his arm, to comfort him.

Priedeux decided to deflect the conversation from his own concerns, 'And do you have children, family?'

'Nay, we were not blest, Madge and I, but for all that she is the best wife I've ever had.'

Madge laughed and started to clear the table,. 'And the only one while I'm alive you old codger you.'

'So who will carry on the baking when you are gone?' asked Priedeux, interested.

'Aah, that be a problem for when I'm not here, but I tell you what Madge and I have planned since we have made a pretty pile with our baking, have we not, Madge?'

His wife stood at the door, dirty crocks held in front of her, frowning. 'Now don't go boring our guest with our private business, Simon.'

But Simon had had too much ale in him and gestured her away, 'Priedeux here is to be trusted, he said so himself.'

His wife shrugged and left the room. Priedeux wondered when he had claimed to be trusted but knew that people did trust him. Anne did. Dinteville and de Selve for instance. Simon leaned forward and put his hand on his guest's sleeve, 'We intend to leave our estate to the monks with the request that they set up almshouses hereabout and called them the Bakers' Alms, for we have seen the old without a roof over their heads and we'll do our bit for them. We have men in our employ who grow old with us and we would want to make provision for them, for they have served us well. The monks know about this and have agreed. What think you?'

Priedeux nodded, 'That's good. Will the monks continue the bakery?'

Simon guffawed. 'Indeed they will, I truly believe they will, for they know a good thing when they see it. Good businessmen are those monks.'

Priedeux smiled with him. Madge returned and stood there for a while. Then she said, 'Stranger, you want to go to Sir Ascham tomorrow?'

'If I can.' He nodded, liking her astuteness.

'Then ye'll go with our blessing and our bread. That'll give you the opening to the household. Very private they are, but you can take a commission from us and that will get you in. What say you?'

Priedeux stood and approached her, took her hand and shook it in grateful thanks. 'Not only are you a great baker, but you are a kind and wise woman, indeed.'

Her husband emitted another genial guffaw. 'Ho, stranger, don't let my little woman get bigheaded now. I'll admit I would not have thought of that as a way to get into the house. Madge, you have said well.'

With that, he suggested they go to bed, even though there was a red glow and noises of work outside, which would continue all night. Priedeux was sure the smell of the baking bread would keep him awake.

He was shown to a good feather bed, obviously the best in the house, and before he drifted into a dreamless sleep, felt a glow of excitement. Despite the roar of the ovens, the mouth-watering smells and the mutterings of the workers, he fell asleep almost immediately without thinking of what the morrow would bring.

Chapter Nineteen

Priedeux was woken by a hand on his shoulder and he shot upright immediately without the need to be shaken alert. It was not yet light.

'Sorry, stranger, but I must wake you if you are to go with the bakers to Sir Ascham's place. They leave early.'

It was Madge, fully dressed as if she had never gone to bed, except for her dishevelled hair, which hung as a great braid loose over one shoulder. He nodded by way of thanks and rubbed his eyes, to dispel the sleep in them. He had been dreaming of demons who drifted in and out of mizzle, coming at him and then, before he had a chance to stab at them, disappearing into the weather. He knew, from his journeyings abroad, that such dreams were made from too much riding, too much of one thing on one day. He would let them drift away from him and concentrate on today's great activity. As soon as Madge left the room he jumped up and looked out of the casement.

The mizzle of the night before had lifted, as his dreams were lifted, but it was still night-gloom. The only glow was from the ovens. No-one worked the kilns now and the soft light he could see was from dying embers which, he was sure would be stoked into life later. He knew the cost of tinder to start a new fire was higher than keeping a good fire alight, for such as bakers and smiths. Especially in a forest area such as this where wood was for the asking. He made ready to leave with the deliverymen who visited all the hamlets around here early before leaving for London.

It was not long before he had been breakfasted and was on his way, with a pannier full of bread, cheese and ale. 'For the knight'll not think to feed ye, you can be sure,' joked Madge.

As he left he offered Madge some coins 'for bed and board' but she shook her head, 'Nay, lad, for to me you are still young. You have paid for the food with your stories. You will reward us one day, I'll be bound.'

He nodded his thanks and did not press the coinage on her, realising that to do so would insult her. He spurred on his horse and followed the deliverymen.

They travelled, saying little, but rode slowly, balancing large wicker baskets, full of the smell of fresh baked bread, before them on their nags. The land climbed gently upwards as they made their way out of the clearing surrounding the baker's home and soon they were in a thick wood, with a clear narrow path through it. There was no sign here of a structured road for rich men travelling, or merchants on their way to a bargain. Here it was for working men, agricultural labourers, woodsmen and charcoal burners. Even Priedeux, from his lowly estate, reasoned that this was indeed a poor area. The men he travelled with said nothing, but seemed to sink into a sleepy stupor in their saddles. It was too dark anyway to see their features. As they rode on, a greyness outlined the shapes of the trees and horizon before them.

'How long now?' he asked one of the men.

'Not long,' was the short answer.

Then they rode out of the forest onto a landscape of fields on either side, some fallow now and others growing early winter greens, their soft growths just starting to curl over into balls. There were a few small cottages, tumbledown. Then, as it became lighter, he could see the church, towering above all the homes of its parishioners like a protective hand, its digit finger pointing to God in the sky. It had a solid Norman tower, and a small nave which, Priedeux guessed, was large enough for this insignificant village. No-one seemed to be up yet although it was now half light, but as they rode along the path that led between the cottages and past the lych-gate, a child crept out from behind rough matting that formed a door of a tumbledown hovel. Their footfalls must have woken her. She stood there thumb in mouth and watched. One of the

223

men fumbled in the basket before him and broke off the crusty end of a loaf with a mouth-watering crunchy sound, and threw it. The child, barefoot, ran to catch it and laughed, her feet making splashing marks in the mud from the previous day's drizzle. She ran back and disappeared inside with her prize.

This indeed was a poor area. It was still damp from the night before and Priedeux thought the marsh was not far; he could smell the marsh mist with its rankness. Indeed, he thought he saw the earth rising to greet him but realised it was probably the early morning mist. They rode on and, as the sun broke through the mist, he saw, through some pollarded trees, a large building set on its own. Strange shaped trees were bounded by a low fence. They came to the enclosure and there, in the middle, was an old stone house, its turret crumbling. It reminded Priedeux of Hever but on a miniature scale, as if someone had tried to copy the castles of old but didn't have the money to build properly. Priedeux's companion bent over the wattle wall and opened the latch of a rough gate. They rode into the courtyard where the morning activity was just beginning. A young girl was emptying a bedpan onto the muck in one corner, an older woman was feeding chickens which clucked and fussed around her. Another stretched up from milking a tethered cow, thin along its flanks, and, ignoring them, walked into the house with her pail.

'The bread's come,' shouted the bed-pan girl to no-one in particular. Out of a corner door came a deep voice, and Priedeux imagined an officious man in charge, 'Good and about time too. When you have a dying man who wants his bread, you give it to him and quick.'

The person speaking then emerged, and turned out to be a thick-set woman with her hair tied back and hidden by a close bonnet, red arms emerging from a short sleeve shift so that Priedeux could see the skin was chapped to the elbows. She was wiping her red hands on a rough towel. They were unusually large hands but shapely. As she strode out, a strong walk, her large bare feet showed beneath the rough hessian of her skirt.

Priedeux guessed she was housekeeper, laundrywoman and cook in one.

'Hey ho, who's this stranger? Where you come from and what you want?'

Priedeux dismounted and stood before her. She was almost as tall as he was. Her face had the florid hue of a person who leaned over hot pans or a turning spit, the heat puffing up the deep set eyes and fleshly lips. Her face was not unkind, but sharp as if the world had treated her badly and she constantly watched for rogues. He was not sure he should give his name or not.

'I come to speak with Sir Askham, for I may have news of his family.'

Her face clouded then, 'Oh, not another one. So many. You rogues.'

She turned into the kitchen and quickly returned with a thick broom, 'Go on, clear out. You, bakers, how dare you guide another one here. Have I not told you, the master is not to be bothered by these adventurers?'

Her arm was held by Priedeux's silent companion who had slid off his nag, unnoticed, and placed his pannier of bread on the trodden down mud before the kitchen door.

'Nay, mistress, Madge said it would be all right. She said to tell you he's all right.'

She stopped and slowly leant the broom against the wall. She stared at Priedeux for some time until he began to feel uncomfortable.

Suddenly she said, 'Come in then, stranger. And you, leave the normal loaves and go.' She turned her back on them and stalked into the kitchen, not waiting for Priedeux to follow. He stood at the entrance and hesitated a second before entering. Inside, the floor was of earth and there was a small spit in a small hearth. Despite the obvious poverty, all was clean and from the ceiling hung a salted belly of pork for the winter and some smoked fish. Jars of pickles stood on a rough wooden shelf, which was propped up with other jars beneath it. A pot bubbled on the hearth, and there were piles of root vegetables on the table. The woman was picking up a knife, about to start chopping them. Priedeux guessed she managed to provide for the household in straitened circumstances.

'Sit,' she ordered, pulling up a milking stool, still holding the knife. Without waiting for him to obey she turned and poured some milk, which was still steaming, and handed this to Priedeux. 'Stay there while I sort the bread and send the men on their way.'

He sipped the milk and could hear her deep voice arguing over loaves and money to pay for it but then her voice dropped as she walked away with the bakers and he knew she was enquiring of him. He waited.

'Tell me then, why you are here.' She made him jump, returning quietly, standing behind him in the entrance. He stood but she put her large hand on his shoulder and pushed him down, not roughly but as if she thought it would be better for him to sit rather than stand. He decided to tell all. What could he lose?

He told of Nan Muncy, of his childhood and a short version of his life since then and, as he explained, he fingered the talisman hidden beneath his clothes.

'I was called Priedeux but I don't even know if this is my true name. I heard a story in London town of a knight who also looked for his family, who used the phrase 'Pray-do'; this could be another way of pronouncing my name and ... here I am.'

He ended lamely for suddenly he had no idea why he had come to this place. No thought except instinct had driven him on. Despite Holbein's tale and the similarity in the pendants, how did he know this was the place? Now he was here it all seemed ridiculous for a grown man to be in such a position. It was the look on the woman's face that made him stop talking. As he spoke she had moved imperceptibly closer, like a fat cat towards its prey and now her face hovered in front of him so that he could almost head-butt her if he felt like it. He could smell her breath, the breath of a person whose teeth are rotten, who does not eat well but relies on sour milk and bread. He faced her, forehead to

226

forehead almost, and there was a silence which he felt he should break. But he didn't, for those sharp eyes had narrowed and there was a look in them that he could only describe as wonder.

Suddenly she snatched out – so fast he could not stop her – and ripped the laced collar of his inner tunic and pulled at his talisman. Stared at it and then stood upright.

Arms akimbo, she said, in that deep voice, 'Come with me,' and turned and strode away to reach the door of the kitchen which led into the rest of the house. She was muttering to herself and Priedeux's sharp hearing, sharpened by the eavesdropping at Court for his mistress, could have sworn he heard her saying, 'If it is not too late, don't let it be too late for him.'

She led him through a dark corridor where all was gloom and cobwebby into a back room with walls of wattle-and-daub which had been plastered on so badly that some of it was falling off, showing gaps to the frame of the wall. There was a pallet of sorts in one corner, heavily draped with cloths and furs of all sorts. Priedeux thought he saw a human shape amongst the drapes but it was so thin he couldn't be sure until he heard the rasping of what sounded like a death rattle.

'Master, I bring someone to you. Come, try and sit.'

Her voice had softened and she sounded motherly, all the sharpness damped down as she leant over the bed and pulled at cushions. A thin arm now emerged from the covers. A figure moved in the gloom, skeletal with thin straggles of white beard hanging from the pointed chin. The features he could see bore only a passing resemblance to the painting of Holbein's, as if Holbein had squeezed the lifeblood from the man. The rasping changed imperceptibly as the weight was lifted from the lungs. The eyes were mere sockets and for a moment Priedeux recoiled. The face was skull-like and the way the old housekeeper held up the body, he wondered if she were not mad and just kept an old skeleton to frighten strangers and the noise was caused by some strange bellows in the room. Then the smell hit him; the smell of stale urine, body-sweat and musty clothes. Dead bodies smelt

227

different. Priedeux knew. He remembered Nan Muncy and her death, this scene taking him back to her last days. The rasping changed and became an ugly rattle.

'What – is – it?' The words were enunciated separately, interrupted by the need to gasp at air.

'Cook.' Another wheeze.

'What is it?' he repeated, as if the difficulty in breathing meant he could find no other words.

The woman whispered again and Priedeux was sure she said, 'The necklet, he has the necklet.'

The gasp became a great groan and the woman pulled him up and shoved some coverlets behind him to give him support, for he would sit up and greet his guest.

'Come … come closer.'

Cook stood to one side and nodded encouragement to Priedeux, who stepped forward slowly.

'Show me. Show me the necklet.'

Priedeux gingerly lowered himself onto the rags on the bed and the old man winced as the bedclothes tightened over his thin frame. Priedeux, despite his disgust at the smell, bent closer, holding his talisman away from his chest, in front of the old man's face. The nose quivered, the lips trembled, the eyes opened wide and the skeletal hands lifted off the counterpane and moved towards Priedeux's neck, the fingers outstretched as if they would wrap themselves round his throat and strangle him. Priedeux did not flinch, but held his talisman still, as if it were a holy relic, protecting him from this apparition.

'Ye...es, the key, it is the key. Priedeux, you are Priedeux, is that the name you hold?'

Priedeux nodded, 'I am known as Tom to most as I serve my mistress as her personal messenger.'

The old man wiped his brow as if he could not take this in, 'Your mistress. Who is she?'

'My Lady Rochford, Lady Anne of Hever. Soon to be a marquess, the highest in the land. Soon to marry his Majesty '

The old man fell back then as if slapped.

'My son. A servant of a queen. Could I wish for more? After all my searchings.'

Priedeux recoiled, shocked.

'Sir. Your son? What are you saying?' Priedeux turned to the cook, showing his astonishment. She nodded and he turned back to the old man. 'What do you mean? You must tell me.'

Priedeux lent forward and took the man by the shoulders, tried to pull him upright as his head fell to one side, but the woman pushed him away.

'Nay stop, he is too weak, let him rest awhile, or he will breathe his last and you'll never know.'

Priedeux released the old man gently, accepting her wisdom.

'Sorry, sir, I see you are old and ill. Rest awhile and I'll wait for your story.'

The old man's head moved from side to side as if he would fight against his weakness. He took a deep breath and pulled himself up, his arm so thin it seemed it would crack with the weight of him. The hollows in the collarbone seemed like dark caves where they showed beneath his loose bed gown. As he dislodged the bedclothes a great whiff of sour urine hit Priedeux but he fought against the urge to move away.

'Nay I haven't much time,' There was a whistling in the breathing now. 'And you must know my story for it is yours as well.'

He paused and took a deep breath and the room was filled with a groaning and rattling and then he began, slowly but not hesitating.

'You *are* my son. My wife she – deprived me – wicked of her. No, she did not mean it, it was the birth sickness. It took her shortly after she hid you. She could not tell from her grave, what she had done with you. The bitterness had started it, all those years ago.'

He fell back and Priedeux waited. Eventually the sorry tale was told. It took the old man several hours, falling back and dozing, in between episodes. His name was Priedeux and he revealed how he came from an ancient noble family.

'Some say we are descended from that great Gaunt, John of Lancaster from the wrong side but I found out that was not true. Our family crest was of de Coucy, his son-in-law, but all the stories are of de Coucy marrying a second Isabella and a secret family was born. We were always Lancastrian, and always supported the white rose but when the Wars came I found the Lancastrians distasteful, forever fighting each other and killing their kin. I had also heard of Owen Tudor, a great leader who lived many many years ago, and when Henry rose out of the Welsh marches I rose too and rushed to his side, for he claimed descent from that Owen Tudor who I had admired in my history books. His claims seemed more genuine to me, from what I knew of our family and its involvement in that distant history. I left behind a young bride who I had not yet tried and she sulked and hated me for deserting her. What I did not know was that a deeper hate grew for she was Lancastrian and forever blamed me for fighting on the wrong side.

'And for killing her brother and her cousin who she loved beyond me. I killed them in the heat of the battle without knowing who they were.' The old man seemed to gather strength as he spoke and the story came out in one great gasping rush. Priedeux did not stop him. After another rest, the old man continued, 'So I returned to my marriage bed triumphant with honours and my wife turned her back on me. For years we fought together until, in her autumn, she produced you, our only fruit. Oh, I was so proud, at last I had a son and heir.'

The father took the son's hand and tried to squeeze it, but he was too weak. Priedeux held his father's hand as he rasped on, 'In the meantime our fortunes had not grown, for somehow all I can do is fight but there was no fighting to do unless I travelled and sold myself for a mercenary. I could not do that for I was locked in a fight to the death with my wife. There was plague in the cattle, scrapie in the sheep and my serfs refused to work and started to desert us, except for Cook here who stayed.'

But Cook had gone, when Priedeux turned round to acknowledge her. The old man fell back and closed his eyes and Priedeux studied the face. The face of his father. It was too sharp to be handsome and Priedeux suspected that had never been the case. The wispy beard on the pointed chin made him look simple but he had a fine high forehead which hinted at some intellect.

Then the cook returned with a pitcher and two tumblers. She poured water into one and sat behind the old man, lifting his head gently so he could drink. He took the help mildly, as if it was customary. Then he seemed to recollect himself and stared at Priedeux. He reached out and Priedeux took the bony hand. Held it in his two hands and the old man squeezed gratefully.

'She swore I would not have the educating of you. 'Twould ruin you, she said. She whispered it in her dying pangs. I argued back, laughing at her. What could she do now, I taunted, oh, I know I should not have done it, but she had sore tried me over the years, and I taunted her and said she could do nothing now for she was finished and I would educate my son to understand that it did not matter who he fought for so long as it was nobly.'

He leaned back, licking his lips to savour the dampness of the water which had trickled over his mouth.

'And somehow she persuaded someone in the household to take you away.'

He looked at Priedeux mournfully then, and there was a wetness in his eyes which he could not control. Priedeux continued to hold his hand.

'They took you away and I have spent my life searching for you. She died, your mother, but she was remorseful. She told me with her dying whispers, before she took last unction, that she had given you the necklet I had given her, a family heirloom. The marks on it are Arabic, I have been told, and swear of true love between the givers. Huh, it did not do that for us.'

For a moment there was a gleam of anger in his eyes and Priedeux imagined the bitterness between his parents before he was born. Not unlike the fighting between Henry and his Queen

231

Katherine now, he thought. But his father was whispering again.

'And I left the manor and travelled. I went to France, to the German states, to Spain and Portugal, but could find you nowhere. I became known as Sir Askham and, ashamed of myself, I took the name.'

He paused, 'Hever, where is that? Far far away ...' His voice was fading as if he too were moving far away.

Priedeux hesitated, what good would it do now, for the old man to know he had been in England, not that distant? Priedeux knew though that he had to respect the dying wishes of his father so explained, 'Hever's in Kent, sir, below the Kentish hills and a short way off the road to Dover.'

The tears flowed then, and the hand pulled itself from Priedeux's, to wipe them away.

'Nay, nay, I cannot believe it. So near, yet so far. Oh, the wicked woman, to hide you in that way. So many times have we travelled that way and never thought to ask in the villages along the road. But stay, let me look at you.'

He pulled himself up on the cushions behind him and Cook helped. He gestured to the window and she pulled aside the old tapestry which served as curtain, to reveal only an open gap, with no glazing in it. Chilly morning air entered and he coughed and wheezed. He stared at Priedeux and Priedeux leaned forward, allowing this man who was his father to survey him.

'Aye you have the noble bearing of your ancestors. That much can be seen. Can you read? Write?'

Priedeux nodded. 'And ride, and use a sword as well now. I move at Court unseen, as a trusted servant. And truth to tell, sir, that is how I would wish it, seeing as how others intrigue and trick each other.'

The old man's face grimaced into a smile and he nodded, 'At Court? Aye, royalty and the rich soon forget those who serve them. Expect nothing from them but trust your own judgement.'

Then there was silence between them, and Priedeux continued to sit, and the old man seemed to sleep. Cook moved gently away, placed her hand on his shoulder and nodded to him to stay while she left.

After a while, the old man opened his eyes and his face twisted into a skeletal smile, but his eyes were soft and he was at peace.

'Tell me, sir, how come you are here, at this place Wilcomstou? Is this the ancestral home?'

'Nay,' he whispered, 'We are of the north, in the lands of Lancaster. But it is all gone, sold now, for what I could get for it to make sure I kept going, my horse and me, travelling to find you. It has been many years.

'This place belongs to a cousin – the Sir Askham was a joke for we have Aschams in the family, respectable people, scholars, clergy who study at Oxford, and a distant cousin gave me this small place to call my own for life. Cook here has always been with us and she is the manager, and cares for me.' He paused. 'When I am gone you must care for her, if you can. It will not be long now.' The old man's eyes closed and his face relaxed.

Priedeux sat a while until he was sure the old man had fallen into a restless, rasping sleep and crept out of the room, pulling the curtain across the opening to keep out the cold.

'You really are his son, I can tell. When you first spoke I suddenly saw my mistress in you. You are very like her.' Then Cook smiled. 'But I hope you do not have her temper, for she was a wilful thing right from the start.'

Priedeux gave a short laugh and thought about it. 'I do not think I am wilful, but I keep my own counsel. I do not do as others do, but what I think is right.'

She looked at him then arms akimbo and nodded.

'Yes, Nan Muncy did a good job. I am sorry for it now, but I confess I was the one who spirited you away. Nan was my older sister and I knew her as a good wet nurse. I thought you would not survive here, with the old man, who was so angry about everything, and I knew Nan could give you good milk.' She turned away, stirring something that had started to boil, and shook her head. 'It was right to do it, it was right, I am sure.'

'But you must have known where Muncy was? Could you not..?'

'Nay, she moved with her family and never got a message to me to say where they had gone. At the time she was in the flat lands of Norfolk, and when I enquired, she'd moved and no-one knew where. I rather fear she did not want to let me know.'

Yes, that was it, he remembered how Muncy had said she would fight to keep him if anyone had come to claim him. Dear Muncy, he could not blame her for what had happened.

Priedeux was amazed at these new revelations, but said nothing. So many things had happened today he felt as if he should go into a quiet room, a monk's cell, and think through all he had learned. It was not possible of course. He would have to stay until the old man, his father, *his father*, died, for he could see that it would not be long. He thought back on Nan Muncy; his mother in all but name, and now he was doing the same for his father, in a bizarre coincidental mirror-game.

It took three days before Sir Askham finally faded away. He sank into a deep slumber the next evening even though he and Priedeux had sat quietly together, only conversing when he had the strength. At the start Priedeux thought he had drifted serenely into deep sleep but it turned out to be his last before death and the son still sat, watching the now still face and knew he was at peace. His last breath came imperceptibly and Priedeux was never sure later how long he sat with a body rather than the living.

* * * * *

He stayed a few days, helping Cook with the cleaning of the place, and settling of accounts, of which there were many. On the last of these days, there was a commotion in the yard and a voice called, 'Priedeux, where is Priedeux?'

The voice was familiar and Priedeux dropped the pile of folded covers off the bed, newly washed and ready to store, and ran into the yard.

'Jonril. What are you doing here? How have you found me? And why come to this far-off place? You're not one to leave your

234

comforts.'

The masque maker jumped off his horse and skipped over to Priedeux, his arms outspread,. 'I have found you at last. What a backwater and filthy too. I have come because your mistress is in trouble. She is besieged near Richmond by a mob of angry women who have refused to let her out until she renounces the king. It is a ridiculous situation and the king, even though he has ordered soldiers to break them up, can do nothing for the soldiers refuse to go in against women.'

'Not again. I love my mistress but why is she so foolish? Did she not learn when this happened in the City last November? What can I do? Jonril, what can I do?'

Cook had come out with her usual pitcher and handed Jonril a tumbler of something which he took gratefully and knocked back. He grimaced, 'Yeuch, warm milk. Sorry, ma'am, I appreciate the kindness, but warm ale would be better.' He turned back to Priedeux. 'You have ideas, you are not known, you would be able to organise something.'

Cook sighed audibly. 'You must go, Tom, worry not about me, I have already arranged something. I know Sir Askham was concerned for me, but I have agreed to marry the miller, a goodly widower of my own age and he has waited long for me. You go but return some time to let me know how you be.'

Priedeux nodded. He knew he could trust her like he had trusted Nan Muncy. Over the last few days he had come to realise how alike she was to her sister, not in looks but in kindheartedness, good sense and the willingness to labour. They had worked well together in tidying up his father's affairs.

He found his horse and soon he was saddled and prepared for the journey. As he rode along with Jonril he said nothing and Jonril did not ask again what he was doing in the tiny country hamlet, but continued to tell his story of Anne's danger. Priedeux knew then that, since that day in the barber's, he had been worried about her but all that had happened had kept his worries at bay. Now he frowned for he had seen an angry London crowd and knew what could happen. Richmond though was a quiet backwater.

Priedeux had heard his mistress being called the whore of Henry and a heretic in the towns he had travelled through in Europe, especially the Mediterranean states that were held by Charles V, where there was little religious dissent. Despite the fact that the king had decided he was no longer married to her, Katherine was still popular, and many people hated Anne for deposing her. He realised Jonril was studying him and grinned back.

'What was my lady doing at Richmond?'

Jonril emitted his high pitched giggle. 'She was celebrating her impending appointment as marquess and travelling with the king with some hunting thrown in. They had retired from Court for a few days while her father organised the trip to France. You have heard of that?'

Priedeux nodded. He urged his horse faster, even though they rode towards the marshy ground of Hackney once again.

'Henry was with his heads of state and she was bored so she decided to visit a friend. Some spy must have spread the news. She has been trapped for some days.' His words were lost on his companion who was galloping away.

'Hey, wait for me. We will reach London town soon enough. When we do, I suggest we take to the water; that is the quickest way to Richmond.'

Priedeux agreed and he reined in his steed and waited for his companion to catch up. As he rode he developed his plans for rescuing his mistress.

'Jonril, before we leave this place we must visit my friends Madge and Simon. I have a mind to borrow something from them.'

* * * * *

They were nearing London town.

'We must plan, my friend, to save the Lady Anne,' Jonril interrupted their silent riding.

Priedeux had been thinking and plotting while they rode. He would have to explain to Jonril what he planned to do. He could come or stay, Priedeux did not mind. He explained his plans and Jonril immediately said, 'Don't leave me out of this. It will be like a real masque, a game. I shall enjoy it.'

'It could be dangerous. We could be arrested by the guard or set upon by the women.'

'Oh that second does scare me. A gaggle of women would be terrifying.'

They both laughed and rode on.

When they reached the city walls they were only just in time to enter before the gates were closed for the night. They headed for an inn and left their horses and headed for the river, sharing their load. At the inn all was gossip of the mob that had ridden to Richmond to rout the king's mistress. As he listened, Priedeux's face darkened, for it was obvious from the talk that the mob was made up of City apprentices, fired by the words of their masters who supported Katherine.

'Dressed as women they won't be identified, and the king won't do anything about it, like that other time last year,' whispered one ostler. Priedeux frowned at him and the youngster turned away with a snigger.

They soon found a waterman, with soft lantern at prow, to take them upriver. The going was slow with the lap, lap of an outgoing tide and Priedeux relaxed for he wanted to arrive when it was quite dark.

They had left the town behind, passed Westminster which was ablaze with lights, and turned the curve of the river where there were fewer houses along the waterfront. They travelled on and soon passed the river frontages where there were moorings. Here there were fewer boats and they asked their oarsman to keep in the centre of the river in the hope that they would attract less attention if anyone watched the water. But there was always the odd vessel moving about so no-one should challenge them.

'There it is,' pointed Jonril. 'That house there, with the new thatch.'

Priedeux could make out the new roof for, as they came closer the moon rose amongst the trees and the soft honey of the roof stood out. The house was at the end of a long sloping garden which reached up to it from the river. It had its own jetty but no boat was moored against it. Then they could see a glow of tapers and there was a threatening murmuring but they could see nothing. The house looked shuttered and they hoped no-one kept guard on the waterside.

Priedeux and Jonril ordered the waterman to lay to and they instructed him to wait. 'But I would dim your lantern if you would for we may be chased when we return with our cargo.'

The waterman grinned as he took down the lantern and placed it carefully between the benches. He too was enjoying what he saw as a jape with these two men who seemed to be bakers' delivery men, for they carried between them one of the large pannier baskets which the bakers had carried, full of loaves.

The two adventurers lifted the basket carefully onto the jetty and then jumped up themselves.

Jonril whispered, 'I am tempted to sing loudly rather than creep up. If there are any spies they will wonder why we creep.'

'No, I'll not warn them. We walk calmly and quickly up to the house and demand entry. No funny business, Jonril, this is serious.'

He felt the basket juggle as the man shrugged. Priedeux realised that his companion was ever the showman, and would never want to do anything quietly. Their friendship was a strange one; his career based on messages that were instantly lost, and Jonril's job to make a great display for all the Court to see. But now they were carrying a breadbasket between them as if it was the most natural thing for both of them to do. They reached the dark shadows of the house, which hid the moon, and made their way to the back door. Priedeux knocked not too gently.

A rough cry from inside, 'Who's there?'

'Bakers, sir, with your bread, sent from the king. Open up.'

'Nay, not tonight, 'tis late and we'll let no-one in, 'tis our mistress's orders.'

Priedeux called out, 'Summon your mistress, for I'll have words with her. Hurry, man, or you'll bear the brunt of her wrath when she hears you have refused the delivery.'

It must have been the sternness of his voice for there was a silence and then, a while later, when both Jonril and Priedeux had almost given up hope, Lady Anne's voice came, imperiously, 'Who is without, and how dare you demand to speak with me at this late hour?'

'Madam, 'tis I a poor baker delivering food, and we must away before we wake those demons at your door. 'Tis a wonder they have not yet come round to see what the commotion is about.'

He thought he heard her whisper, 'Priedeux, thank God,' but it might have been the wind in the trees. No more was said. Soon there was the scraping of the door as it was opened, and Anne was silhouetted against the light of a handheld taper.

'Priedeux.' It *is* you.' She held the door wide open but he took her hand and said quickly, 'No, Madam, we must away, we have a boat waiting. Come.'

Suddenly there was a loud calling. 'Dames, come here, there is movement at the back door. The whore will escape out the back way like a servant emptying a piss pot. Come quickly, we'll have her now.'

'Quick, get into the basket.' Priedeux was throwing out the loaves deliberately spreading them all over the path from where the calling had come. Anne understood at once, climbed in and Priedeux and Jonril between them disappeared into the darkness of the garden's shrubbery with their heavy load.

'What, man, what are you talking about? I am but a poor baker just collecting stale loaves for the pigs and delivering new ...'

'Come back here and give us some then.' called one of the crowd as Jonril and Priedeux moved away with their load.

Priedeux laughed loudly. 'What? And have you beat us up? I know what women you are and I'll not be a part of this charade.'

Jonril and he walked faster but the apprentices seemed unsure and they could be heard debating amongst themselves.

'Wait, they're probably decoys, she may go out the front.'

'The door's open, surely we should look inside first ... Quick those inside are shutting up again ... Quick round the front. The king's whore's making her escape that way ...' All was sudden confusion and flashing tapers.

As they reached the jetty they heard swearing and cursing coming from the coarse women who were so obviously apprentices dressed up. Priedeux grinned. Their pursuers were falling over the loaves he had discarded. They had plenty of time to board the bobbing boat and order the waterman away.

Chapter Twenty

It was some days later and the Court was all a-bustle with preparations for the journey to Calais. Anne was none the worse for her experience on the river and mentioned it to the king as a passing escapade.

'It was undignified. But I managed to leave eventually.' She did not elaborate on how, but continued, 'Now I am the Marquess of Pembroke, I'll not fear such events.'

Henry had hugged her to him and said, 'You shall not be so foolish as to gadabout on the river on your own now! You shall have a guard with you.'

Anne did not refuse him. Despite her bravado, she was growing a shield of dignity and coolness to those courtiers who flocked about her, suspecting them of spying on her and informing her enemies where she would be, and then inciting trouble. It would be good to have her own guard, who could keep the rabble at bay. She held her head high and swept through the corridors of her life as if she was born to be powerful. In reality she was afraid of the animosity against her, surprised at the strength of ill-feeling. She would never show that fear though, least of all to her enemies. Only with Priedeux was she friendly and open, it seemed to him, trusting him implicitly since the night of escape.

She had not accepted the King's offer of revenge.

'I'll tear down their hovels and make them go to live in the mountains of Wales where the cold damp valleys will drive them mad.' he'd said, but she had calmed him, 'Nay, Henry, it will further antagonise the people against me. Leave be and look to the future.'

Henry had kissed her and called her his sweet Bub, fondling her and pressing himself against her, all in front of courtiers who marvelled at his constancy to this woman. It had been six years now and, if anything, his ardour had waxed greater as the years passed.

To Priedeux, in private, she had confided, "'Tis mighty strange how the likes of Norfolk and Suffolk laugh with me in the King's presence and gifts are sent to me. I did not believe my father's warning but now I shall heed it. I'll trust them not, Tom, and I know you will watch out for me. But to business.'

They were in her antechamber where she kept her private books and papers. Here was the tiny book of hours that she had acquired in France, the multi-coloured illuminations her pride and joy. Here was the English Bible, and the French, which she read and compared. Amongst her most greatly prized possessions was the Lutheran hymn book de Selve had sent from the German states, when he had been ordered there to placate the reformists. The notes were dark and plain, the words ordinary and in German, not in the mass-Latin. She smiled to herself as she moved the book away from the papers she now wanted to consult. It had been a good manoeuvre to ask Holbein to include such items in his great picture. The room was cluttered for it was a withdrawing room, much smaller than the state rooms where Anne and Henry lived their public lives. It was comfortably decked out with dark oak panels and a good fire in the hearth to keep out the early autumn chills. A large table dominated and they sat at it as equals, facing the fire. After she had poured them some wine, she began to outline what she wanted him to do as part of the preparations for the journey to France.

'I'll have you wrap up that great painting of my ambassadors. It is in panels so you could try folding it.'

He interrupted, 'Anne, you are taking your bed with you?'

Anne, ever quick, nodded, 'Of course, I see what you are getting at.'

'Aye, it can be the base of your bed and no-one will question it, but tell me further what you plan.'

'We will show it to de Selve, he will be surprised at the likeness

242

I am sure. He will be at Calais, I understand, as one of the clergy.'

Priedeux nodded slowly. 'And how go the negotiations? I know the queen won't attend, not surprisingly as she is the sister of Charles. Will Marguerite of Navarre be part of the French party?'

Anne shook her head and for a moment there was a gleam of anger in her eye, but she was smiling when she answered, 'Sadly she has refused. I knew her when I was at the French Court and she was a friend, although a fickle one. She liked not my creeping off with Dinteville and de Selve. We never knew whether, as the king's sister, she would report what we said. She was a little older than us, too, Tom. You know how it is with children; a year makes a big difference.'

Anne put her chin in her hands and stared into the fire, thinking back. 'I realise now she must have thought we were precocious, wanting to be friends with her, for she was old enough to attend the banquets at her brother's side whereas we were just displayed as pretty children.'

Tom realised Anne was hiding her disappointment at the way in which the highest of the French ladies were avoiding meeting her. It was obvious why the queen would not attend, being sister of Charles V, but surely the others? Those who had known Anne as a lady-in-waiting in the French Court?

Anne explained the excuses given. 'Francis has said he could not travel. But Henry had insisted that I be by his side and form part of the festivities. Tom, he is proud of me, so he says, not only for my beauty but he knows I can speak French as well as any in France and he wants to use my language skills with Francis.'

She stood up and started to pace in the excited way that Priedeux remembered and continued, 'Francis had agreed to this, sending a letter where he said he remembered "the young Lady Anne well from her time at the French Court. But he very much regretted ..."

'He has dared to suggest that they, the two great Kings, meet together as brothers and forget about women. Henry, the dear, has ignored the suggestion. He raged and thundered and ordered that I be included in the travelling party.' She stood behind Priedeux and clapped her hands. 'So the diplomats have had to cross the Channel once again and the meeting has been postponed. Now Francis has capitulated and agreed to meet with me on English soil, in Calais, which I accept as a great honour. Think on it, Tom, dear Tom.' She was clasping his shoulders now and staring in front of her, 'I shall meet that old goat Francis as an equal. I'll not remind him though of his failed seduction.' She clapped her hand to her mouth. 'Nay, I'll not say more.'

This meeting was the longest that Priedeux had had with Anne for many a month, for she had been involved in ordering clothes and jewels for the journey to France, being convinced of the successful outcome of the negotiations. Now her face changed, and she suddenly seemed to see Tom. She said, 'You have not told me about your private journey? How did it go? Is it a woman?'

He smiled and stood up to face her. She asked kindly, dropping the imperious lady demeanour. Or the triumphant schemer that had just finished boasting of her success in the diplomatic negotiations. He remembered the time when he had been searching London and she had screeched at him on his return. Now she asked softly. He marvelled at the way she could change so quickly. He felt that they were equals, he and Anne, and she asked him now, as an equal. Perhaps she recognised the new dignity in him, at the knowledge of his forebears.

He was not sure whether he should tell her or not. He closed his eyes and thought hard. There was a silence in the room but he suddenly felt that soft hand on his arm.

'Come, Tom, you know you can trust me like I trust you. Tell.'

So he did, starting with revealing the talisman around his neck. She laughed. 'Oh, I remember playing with that and holding it to save myself from the storm when you took me to France all those years ago. It hurt my hand, I held on so tight. Indeed, I do recall it now.'

He tucked it back into his jerkin and told his story. As he spoke her face changed from interest to sadness. He could not know she was thinking of her own secret birth. Unlike his story which had a successful ending, hers could never have one. Priedeux had found he was of good birth, but Anne would always feel tainted if she ever thought about how she came to be.

When he had finished there was a silence which she broke by saying decisively, 'You shall have a manor to go with your status, now I am marquess. We shall find you a good one, with fertile land, animals and income, not far from London. You will become a landed gentleman again, as you should be, my good honourable Priedeux. I shall not mention this to the King; it will be my bestowing.'

Priedeux nodded, accepting the promise silently. They returned to the detail of their plans for the painting which was to become a bed before it was shown.

The trip to France took five days, three to travel through England, stopping at houses on the way for rest and refreshment, and seven hours across the Channel, in a balmy sunny October where the Channel was as still as one of the King's fish ponds. At Calais they were greeted with enthusiasm and great feasts and celebrations. A few days later Henry rode off to meet with Francis near Boulogne, leaving Anne behind. She did not mind, for she had her own plans now and made arrangements to entertain her old French friends.

Priedeux was sent with messages to de Selve and he promised to visit Anne again. Priedeux wondered why. He could not believe the priest was an innocent, and thought that he too had other motives for keeping in touch with the English king's mistress.

When he returned to Anne with the acceptance he said to her, 'Be careful, Anne, I do not trust de Selve. He has made it plain to you that he does not like the way you are moving the English church forward. He has said his position is jeopardised. Why then does he risk all to come to you? We all know that in a temporary camp like this, the comings and goings of people are watched and

245

talked about. Even if he comes at night, disguised, he might be recognised. So why does he risk it?'

Anne nodded, turning away from Priedeux, 'I accept all that you say. I suspect he has been told by his papal masters to keep an eye on me, to engage in talk and report back. That worries me not, Tom, for I shall always tell him the truth and if that worries the Pope, then good, and I hope His Holiness listens and thinks about what I am saying. If de Selve is brave enough to repeat what I say,' she laughed.

'I believe that de Selve will do my bidding soon. What I want you to do is to stand the picture in the room we dine in, but behind a curtain. I have brought those green drapes of mine, to remind me of my rooms at Court,' she said it ironically. 'We will dine and then ...'

Priedeux set up the room as instructed, placing the picture on a stand. He stared at it and was, once again, full of admiration for the way Holbein had captured the likeness of the two men but also the way he had placed them, either side of shelves where there were symbolic timepieces or geometric instruments. The picture was illuminated by covered flares in this temporary home and Priedeux admired how the painting gleamed and the light reflected from the insignia worn by the men, and the whiteness of the pages of the books on the lower shelves. Holbein had explained what they all meant even down to the hymnbook with its discordant hymns displayed. Priedeux grinned, for he could imagine de Selve's face when he saw the painting. Priedeux stood to the right of the painting to appreciate the way the twisted greyness at the feet of the two men became a skull – a symbol of death. The servant wondered for whom this signified. The effect was uncanny and he involuntarily shivered. Would de Selve also shiver when he saw it?

He checked the preparations and then left to order food for the small party his mistress was organising. He had some hours to prepare for the strange event. .

* * * * *

Anne relaxed with a sigh and wiped her fingers delicately on her napkin. She must remember to congratulate Priedeux, for the meal was almost as good as the last one she had shared with Dinteville and de Selve, despite the temporary lodgings. They too were pushing their plates away and smacking their lips.

'A good meal, my dear,' Dinteville said, 'and in difficult circumstances.'

She smiled and then said gently, 'I have something that I would show you both.' She stood and, taking her glass with her, moved around the table to the dark drapes that formed a corner of the chamber. The men stayed where they were, leaning forward expectantly. She pulled back the heavy curtain with both hands, her back to her guests. Then she turned to face them as the picture was revealed. She watched de Selve.

There was a silence in the room broken only by the soft sound of musicians playing in the distance, a gentle dancing tune. De Selve half rose and almost knocked the table over as he stumbled around it to get closer to the picture. As he did so the mark that tore across the tessellated floor moved and came into perspective. A skull. He stared; he had caught the full effect from the right. De Selve visibly shuddered at the portrayal of mortality. He stopped a few feet from the canvas. He stepped back, almost falling on the table, and gazed at the full height of the painting.

'Nay it cannot be! I bethought at first it to be a bizarre mirror because the table is covered by the same oriental rug as on the table we have just dined from.'

Dinteville had also moved so he was standing to one side, the same side as in the portrayal of him. Anne was pleased by the effect. The ambassador immediately appreciated the implications and stood back, also watching de Selve.

Then the bishop stepped forward to examine the picture. He ignored the geometric instruments on the top shelf for he could see no significance in them but bent to examine the hymnbook below them, positioned close to him. He then knew what the picture meant for it was open at the two hymns he had recommended to

247

Anne when he'd sent her the book many years ago. She probably still had the accompanying letter. He had been careful, when he was travelling on his papal duties not to have such Lutheran publications on his person for very long. But if it was discovered by his papal masters that he had acquired a Lutheran hymnbook *and* sent it to the mistress of a king who was arguing with the Pope his career would be in ruins.

De Selve said slowly, 'It is interesting that Dinteville's image is placed firmly on this circle on the floor whilst I am set back; nobody can tell what my position is.'

'On the contrary, dear Georges, all can read the symbols around you; they imply you would want to break up the Church, do they not?'

Anne waited and let him savour the thought. As he stopped and turned round, she came forward and stroked the painted beard on the painted de Selve, 'A very good likeness, I am very pleased with my painting. It could be displayed in my royal apartments, for all the world to see, when I return to England. Although I fear Holbein has painted your face a little too brown, de Selve, for you look quite pale now. What think you, my dear friend?'

Her voice was a whisper which seemed louder than normal speech. The music outside was increasing in tempo, the drum beating wildly, mirroring the very beat of de Selve's heart.

'Why, Anne, you would ruin me. You know that my work depends on not being known as a reformist ... not being friends with Dinteville here. Or with you.'

'Indeed. But I would wish you to do something for me if this painting is to stay private.'

'What? What do you wish me to do?' He came towards her eagerly, not looking at the painting as he passed in front of it.

'I would have you persuade the Pope to use his holy influence on the great men of Europe, including the Emperor, that England is not worth invading. If my king should marry me and declare himself head of our church.'

'But Anne, I cannot do that. How, think you?'

'I don't care how you do it. I believe you take information back with you, do you not?'

De Selve's colour changed now, as he blushed, and looked down.

'Yes, of course, you play a double game. So, you can persuade them that the whole country is behind Henry, that his naval fleet is great, which it is of course. Or that the land is laid waste and there is no food for a great army. Tell them that there are witches who make two men come out of the land for every one that is hacked down. I know not how you will persuade your masters, but you must if you wish to keep your bishop's hat.'

De Selve still looked down, and rung his hands. He turned to look at Dinteville, but he shrugged in a typical French manner, in a way that de Selve remembered from their childhood together, and sipped his wine.

'And, dear young Georges, look at the date – Easter Friday 1533 – I intend to be married and with child by then. I would expect you to carry out your mission by that date, or the picture is shown to the whole world.'

'And if I do what you ask?'

'It will be kept private, behind, well, let us say green damask curtains.'

'But Anne, if you keep this picture, how will I know it is safe? If you die it might then be displayed.'

Dinteville stepped forward and agreed, 'Anne, he is right. If this painting returns to England, his life will always be in danger. May I suggest ...'

But Anne turned to him then, her eyes slit like a cat's, staring at him. Was he in league with de Selve? But he stared at her, open eyed, and eventually she nodded. 'Carry on, my friend.'

'May I suggest that as the painting is already in France, I transport it to Polisy, our main chateau, where my family will protect it and, while I and my brother are alive, it will not be displayed. If you survive, and there is an invasion and you do not succeed, give me orders and I will return it to you for display. If you never send for it, I will leave specific instructions that it should not be hung for three generations and such instructions will be carried out. Especially when they see that skull.'

Anne put her head to one side. She knew both men were right. If she was to satisfy Henry she would, she hoped, soon be with child and child-bearing was dangerous. If she left a son, who would be king, she would die satisfied, but she would not want to endanger her friends for no real reason. If de Selve did manage to persuade the Pope, and through him, Charles V not to invade England then there was no reason to ruin him.

While she was thinking, de Selve moved to his French colleague and kissed him on both cheeks, and then turned back to the Englishwoman. 'If you agree to this, I will do my utmost to ensure no invasion. I am sorry you are going down the route of schism like the German states. I know my fate must be with the Catholic Church and the Pope but I will always love you as a great stateswoman, dear Anne, for I recognise this clever ploy as yours only.'

Anne stood a while. The music that wafted from outside was silent now. Then she nodded and returned to the table to collect the wine flagon. She poured for all three of them and they clicked glasses to seal the agreement.

'All for one and one for all like we were as children!'

The picture would stay in France. England would not be invaded and Anne would become queen.

* * * * *

Henry returned from his meeting with Francis and immediately went to Anne's apartments where he flung himself into a chair. In the end Anne had been forced to wait in the English port of Calais, while the first courtesies were carried out. Henry looked weary and Anne said nothing, but snapped her fingers for an attendant to bring wine. She took it from the servant as he entered the door, hiding the slumped figure of his king from him. She poured a glass and placed it before her lord. He greedily grabbed it and gulped it down. She poured him another, saying nothing, standing quietly by his side. He stopped gulping and sipped the second offering more sedately, smiling up at her.

'My dear Bub, you know how to please a man.' He stretched forward to stroke her breast but she slid away and put the tankard of wine on the table. Then she moved behind him and stroked his brow in the way he liked, sliding her hands gently down to his bull neck and kneading the muscles which were knotted like ship's rope. Henry sighed and grimaced.

'Aah, that ride across French soil has left me full of aches ... ooh, that is good, my dear Anne ...'

He was stroking his thighs, reaching awkwardly to his knees, and Anne could almost see the aches, like a dark band around his body, squeezing. As she massaged, so he slowed the stroking of his thighs to keep to her rhythm, and then stretched behind him and pulled up her skirts and caressed her legs. Slowly his shoulders relaxed, his eyes closed and Anne knew she could now persuade him to do anything, if she wanted. Tonight she would not ask for anything. Later, or tomorrow, would be time enough to tackle him with the next step in her plans.

Now she was sure of de Selve, and as certain as she could be that her country was protected, and she and her king were safe, as safe as possible in such a shifting sand of politics, she would now press for the ultimate; to be queen in title, to rule beside Henry.

'How did it go, with the French King?'

Henry stiffened and looked up at her. 'Not now, my Bub, I would forget for a while.' His eyes closed again. Then he struggled under her hands and pulled her round to sit on his capacious lap. Anne was not strong enough to resist. She saw that Henry's eyes were cold, and knew then that he was angry and had been angry ever since he had come into her chamber.

'What ails you, my dear one?' she asked gently, still stroking his neck, but he pulled her hands away and held them both in his. He did not look into her face but said, into her chest, and the words came out muffled. 'He showed me his three sons, all hale and hearty, all dressed to the hilt in velvets and lace, with their own little swords, all possible heirs and future kings. He was smiling, my coz, and affable. Affable as a father of sons can be to one who has no legitimate heirs. Francis will have successors and his line is guaranteed to continue. I introduced Fitzroy and he was as noble as can be but – but it was not the same at all. I felt as if the French king was laughing at me, Anne, me, the great sovereign over all I behold.'

He paused for breath and reached for his wine, gulped but Anne slowed him, knowing he might get cramps if he drank so quickly. He continued, 'Oh he was a great host, most magnanimous, and promised me all the help a kindred spirit could give to his brother, but he has a triumphant sneer that belies his magnanimity.' Henry's face softened. 'His sons are great little princes. Anne, we will have such as they, shall we not?' His face changed again, 'But when, when, Anne?'

She leant forward and bit his ear. She took the wine from him, placed it on the table behind her, and whispered, 'Within the year, God willing, I promise you that if you will plant your seed within my ready body such seed will grow a son.'

She started to stroke his neck again, tickling behind his ears and pulling at the corners of his beard. His face was buried between her pert breasts, and his hands were busy on her buttocks and thighs, and she could feel the heat of her body rising.

'Why, Anne, you will give yourself to me?' His head moved sideways and looked at her, smiling, hopeful, but surprised as well. Anne knew well why. She stared back at the mature, strong visage, the sharp eyes, the gristly beard, and knew she had to allow him to take her, for her own sake if not for his. She knew that the sudden angers that welled inside her were made of sexual frustration. She did care for him, and they shared a common aim. They had spoken of it often in the privacy of their chamber: to reform the church, to find the true way for their people. He was still attractive, despite his age. She licked his face, his eyelids as they closed, found his lips and forced them open and tongued his

252

tongue in the French way which he liked. Before today she would have slid down from his lap and satisfied him with such lickings and suckings but she could feel herself opening up to him and knew that, even if she had not felt so confident in the way she had arranged their future, she would have to give herself to him to satisfy her own inquisitive lust. Then, as he found the source of that lust with his fingers, she knew, as in a vision, that her machinations with de Selve would succeed and this brought an excited triumphant feeling which seemed to melt all her resolve to remain a virgin until her legal marriage.

'Hey ho, he will marry me now if I grow with his child,' she thought, as she yielded to him. She and Henry had played like this before and she had managed to contain herself and satisfy him at the same time but now she too, like Francis, was feeling victorious and this made her want more than titillation. Now he was playing with her nipples and she fell back against his strong arm in an abandonment she had never allowed herself before. She could feel his excitement, hard against her, and suddenly she was grappling with the laces of his codpiece, while he lifted her skirts. She straddled him in a way new to her and knew she would not be able to stop. She positioned herself over him and paused a second before she lowered herself on to him. Henry was grunting and pushing into her and she cried out with the initial pain of it and the rising excitement thereafter.

When it was all over she fell on Henry's chest and found tears in her eyes, satiated, and now totally triumphant at the thought that she could enjoy this so much. They stayed like that for some time, neither of them speaking but then Henry raised her head gently and looked at her. It was a look of deep love and admiration, 'Well, my young Bub, was it worth the wait?'

She pulled his beard gently and nodded, unable at first to speak.

'We must do it again soon.'

He laughed at her response, and pushed her off him to reach for the wine which he offered to her. She sipped and held it for him to sip too.

'Why now, dear Anne? After so many years?'

'I could see my king was desperate for his sons and I would honour my king by giving him what he wants. The time is ripe, yes? And I would dance with the French king when he comes, yes?'

He laughed, 'So long as that is all you do. After this I wonder if I can let you out of my sight.'

They laughed together. Anne said nothing about her plans, for she knew Henry would not like to think that a mere woman had helped him to keep his throne against a hostile Europe.

* * * * *

A few days later Francis and Henry were still ensconced with their advisers, Cromwell and others, including Anne's father. Anne fumed, furious at being ignored.

'But my dear little Bub, it is important that you are introduced with due ceremony. When the official banquet is held in the hall of the Exchequer, then you will be victorious. Wait, we must settle the protocol, and, in the meantime, your father represents your true interests, I can assure you.'

She bowed graciously and accepted the explanation but it was not until two days later that she had the opportunity to meet the French King, and it was not without some trepidation. Did he truly remember her? Would she be treated like the Marquess she was, or as the King's paramour? She would know the difference, even if the men around her, Henry, her father, her brother, even Cromwell, would miss the subtle nuances in Francis' behaviour which would tell her.

In the meantime, Anne found herself without much to do. She read her book of hours; scribbling in it '*my time will come*' in the Latin she disliked so much, so as to disguise it. She scanned the treatises which she had recently obtained but she could not concentrate on the obfuscations of religious argument at the moment. She opened the rosewood box the king had given her and fingered the crown jewels which had been delivered by a reluctant Katherine after the king had had to order her in writing to release them.

She ordered her maids to prepare for a great dinner, designed to show the French monarch that the English could cook and entertain as well as he. Eventually it was time to dress for the evening and she ordered her maids to add extra petticoats, more satin bows and special lace.

Still, she was not allowed to eat with her king, sitting at his right side. Instead, she and seven of her ladies-in-waiting dined early and then arrayed themselves in their gorgeous costumes of cloth of gold, silver and crimson satin.

Anne's costume was more elaborate than her ladies with more embroidered gold work and she paraded before them as they admired her and preened themselves. Then they donned masks and Anne led them to the banqueting hall. At a signal from Jonril the doors were ceremoniously opened, the trumpets blared, drums rolled and Anne and her ladies danced in. As agreed, Anne stepped straight to the French king and invited him on to the floor. He looked towards Henry who nodded, smiling, as he moved to another of the ladies.

Anne took Francis' hand and led him to the head of a row and they started the steps of the formal Court dance. He was entranced and watched his lady as she moved, stepped away from him, came again and swung round, her small toes showing beneath the gorgeous costume. As he walked in a circle away from her he turned his head and at all times kept his eyes on her, a look of ironic admiration in them. When the last notes died away, Anne curtseyed, as did all the ladies to their men, and then they took off their masks in unison.

Francis clapped his hands, 'Encore, trés bon, my dear marquess, we must dance again. What a wonderful surprise.' He spoke in French and Anne answered in the same language with the impeccable accent she had developed in her many years as a child at his Court.

'My dear King, you look as young as when I last saw you.

Come, let us talk and let the dance continue.'

The music struck up again and the others moved and reformed for the next dance.

She led him to a settle beneath a curtained window and they sat, Henry ignoring them and roaring with laughter at something his lady whispered to him.

'Well, madam, you are elevated beyond my wildest imagination; it suits you.'

She bowed, saying nothing.

'And the entire world knows how my brother, the great king of England, follows you around like a lapdog.' She looked at him sharply but he was smiling, and she smiled back, acknowledging what he said as a compliment.

'And I would follow him, my Lord, and hope to be his wife soon.'

He nodded but said nothing. After a pause, he said, as if he were reciting well-remembered lines, 'I would send greetings and regrets from my sister of Navarre who is sorry she cannot be with you today. Perhaps when you are queen ...'

Anne knew what he meant and chose to ignore the subtle insult, for she needed to have this king on her side, to protect her future and that of her country. She merely smiled and looked down in seeming modesty and left him to continue.

'So, my young Anne, I remember you well from my Court and you have developed the grace and wit of a French courtier, so I have been told and now I can see for myself, 'tis true.'

Anne laughed quietly and raised an eyebrow. 'One tries to entertain one's master how as I was taught.'

Francis placed his hand in the folds of the rich cloth of her skirt which touched his leg and squeezed her thigh.

'Indeed I remember you were taught but did not practise, n'est-ce pas?'

She laughed again, as she took his straying hand and raised it from her skirts and stroked it. She looked down as if examining the rich ruby ring on his finger, before returning it firmly to its

256

own lap.

'I would retain my modesty,'

'How so?'

'Only when it is worth giving the prize would I give away my greatest gift. Perhaps now when I have jewels, position, and authority.'

He nodded in approbation of her reply.

'Even so, I wish for something Henry cannot give me ... nay, not what you think.'

'Yes?'

'Something you can give me. For old times' sake?'

Francis laughed. 'You were cold to me, why should I give you anything?'

'I will give you something in exchange.'

'And what would that be?'

Anne put her hand on his leg now, barely touching the hand which had rested in her lap.

She looked away at the dancers, and tapped her fingers to the music.

'Has it occurred to you that if my king breaks away, you too could do the same? We could show you how 'tis done.'

'And? What do you want from me? I know you give nothing unless you get something in return.'

Anne said quickly, 'I would have the knowledge that the Holy Roman Emperor does not have the ability to raise an army against us. I know the Pope is weak and does not have power to order a holy army against us; gone are the days when he can command all Christendom to lock up their ladies and leave for holy crusade ... but the emperor? He is now your brother-in-law. Being so bound, would you obey him if he ordered an army across the Channel?'

Francis looked at her and then again surveyed the dancing company, as if he saw them like an advancing army. The music and the dancing were sufficient to provide them with absolute privacy, almost more than could be expected behind locked doors.

'Indeed, the Emperor is an ally for now, while I have his sister, but he is cold and calculating and I would only trust him from day to day, as the wind blows. I married his sister under duress you must know – after I was deceived at Pavia.'

Anne smiled at the euphemism. The Battle of Pavia. The decisive battle where the Emperor showed his might against the other European sovereigns who thought they could work together against him. France now would have to fight again for their part of Savoy. It must have been deeply humiliating for this king to have lost a battle, been captured and kept prisoner, no matter how well he had been treated. Now he was frowning and his face was all lines.

'I will not speak of such a time, it was deeply unpleasant. So, my pretty one, what are you angling for?'

'The Emperor, he could find himself tested, so he could not watch you and my Henry?'

Francis looked puzzled. Anne sighed and explained, 'Supposing he had pressing matters on his eastern borders? With the Turks threatening invasion? He would not like his Vienna to be invaded by those hordes?'

'They have made moves, 'tis true but not so as to worry Charles.'

'But supposing they were given hints and stories by western lords that, if Charles were so minded, he would invade their way? And the assurance that help would be given the eastern hordes if they invaded as a defensive measure?'

The king looked surprised, his creased face deepening.

'Anne, what have you heard?'

It was her turn to look surprised now.

'Nothing, but you must know I am aware of what can happen. Tell me if I guess right.'

Her hand was on his sleeve in that gesture of entreaty. Francis did not hesitate and Anne realised, as he explained, that he was such a vain man, he would give away secrets in his boasting.

'You must be a witch. You have guessed well but I hope you will keep my secret. It is true I have sent envoys east; they have

258

spices, rich perfumes and the jewels that I crave. There have been talks, of a diplomatic nature, you understand. It is possible that Charles' eastern boundary would need some shoring up. This is a way for me to protect my French soil from my brother-in-law's avarice, for he fights on all fronts to expand his boundaries; if all goes well it will not be an expansion but a defending of what he has from unexpected quarters.'

Anne nodded, satisfied. She smiled radiantly, looking up into the face she had hated as a youngster. Now she saw it contained a sardonic cunning which was so self-absorbed that she felt confident she could now match him.

'Indeed, Francis, you and I understand each other well. Come, let us dance together again.'

They rose and moved as one, but soon Henry came and joined in with them and all the courtiers stood back to watch the royal trio, dancing an impromptu jig, the musicians catching the movements and speeding their tempo. Anne was spun from one to the other and back again, laughing loudly as she moved fluidly between them, accepting the implication that she was on equal terms with these two great kings. For the first time she felt truly royal. Then Henry shouldered his fellow king aside and claimed Anne as his partner for the next rill.

Chapter Twenty-One

It had been as they sailed back to English soil that Anne felt sure that soon she would lose the moon's blessing and her belly would grow. The slow rhythm of the sea had rocked her into a dreamy mood, unusual for her. The soft lilting of the ship, its sails only just bloated with a gentle breeze, had then made her queasy. She was hardly ever sick and knew that the sea was not rough enough to affect her. With a quickening she realised. Was she pregnant? She did not believe so but with the stillness that the channel crossing enforced upon her, and her new found womanhood, she found herself dreaming. The languid feeling was so unusual that she wallowed in it. No more did she rant against her fate, as a woman waiting for her life to begin. She sat on deck, at the prow, on a cushioned chair, open to the sea breezes, and watched as the sun set to her left making the slaty waves colour with amber-gold in a long stripe which seemed, to her, in her dream-like state, to be a path from heaven to her.

As if God is confirming that I do right and is providing a path for my son to come and grow inside me, for the King's sake, and for the sake of the Lord's own church which will be cleansed and righteous again in our land, and if I cannot achieve it then my son will. A gilded righteous path to glory. Truly he will be a golden sun-king, she thought, fingering the belt which lay across her belly, thinking that it had moved with a kick from inside. She knew it was too early yet, even if she had taken the King's seed, and that the movement was a mirror image of the movement of the ship making her slightly nauseous.

She could see the vague shape of her now beloved country rise before her like a dark shadow on the horizon. As she watched, slowly, very slowly, the white cliffs appeared and then stayed steady before her, gaining in size so creepingly that she could not perceive when they became so large that the ship was but a tossed toy against the wash of the tide against the shore. She recalled her fear when she had travelled away from her home as a child and then returned all those years ago. Now she felt sure of herself, sure that her chosen path was true. As the cliffs grew, so the sun dipped over the horizon, and the golden path across the grey tossing water dimmed and then disappeared and all she could see was the great white cliffs around Dover. As they edged beneath the cliffs, nearer land, the ship tossed more.

Henry was suddenly there, standing behind where she sat, placing his hands on her shoulders. She acknowledged his presence by touching his fingers gently, but he said nothing. Perhaps even he felt something spiritual and was silenced by the moment. They both watched as the boatmen hauled and ran up and down the rigging to tack the sails and start the oars so they could steer into Dover harbour. Small boats now came alongside, lit by tossing lamps, as those who lived in the port put to sea in an effort to spot their king and his courtiers. There were shouts of excitement but Henry stood there, not waving, just smiling and nodding. Lights had been flared along the deck of their ship and Anne realised that they could only be seen as two large shadows. She turned and saw that Henry's rich robes and medallion of state glowed. Perhaps the occupants of the tossing boats could see the gleam of these and guessed it was their King. As they stayed there, the evening closed in and tiny lights and flares from the town became visible, seeming to wink as more were lit. There were shouts from the helmsman, the ship's rigging creaked and the salty smell of the sea was lost in the freshness of herbiage wafting to them from the shore. The smell of fresh cut grass and hay, Anne thought, remembering that this would be the time of harvesting the winter feed for the cattle.

'I smell a good roast,' exclaimed Henry enthusiastically, breaking the silence and then she too could smell the familiar strong odour but the nausea had passed and she knew she was hungry. Hungry for me and the babe, she thought. She would not tell Henry until she was sure. They were to be royally entertained by the Dover Castle lieutenant and for a moment Anne felt a twinge of disappointment for she wanted to have Henry to herself, away from all the courtly ceremonies that had taken up so much time recently. Even as she felt the quickening of her child, she could feel the excitement of lust for this king of hers, now that she had experienced true coupling.

Her wish to be alone was not to be fulfilled for some time. Henry wanted to stay in Dover and inspect his fleet and castles there and accepted the hospitality of his local officials. When they landed they were escorted to the great black mass on the top of the cliff which was Dover Castle, and Anne shivered as they were shown into its royal apartments, by the light of great flares, for it was quite night when they reached it.

'If anyone is to invade us, this will be the port from where my ships will sail, and I do not trust your Francis, even now, to stay true to us. Since Pavia, he has been beholden to the Emperor, we must face that,' Henry explained as he left her the next day for the port's boat building area.

She said nothing, not contradicting him, although she was sure he was wrong. When he left, she languished in her own apartments with her thirty ladies who had accompanied her to France, gossiping with them and now, now that she knew what congress was all about, discussing the implications of love poems from Ovid and the love songs in the Bible with her sister Mary. They laughed together, but it did not stop her yearning.

'Oh, Mary, I would have Henry a-bedding me again and again. Not just for a lovechild, either. But I would hurry it, for I know Hal grows weary of his lack of an heir and it turns him bitter sometimes, even with me.'

Henry came striding back hot and dusty, 'Tomorrow we leave for London, Eltham first and then on to Whitehall, all is good there.'

'Could we not stop at Stone on the way, dear Hal, and see our friends the Wingfields?'

Henry laughed and agreed. They rode to see her friend Lady Bridget Wingfield at her home at Stone where there was no grandeur and no attendants. They spent a quiet day eating and laughing, her friend's children flocking around them, excited at seeing strangers. Little Annette, Anne's god-daughter, sat on her knees, showing her wooden doll and explaining how she could dress her, and suddenly had turned and buried her head in Anne's breasts and whispered, 'I love you, for you are like a queen.' Anne stroked the soft golden curls and tears had watered her eyes. Henry witnessed the scene and smiled broadly at her.

Bridget had called her away to look in at the nursery and Anne went eagerly, for her friend was adept at having babies. As they leant over the wooden cradle, which Bridget rocked gently, Anne whispered, 'How does it happen, dear friend? How does the babe grow inside? Can one be *sure?*'

Anne still looked down at the sleeping infant and did not see the look of astonishment on her friend's face. 'Why, Anne, you're not ...?'

'I'm not ...' she stopped, but her curiosity got the better of her discretion, '... not sure, and not for the sake of trying, Bridget.'

'Really, Anne, and you not married. You'll lose him and be like your sister Mary.'

Bridget stroked the soft cheek of her babe and looked over the cot at Anne.

''Nay, not that. I'm sure Henry would be true to me; if only I could be sure of the quickening of my loins, then I'd be certain of him. He is desperate for heirs.'

'You will know soon enough. What makes you believe you are now?'

Anne shook her head. 'I just feel different. And slightly sick and I am never sick.'

Bridget laughed. 'No, you are frighteningly healthy, except for your so-called catching of the pox.'

Anne looked at her. 'Well, what do you think?'

'Have you mentioned it to Henry?'

Anne shook her head.

'Then wait and tell him first, that is all I will advise. But you must look after yourself if you are to bring into the world a healthy babe.'

The mother leant nearer to her friend and, although there was but a sleeping babe in the room, she whispered some hints, of herbs to use, incantations to say and movements to make, to ensure that the man's seed would hold. Anne nodded and they held hands and kissed each other and joined the men.

Shortly after, she and Henry waved goodbye and rode on together, meeting up with the royal household some way along the main London road, and Henry held her hand and played with the rings on her fingers but said nothing. They reached Eltham late on a cold winter's evening. Anne imperiously gestured everyone away and took Henry to her bed, eager for his love and he followed her willingly, laughing at her eagerness. The memory of the cuddly children, the complicit looks between Bridget and her husband at their brood, and the wish for this to be her lot, made Anne ardent and this flamed Henry's passion so that they did not sleep all night.

It was after the great banquet for Christmas that Anne was sure that she was pregnant. She had missed two monthly bleeds now and all the rich food of the season had left her feeling jaded and sick in the mornings. She had not risen early enough to accompany Henry on his morning hunts but languished in bed. Henry returned on new year's day and rushed into their private chambers, yelling for her as usual, 'Nan, Nan, we have caught a goodly fox but nothing for the pot today. Nan, why do you stay in chambers? And every morn this Christmas.'

He sat on her bed and took her hand.

Anne, although warm from being well wrapped indoors, ordered mulled wine and oatcakes. Still she had not told him that she was with child for she was afraid of losing it, but soon it would start to show. When Henry had disrobed and partaken of some of

264

the cakes and was waiting for the steaming brew to cool, she opened by saying, 'I have something to tell you, dear Hal.'

He had carried on eating, breaking the cake so crumbs scattered, nodding. 'Go on, then, surprise me as ever, dear Bub.'

She moved closer to him and stopped his hand and wiped his fingers with her napkin, sitting on his lap between him and his food. Playfully he tried to stretch around her but she stroked his beard and his face until he was forced to take her hands away and said, laughingly impatient, 'Come, out with it, dear girl, and let me to my food.'

'You are to have a son. I swear it. Feel it.'

He almost dropped her from his lap but then caught her in a great bear hug, hiding his face in her linen collar so that she shuddered with the stinging of it as his beard grazed her long neck. He moved away and stared at her. 'Are you sure?' He put his hands gently on her belly and she nodded.

'As sure as I can be. I am ever regular. I swear.'

He stood up then, holding her in his arms, his strong body not flinching as he moved her through the room and into their private chamber where he deposited her on the bed.

'You must rest, you can have all the best foods. We must nurture you to ensure that you have a healthy child. And we will be married, soon, and you will be queen. We will have many sons and all will be legitimate and good princes to continue my line.'

He continued to talk as he fed her dainties. 'My queen; my prince's royal mother, all riches will be heaped on you. To think, you have quickened my seed.' His face darkened. 'Now the curse will be lifted; married we must be and soon.'

Then he said what he had never acknowledged before, 'My marriage to Katherine never was; it was but a farce and I'll not wait for some Italian weak-kneed prelate to tell me what to do.' He paused, then repeated, 'The marriage never was so we do not have to wait for their decision. We will marry now. Now, I say.'

Anne was astonished. For nearly six years Henry had insisted that he needed a papal bull to say that his marriage to Katherine was a nullity. Despite evidence, Anne's arguments and Cromwell's machinations, the spreading of gold across the continent, consistory courts held in England, emissaries to the Vatican, and many discussions in Rome, Henry had refused to set aside the old queen without that papal bull of nullity. Now he had turned about face so quickly it took her breath away. Anne knew it was because he was desperate for an heir and she was confident of providing that heir. But now she wondered why she had not given in before. Why, she could have had several children by now. But she did not look back. She was too exhilarated at the turn of events.

Ever careful and politic, she stopped him in his enthusiasms. 'Wait, Henry; cannot we wait until we are sure of our position? We have to follow protocol. And who is there to marry us here?'

He nodded, as he stroked her belly gently and said after a pause, 'You are right and I would that we marry before gentry of the Court. I'll not have any say that our marriage is not legal, that my sons are not legitimate. We must think about this.'

Anne said, 'Cranmer, who is my family priest, he is kind. I would like him to carry out the ceremony but now you have made him Archbishop that cannot be.'

'But, dear Nan, why not?'

She sighed and stood up, her bed robes loosened around her. Before she spoke she moved them further around her shoulders and pulled them close. She said, quietly, slowly, 'You have now said the Pope has no jurisdiction in this country, and that you are the head of the Church in England. So the Archbishop is going to be your chief judge and jury, still part of the established church.'

'I see now,' he interrupted, 'if he marries us, he can't then pass judgement on my previous liaison with that Spanish witch.'

'Nor could he judge our marriage legal if he conducted it. It would be a travesty.'

'So, Anne, who?'

Anne thought. She realised the marriage itself was only a small stepping stone to her being made queen but she would still want the ceremony to have the dignity of a royal wedding.

'I shall ask Cranmer who it should be. He is my spiritual leader, he will tell us of the right man to use, though I swear he will be disappointed that he cannot carry out the ceremony. What say you?'

Henry agreed. 'Don't leave it too long, my love, I would have you as my legal wife today, if it were possible.' He hugged her, smothering her face with bristly kisses, stroking her back, her arms, her whole body as if he would possess her but with a love transcending the passionate lust that had begotten their child.

* * * * *

Anne sent for Priedeux and explained what was afoot. She told him of the pregnancy and the proposed marriage. He congratulated her but it was half hearted. 'Why, Tom, are you not pleased that all our plans have come to fruition?'

'Indeed, yes, but once you are married you'll have need of wet nurses and handmaids, and not want loyal messengers such as I.'

She surveyed him, a finger holding her chin upwards in that familiar way she had, giving her a look of great thought.

'Tom, I shall always have use of your eyes and ears. 'Tis true you may not be able to be part of my royal entourage and for that I shall reward you with the manors I promised you, but I know you are loyal and I would ever trust you.'

She removed the signet ring she wore on her finger, the one with the falcon, the sign of her family, which she had inherited from the Ormonds, for her father had eventually won the case. She held it out to him. Slowly he stretched forward and took it from her.

'This should always ensure entry to my presence wherever I am.'

He nodded and bowed his head then, ashamed that he should think she would forget him. He remembered what Jonril had said on the way back from Essex, that it was known Anne would not fail a loyal servant. How could he have thought she would abandon him? As he took the ring she said, suddenly businesslike,

'But now you will take a message for me to Cranmer. Explain what I have told you and ask him who should officiate at the marriage. A discreet churchman who would have no dealings in the Court which sits next year to decide on the nullity of my dear Hal's betrothal to Katherine!

'You see, dear Tom, despite my dear Harry breaking from the Catholic church, and making himself the head of a new English church, he is still minded to ensure that a declaration of nullity is made. Strange, do you not think? So I must ensure all areas are covered. You should know that Cromwell has drafted the Appeals Statute now and soon there'll be no more running to Rome from this country on matters to do with inheritance, marriages or divorce. It will be treason to ask Rome for a decision.'

Priedeux set off to make enquiries and soon returned with the name, Rowland Lee. Cranmer had begged a favour of his patroness. Priedeux explained using his excellent rote memory what Cranmer had told him, 'He is a goodly man and has like beliefs to myself but he needs some promotion and I verily believe that the bishoprics of Coventry and Lichfield will shortly become vacant and if your Goodness can see it in your heart to promote him to the see then this will be a good reward for conducting such an important ceremony.'

So on the 25 January 1533 without great ceremony, Rowland Lee, churchman, shortly after Bishop, married Henry and Anne before witnesses Henry Norris and Thomas Heneage of the Privy Chamber and Anne Savage who was later to be rewarded by her own marriage to the Sixth Lord Berkley. Anne shivered throughout the ceremony which was carried out in the early morning in the west turret of York Place. There was no fire and she only had her furs and velvets to warm her. No feast followed the ceremony but those taking part scurried back to their jobs as soon as she and Henry had plighted their troth.

Henry developed sudden energy and met with ministers and churchmen and spent many hours ensconced with Cromwell. Parliament was summoned. Priedeux was sent to visit old parliamentarians, entrusted to ensure that gold changed hands, and that old loyalties and debts were called in.

Henry would visit Anne to brief her as she rested, while he impatiently paced up and down before her, his arms akimbo, the great shoulders of his cloak swinging round each time as he turned, 'We should persuade Parliament soon. And rumours are spreading so you must be crowned before the child is due. The child must be born not only in wedlock but with you as my crowned consort. Once Parliament has passed Cromwell's Appeals Statute then we can start Cranmer on the formal inquiry. And *this time* there will be no machinations, or Popish arguments. This time, I will have my way.'

Anne shivered and felt for the child within her. She had known Henry for nearly ten years now, several as an eager but unrequited lover and now as her true husband, but this sudden angry impatience was new to her. Impatient he had been in the past but not with this bitterness and urgent imperativeness that he now displayed. She realised what it was: the desperate need to legitimise their unborn son. Even though Henry was truly a great, powerful king who always had his way, there was one thing he could not achieve and now he felt that it was truly within his grasp he was greedy for the reality of it: a legitimate heir.

'We shall organise the coronation, for it takes some preparation. Unless we tell the guilds in the City and their companies, they will not have time to commission their pageants and I will have a great coronation for you, my dear queen in all but name. It shall be greater than that gone before.' Anne knew he meant Katherine's coronation and nodded in agreement, stroking his unruly hair where he had combed his hands through it in excitement at all he told her. He was kneeling before her now, his bear hands stroking her belly.

'We shall have three days of festivities before you are crowned, and all those intransigents who have bullied us and shouted at us will come to heel. Wine will flow in the City of London and all will rejoice. That I'll be sure of.'

'But, dear Hal, if the crowds hate me so, will it not be dangerous?'

He stood up and started the restless pacing again.

'Nay, the people love great ceremonies, the conduits flowing with wine. The more spectacle there is the greater you will be seen in their eyes. Trouble not, Nan, I've been king for over twenty years now and I *know*.'

He moved away restlessly, as if her opinion was of nought, and consulted a calendar, counting days and weeks and suddenly he was off again. 'Cranmer must be finished by the middle of May – your coronation will be on the 1 June – a summer coronation where it will be fine and your royal barge will be blessed by the sun. And if we tell Cromwell this he will sweat blood to make sure it comes to pass, what think you?'

Henry was grinning for he had a despot's humour and sometimes liked to see his advisers be flurried by his orders as they strove to carry out his wishes. Cromwell, the butcher's son, would sweat and Henry would laugh quietly to himself. Anne said nothing, for she was excited and fearful at the same time. Everything was happening too fast now and all she wanted to do was languish, allowing the babe to grow inside her.

He strode off, muttering to himself and without asking his wife what she thought of his plans. Anne wondered what she had entered into. Although she too loved ceremony and fetes, masques and dancing, she was in no mood to partake in them now.

* * * * *

Her wedding, so long anticipated, had been conducted almost in secret. Her coronation, on the other hand, was organised as a three day event, of feasting and merry-making, including a great procession through the City of London, with all the guilds ordered to provide entertainments. It was to be held with great pomp, and Henry decreed that any disaffected citizens should be kept firmly away from the ceremonies. Anne worried about those rumours of resentment, interpreting them superstitiously as foreshadowings of future doom.

She was surprised at how quickly and efficiently Cranmer had despatched the inquiry into the validity of Henry's marriage with Queen Katherine. The marriage had been declared 'null and absolutely void and contrary to law'. Five days later, and a day before the coronation began, it was pronounced that the marriage of Henry and Anne was valid.

On the first day of the coronation ceremony, she was transported upriver from Greenwich to the Tower of London where she was to spend two nights with Henry. The official ceremonies commenced as she was escorted in the royal barge, devoid now of the Spanish pomegranates and adorned with Anne's crowned falcon. The escort consisted of fifty vessels decorated with festive flags, streamers and banners. Boats full of musicians surrounded her entourage, and music echoed around her from all corners of the river, the water affecting the sound of the tabors, trumpets and drums so that, even when she could see the musicians' barges, she could not be sure that the sound wafted direct from them. She was greeted by Sir Steven Pecock, Lord Mayor and of the Haberdashers Company.

He bowed so low as he stepped into her barge that he nearly fell out as the boat swayed. She remained seated, not rising to greet him, but merely nodded and gave him her hand in a languid manner. As the entourage moved slowly away, she gestured to him to sit on the cushioned seat opposite her and made desultory conversation with him but she found him embarrassingly obsequious. She was glad to reach the tower and say farewell to him, and managed to say it graciously despite the fact that she desperately needed to urinate. As she was led to the tower and handed over to her uncle, Norfolk, who had been put in charge from now on, she shuddered at the grey bulk of the battlements. As the great doors swung shut behind her, her legs felt weak and the baby moved within her so that she asked if she could sit down.

Norfolk, her uncle, snapped his fingers and a chair was found and brought to her, in the green outside her apartments.

'Pull yourself together, girl, you have nearly attained your ends, and I hope it turns out well for all of us. If you have overstepped the mark, it will be the downfall of the whole family, you realise that?'

She looked up at him witheringly. Her uncle, her mother's brother, had never been a favourite of hers, for he seemed to blow whichever way the wind was favourable. She had heard the story that Chapuys, the Spanish ambassador and a known spy of the old queen, had boasted on the continent that Norfolk felt upset about the setting aside of a good Catholic queen and did not favour his niece's presumption. For now, though, he did his King's bidding and was in charge of the coronation ceremonies.

'If anything goes wrong in the next few days, I truly believe it will be you, dear Uncle, who will suffer a downfall. Not me.' And she stroked her belly to show him what she meant. He stalked off, muttering something about arrangements and gestured to an underling to show her to her apartments.

Anne sighed. Was there never any peace? She was always having to look about her and trust no-one. She wanted Priedeux to be here but it was impossible, she knew that. She grew weary because of the growing child and pulled herself up and nodded to the servant who guided her to sumptuous apartments. She had insisted that the tower be renovated and painted for her visit and Henry, the compliant father of her child, indulged her.

It had been a bit more difficult over the barge for he had pretended to find it distasteful that she should want to ride in the old queen's pleasure craft. But Anne had her reasons.

'I would show the people, dear Hal, that I have the same ways as Katherine, but with more refinement, with more Englishness if you like.'

He had smiled at this and sent the order. to redecorate Katherine's barge. So she had managed to have her own way. Tomorrow, she thought gleefully, she would be sailing up the River Thames in the barge which had once been the personal property of her predecessor, not a gift from Henry, now decorated with the coat of arms of Queen Anne, with the pomegranates of the former queen discarded.

Still tonight, she had to sleep in this great dungeon of a place, and she shivered again, as the stone building was resonant with a chill that contrasted with the heat of the day. Then Henry was there, his usual bluff self, striding along the long dark corridor like a great blundering comfortable dog. 'Why, dear Nan, you're not tired by a ride from Greenwich. Come you'll soon be revived when you see our royal apartments for they are decked with your favourite pictures and drapes.' He helped her up and led her to their private rooms, but as the heavy door closed behind her she still felt the coldness, a smell of damp as if the river itself oozed within the very walls. She could not hear the noises from the river from here but she could feel it. Their quarters were indeed sumptuous and a fire burned but it was some time later, after a hot meal, that Anne warmed to these foreboding surroundings.

She was glad when it was time to leave the next day. Her ceremonial clothes had been designed to ensure she kept cool in the heat of summer and, she thanked God, her hair would be loose around her shoulders as befitted one who was to be brought before the Lord's anointed, who would, in turn, anoint her his Queen. It showed innocence and humility. Her surcoat was of white cloth of tissue, light and cool, with a cloak of the same, edged with ermine, the royal fur. All she wore on her head was a circlet of rich stones.

Henry left her and it was Norfolk and his minions who led her out to begin the journey through the City of London before joining the royal barge further down the Thames. She was shown to the litter, embellished with white cloth of gold and silver bells. She inspected the palfreys which were to pull the palanquin through the City of London stroking their haunches. In her condition it would not do for a horse to bolt. Satisfied, she allowed herself to be helped up and nodded to show she was ready for the state occasion to begin. But then she waved her hand to stop the train.

'Wait. Where is Bridget, my maid?'

There was a-muttering and scampering and then Bridget was there. 'Here, Madam, what can I do for you?'

'Make sure there is a chamber pot amongst your robes, and when I call, bring it. I will not bear another day like yesterday. The babe presses on me and it's devilish uncomfortable.'

Bridget had to lean forward to hear what was said but when she heard she smiled, and Anne laughed her manic laugh with her. Bridget was still grinning as she ran back into the tower and emerged, a little plumper herself with the bulge of the essential item.

The day proved as tedious as Anne had anticipated despite Hans Holbein's efforts at decorations on arches she had to pass under. The pageants and their poems were banal. They moved slowly down Fenchurch Street as the day warmed, the gravelled streets making the horses' hooves scrunch. The noise nearly drove her mad by the end of the day. The horses' sweat sent a rancid odour wafting back to her, accentuating her daily nausea. When they stopped at the pageants, at first it was a relief to be stationary but then the whining voices of untrained children reciting verses to her made her think of cool drinks and a cushioned bed. The litter, although it sheltered her from the rays of the sun, became stuffy with the smell of the horses, and flies soon gathered around their haunches and then around her.

When they reached Gracechurch Street she was led under the arch prepared by Holbein and noticed the eagle which topped it, above her now-crowned falcon. It was supposed to be a replica of Parnassus and had been sponsored by the ironworkers who relied on royal patronage for their work. She smiled graciously and closed her eyes as if to enjoy the poetry more, but in reality she found it execrable.

'Truly the City needs a Jonril to teach them what to do,' thought Anne. 'Even with such a short time, he could have created something better than this.'

But more disturbing was the quiet sullenness of the crowd. Not many hats were raised and only those in the merchant companies who sang her praises officially gave some atmosphere of enthusiasm.

At one point where there was a garland of entwined flowers with hers and Henry's initials, H & A, the crowd started to chant 'Ha! Ha! Ha!' in a maniacal pretence at laughter. Anne looked stonily ahead. A choir of young children were trying to make themselves heard over the chanting and Anne dropped a few coins onto the outstretched hand of the youngest, smallest child. The whole charade was excruciating but she could not even ask the cortege to move faster for there were a hundred men at arms in front, with a great army of ambassadors and courtiers. She passed on, nodding at the still performing group.

At Eleanor's cross at Cheapside she was presented with a gold purse with a thousand gold marks and she thanked the guild with graciousness, tucking the purse inside the extra band of her skirts which had to be inserted to accommodate her pregnancy. Then she was led through St Paul's Gate into St Paul's churchyard and they were moving slowly through the crowds down Ludgate. Here the horses slithered. She was glad of the stop at Fleet Street and gestured to Bridget, for the journey had taken some hours and she needed that chamber pot, which she slid gracefully under her skirts and then handed back to Bridget, who poured it into one of the conduits in the street. The crowd said nothing.

At the end of the day her ankles were swollen despite the fact that she had not stood much, the baby kicked as if it wanted out, she felt sick, the cloth of tissue stuck to her where she had perspired and she knew she smelt. The only consolation had been the chamber pot which meant that she did not have that terrible aching need to urinate that she had experienced the day before.

After refreshments in Westminster Hall of spiced delicacies and cups of Hippocras, the ceremonies were at an end and Anne hurried back, as fast as she was able, to the Thames and travelled to York Place by the waiting royal barge to be with Henry again. She had expected to feel triumphant at riding this vessel which had once belonged to her rival, but all she felt was disappointment and exhaustion. Even the cool of the water in early evening could not rejuvenate her and by the time she met with her king she was fuming.

'It was humiliating. The silences were worse than the mutterings, dear Hal.'

'A queen must endure. They will learn to love you, especially when they see the fruit of your womb, dear Nan.' Henry lay beside her and caressed her and kissed her neck and soon their lustful intimacy numbed the memory of the day's events. At least, she thought, as she drifted into sleep, her king loved her and would cherish her and their sons would be great kings.

The next day was the triumph of her life. Dressed in crimson, ermine and purple, the traditional royal colours, she was led into Westminster Abbey and there, amongst the peers of the realm, she was ceremoniously crowned Queen, with a ceremony that was new, devised for the new Church of England. Cranmer, as Archbishop of Canterbury and leading churchman of all England, anointed her with holy water and the crown of St Stephen and handed her the sceptre of gold and the rod of ivory. He smiled benignly at her, as he lowered the crown gently on to her head. She realised there was a hint of pride in his look as well, pride in his benefactress achieving her ultimate goal. Anne knew that no other queen of England had been so honoured. For no other queen of England had been anointed by the religious head of church. In the past that head had been the Pope and he had always been in Rome appointing papal legates to carry out his orders in the outskirts of his religious realm. Anne was anointed directly from God through the Archbishop. She was *God's* anointed queen, equal to the king, an honour far greater than Katherine had received. She remembered what she had said to her friends in that gallery, so many years ago: *I will be queen.* Dinteville, she knew, was in the audience, as representative of Francis I and she was sure he would be proud of her.

She watched as, through the thin smoke of incense which caught in her throat with the strength of the smell, her subjects bowed down before her. The trumpets blared, drums rolled, and all the agony of the last few days, the jolting of the uncomfortable litter, the even more agonising time of listening to bad eulogies and trying to be graceful, were forgotten.

She was queen of England, the bearer of great kings for the future.

The banquet that followed, where she presided as the main guest, a monarch in her own right, lasted several hours and she knew that Henry watched it from a balcony. She was triumphant and wished the day would never end. She bethought that the cold of her wedding day was one thing, but the richness and warmth of this her coronation was worth a thousand wedding days; to be queen was all she wanted, to be able to influence her king to reform and make good the Church and in that she had almost succeeded.

Chapter Twenty-Two

Henry had finally broken with the Roman Church by accepting the nullity decree. He and Anne had spoken about the English vernacular Bible being introduced into every church in England, so that the priests would read to their congregations in a living language that they understood. Anne could not believe the long wait was at an end. So much had happened, her wedding, the coronation, and now this: the culmination of all she had planned. England would soon be truly Protestant, cleansed of all the papal taints.

There had also been the excitement of ordering new brocades, velvets, muslin and ermine and seeing the dressmakers stitch double time so that the gowns were ready for each part of the coronation. She smiled to herself secretly at the times they had to adjust the front panelling as her babe grew inside her. Now the long nine months was nearly at an end.

In addition she gloated over the gifts that Henry had showered upon her. Even in her early birth pains she felt triumphant. Henry had made her a very rich woman with manors and gold and castles and farms of her own. She had achieved the highest status of any female. It had pleased her to help those who had helped her achieve her aim. Priedeux had been given lands in Essex and she had been proud to say farewell before she was taken to this withdrawing room. He was given a good horse, gold and parchment deeds to prove his ownership.

But Priedeux had not yet left Court. As he checked the tack for his horse from the stores and collected provisions, he chewed on a piece of straw, anxious to be gone, but anxious too for his mistress; her time was near. Suddenly he heard a rustle behind him. He jumped and turned quickly, always alert to danger even though it was mid morn and full daylight. There stood the thin shadow of Jonril, outlined in the entrance. He held up a hand. 'At peace, my friend. I'll not be stabbed through the heart by you.' Priedeux dropped his hand from his scabbard. He realised he was being infected by the nervous excitement at Court. There was an air of anticipation surrounding the coming of the new heir.

'Jonril, welcome. But you are never seen at this hour; are you ill?' Priedeux said it jokingly but they both knew Jonril was a man of the night. The only time he was seen to take daytime exercise was when he had come to find Priedeux to rescue their mistress. Priedeux realised why his friend seemed so pale and eye-sunken in today; this was a most unusual outing.

Jonril shrugged and answered, 'I came to bid you farewell ...'

He gestured for Priedeux to join him and, as he did so, Jonril placed a bony hand on his sleeve and led him to a trestle where they could sit astride, as a saddler would have done while he polished and mended the leather saddles. Once they were settled Jonril looked round and said in a quiet voice that he had rarely used before, 'I come to warn you, my friend, these are troublous times. The Norfolk faction are encouraging the spark the king has for that young Jane Seymour, despite the Seymour clan being enemies. I tell you that if Anne is not delivered of a boy, then there is danger, not only for Anne herself, but for all those who have tied themselves to her train, such as you and I.'

Priedeux interrupted him. 'I know that, Jonril. I am leaving, as you see, for the manors that Anne has bestowed on me. The charters show they are restored to me as the next of kin of my father. I think I can prove they are mine, even if there is some local opposition, with the support of my friends, the bakers in the forest, what say you?'

Jonril smiled, satisfied.

Priedeux added, 'And if you ever feel like retiring quietly, for I'll swear you'll not be able to persuade my bakers to put on masques, then you can come and stay.'

Jonril jumped up and made a fine bow, in thanks, and just as

279

suddenly sat down again leaning towards his friend. 'Nay, I'm not ready for retirement just yet.' He was bursting with excitement. 'I have had an offer to go to the French Court. Dinteville will introduce me. What say you?'

'Indeed, you will brighten up that great place. But the intrigue there is just as bad.'

Jonril nodded. 'I know that, but what excitement. So, my friend, if you hear that Anne is delivered of a girl, pray for my crossing of the seas.'

They looked at each other and placed their hands on each other's shoulders.

'Go in peace, dear Jonril, and I'll hear more of you, God willing.'

Jonril jumped up with his usual quickness, suddenly embarrassed. He said nothing, but walked quickly across the stables courtyard, raising one hand in farewell as he disappeared through the arched exit.

Priedeux thought of Anne. Rumour had it that the pains had begun.

* * * * *

Anne felt dragged down with the ache in between the stabbing pains. She thought of the days since June, the long hot days of July and August, when her king had wanted to be out, riding or, as she found to her disappointment, a-whoring. She understood this, knowing him to be a lusty man, but it still hurt. They had dragged for her, those days. She had dragged with the days, her body changing, her breasts growing heavy and pendulous on the mound that was her stomach stretched tight with the growing thing inside her. Parts of her body, her hands and ankles ached. She could not see her legs but she could feel them and they seemed to throb not only with the heat of the days but with the weight of it all. Nights had been sleepless as she tossed and the baby kicked and struggled. She would lie there, whispering to the child within her, telling him of his greatness, of his destiny and of his history. Sometimes she felt as if the child responded with a gesture of a fist.

She had been left in this withdrawing chamber for some days, with Henry banned as was the custom. She thought to herself, now she was queen, she would change this practice for she hated to be with women only, and missed the gruff laughter and teasing of men around her; she missed Mark Smeaton's lute-playing, Wyatt's poetry and, more than anything the freedom of being able to send messages to anyone by Priedeux. She ached for Priedeux. He had become so much a part of her life. She was bored and lonely, despite the attentions of her waiting women, despite her Book of Hours, her religious tracts from Germany, and the card games that her waiting women insisted on playing. Oh, how she missed Henry, and all the courtiers around him; she missed the quick repartee, the flirting laughter and was thinking that this enforced withdrawing was giving her indigestion when she realised the slow pains were sharpening and coming regularly.

Her waters burst and she knew that soon she would be delivered. She wished Mother Muncy was with her. She thought long on her wet nurse and the unconditional love that had come from her. This did not stop her from screaming as the almost constant pains seared through her body making her back arch and her hands to crab into tense fists around the heavy wooden bedposts, as the baby shoved and struggled to come into the world. Irrationally, she wished she could have Priedeux by her side now. She laughed hysterically to herself as she imagined the shocked faces of those around her if she suggested that a man, and a man they would consider of the lower orders as well, should be her companion at such a time. One person she certainly did not want to see her like this was Henry but she knew that, as both king and a husband, he would not come near her at such a time. This was woman's work and all involved knew it. Instead she had her maids and strange women who surrounded her, urged her to push, and rubbed her belly, and bathed her brow and could see her in all her indignity. At one point she was given a foul smelling drink, which seemed to send her into a strange dreamlike time with the pains coming from a long distance away, but they were still in her body and she still suffered. She did not mind that her sister Mary was with her for she had suffered like this and at the King's behest too. Again Anne gave a maniacal laugh, half scream, at the thought of it.

The pains strengthened and she released the bedposts and flung her arms forward, and then found Mary's hands moving around her, and she gripped those as if she were drowning, digging into the flesh until Mary yelled, 'For the love of God, dear Anne, desist. Come let me bathe your brow.'

The night wore on and morning came.

September the seventh and the child was born, crying lustily.

Anne cried, 'Praise the Lord, for his work is done. How is my son?'

There was no answer.

One of the maids lay the infant in her arms. Anne looked down at the naked babe who had not yet been wrapped in its swaddling. A girl.

Silence. Disappointment. Wonder that Anne, the all powerful, confident, successful queen, had not produced what she had promised.

Henry visited and looked at his daughter, and then at his wife. He smiled, but Anne knew it was a fixed smile. After a while he took the babe from its cradle and inspected her. She had red hair, startling blue eyes, an alabaster complexion.

'Indeed, she is my girl. Mayhap this promises more to come, a son next time.'

He gently laid her down and left the room.

Anne cried bitterly; she felt for the first time in her life as a hollow shell. She could not even find it in herself to pray to the God to whom she had trusted in so much, who she thought had guided her so far. She turned to the cradle and picked up the child, loosened the tight swaddling clothes with which she had been bound before the king arrived.

'Elizabeth, you shall be named after that good woman, my father's wife, and your father's mother.'

282

She looked at the child and the babe looked back, which Anne in her exhaustion thought was a look of deep wisdom. In those babe's eyes Anne imagined she saw something of her own determination. The little chubby fingers, with their tiny soft fingernails curled round Anne's finger as if this was a sceptre and the child would grasp what was hers as of right. The veins could be clearly seen beneath the alabaster clear forehead, as if it was paper-thin, and the deep blue of royal blood showed quite clearly, throbbing regularly.

Anne looked into those eyes and said wonderingly. 'Indeed you have the brain of a man, I sense it. You will need to be as brave as a lion to survive this disappointment of your father's, but I know you will succeed in the future where I may fail.' She whispered as in a dream, but, as her eyes closed in exhaustion, she could see quite clearly her daughter's destiny. It was the only time in her life that Anne admitted failure herself but even this was tinged with this strange foreknowledge. Already she was besotted with the babe and wanted to hold her and keep her safe forever even though she could feel sleep overtaking her. She continued to whisper to her, 'If I bear no other child for my lord you must carry out my aim and ensure that the Catholic Church never takes hold again in this island; that all can read the Bible in English, and all can make their own decisions whether good or bad. You, my child, will be educated well, I will make sure of that.'

Elizabeth was christened soon after, but neither Anne nor Henry was present. The babe was held at the font by Dinteville, standing in for the godfather, Francis 1. He looked down on the child and felt, even though he knew it was irrational, that he, de Selve and Anne had done their work; they would succeed in creating a new, better church.

Epilogue

'Well, de Selve, are you satisfied now?'

'Indeed, dear Jean, a good tale well told – and me safe at the end of it.'

Dinteville sighed. 'You were always watching your own back, you old pope-toady. But the story – it was supposed to be our story. I confess to being somewhat disappointed.'

De Selve put down the goblet he was about to raise to his mouth and licked his thick lips.

'Disappointed? Why?'

'It was all of Anne; how *she* caught her man, how *she* reformed the English church. I mean, didn't we do our part? It may not have been so obvious as hers, but the French king became a little tolerant afterwards, did he not?'

De Selve then took his draught of good wine.

'But I didn't want to be known to be involved, and that *has* been revealed. Except for that terrible picture, my part would never have been known, would it? No-one would ever have discovered I was mixed up with that minx.'

'But she comforted you, de Selve, in the hour of your greatest need, did she not?'

'Hah, plotting at the same time!'

Dinteville turned away from his friend and looked out of the window of his study at Polisy.

'Indeed, she did plot, but she was a great lady and I for one am pleased to have known her – with her we have lived, become famous, just because of the painting of Holbein's – nobody knows us for the work we did, I as a diplomat, you as a bishop, do they? All they know of us are as 'Holbein's Ambassadors.' In many ways I wish we were called 'Luther's Ambassadors', but you

284

would not agree with that, would you?'

De Selve shook his head. 'Ambassadors for reform perhaps.'

'Or perhaps, The Queen Anne's puppets.'

His companion smiled ruefully. 'Anne would want us to be known as Luther's Ambassadors.'

Historical note

As far as possible I have stuck to actual historical facts, Anne's life at Court being well known. For instance, Henry VIII's letters to Anne are well documented and studied; but there are no letters from Anne to him.

Although I have not found any historical records to say that Anne Boleyn knew de Selve or Dinteville they were very close in age and must have known each other as children in the French Court, because high born children such as these two men were invariably sent to the King's Court to be trained and it is known that Anne spent her formative years there. In addition it is true that Dinteville stood in for Francis I as godfather for Queen Elizabeth at the baptism, which shows a close connection.

The story of Holbein's Ambassadors is well known in that there is no record of why or who commissioned it and it appeared never to have been displayed in the sixteenth century when it was painted, but was discovered at Polisy in the nineteenth century. For the facts surrounding the painting I have to thank the National Gallery in London for holding an excellent exhibition in the early '90s where I first derived the idea for the novel and for giving me hours of pleasure with the painting.

Jonril and Priedeux, among other characters, are of course fictional; Priedeux has already appeared in my first novel, *The Gawain Quest* and will appear in *The Nine Lives of Kit Marlowe*. My future novels will continue to move him through the centuries.

Also available from Goldenford

Fiction

Esmé Ashford
On the Edge
Tramps with bad feet, a sheep rustler, a busker invited to dinner; a monster who devours a nasty husband and a child who learns from a visit to the fair; limericks and blank verse; it is all here.

Irene Black
Darshan, a Journey
The start of the new millennium harbours danger, even in Oxford, that most English of cities, where a naïve but spirited Anglo-Indian student sets out on a quest to reassert her British identity She is determined to find her estranged Welsh father and to escape the prospect of a safe but passionless arranged marriage in India. Her turbulent journey takes her through three continents via a morass of perilous affiliations, betrayal and heartbreak before coming to a momentous conclusion.

The Moon's Complexion
Bangalore, India 1991. A young Indian doctor has returned home from England to choose a bride. But who is the intriguing Englishwoman who seeks him out? Why is she afraid and what is the secret that binds them together? The lives of two strangers are turned upside down when they meet and the past comes to haunt them. *The Moon's Complexion* is a tale of love across cultural boundaries. It is also a breath-taking thriller played out in Southern India, Sri Lanka and England.

Anne Brooke
Thorn in the Flesh

Kate Harris, a lecturer in her late thirties, is attacked in her Surrey home and left for dead. Continuing threats hinder her recovery, and these life-changing events force her to journey into her past to search for the child she gave away. Can she overcome the demons of her own personal history before time runs out?

Pink Champagne and Apple Juice

Angie Soames is determined to leave her home in the idyllic Essex countryside and set up her own café in London, but before she can achieve her goal she has to overcome potential disasters in the shape of a glamorous French waiter, a grouchy German chef and her transvestite uncle. And, if she manages to keep the lid on all that, what will she do about the other hidden secrets of her family?

Jacquelynn Luben
Tainted Tree

A surprise bequest from an unknown benefactor leads American adoptee, Addie Russell, to Surrey on a journey to discover more about her mysterious English family. She does not know that her search will uncover secrets that will both shock and thrill her. Nor can she imagine the emotions and events which await her.

A Bottle of Plonk

It's 1989: Liebfraumilch, Black Forest gateau and avocado bathrooms are all the rage, and nobody uses mobile phones. When Julie Stanton moves in with Richard Webb everything is looking rosy. She certainly doesn't expect their first romantic evening in the flat to end with her walking out clutching the bottle of wine with which they were to toast their new relationship. But then Julie and the wine part company, and the bottle takes the reader on a journey through events revealing love, laughter and conflict.

Jay Margrave
The Gawain Quest

Priedeux – a character who changes the course of history …
In the first of a trilogy Priedeux sets out for the wilds of Wirral on a quest to discover the writer of *Gawain and the Green Knight*, a seditious poem with a hidden agenda - a call to rebellion against Richard II. Can Priedeux find the writer in time to stop the rebellion and save his own life?

Non-Fiction

Sold … to the Lady with the Lime-Green Laptop

The author has used the experience gained over five years of trading on eBay to describe one hundred of her most interesting, entertaining, sometimes lucrative and occasionally disastrous sales. The book is dotted with hilarious, fascinating and sometimes useful observations.

Forthcoming Publications

Jay Margrave
The Nine Lives of Kit Marlowe (Spring 2009)

In the third part of the trilogy Priedeux is the friend and chaperon of Kit Marlowe, who does not die at Deptford but escapes to the Continent, dressed as a woman. He still writes plays but can't use his own name so uses a hack actor, Shakespeare, to get them performed on the London stages. Kit's many escapades mean he sorely tries his friend Priedeux … Will he stay loyal to the mercurial Kit?

GOLDENFORD

info@goldenford.co.uk
www.goldenford.co.uk